"On the surface, *Behind the Crimson Curtain* is a lyrically haunting love story—love of freedom, love of another, and a daring love of self. Underneath it grapples with oppression-bred desperation, classism, and the historical use of theater as a dominating and deadly tool for political warfare. Masterfully straddling the line of scathing critique and hopeful beacon, Golden weaves past and present to build to a heart-pounding conclusion that will enrapture genre fans. Behind the Crimson Curtain anchors Golden as a standout new talent whose lyrical, historically-informed prose is perfect for readers who love their fantasy razor sharp."

—J. Elle, *New York Times* bestselling author of *House of Marionne*

"In *Behind the Crimson Curtain*, E.B. Golden layers political intrigue, mystery, and romance like layers of a pastry. This story isn't what you think and neither are its characters. Stellar prose carries a tormented and morally gray protagonist through a polarized city, where her struggle to survive threatens to unravel the very threads of her identity. This is a thought-invoking and compelling read that will appeal to readers inside and outside of the fantasy genre."

—Charlie N. Holmberg, *Wall Street Journal* and Amazon Charts bestselling author

"I cannot wait to own a copy of *Behind the Crimson Curtain*! I truly cannot believe that this is E.B. Golden's debut. Her prose is stunning, her world building gripped me from the very start, and on top of that she gave us a steamy, epic romance with two backdrops—a revolution and the theater—that somehow work perfectly together. Firin is the specific kind of resourceful, intelligent, morally gray female main character who has me wanting to know everything about her story, and

I love to see characters like her paired with male main characters like Bregan, who are steadfast and loyal and righteous—until they cannot be anymore and end up breaking their own hearts. I adore the chemistry and the ideological tension, the way circumstances drive them together and apart, and the intrigue and machinations they weave through. I cannot wait to see what happens next in this series. Both fantasy and romance lovers will fall for this book!"

—Ali Hazelwood, *New York Times* bestselling author

BEHIND

THE

CRIMSON

CURTAIN

BEHIND THE CRIMSON CURTAIN

E.B. GOLDEN

Text copyright © 2024 by E.B. Golden
All rights reserved.

No part of this book may be reproduced, or stored in a retrieval system, or transmitted in any form or by any means, electronic, mechanical, photocopying, recording, or otherwise, without express written permission of the publisher.

Published by 47North, Seattle

www.apub.com

Amazon, the Amazon logo, and 47North are trademarks of Amazon.com, Inc., or its affiliates.

ISBN-13: 9781662523243 (paperback)
ISBN-13: 9781662523236 (digital)

Cover design by Natalie Sousa
Cover image: © David Matthew Lyons / Arcangel; © faestock, © YuriyZhuravov, © ZOOM-STUDIO, © Yuran1 / Shutterstock

Printed in the United States of America

To 14 School Street and Al Miller.
Thank you for everything.

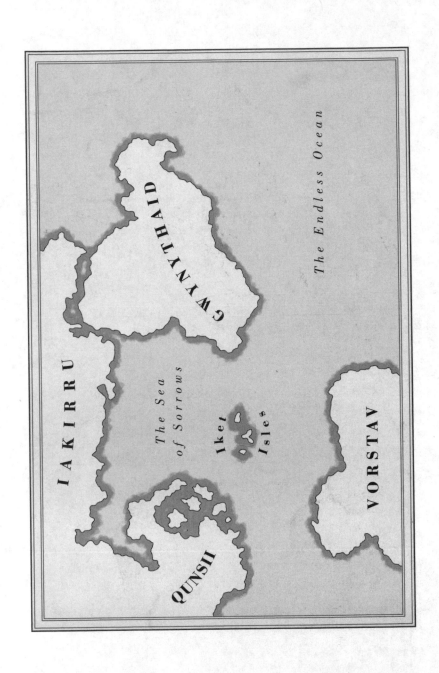

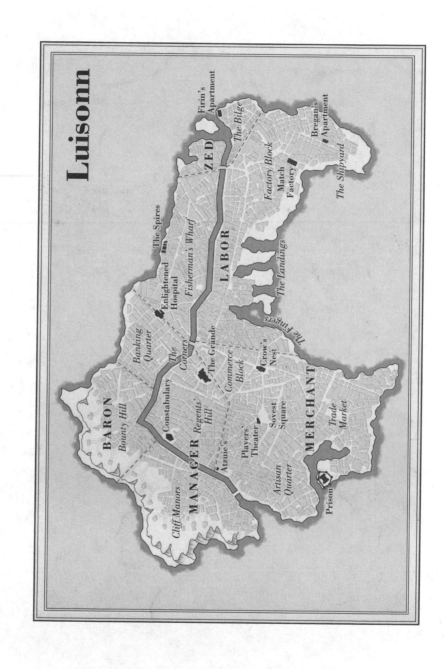

ACT I

ONE

Firin

The tiny apartment smelled like death.

I held the sleeve of my linen dress over my mouth and parted the curtains just enough to peer outside. A unit of Stav soldiers marched down the street below, scattering Merchant-class citizens in their wake. The soldiers didn't look up, and there were no signs I'd been followed, but my pulse didn't slow. Anyone in this city could be an agent of the Stav Regime.

Dropping the curtain, I turned to face the room. On a high-back bed in the corner, a woman moaned incoherent words through purpled lips. Sweat dripped from her fever-yellowed skin to her tangled quilt. She'd be dead by morning, and with her, any memory of my presence.

In the meantime, her death was going to buy me a life.

The Stav had caught on to my schemes, and if they caught *me*, I'd be hung before dawn. I had to get off this island tonight.

With steady, practiced hands, I searched every crevice of the apartment. The dresser and table were simple but fine. Painted pottery decorated a hutch against the wall. Clothes packed the wardrobe, tailor made and unstained. The signs of the woman's comfortable Merchant-class life clashed grotesquely with the black cloud of her mortality, but death came for everyone.

I slipped on a nice moleskin jacket—purple, with gray embroidery—and turned to the dresser. The drawers didn't squeak. Inside, a thick, folded piece of paper lay atop a pile of sweaters. I read the Stav's identity designations:

CLASS: MERCHANT

OCCUPATION: WEAVER

Stuffing the papers in the pocket of her coat, I eased into the putrid cloud of the weaver's looming death. I'd had the salt fever as a child, so I was safe, but superstition made me cover my mouth. As she muttered into her pillow, pain wrinkled her face. A few gray strands curled in the thick black hair pasted against her pale brow. She was around forty years old but had hours, maybe, until her last breath.

Upper-class physicians could have healed her, but they wouldn't. At least she had a pillow and a bed, privacy. In the Labor District they'd have thrown her into the street. In the Zed District they'd have used her as an excuse to burn the whole building down with everyone in it.

A green leather wristband encircled her bony wrist, marking her as Merchant class. I slipped it off.

Fingers snatched my forearm.

I rocked back on my heels as the weaver pinned me with a lucid blue-eyed stare. She scanned my face—her estranged daughter's face—and my mouth went dry. I'd donned her daughter's features as a precaution, in case anyone saw me enter the premises, but I wasn't her daughter. Her grip was wet on my flesh.

"You're here," she croaked, blood coating her lips. I stood, and her arm thumped to the mattress. "You actually came."

When a tear slipped through her lashes, mixing with rivulets of sweat, the emotion in her fever-bright eyes thickened to something heavier than an ocean. No one had looked at me that way in years, maybe not ever. I pocketed the Merchant-class wristband with her papers. I was running out of time I didn't have.

"Wait," she gasped.

The word halted me at the door, reverberating in my skull, evoking a memory of my father groveling to me on the other side of a prison-cell door.

"Please forgive me," the weaver pleaded.

When I closed my eyes, Father's many faces and their sneers spun on the back of my lids. I opened them again. He didn't deserve space in my thoughts. Maybe the weaver didn't either. I knew little about her, and even less about her daughter or why they were estranged. I shouldn't have cared. I didn't. But she *was* dying.

"I forgive you," I muttered.

Then I burst from the room and slammed the door shut on it like a crypt.

The Merchant-class residents were off to work, so nothing but dust floated in the apartment building's hazy, sunlit hallway. Racing down the steps, I gripped the weaver's identity wristband and papers. If I could pull this off, I'd sail to Qunsii tonight with a new name, a new past, and a new life. One free of Father's wretched legacy.

I pushed open the front doors and nearly barreled into a broad chest covered in black leather. I lurched back. Only the Nodtacht, the Stav Regime's elite secret police, wore leather in Luisonn.

"Everything all right?" the man asked in a familiar gravelly voice. He surveyed the apartment building, throwing the hook-shaped scar that split his beard into the sun's spotlight. The knife in my sleeve popped into my hand.

He wasn't just any Nodtacht. He was the one hunting me.

I dropped my eyes. "Yes, sir. I'm sorry."

I stepped around him. When he didn't stop me, I quickened my pace, ducking down an alley. I ran for several blocks before I dared to stop, sequestering in the darkest corner I could find. My sweat chilled against my skin.

Too close.

How was he *here*, today of all days? Was he onto me? I pressed a steadying palm to my abdomen, forcing deep inhales. The Nodtacht had seen me wearing the weaver's daughter's face, but if he searched the building and found the dying woman's identity papers missing, he might put two and two together. I swiped my sleeve across my mouth. It was a risk I had to take.

With shaking fingers, I pulled my silver pocket mirror from the neckline of my dress. The weaver's daughter blinked at me in the glass. For the briefest moment, I imagined the face imprisoned beneath her, the one that hadn't seen sunlight in four years, not since the Nodtacht had caught on to my identity and crimes.

Soon. Across the sea I could set myself free, but I had to get there first.

I trained my focus on the cord of illusion behind my heart and tensed it like a muscle. I visualized a new face, and with a mental tug, my blood rushed hot. My skin prickled, my bones throbbed, and the face in the mirror shifted. When I finished, dark hair hung around a soft milky-white jaw, sprinkled with flecks of gray. A few freckles winked beside my left eye.

I was now the weaver. Healthy, whole, and alive.

It was time to buy my way off this island.

TWO

Firin

Then

My father transformed with every sunrise. As a child, boxed in by windowless walls, my first and most important mission every day was to discover who he was.

One morning, when I was six, maybe seven years old, I slipped from the scratchy embrace of the pile of blankets that made up my bed and felt my way through the racks of costumes hanging like limp bodies in the dark. The Zed District tenement creaked around me with the subdued sounds of an early-winter morning—boys whispering next door, someone pacing upstairs, distant cackles of a drunken street crowd.

I hesitated with my fingers on the frigid latch, imagining. Beyond the door, the gas lamp would flicker, illuminating nothing but Father's face, as if the world were a canvas and he were the paint. I might find a hook-nosed pirate, a mustached businessman, or a gaunt-cheeked chimney sweep. As my toes became icicles in my ripped socks, I prayed that today Father would be one of the safe personas rather than one that scared me.

I cracked the door and stuck my nose out. A strange, round face beamed in the circle of golden light. I froze. I didn't know this persona.

"Good morning, dear," Father said, seated at our table. His new mustache twitched. A watch chain gleamed across his brightly striped waistcoat, and a short top hat perched beside his folded hands. Fancy pieces of a Manager-class man's costume. He was too clean for the smoke-stained walls, too fleshed out for the empty rations bin. But Father rarely looked like he belonged in our apartment, no matter what face he wore.

I looked at his eyes. They were a dull wood brown like mine. Illusion couldn't change eye color, so I always searched his for signs: a glint of anger, a flash of instability, a stillness of calm. That morning, he sparkled in a strange new way. I pinched the doorframe.

"Who are you?" I asked.

The strange persona's smile softened. "My name is Mr. Finweint, and today you are Afyn, my daughter."

My head spun. This was it. After practicing for longer than I could remember, he was finally going to take me out with him.

When I didn't move, Father rounded the table. He crouched and I recoiled, but when he took my hand, his touch was so gentle I shivered.

"It's time, Firin," he said, sliding a blue Manager-class band out of his pocket. The Stav Regime required every documented citizen to wear class bands. Father and I weren't documented, but we had bands of every color anyway. After securing it on my wrist, he pushed up the sleeve of my nightgown, revealing the thin X-shaped scar on my upper arm. "What is this?"

"My illusion mark." The scar gave us our face-changing powers. It was the only thing, other than eye color, that Father shared with me and that couldn't shift with illusion.

"And?"

"Don't show it, or my illusion, to anyone, ever," I recited. It was Father's first rule. He had ten of them, and I'd numbered them long ago. This one was the most important.

"That's right." He dropped my sleeve. "Do you know why?"

"Because people would hurt us."

"Exactly. If people knew we could do things they only hear about in legends, they'd use you, kill you. Do you understand?"

I didn't, as Father never told me legends, and I wasn't allowed to leave the apartment, but I nodded anyway.

"Show me," he said.

Closing my eyes, I searched with my mind for what felt like a rope near my heart. I imagined my ratty brown hair turning black and clenched the muscles of my chest, squeezing the cord as Father had taught me. Warmth radiated through my veins, heating my ribs, sliding over my bones. The top of my head tingled, and when my eyes flicked back open, Afyn's lush ebony curls draped over my bony shoulders.

Father's mustache crinkled in a grin, a sight as rare as stars in Luisonn's smoggy skies. "Can you hold it?"

"Yes."

I'd practiced every day for as long as I could remember, holding my transformation for hours at a time, praying he would take me out with him. In the depths of that winter's cold, I'd nearly given up. But now he was here, now he was Mr. Finweint, and today was my test—one that would determine if I was ready to help him or if I'd spend more untold months in my room.

I wasn't going to fail.

Since illusion could transform only skin and bone, Father spent the morning preparing me. He scrubbed me until my skin burned and my nails were clean, dressed me in the nicest costumes we possessed, and pulled a cloak over my hair.

Two hours later, he led me down our winding tenement steps into the coal-choked streets of the Bilge—the block of the Zed District where the Stav stuffed all the city's bandless residents like pigs in a too-small pen.

The sky was bloodred as Father guided me down a thin alley between sunken tenements and moldering rear houses. Except for the handful of times when Father let me take our chamber pot to the canal, I hadn't been outside since summer. On a swelteringly hot day, he had brought me to the Landings, where ships from the continents harbored. He'd spent the whole day teaching me which ships carried what. I still remembered.

Gwynythaid sent us food on red-sailed cargo ships; Qunsii sent machines and other innovations on massive steamboats; and Iakirru's blue-sailed vessels provided us with coal, silks, and tobacco. The dark-wood, black-sailed Vorstav'n ships took most of the goods to the southern Empire before they ever had a chance to dock on the Iket Isles.

I'd relived that day in my dreams for months—the busy energy of the docks, the strange new smells and sights. I'd begged Father to bring me back again and teach me more, but he hadn't given in until now.

Yet Father didn't head for the Landings. Instead, he headed north, toward the Centre Canal. I gripped his hand to keep from tripping as we squeezed past a woman wrapped in layers of mismatched clothing, her teeth chattering against the chill, then stepped around a sleeping body whose feet were edged with blue.

I clung to Father as we emerged at the edge of the canal and into a maze of Zed-class people lining up for rations of half-edible waste redistributed from the upper-class districts. Every morning I watched the line form from our kitchen window. Up close it was far louder than I'd expected, the stench of bodies fouler even in the crisp winter air.

I looked back, trying to find our apartment window. Our tenement had once been a pirates' inn, but in the last forty years under the Vorstav'n Empire's occupation, it had rotted from the inside out. The Stav Regime cared little for the Labors whose factory work filled their pockets. They cared even less for the jobless Zed. I couldn't tell which of the once-elegant buildings was ours.

I tucked into Father's side as he broke free of the food lines and flagged an early-morning gondola. When a man rowed over, Father flashed a piece of gold that could be spent in only the upper-class districts. It was money he'd brought home last night from one of his jobs—money we had to replenish today.

I peeked out from my hood as the coal-streaked gondolier scanned the pieces of Father's fancy costume. He raised an eyebrow. I tensed, waiting for him to demand Father's identity papers, but the man just sucked his teeth and took the money.

Father lifted me into the flatboat, and we pitched into the middle of the canal. The gondolier rowed us against the current, through a curtain of smog. When Father crouched, my hood blocked out all but his strange new face.

"Now, Firi," he whispered.

I clenched my illusion cord, and my stringy, wet hair became Afyn's thick, damp curls. They froze against my neck, and my cheeks burned from Father's scrubbing, but I didn't care. The layers of the woolen skirts Father had stuffed me into kept me warm enough, and I was outside. We were going somewhere new. I held the cord tight.

Minutes later, a bridge appeared over the canal, decorated with fresh corpses. Purple ribbons dangled from the ankles of several bodies, even one as young as me. Purple meant stealing. I spun the Manager-class band Father had affixed to my wrist. We didn't steal. *It's not stealing if they give it to you,* he always said.

The gondola skimmed beneath the display of death, and as we crossed from the Bilge into the Labor District, farther than I'd ever been, I recited our script in my mind, over and over. I would say everything perfectly. I would prove to Father that I could help. The sun rose as huge factories popped up along the canal, spewing black smoke, before giving way to squat buildings, parks, and fine architecture.

When we pulled to a stop at the Corners—an intersection of the Labor, Merchant, and Manager Districts—Father lifted me out of the boat, removed my cloak, and smoothed the sleeves of my costume. At the center of the huge square, a statue of Emperor Dreznor'proska'ed'nov cast a long shadow over the bustling crowd. He was the ruler of the Vorstav'n Empire on the southern mainland and of the Stav Regime that occupied us. There were statues of him in every square in the city. This one was as tall as a building. His beard alone was nearly my height.

We joined other newcomers in kneeling before the statue's feet, as the Stav soldiers expected. When we straightened, Father took my hand and walked confidently toward the road to the Manager District, as if he belonged among the business tycoons, factory owners, and government officials around us. When we passed the huddle of Stav soldiers manning the checkpoint, he flashed his blue band, and they nodded us through without question.

Father led me into a well-manicured square. Every part of me tingled. The Manager District was empty of bloated bodies and cackling loiterers. The buildings shimmered. The winter air tasted crisp. Even the sky seemed bluer. I swiveled, taking in each painted storefront and coiffed resident.

A cloud of sweetness grabbed my stomach. I turned. Behind the clearest window I'd ever seen, shelves of pastries steamed, piled high, begging to be taken. In the Zed District, food came off ration boats smelling of mold, not sugar. Inside the shop a little girl bounced on her toes. The skirts of her fancy dress flared as she pointed to a pastry. When her mother laughed, something sharp dug into my chest. Did they live here?

Father snatched my chin.

Whatever you do, don't break character. That was rule number six.

I bit my lip. Today, I lived here too. This place wasn't strange to Afyn, Mr. Finweint's daughter. Very few of Father's personas had a daughter, so I melted into his side as we continued across the square.

Finally, Father halted under a shop's awning. "I have a quick meeting," he said in a lilting Gwyn accent. The first line of our script. I straightened. Who was our mark? Father brushed a curl behind my ear, regaining my attention. "Promise you will be sweet and patient?"

"Promise," I recited.

"Maybe, if you behave, I will show you the surprise after."

I gasped. "What surprise?"

"If I told you, it would not be a surprise."

There wouldn't really be a surprise, I knew that, but bumps still erupted on my arms. We'd rehearsed this conversation in our apartment many times, but always with one of his training personas. Now we were actually outside, in the magical streets of the Manager District, and Father *was* Mr. Finweint.

When his gaze flicked behind me, I followed it to a man heading down the sidewalk toward us. An orange wristband peeked out from the sleeve of his worn but well-kept flannel shirt and wool jacket—the Gwyn-style uniform of the Labor class. He was the only Labor in sight. Fleshy windburned cheeks pushed up above his stiff frown, and his oily hair was slicked into submission.

He wiped stained hands against his thighs again and again, appearing more out of place than a fish on land.

When the Labor-class man drew close, Father veered into his path.

"Look where you are going!" Father barked.

The man gasped apologies, tripping over himself to back away. Father huffed. I curled against him as if I were afraid, but my head was light. I counted, waiting for the next prompt.

One, two, three—

Father patted his thighs. "Thief! My purse!" He pointed at the Labor-class man, who gawked as the checkpoint soldiers launched after him.

"It wasn' . . . I didn' . . . ," the man sputtered as they patted him down.

"Sniffles, Firi," Father whispered. Tears poured hot and burning from my eyes, as we'd practiced, as I'd perfected. "It is leather!" Father shouted over my wails. He cupped a hand against the base of my skull. "Othan Finweint. My name. The name. It is engraved . . ."

"I didn't take no purse. I've got papers to be here," the man protested. "I've got a summons to the Baking Quarter." He tried to reach into the folds of his jacket, but the soldiers wrenched his arms back. Then one pulled Father's expensive leather coin purse from his pocket—the purse Father had planted when we'd run into him. The Labor's eyes bulged. "Tha's not mine. I swear. It's—"

A Stav soldier punched him in the jaw. His knees gave out. "One invitation to the Manager District and you steal? Piece of shit." When the Labor-class man lifted his chin, red stained his top lip. My stomach squirmed in a way that didn't feel like hunger.

Father popped open the purse. Only his forged papers were inside.

OTHAN FINWEINT

CLASS: MANAGER

OCCUPATION: VICE PRESIDENT, SKERTZA BANK

"My money." Father thrust the purse back at the soldiers. "Ten pieces were inside. Give back the money, you thieving—"

I shrieked. My illusion cord twanged, sparking panic. If my curls bled limp or brown, even for a moment, Father would never let me help him again. My tears gushed faster.

A soldier approached with his palms up. "Please, sir," he said in broken Iaqun. All the Stav soldiers were from the southern continent, and few spoke the language of the northern countries well. "I get your money. Take your daughter to safe place."

Father hesitated, cheeks red, but then led me to the sidewalk to wait. Behind us, the Labor-class man argued and the soldiers interrogated. Managers all over the square stared at the scene with straight backs and upturned noses. I clung to my slippery illusion. Sweat beaded on my forehead. If I failed now, I'd be locked back up in my room forever.

Calloused skin brushed my wet cheeks. I shuddered, waiting for angry fingers to pinch my jaw, but they didn't. When I looked up, Mr. Finweint's frown was soft. "Are you all right?" he asked, running a thumb down my cheek.

He'd never looked at me like that before, not with any persona.

When he kissed my forehead, he erased reality. I forgot that Mr. Finweint and his daughter were fake, that there had never been any money in the coin purse, and that the Labor-class man hadn't truly robbed us. In the softness of his concern, I became Afyn, daughter of Othan Finweint, and Father's love became real. I tensed every muscle in my chest. I would not release Afyn for anything.

"Here, sir," the young soldier said, returning with Father's coin purse. Beyond him, another soldier kneed the writhing man in the gut. My stomach tightened again, but I made myself whimper. Afyn was afraid. Afyn had just been robbed.

Still gripping my hand, Father took the purse, now full with ten pieces that had never been ours—money the Stav wrongly assumed belonged to the wealthy Mr. Finweint, not the destitute Labor-class man. It was probably most of what the man owned. I wondered how much food it would buy us.

"Take him to Central," Father demanded. "I will call on the admiral to press charges myself." The man's limbs twitched. He twisted, shouting as they dragged him from the square.

Father knelt, blocking my view. "Well, we are late for the appointment now, but perhaps it was not that important. Perhaps you are more important." His finger bounced off the end of my nose, continuing the script even though the soldiers were walking away. *Always assume you're being watched.* That was rule number four.

"Really?" I recited. A shudder zipped through me, followed by a twang of dread. The surprise wasn't real. These were just our last scripted lines, signaling it was time to go home. But I didn't want the act to end.

Father took my hand and led me across the square. My feet grew heavy. Had I done well enough? Would he take me out with him again tomorrow?

Then, in a flash of shock, I realized Father was marching us uphill, *away* from the Zed District. We approached the marble front steps of the biggest building I'd ever seen. Entry columns shone elegant and imperious. A huge canvas advertisement hung between them, depicting two Vorstav'n dancers in perfect mid-twirl. Father started climbing the steps.

I glanced back over my shoulder. We were supposed to go home now.

"This is the Grande, Aza Veska'nora's dance hall," Father said, following a trickle of Managers into a cool foyer. The thrill of voices bounced between marble walls.

Who is Aza Veska'nora? I wanted to ask, but this wasn't part of my script. Father's polished shoes approached the ticket counter. He said, "Two, please," and gave the girl some of the money we'd just gotten from the Labor-class man.

By the time we entered the dimly lit theater, my head was spinning. Questions tangled in my throat, but I was afraid of breaking character, of saying something wrong.

"They do serdzat dances here," Mr. Finweint said. He gestured me into a wide velvet-cushioned chair. "It's a refined dance form that comes from mainland Vorstav."

I couldn't speak.

Father touched my cheek. "We're here to watch the dance. You've earned it."

The air punched out of my lungs. "A real surprise?"

His strange, low laugh drenched my shoulders. I straightened as high as I could. Father had sat us in the very last row, near the doors, but over the sea of expensive hats and intricate hairdos, I could see the whole stage.

When the lights went dark, silence pressed on my ears. I leaned closer to Father, and our arms touched. He squeezed my forearm, then left his hand there, a warm weight. "Watch closely, they're going to tell a story."

Music amplified and the stage lights shifted. Then Father's touch became an anchor as dancers spun onstage and swept me away.

They moved with seamless perfection, bodies twirling and tapping out a story before my eyes. I clutched my illusion cord so hard my rib joints protested. My knuckles turned white around the armrest. I'd never known something so beautiful could exist. I wanted to hold it, consume it, make it part of me.

But my illusion cord was like a sea snake wriggling in hands that were too small. Sweat soon soaked my neck. By the middle of the show, I was shaking.

"Afyn," Father murmured. Onstage, the head dancer spun into her lover's arms. "Afyn." His face swam in my vision. To any onlookers, I'm sure he appeared the concerned parent, but he was looking for signs.

The ends of my hair flickered brown. I shook my head. I could hold it. I just had to grip harder. I writhed, trying to get a better look at the stage.

Father stood. His grip turned lethal. I swallowed my cry on instinct. Fabric rustled as nearby audience members glanced at us, but when Father pulled me to my feet, I tried to yank my arm away. Just a little longer, I could do it.

He dragged me to the exit.

THREE

Firin

Then

Father's fancy shoes echoed down empty halls, and I tripped after him, grief gurgling up my throat.

"Now, now. No need for that," he said, pulling me back outside. Sunlight accosted us, fluttering my lashes and hitching my tears. I kept my eyes on the cobblestones, afraid of what he'd do if other Managers saw me crying.

Waving his fake Manager-class band at the checkpoint soldiers, he led me downhill, into the Merchant District. In the shadows of an alley, he sat me down on an overturned crate and replaced my blue Manager-class wristband with a green Merchant-class one.

"You did incredible, Firi," he said.

I heaved tiny, strained breaths. I didn't want to be Firin. Father locked Firin in the apartment. He trained Firin but never let her help. If I was Firin, Father would be someone else with harsh words, someone whose touch hurt.

I wanted to be Afyn. I wanted him to be Mr. Finweint.

"Can we do it again?" I whimpered.

"Of course." He pulled me to my feet.

After shedding the most conspicuous layers of our costumes, Father led me east back through Luisonn. At every District checkpoint, he gave me a new wristband and presented the Stav soldiers with a new set of identity papers.

Wide streets narrowed. Winter winds picked up speed. Cobblestones gave way to mud, and buildings tilted inward, as if pulled by the lines of laundry hung between them. When we reached the edge of the Zed District, my legs trembled, so Father picked me up and carried me past frozen beggars and corpses, caked in coal dust and grime, back into the nightmare of our reality.

I was asleep before we reached the tenement.

The next morning, I woke before the sun.

I picked at shreds of wall plaster from the inn's previous life and waited for signs of Father. When the boys next door stopped arguing long enough to murmur their morning prayers to the Gwynythaid saints, I joined them. The Stav outlawed public worship of any religion that wasn't their own, and Father didn't pray to any deities that I knew of, but he'd taught me about all of them anyway. Compared to the vengeful Kirru gods, the horrid Vorstav'n ancestors, and the Qunsiian's judgmental Enlightened, the protective Gwyn saints seemed most likely to answer my prayers.

That morning I begged for Father to be Mr. Finweint again.

When candlelight flared under the door, I tore off my blankets. Father slouched at the kitchen table. His neck swiveled at the squeak of the hinges, and one of his semiregular personas glared down his arched nose at me. My heart sank.

Sniq was one of my trainers, a persona who'd once lived with a Qunsiian circus. I hated everything about the illusion, from his ragged hair to his bowed legs. When he slid a napkin of fresh buns across the table, the steam danced in the cold air. My stomach rumbled. Distantly,

I understood there was pride in his sneering smile—*I'd* helped us get this food—but I stayed in the doorway.

"Tell me about the neighbors," Sniq said.

A routine request. Father had me report every morning on the neighbors' activities. *To practice observation.* I wanted to ask about yesterday, but I knew better than to disobey, so I swallowed and said, "The third brother's got a chimney-sweep job, and his pa is happy about it."

Sniq grunted. "Why's his pa happy about it?"

The answer seemed obvious, but Father was always asking me why people did what they did and said what they said. "Because if he does a good job, he might get made a Labor."

Sniq nodded, then pulled a cigarette out of his striped shirt pocket and lit a match. A winter breeze gusted through the window, dispersing the fumes. Rancid low-tide canal refuse wafted up my nose.

I curled my toes, regretting my lack of socks, and tried not to breathe too deep as a question clawed its way up my throat. I willed myself not to say it, but the question didn't obey. "Why can't you be Mr. Finweint again?"

Sniq went deathly still. He took a drag of his cigarette. "What have I told you about faces?"

"You change too much," I choked out. "It's not fair. Why can't you just—"

"What have I *told* you?"

"Please—"

He banged a fist on the table. Stood. *"What do we say?"*

I clenched my teeth together as he loomed over me.

"Say it." His horrid, cracked Sniq fingernails dug into my chin.

"It's not safe," I muttered.

"What isn't?"

"One face. I can't . . . can't be predictable." That was rule number three.

Sniq sniffed. Something very *un*-Sniq-like softened on his face, but then he exhaled, and it vanished.

"You said we could do it again," I pressed.

A cloud of warm smoke descended over my face. "You did all right yesterday." I scowled. Mr. Finweint had said I was incredible. "Afyn is a dangerous role to play. If you want to be her, you need to *become* her, you hear me?"

"Yes." I'd never wanted anything more.

"Good. Now, I've a job to do. You stay here'n train." He tugged one of my braids and grabbed Sniq's signature red jacket.

As he stepped toward the door, I blurted the other question that had plagued me all night: "But what will happen to the Labor man?"

Sniq squinted down at me. "He'll be fine. He's a Labor. He has real identity papers, ones that the Stav Regime can confirm in their registries. That means he can work at a factory—not like us. That's why I must do what I do." He sniffed, then crouched in front of me. "We only have two choices in this life, Firin: we can grovel to the Stav and try to get assigned to the Labor class, like those boys next door, or we can do jobs like yesterday and get enough money to sail far away from the Stav. Wouldn't you rather do that?"

"Yes," I said, my fingers curling into fists.

"Good. We get enough money, we can sail wherever you want, *be* whoever you want. Now, go practice."

I listened to him plod down the stairwell, then snatched the bun he'd left me and the oil lamp. Chewing ravenously, I dug through the blankets that made up my bed and found the silver pocket mirror Father had given me long ago. I set the lamp down just so and sat cross-legged on the floor. Firin's face squinted up at me in the little glass circle. Her limp brown hair frayed from its twin braids, her round nose perched between two sharp cheekbones. She looked like something that lived in the dark. I shut my eyes and willed her away. My illusion cord shivered. Bumps rippled up my neck, over my skull, and when I opened my eyes, Afyn's ebony curls gleamed in the lamplight.

Hours passed. The sun rose. Thirst dried my lips. Sweat broke out on my neck as all the muscles in my torso strained, but I held on to the curls until my vision swarmed and my body shook.

I would perfect my illusion. I would help Father—and one day, I would truly become Afyn, whatever it took.

FOUR

Firin

Now

Nine people.

Nine people stood between me and my ticket off the Iket Isles. I gripped the strap of my bag as the family at the head of the line stepped into the square-jawed quartermaster's steady gaze.

Six people now.

I chanced a glance behind me. Over the heads of bellowing lower-class dockworkers and frantic upper-class passengers, I counted at least two dozen Stav soldiers. They dotted the congested Landings like rocks in a rising tide. At least four of them wore black Nodtacht uniforms. Chaos erupted as they dragged people from lines. Each time they searched their targets, they found a way to check their arms.

They were looking for me.

Putting my back to them, I tried to breathe. The weaver's identity papers crinkled in my fist inside the pocket of her purple coat. The Nodtacht with the hook-shaped scar wasn't here. As long as he hadn't checked the weaver's apartment, the soldiers were just guessing which face I wore.

Thankfully, the docks were extra crowded with mid- and upper-class citizens bundled against the early-spring cold. Most people didn't know how strong the old anti–Stav Reformist movement had regrown in the shadows, but they sensed it anyway, fleeing like animals at the first pressure change before a storm. As soon as the Reformists decided to strike, the Vorstav'n Empire would send more soldiers and Nodtacht from the mainland to punish anyone who looked at them sideways. I intended to be far away before that happened.

The dockyard clock ticked. Between the planks under my feet, a Stav pamphlet floated in the water, declaring new taxes on Labors, arrests and executions, reminders of curfews. In front of me in line, a Merchant-class child released an earsplitting shriek. I cringed.

"I don't *want* to go to Qunsii," he sobbed. He'd been a mess for hours.

"I know, love," his young, tired mother said, crouching down. "But it will be an adventure." Behind her, a younger boy clutched a bun in fleshy fists that barely cleared the sleeves of his thick wool coat. His wide eyes hadn't left me since I'd joined the line.

I gripped my purse and glanced west, toward the Bilge, then quickly looked away before my mind could fill with poisonous thoughts of Father. In the bay, hundreds of ships dotted the skyline. Most carried imports of raw goods and food from the northern-continent countries: to fuel the factories, the people who worked them, and the Vorstav'n Empire's greed. While a majority would continue south to the empire, a few prepared to head back north, loading up on passengers in lieu of cargo. Soon I'd be on one, heading for Qunsii, where I could finally stop surviving and *live*.

An older couple stepped up to the quartermaster.

Four people left.

A scream of true distress split the din of the dockyard, shocking even the child into temporary silence. His younger brother flinched. A Stav soldier was pulling a Merchant-class woman from a line just four docks down. He yanked the neckline of her dress, ripping the buttons in the back, and I resisted the urge to grab my bicep and cover my scar. My knuckles turned white around the strap of my bag.

As I stepped forward, a cart full of suitcases barreled toward me, parting bodies in its wake. "They're swarmin' the docks today. You think they know?" one of the dockworkers pushing it muttered over a toothpick.

"Nah, they're looking for someone specific," the second man rasped. I spun toward his sweat-soaked back. "But they've got the wrong direction, if you ask me. Everyone's with the Players tonight. You're goin'?"

"To Sovest? Absolutely."

The crowd swallowed them.

I stopped breathing.

The Veiled Players.

The name of the old, illegal theater troupe—which everyone called the Players—hooked into my windpipe. Years ago, before the Stav discovered what I'd done and what I could do, I attended the Players' every underground show. But I hadn't heard a word about them since they vanished with the Reformists four years ago.

Sharp pieces of an old life sliced through me with the scent of oil lamps; the sound of violins; a crooked, knowing grin on a freckled face; and the brush of calloused hands on skin. A shudder split me from head to toe.

Sovest.

If Bregan was alive, I knew, for the first time in four years, exactly where he'd be.

"Ma'am?" The Merchant-class mother frowned at me. "Ma'am, are you all right?"

"Yes, I'm . . . I'm fine."

Her older child released another scream, yanking her back to her knees by her skirts. The toddler kept staring at me.

"Next!" the quartermaster shouted. The young man ahead of the family stepped up. Before greeting him, the quartermaster added, "Got four tickets left! Just four!"

My heart fell. Groans exploded from those in line behind me. The mother and her sons would wipe out the rest of the tickets.

When I glanced back, I froze.

The Nodtacht with the hook-shaped scar stood like a broad-backed tower at the edge of the Landings, encircled by Stav soldiers. He gestured as he talked, miming a high hairdo, then signaling a bag. He was telling them about me, about what I looked like as the weaver. The child's continued single-note wail grated down my spine.

I had to get on this ship *now*.

When the next cart, this one full of sacks of food supplies, rolled down the dock, my stomach twisted viciously. I looked down into the silent toddler's eerie, unblinking stare. While his mother was consumed by her other son, I crouched down, hating every piece of myself as I said quietly, "Watch this."

I flipped a coin through my knuckles, hypnotizing him.

Then I hoisted him onto the cart.

As he sank into bags of flour, his brother's pathetic wails drowned out his shocked cries. The cart rattled down the dock.

"Next!" the quartermaster shouted.

The mother stood up. She took her older son's hand, then turned to look for the younger one. All the blood drained from her face. She screamed his name.

I grabbed her shoulder. "Ma'am, I think he climbed on that cart." I pointed down the dock, to where the cart was still just visible. The mother seized her other child and ran. She would find him, but not before I took a ticket. They were Merchant class. They would find another ship to board. I would not.

When I staggered up to the quartermaster, sweat dripped down my temples.

"Where're you headin'?" she asked.

"Qunsii." I passed her the stolen identity papers.

She squinted at them, then at my face—the weaver's face. "Eight hundred."

I pulled out the money I'd saved for four years: hundreds of coins condensed into four sleek bank-issued gold bars. The quartermaster counted, nodded, then shoved my papers back with a ticket. I stared at it, overcome with a strange, sudden urge to throw it in the water lapping beneath our feet.

"We leave at sunrise."

"Sunrise?" I choked. I didn't have until sunrise.

"We don't have rights to leave the harbor until then. That a problem?"

"No," I forced out. "No, that's not a problem." I wouldn't get on another ship tonight. This would have to work.

Flipping up my hood, I retreated down the dock. On shore, I wove through bodies, heading west where fewer Stav patrolled. I didn't dare lift my gaze from the cobblestones as I pulled on my illusion, gouging wrinkles into my cheeks and thinning out my hair. With luck, I could get out of this square alive, but if the Nodtacht suspected I had stolen the weaver's identity, how long would it take them to check every ship's roster for her name?

A terrible idea bloomed in the back of my mind, like a flower in the dead of winter. I could go to Sovest Square and hide at the Players' show until my ship was ready to leave. My fractured heart strained, deepening years-old fissures, but I thought past the pain, groping for logic. The illegal theater, with all its protocols and protections, would be a safer haven than most crevices of the city tonight. I could allow myself one last glimpse of Bregan, if he was even there. As long as I didn't talk to anyone or show my real face, I'd be fine.

I glanced up. The dockyard clock read twelve hours until sunrise. If I could just—

My gaze clashed with the scarred Nodtacht's across the docks like steel against steel. In the surprise of it, I flinched, and all at once I realized that, though I wasn't wearing the weaver's face anymore, I'd forgotten to ditch her purple coat.

The Nodtacht's brows rose.

Before orders could leave his lips, I bolted.

FIVE

Firin

Then

One dreary spring evening when I was sixteen, I slipped down an alley between Fisherman's Wharf and the Banking Quarter. My expensive embroidered skirts and long silk dress sleeves were rumpled. In the glass of my pocket mirror, I tweaked my illusion—thickening my eyebrows and sharpening my chin—based on an illustration of my mark's long-dead sister.

Today's con was a fake business deal, one that required charm on my part, and if we were successful, it might be the last con Father and I ever had to do.

I peered around the corner. The year's first big harvest had arrived on ships from Gwynythaid. Crops didn't grow on the Iket Isles' rocky shores, so it was one of the busiest harbor days of the year. Under a gray sky, people flowed north on the bridges that arched over the Corners, carrying goods up from the Landings. Merchants and Managers, accompanied by their Labor-class servants, knelt before the statue of the emperor before veering off to their respective districts.

As I sought my mark, my eyes snagged on a poster blowing in the crisp wind. THE DEBUTANTE OF TERZAT, it announced, AT THE

GRANDE. Behind the words, a sketched Vorstav'n dancer beamed mid-twirl. It was *the* show of the year, starring Aza Veska'nora's new talent, a dancer named Sochya'tov. If this evening's con was successful, Father and I would go see it to celebrate.

I'd studied every dance we'd ever gone to see, practicing the moves in the apartment when Father was out. When we left Luisonn, I would be a dancer. Not a serdzat dancer, as that style was solely performed in Vorstav, but I would do a similar Kirru-style dance I'd learned about from a Merchant-class man we conned a few months back. As soon as we arrived in Iakirru, I would learn it.

It had taken Father and me longer than I'd hoped to save up the money to leave Luisonn, as preparing for and pulling off cons required reinvestment of most of the money they made us.

Today, that would change.

For years, my training and our cons had consumed my every waking moment. I apprenticed to a dozen of Father's personas—magicians, artists, soldiers, and spies. With their guidance, I perfected changing the composition of my hair, the angles of my face, and the shape of my body. I learned basic Vorstav'n and practiced diction until I could speak Iaqun—the language of the northern continent—in Qunsiian, Kirru, and Gwyn accents with ease.

I put up with the training personas' disdain, rage, and indifference, and in exchange, once in a while, we followed our most intricate cons with luxurious outings as Mr. Finweint and Afyn. It was the only time I ever got to just *be*.

Months had passed since our last big con, months where Father had been away more than he was home. He never explained what he did when he left me alone, but I suspected he was planning our trip. After today's con we would have enough money to sail north. Then Father could get a job, and I could become a dancer, and we could finally breathe.

I wrung my shawl in my fingers—which I'd manicured with illusion to look like a Manager's—and scanned the Corners. It seemed pointless, searching for one face in a sea of enriched pockets, but our days of manipulating wallets were long over. Father's more lucrative fake business deals could take months to plan. He made me research my marks: asking up on them around the city; spying to learn their histories, interests, and hearts' desires. I enjoyed the work, mostly because it allowed me to leave the apartment.

Over the last month, I had learned that today's target, Baron Ihan Hulei, owned the biggest factory in Luisonn's Shipyard, the Iket Isles branch of his Qunsiian father's business, and a theater on the continent. He had three brothers in Qunsii and a sister who died as a child. I'd even read that a few years ago, he had lost his wife to drink and his son to a shipwreck. Amid all that tragedy, he'd waded through a controversy when a girl died in one of his factories. He raised wages for all his employees to mollify them.

I'd considered using my illusion to mimic his late wife, but I wanted to provoke more empathy than grief, so I landed on his sister. I found an old illustration and tweaked my illusion to look like her *just* enough to snag his attention.

Barons never came down from their mansions on Bounty Hill, so this was a rare opportunity. If all went well, Father would invite him out to dinner and corner him in a fake deal that would score us enough money to leave the Isles. Then we'd go celebrate at the Grande.

In the square, people glanced repeatedly over their shoulders, their hair and clothing whipping in the growing winds. Tension stretched over my skin, but it was more than just the storm brewing on the horizon; it was as if behind the harvest jubilation, a dangerous current churned. Then I saw why.

Stav soldiers were *everywhere*, posted at every corner, creating ebbs in the crowd's flow as people gave them a wide berth. The Vorstav'n Empire had sent more soldiers from the mainland in response to recent Labor protests. But it wasn't the blue-uniformed soldiers who made my heart clench; it was the dozen black leather–clad Nodtacht among them, scowling out at the square. The empire's security agents usually worked undercover, but in the wake of rising strikes and riots, they'd started showing themselves plainly in public to frighten people into obedience. If anyone could sniff out Father's and my schemes, it was them.

If a Nodtacht is near, abort, no matter the mission. Rule number eight.

Years ago, I'd unknowingly conned a Merchant-class man right in front of a Nodtacht. Father had abandoned the con, dragged me home, and locked me in the apartment as if I were seven years old again. After three months of staring out the kitchen window, there'd been stretches of days where I hadn't even gotten out of bed.

But this was the first baron we'd ever conned. Barons were *the* wealthiest inhabitants of Luisonn; they owned conglomerates of businesses, many of them international. Most had primary homes in other countries. This was our best chance at securing the money we needed. I adjusted my sleeve around my hidden knife. I couldn't abort.

There.

A man sauntered over a bridge. Thick yellow hair and fair skin. A shiny top hat, crisp blue suit, and bright-green waistcoat. Even without the white band gleaming on his wrist, Baron Hulei would have looked out of place. A pillar among weeds.

I bit my lip, then glanced at the Nodtacht agents. My pulse thumped in warning, but I took a deep breath and pulled up a memory of a Labor-class girl I'd once seen while out doing reconnaissance. Her brother had talked back to some Stav soldiers, and while they beat him to a pulp, she exuded a raw, hypnotizing, writhing kind of horror. As Father had taught me, I channeled the memory of her panic into my limbs, then surged into the square.

I vaulted straight into my mark.

"Oh, I'm so sorry," I gasped, dropping my shawl.

The baron grabbed my shoulder, and when I looked up, his lips parted with the slack shock of having seen a ghost. A thrill of conquest shot to my core. "No apologies necessary," he said with a slick, polished

Qunsiian accent. "Are you all right?" He was older than I'd expected, and his round, fleshy features looked nothing like the news illustrations.

I glanced at his wristband, then stepped closer, and spoke with the melodious timbre of a native Gwyn. "No, actually. I've lost my father. I don't . . . don't know where he . . ."

"Relax. You're safe now." He removed his towering top hat.

The nearest Nodtacht—a woman with a braid thicker than rope—glanced in our direction, then returned to her conversation with a couple of Stav soldiers. I exhaled.

"Where did you see him last?" the baron asked, picking up and dusting off my shawl. His eyes sparkled like a bluebird sky over a cerulean sea.

Father and I didn't use scripts anymore, now that my improvisation had improved, but I pulled from the story we'd agreed upon. "He said he was going to a jeweler, but I got distracted and went into a bookstore because I saw they had a copy of a Sumni book," I rambled. "I just stepped in for a minute, but then he was gone."

"Ah, I have an idea where he headed. I can take you."

He started across the square with the smooth surety of a man who held solutions to problems in his purse. When I glanced over, the Nodtacht woman was gone. The con was working. I wrapped myself in my shawl with a pathetic sniff.

"You like Sumni?" The baron tapped the rim of the top hat in his hand.

"Yes." I'd read that Sumni was his favorite philosopher. "My grandfather was from Qunsii."

"I see. Well, the jeweler's is just—"

A wail shot across the square. "Afyn? Afyn!" Father bolted for me with his expensive suit askew, hair mussed.

"Papa!" I gasped as he enveloped me in a frantic embrace.

"Oh, my Afyn, I've been looking for you everywhere," he said, pushing me to arm's length. Worry etched lines around his frown. "What happened to you?"

"I got lost. This man helped me." I held my breath, but Father didn't seem to have noticed the Nodtacht looming nearby.

Father's eyes flitted to the baron's white band. He half bowed. "My gratitude knows no end. Othan Finweint." He held out a hand.

The baron inclined his head as he shook. "Ihan Hulei. Truly, I did nothing."

A shadow fell over us, stretching long in the dim evening light.

"Is there a problem here?"

The deep voice belonged to a man built like a stone building. A ragged scar shaped like a fishhook sliced his thick beard in half. When his pale eyes met mine, they shattered my insides like a hammer to ice. Behind him, two additional Nodtacht agents, all in black leather, rested their hands on their gun holsters. I popped my knife into my sweaty palm.

Father's grip spasmed on my shoulder. "Well, we were just—"

"No," the baron said. He squinted. "Everything is fine."

A vein throbbed in the Nodtacht's temple. Wind whipped around us as Father glanced between them. "It's true. My daughter is a wanderer. But we are fine." Then he *smiled* at the Nodtacht with all the naivete of a Gwyn traveler out of sync with the dangers of this regime. I held my breath.

"Papers." The Nodtacht outstretched a beefy hand.

"Of course, of course." Father reached for a pocket inside his jacket. When I pulled my own fake papers out, my fingers shook.

"This is unnecessary," the baron insisted.

I peered up. His confident composure hadn't changed, but a harsh light shone behind his eyes, like the sun through a keyhole. The Baron class was the highest in Luisonn, but Baron Hulei was Qunsiian, not Vorstav'n. The Nodtacht served the Vorstav'n emperor, outside the laws of the Stav Regime. It was unclear, in this situation, who held more power—and yet, the baron was defending us, complete strangers a class below him, as if he were personally offended by the Nodtacht's behavior.

"Papers," the Nodtacht repeated.

"It's fine, it's fine," Father said, brandishing our forged documents.

The Nodtacht surveyed them, then sniffed. "Welcome to Luisonn." With one last assessing glower, he disappeared.

A gasp rushed out of me. The baron looked down, and with the swiftness of blowing out a candle, the storm of his rage died. His eyes crinkled.

I made myself smile at him. "Thank you, sir. For helping me."

Father watched the Nodtacht's receding back. His fake geniality had frozen on his face. *Please don't abort,* I prayed. We could still take the baron to dinner, work a fake business deal, celebrate at the Grande.

"Well, I wish you the best," the baron said, donning his top hat.

"You look familiar," I said, improvising. I tilted my head to give him a full view of the features I'd chosen to look like his sister's. I could not let him leave. "Have I seen you in the papers?"

Come on, Father.

"You read the papers too? Smart girl."

"You are of the Hulei and Hulei family!" Father finally gasped, returning to the plan. Thank the saints. "Out of Qunsii?"

"Yes." The baron's eyes glinted. I fought the urge to fidget.

"This is fortuitous," Father said. "I am with Thayne United. Out of Gwynythaid. It is a new timber operation. I would love to talk to you. I owe you for helping my daughter. Would you join me for a dinner?"

The baron glanced at his golden pocket watch. "All right. How about Atzuie's? It's just around the corner there, on Seventeenth."

My joy leaped like a fish clearing the surface.

"Perfect." Father squinted at the clouds gathering in the sky. "I will meet you there. Let me just send my daughter back to our lodgings."

What? No. Father was supposed to bring me to dinner. My job was to distract the baron if he got suspicious.

"Come, Afyn," Father said.

"Can I come with you?"

Father laughed, but there was an edge to it. "No, this is a meeting for gentlemen. See you there?" He nodded to the baron, then steered me out of the square.

When we turned down an alley, I yanked off my ridiculously expensive shawl. "Why aren't you taking me to dinner?"

"*You* are being reckless," he snapped, impatience uncharacteristic to Mr. Finweint slipping through his mask.

"Is this about the Nodtacht? I didn't see them," I lied. "It doesn't matter anyway; we tricked him, and the baron." Two of the most dangerous people in Luisonn.

"You think you know everything," Father said, "but you don't. Now, please go home." He pulled at the lapels of his jacket and rolled his shoulders, as if adjusting his Mr. Finweint personality back into place. Unease writhed in my stomach.

"You're still doing the con, right?" We needed the money.

"Yes."

"What about *The Debutante*?"

His brown eyes flared like flint on steel. "That is not possible anymore."

This was a punishment, then.

We glared at each other for several painful heartbeats. Each thud threatened to fracture my bones. I was *good* at conning, and I had *hours* left of Afyn in me. I could help him cinch this deal and get off this cesspit of an island. But when Father made a decision, nothing I did or said would change it. Fighting would only make my life more miserable.

A familiar wave of exhaustion crashed over me as I bled back into Firin. I clenched my fists against it.

"Good." He crossed his arms. "I'll be back in the morning."

I turned on my heel and stormed out of the alley, feeling his eyes on my back. I headed toward the Zed District, as he expected me to, but with every step, I traced the edges of Afyn's papers in my pocket.

If he didn't want my help, fine.

I wasn't missing *The Debutante*.

SIX

Firin

I made it halfway to the Bilge before I dared change course. By then, the clouds promised to crack open at any moment. Winding from alley to alley, I returned to the Manager District. I peeked around every corner for Father and didn't see Mr. Finweint anywhere, but to be safe, I slipped on a new face—neither Afyn's nor my own—and became just another pretty Manager with smooth, unblemished skin.

When I stepped onto Regents' Hill's polished cobblestone streets, the very air calmed. Less chatter. Smaller crowds. Even the storm seemed to consider leaving the place be. I lifted my chin, mimicking the Managers around me, but my mask of ease strained. A Stav soldier smoking a cigarette at the district checkpoint pushed off the wall as I approached. I slid up my sleeve, showing him my blue wristband, and he slouched again, unconcerned.

I hurried past him, exhaling as I knelt before the square's small marble statue of the emperor. Across the plaza, a massive advertisement for *The Debutante* rustled in the wind outside the Grande, making the sketched woman look as if she were dancing.

This was risky. I'd sneaked into the Grande a handful of times before, but always when I could rely on Father being gone for several days. This time, he was only a few blocks away. If I was caught by the Stav, I'd be imprisoned for trespassing or hung for attempted theft. But I was good at slipping through their fingers. If Father found out, however, he would kill me himself.

Panic is the enemy, he always said. *Confidence is key.* I wiped sweaty palms on my skirts and stood to face the Grande. I could do this.

A ribbon of well-dressed patrons snaked through doors guarded by Stav soldiers. Setting my shoulders, I wove through the line with an air of confidence. It took effort to move slowly and not draw attention. After what felt like an eternity, I rounded the building and swung myself up to its fire escape.

Wooden steps groaned as I climbed. At the top, I grabbed the lip of the Grande's gutter and swung myself to the roof. Just above me, a row of five small windows dotted the side of the roof's next tier. The hinges of the leftmost one squeaked, then submitted, the latch still broken. Sticking my head between the curtains, I peered down the dark, low-ceilinged hallway, then dropped to an unfinished floor. Velvet and oil, tainted with sweat and perfume, thickened the dusty air, plush and exhilarating. The floor hummed beneath my boots. The curtains fell, veiling me in darkness, and I ran my hand along the inside wall until I found the maintenance door. Its rough surface stuck me with a splinter. I hissed, sucking my thumb.

The door opened on a sheer drop, like a cliff on the edge of a sea. People milled below. Voices stirred with the rustle of clothes. Oil trays lit at full blast shone on a gilded stage. I shivered from head to toe. I'd made it on time.

Just in front of me, a wide beam jutted out over the audience, connecting with the latticework that held the building together. I crawled out and hugged my knees to my chest. From up here, I could see the stage more clearly than I would have with Father. The thought punctured my chest, but I gritted my teeth.

He had cut me out. He didn't want to be here. I wouldn't miss him.

Another advantage to hiding up here was that no one could see my face. I released my illusion and relished the cool relief that crawled through my bones. At least I wouldn't have to keep half my focus and energy on preserving it during the show.

When the theater darkened, the audience quieted. Then the stage lights flared on *The Debutante*. From her first leap, Sochya'tov snatched my heart. As she pirouetted from suitor to suitor, melding to each dancer's steps before dismissing them, I felt their thirst in every limb. Gasps and laughs ebbed in the audience like water beneath the docks. I drank in every move, branding them to memory so I could practice them later. At one point, I turned to ask Mr. Finweint about the style of serdzat and how it compared to Kirru dances, but my glance met darkness. I dug my nails into my palms and refocused.

When the debutante's true love finally spun out, the music slowed and the dancer's movements elongated, as if time itself had come to a standstill. The newcomer matched Sochya'tov's moves, hesitance in every mirrored curve of their pliés.

"What are you doing?"

The whisper yanked me from my skin.

A man squinted in the small doorway. Claws of fear ripped through my chest. I hurtled off the beam to squeeze past him, but he snatched my shawl. It tightened around my throat. Twisting free, I ran, leaving him with the fabric.

"Wait." Boots scraped the wood floor.

I groped in the dark for the right curtains. If he caught me, he'd hand me to the Stav.

"Hey, wait!"

Yanking the broken window open, I scrambled out onto the wet roof. The air had thickened with a post-rain humidity, and I slid down newly dampened tiles toward the fire escape. Before I reached the edge, fingers clamped around my wrist, halting my descent. My boots skidded. I leaned into the man's hold to stay upright, knees shaking.

"What're you doing up here?" he demanded.

My shawl dangled from a hand with bruised and cracked nails. A faded orange band nestled on his wrist. Relief blew through me as I looked up into a pair of tired eyes.

He was Labor.

He was young, a few years older than I was, with rust-colored curls that stuck out beneath his flatcap. Dark freckles smeared across his cheeks.

"You're not supposed to be up here," he said.

"Neither are you," I responded in Afyn's Gwyn accent.

"Of course not." His smirk sliced like a crescent moon. "I've seen every show anyway, but I've never seen you."

I tugged at my captive wrist. "Let go of me or I'll scream."

He laughed. "Then what? You're clearly not a Manager. Any Stav will see through that." He scanned my expensive boots, then my embroidered wrap skirts and my silk shirt, landing on my calloused hands—hands that weren't Afyn's—and I remembered.

I'd released my illusion.

He was looking at my *real* face.

I stumbled back, toward the edge of the roof, the streets, anywhere to escape this unforgivable mistake.

"You might not want to do that," he said. I froze with one leg over the edge. "The audience is inside now, so the soldiers will be in the square. Especially today. The Nodtacht'll be with them too. They see you climbing down, and they'll want to know what a nice Manager girl was doing on the roof." A dimple appeared in his freckles, but the smile was stiff. "It'd be a shame if they discovered the broken window, don't you think?"

My gut sloshed. I glanced between him and the fire escape. Instinct urged me to move, to run, to get away. If I was still wearing my full Afyn illusion, the Stav would probably help me. Especially if they saw me with a Labor-class man.

Everyone is out for themselves; you should be too. Rule nine.

I glanced at the young man, and my stomach clenched. I clung to reason. If I went to the Stav like this, they'd see through my facade. But I couldn't change into Afyn, not now that this Labor had seen my real face and my worn hands. I might have chanced a lot in coming here, but I could *never* risk anyone seeing me transform.

Father refused to talk about illusion.

When I was younger and asked about how we'd gotten it or who else could do it, he had always slammed the door and locked me away. When he started allowing me to do reconnaissance for cons, I searched on my own but found little to nothing. It seemed like we were the only two people in the world who could change our faces.

Eventually, I discovered legends that the Kirru's eight gods could impersonate people, conveying divine messages while wearing the faces of one's family and friends, but Father and I weren't gods. At first, in my childish naivete, I feared that Father had angered one of the gods, that maybe our illusion was a curse. Soon, I stopped caring. It didn't really matter where we'd gotten our powers, only that they were dangerous. The Stav brutally punished the worship of any god that wasn't their emperor. I once watched three Stav soldiers beat a woman living in the alley below our kitchen window because she claimed she could talk to the Gwyn saints.

If the Stav knew I could change my face, they'd call me cursed. They'd pull me apart, piece by piece.

I eased back up on the roof. The Labor man exhaled, then shrugged out of his jacket and threw it down at my feet. "Sit on it," he said, plopping down just out of arm's reach. "It'd be a shame to ruin that dress."

My cheeks heated. He clearly thought I'd stolen it. Technically, I hadn't. I bought clothes for my Afyn costumes from a tailor in the Manager District, but the money I bought them with was a different story.

I sat down on his jacket. Around us, rooftops stretched out in waves, undulating up toward the barons' mansions on the hill and down to the slums at the edge of the sea. The receding storm painted a sunset that glittered over the ocean.

The Labor took his cap off and squinted at the horizon. He had the gaunt, edged countenance of the lower classes, but there was a rare, sleek ease to the way he held himself, like he was completely at home in his body. On the wrist opposite his class band, he wore a watch that appeared to be broken. When his head turned, he caught me staring, and heat swept across my collarbone. Something sparkled in his eyes.

"You're a good actress," he said. "Almost believed you were a Manager. I'm Bregan, by the way."

I studied the worn edge of his jacket sleeve. The olive-colored moleskin was standard Labor-class issue—roughly hewn, but thick and warm. I couldn't remember the last time I'd talked to someone without a motive. The only conversations I had with people were part of my reconnaissance or our cons. For the first time in my life, I felt unprepared. Unscripted. It made my skin crawl. If I couldn't hold a conversation here, what would I do when I finally made it to Iakirru?

Bregan stretched out on his back like a cat, one knee propped. When he crossed his arms behind his head, the bottom edge of his linen shirt drew up, exposing a stretch of freckled skin. My heart tripped.

If you don't know what to say, ask questions.

"You . . . you come here a lot?" I asked, dropping into my natural lower-class Iket Isles accent. He already knew I wasn't a Manager or from the continent.

"Every show," he said. "Sometimes a few times, if it's good. How'd you find the window?"

A few years ago, when Father had been particularly absent, I'd explored every inch of the dance hall for a way in. It had taken me weeks to find the broken window. I shrugged. "It wasn't hard."

He huffed a soft laugh. Seconds stretched. It grew so quiet I could feel *The Debutante*'s music vibrating beneath us.

Bregan sighed. "I hate that dance."

"Why?"

He snorted. "All the debutante does is lie to people, lead them on, and then leave them shattered in her wake."

"She's not lying. She's looking for her match."

He gaped at me. "How's she supposed to find her match if *she's* matching everyone else's dances? Sochya is good, I'll give her that, but the story is wretched. The fifth act is absurd. They should've made it a tragedy."

I wrapped my fingers in my skirts. I barely knew about serdzat. I certainly didn't know anything about "fifth acts" or tragedies. I eyed the edge of the roof. If I didn't get home before Father, I'd never see another show again.

"Why did you come to see it if you hate it so much?" I asked.

"Just something to do." Bregan shrugged at the setting sun. "But it's still a bad show. Now *Qoyn & Insei*, that's a good love story. Or *The Matchmaker's Heart*. Even *The Widow's Tears* is better than this one, and it's sad enough to make a Stav cry."

I'd never heard of any of them. "How's a Labor know so much about dances?"

"Oh, those aren't dances. They're plays."

A chill poured down my spine. Anyone performing anything other than serdzat could be executed for treason. "Plays are illegal."

"They are." The sunset danced on Bregan's face as he watched me with a kind of captivation, as if I were a show he didn't want to miss a beat of. No one had ever looked at me that closely before. I shivered but didn't turn away. "You know any other accents?" he finally asked. "I've always been bad at them. My ma's trying to teach me Kirru, but it's ridiculous. How do they manage to hit every single consonant?"

A smile teased my lips. "It's not that hard."

"So you do know it?"

Our eyes met. This was incredibly dangerous, yet something fluttered deep inside me that somehow didn't *feel* dangerous. It felt wonderful, just letting a conversation take me where it wanted to. A divot appeared in Bregan's forehead that looked an awful lot like a question mark. He opened his mouth to say something, thought better, then opened it again.

Pop. Pop. Pop.

Distant gunshots jolted me. When a second round answered, I leaped to my feet.

"It's just the strike down at the shoe factory," Bregan said, but unease laced his voice.

A strike. Saints, I should have guessed it. There'd been Nodtacht and soldiers everywhere today.

"I guess they started early." Bregan glared in the direction of the sounds. I blinked. Was he a Reformist? The Stav hated the Labor-class radicals.

"I have to get home." I threw my legs over the lip of the roof. It didn't matter when or where or what Father was doing, he always came home during strikes and riots. If I didn't get back *now*, I would never see the light of day again.

Bregan grabbed my arm before I could drop to the fire escape. "Where's home? Roofs'll be faster. I can get you past all the checkpoints." His dark eyes burned, as if he cared that I got home safely.

The strangeness of his touch fogged my thoughts. In the square below us, a soldier shouted. Managers streamed for the safety of doorways, clogging the streets. I could trust Bregan or risk Father's wrath.

I slipped my hand into his.

"Edge of Landings and Factory," I lied. "Fifteenth and Seventh." Close enough that I could go the rest of the way myself. When he squeezed my fingers, something deep inside me tightened.

Our feet pounded roof tiles. We leaped from the Grande to a neighboring apartment building, then across its roof to another. We traversed the top of the city as the sky bled from bright pink to bruised blue. Bregan led me in circular, clever routes, just out of sight of the district checkpoints, as if he knew the city's ceiling like the back of his own hand.

Long after the sun had slipped below the horizon, he dropped into an empty alley and reached up to grab my waist. As he set me on the cobblestones, his hold loosened, palms sliding to my hips. A honeyed hearth-smoke scent wrapped around me—almost like a bakery—and every part of my body cinched.

His face hovered above mine. The apartment building I'd lied about loomed behind him. A real home for many, but not for me. When that divot returned to his brow, I stepped back. His hands fell, and instantly, the night felt colder.

"Thank you," I said.

"It's no prob—" I lunged toward the street. "Hey, wait."

Despite everything I'd already risked, I halted, turned.

Bregan rubbed his neck. "What's your name?"

My mouth went dry, and with it, my brain. "Firin." My name, so rarely spoken, sounded wrong but tasted right. Forbidden but true.

"Firin," he repeated, as if tasting the shape of it.

My head swam.

He stepped closer. "There's a play opening tomorrow night, three hours after sunset, a few blocks south of here. I could get you in if you want to come."

I tried to inhale. An illegal play? At night, with another person. Someone I'd just told my real name. Someone who sent a thrill into my very bones. None of this felt real. None of it felt possible. It was like a dance on the Grande's stage—a story told but not lived, at least not by me. But maybe in Iakirru things would be different. Maybe this was a chance to practice living a *real* life before we set sail.

"I . . . I'll try."

"Good." Bregan took my hand. His eyes met mine as he raised it, lips brushing my skin. "I'll see you tomorrow. Meet me outside the match factory that burned a few years back, on the south side of the Factory Block." He tipped his cap, then hopped up on a discarded crate, clamored to the roofs, and disappeared.

Heat pulsed through my veins.

Then a gunshot sent me running.

Even my alley shortcuts were congested. Children cried, parents shushed, and doors slammed. Urchins zigzagged across the streets. I pushed upstream of the fleeing Labor-class citizens, toward the Zed District, and as I ran, my skin burned for all the wrong reasons.

It was full dark when I crossed the canal into the Bilge and felt my way up our tenement steps, praying I wasn't too late.

I eased open our door.

The kitchen was empty. Only starlight framed the window.

A laugh bubbled out of my chest. I'd gone to the Grande; I'd met someone; I'd held a normal, real-life conversation—all right under Father's nose.

Tomorrow night at sunset.

I had to try again.

SEVEN

Bregan

Then

Ma was going to be pissed.

Indistinguishable voices chanted across the Factory Block, a chorus of indignation against a swiftly darkening twilight. Bregan had intended to be home before the strike started, but he was already at least an hour late. He raced across the flat roof of the soap factory, then jumped down to the adjoining apartments, picking his way south toward home, trying not to flinch at the Stav's warning shots.

Pa was out there, striking for Labor-class rights and flirting with arrest, but Bregan kept his thoughts on Firin: the blush of her defiance, the glint of her eyes, the citrusy taste of her hand against his lips.

Perched on the Grande's roof, she'd acted as jumpy as a mouse, but he'd sensed something with talons behind her skittishness—brave enough to threaten him, daring enough to steal clothes and pose as a Manager, brash enough to sneak into the Grande.

Yet, when the strike started, she'd been clueless. Somehow, he'd forgotten that there were people out there who didn't dance with revolution day after day, people who lived free of the fear that their choice to fight back could fall like a guillotine on their family's throats at any minute.

As a general rule, Bregan didn't get to know people outside the Reform movement, but he needed to see that *look* on Firin's face again, the one she had worn in the rafters before he spoke: an unblinking, finger-tapping hypnosis of adoration. It was a singular captivation that most people weren't capable of. She deserved to see a performance *worthy* of that awe.

Shots rang out, closer together. Bregan slowed.

A few blocks away, he could just make out the strikers, packed into the square outside the shoe factory. Wooden picket signs poked up above their heads. A line of uniformed Stav soldiers bore down, pistols pointed toward the sky. Smoke billowed in a plume behind the factory, filling the night with the burned-hair scent of leather. Bregan's fists clenched. Were the strikers burning factory supplies?

It'll be peaceful, Pa had said to Ma that morning.

An empty promise, every time.

Turning his back on the chaos, Bregan swung from a fire escape to the roof of a tavern—and he saw them.

Two dozen soldiers wearing black leather huddled on the roof of the hat factory across the square, out of sight of the protestors. Nodtacht. The Nodtacht were the heart of the Stav's violence, the purity of their evil and their most loyal and mysterious agents. They lived to oppress, and right now they each carried rifles. Long-range weapons, not warning pistols.

They were going to shoot down on the strikers.

Instantly, Bregan changed route. Racing back up the fire escape, he rushed for the shoe factory instead. When he dropped into the square, mayhem swallowed him, muting the thunder of his heart.

"No wages, no work!" people chanted, so loud his ears ached.

Bodies pressed in, suffocating with the stench of sweat, soot, and smoke. He kept his elbows out, trying to stay upright, as he wove toward the back of the crowd, searching for his father or any of the other Reformist leaders. With each shove of the Stav soldiers' line, the crowd undulated like a wave.

The Stav were surrounding the strikers, penning them in.

Bregan spun back to scan the hat factory, nausea roiling, hair standing on end.

"We are Luisonn!" a deep voice chanted. "Freedom or death! Freedom or death!" The speaker was a ruddy-faced older man soaked in perspiration, propped up on an overturned crate, brandishing a wrench covered in blood. Bregan's lungs seized. Why did Taidd always have to escalate things? He pushed toward him. Pa would be nearby.

"Bregan!" someone shouted. "You finally decided to show up." Addym Taidd, the speaker's broad son, beamed down, as red faced as his father. They'd grown up together, but Bregan hadn't seen him in months. On purpose.

"Where's my pa?" Bregan shouted.

Addym shrugged. "Come on, we're going to try to push back the line." He shoved something hard into Bregan's breastbone. A pistol.

Bregan stared at it. Shook his head.

"Then why are you here?" Addym sneered.

"There's two dozen Nodtacht up on the hat factory," Bregan said, pointing. He backed away from the pistol. "They've all got rifles."

The color drained from Addym's face. "Are you sure?"

"Positive. Go tell the leaders."

"Why don't *you?*"

Bregan shook his head. "I just . . . I can't." He had to get home. Before Addym could protest, he vanished into the crowd.

He scaled a tavern's balcony and climbed back to the relative safety of the roofs, taking the familiar route. His blood rushed to his head and his knees were weak. A few minutes later, the three-chime bell sounded—the strikers' internal signal to disperse. There was a hanging moment; then all hell broke loose.

Shots fired.

Screams erupted.

Hundreds of boots hit the pavement.

Bregan didn't look back. Didn't let himself think about Pa. Didn't slow until he reached the Shipyard. Massive steamships swallowed his view of the bay as he headed straight for his apartment building's fire escape instead of the front doors. Bregan hadn't used the main stairwell in years, not since the Stav arrested his uncle's family in retribution for his misfired bomb. He usually avoided passing the doorway where the Stav had dragged his innocent cousin out by his neck, so he didn't have to think about it, but the memory accosted him now—the screams, the blood, his mother's broken sobs.

Bregan swung up and raced for his apartment window, yanking it open.

"Where *were* you?" Ma screeched, flying across the room like a living flame.

"I was—"

Nails snatched his biceps. "You went, didn't you? You went to the strike."

"Ma—"

She shook him. "You're not a factory worker. It's not your job to—"

"I didn't go to the strike, Ma," he snapped.

She froze, still breathing hard. A wave of cold swept up through Bregan's chest.

"Oh, baby," she breathed, pulling him in.

He hugged her back, and when his nose filled with the sharp scent of her lavender soap, a tiny part of him unraveled. She was safe. They were safe. For now. When he let her go, he didn't meet her eye; instead, he threw his cap on the table and pulled out the pistol Pa hid behind the coal chest.

Behind him, Ma inhaled. "What happened?"

Bregan checked the bullet chamber, then snapped it back in place. Pa would have shrugged the question off, pretended it was somehow easier or safer to keep her in the dark. But Bregan was not his father.

"I saw a dozen Nodtacht headed for the shoe factory," he said. "They had rifles."

When he turned back around, Ma was as stiff as a board. "Your pa?" The truth swam in her wide eyes: she still loved Pa, even if it took the fear of him dying for her to show it. Somehow, that didn't make Bregan feel any better.

"I got a warning to the leaders," he said, sitting at their one-room apartment's kitchen table. "I'm sure he'll be home in a bit." There was nothing they could do but wait.

"Good." Ma tightened her shawl. "That's good."

Hugging herself, she pressed the braided prayer bracelet he'd made years ago to her lips. She never wore the bracelet, as it was illegal to do so, but she clung to it during strikes. Bregan's grandmother had helped him braid it out of fishing rope when he was a child; together they'd imbued it with a prayer to Saint Chyira, the Gwyn protector of loved ones.

Protection for a family united in blood, heart, and soul.

One strand for all three. Bregan didn't understand why she kept it. Saint Chyira hadn't been there for his uncle and aunt, or his cousin.

The walls muted another round of distant shots and shouts, as if they were underwater, and Ma's focus floated toward the window. Her eyes went glassy and distant. When she wasn't onstage or fighting with Pa, she withdrew like this. Sometimes for hours. Days.

Bregan blamed Pa.

Years ago, when Ma found out he was back in with the Reformists, Pa had promised not to do what had gotten Bregan's great-grandfather hung, his aunt exiled, and his uncle's family shot. He had promised to fight the Stav with as little violence as possible—strikes instead of bombings, protests instead of attacks.

But lately the strikes had veered toward riots, and the Reformists had started to whisper about revolution again. A few weeks ago, when Bregan had asked Pa about it, he'd said, *Luisonn runs on the wealthy's money. If we can get them behind us this time, we might be able to push the Stav out altogether, with little to no violence.*

Bregan knew better. With the Stav, everything ended in violence. If Pa didn't accept that by now, Bregan didn't think he ever would. Three waves of Reformists had tried to overthrow them before, and every failure had ended in the spilling of his family's blood.

Ma wasn't ignorant. She refused to participate in the Reform movement, but she knew what was going on. She saw through Pa's dodgy promises and half-truths, and the distrust ate at her. Pa had promised Bregan that he would tell her about the new plans to push for revolution, but he hadn't yet.

If he didn't soon, Bregan was going to do it for him.

"I went to the Grande," Bregan finally said. "I'm sorry I was late."

She turned away from the window. "To see *The Debutante?*"

"Yeah."

A flame danced to life in her eyes. Sitting across from him, she leaned into her elbows. "Isn't the ending positively *awful?*" When she flashed a smile, he couldn't help but return it, if shakily.

"I don't know, actually," he said, trying to take a deep breath. "I didn't get to see the end. I, uh . . ." He rubbed his palms on his thighs. "I met someone."

"You were seen?" she hissed.

"No, no. She was in the rafters. Found the broken window, I guess."

"Oh, was she?" Ma's eyebrows raised. "Is she pretty?"

Despite himself, Bregan blushed. "Ma, c'mon."

Her grin widened. "Tell me *everything.*"

Bregan spun the pistol on the tabletop. "She's not in the movement."

"So? You can still have a life outside it, Bregan."

But could he?

EIGHT

Firin

Now

Shouts crackled behind me as I fled the Landings, but I'd spent my entire life deceiving the Nodtacht. I ditched the weaver's coat, shook my hair loose, and took another face, then disappeared down old rooftop routes across the city. Scaling building after building, I headed inland. The sun slipped over the horizon. The temperature plunged.

Dread pulled at me like an anchor. If the Nodtacht figured out which ship I had bought a ticket for, my escape would prove much harder. But that was a problem for the morning.

First, I had to survive the night.

When I arrived at Sovest Square and crouched in the shadows of a storage-facility roof, I detected the location of the Players' show immediately. A massive, abandoned Kirru temple and a tall, slim bell tower consumed one whole side of the block. The stained glass windows were boarded, but a faint glow emanated between the planks. The echo of shifting feet and voices rumbled through the air.

I watched the temple for about an hour, carefully cataloging the faces darting in and out of side doors. Some were painfully familiar.

Most were strangers. None were Bregan. A knot in my chest tightened every minute that passed without sign of him. I ignored it.

This was definitely the right place, but unease burrowed in the back of my mind. The Veiled Players' director had always been careful to conceal her stages. Here, evidence seeped through the cracks. The troupe had gotten either sloppy or bold.

Audience members started to arrive in pairs and small groups. They slinked in through back and side doors at sporadic intervals. I popped my mirror open and shifted my features to mimic those of a girl I'd seen come in and out several times: soft curves, small features, and thin blonde hair. If someone saw me in the light, they'd note the differences, but no one would see me.

Emerging from my hiding spot, I rounded the square from roof to roof until I reached the temple. I scaled the sloped tiles and climbed into the bell tower. Underneath the burnished bell, I lifted a heavy hatch door. It creaked, releasing the roar of an audience and a deluge of memories: actresses circling one another, a room of hearts being tugged along as one, the heat of Bregan's body at my back. The images pricked like needles, but I shook them off.

My future was across the sea.

At the bottom of the bell-tower ladder, the outline of a door glowed. It stood cracked open on a balcony, which would be the perfect vantage point from which to watch the show—but just as I started to ease it open, the walls stopped vibrating. The crowd fell silent.

"Ladies and gentlemen," someone said, "the day of retribution has finally come."

Cheers cleaved the tension. Through the crack, I could just make out suited men and women staring imperiously down at the pews where Labors, Zeds, and even Merchants jeered, lifting weapons to the broken stained glass windows. Harpoons and knives. A dozen styles of guns.

I reeled back. This wasn't a play.

"More Stav tyrants are on their way!" the man inside shouted. "But this time we are ready. This time our neighbors are behind us. We will capture their leadership. We will make an example of them." A chorus of hunger shook the walls and rattled my rib cage.

This was more than a Reformist riot.

This was an insurrection.

I had to get to my ship. If the captain smelled a battle, she might leave early, harbor permits or not. I might even have a chance to slip on board while the Stav were distracted. I never should have come here. I never should have strayed so far from the docks. I heaved myself back up the ladder and slipped halfway, slamming my chin on a rung.

Focus, Firin. I licked my bloodied lip and scampered out of the tower.

"Suri?"

I tripped, nearly tumbling over the edge of the roof. Bracing on all fours, I looked up. A lean red-haired man straddled the angled peak of the roof, rigid with vigilance. The edges of my vision pulsed.

Bregan.

The sheer closeness of him, after so long, flushed through me like a brush with death. For the first time in four years, I felt viscerally, palpably alive. I rose toward him, pulled by some kind of gravity.

"What're you doing here?" He squinted and I froze. "I thought you were with Mezua, at the docks."

Suri. The face I'd stolen. The face I was wearing.

"You better leave. The Stav are about to walk into our trap."

I couldn't have responded if I wanted to. I couldn't move, couldn't think. I could only take in the strange broadness of him, the new lines etched in his brow, how his curls were shorter beneath his cap than I'd ever seen them, and his freckles pulled downward in tragic, unfamiliar ways. His olive-colored jacket was heartbreakingly familiar, but his Labor-style linens were stained and ripped, as if carelessly disregarded. It was him, but it wasn't.

An ache struck through my bone marrow. I itched to touch him, to explore this new shape of him, to force all the wrong edges of him to make sense.

"*Go*, Suri." He hoisted a gun to his shoulder with ease, as if holding a weapon were the most natural thing in the world.

I broke. Acid burned through my heart, blasting fumes into my eyes. I couldn't let him leave. *I* couldn't leave. I'd been a fool to think coming here wouldn't make me want to stay on this saints-forsaken island.

My grip on the Suri illusion weakened. "Bregan . . ."

"Shit. There they are."

He glanced beyond me, and my chin followed like bait on a thrown line. Ships. Dozens of them, with a rainbow of sail colors and brands, lined the horizon. They spewed hundreds of boats into the harbor, spilled thousands of soldiers onto the docks.

A barrage of cannon fire split the night like thunder and lightning.

Then closer, much closer, a dark-blue wave of Stav soldiers poured into Sovest Square. The temple doors flew open, tossing the onslaught in blood-orange light. A Stav threw up his weapon and fired. A dozen Reformist guns responded.

"Get out of here, Suri!" Bregan bellowed.

In the square below, the two warring sides collided.

ACT II

NINE

Firin

Then

Father didn't come home the morning after we conned Baron Hulei.

It was the first time I could remember that he hadn't come to check on me during a strike. At first, I reasoned that he was with Baron Hulei. This time he had a pressing reason to stay out late. But by midday I was pacing. By late afternoon I could barely breathe. The rush of my panic had all but eclipsed the exhilaration of meeting Bregan by the time footsteps sounded down the hall.

A familiar, uneven cadence. The adrenaline flooding me twisted into something barbed. *Mizak*, his dockworker persona. Mizak was a guardian, not a father or a training persona. He was nothing to me, and I was nothing to him. We simply shared space.

If Father was Mizak, he didn't intend to discuss the Baron con—or how he'd kicked me out of it—at all.

"Fuckin' Reformists," he slurred, falling into the door as it opened. He swayed on the threshold, his illusion's hair greasy, the creases of his torn clothes stained with soot. He regarded me with glassy eyes. I doubted he was drunk, as Father never lost control, but the sight of him made me clench my teeth.

Where were you? I wanted to scream, but I knew better than to provoke this persona.

Mizak lumbered toward me. I shifted out of the way as he passed into the bedroom, waiting for him to pull up the floorboard that hid the money we gathered, to show some indication of whether he'd been successful with the baron last night, but he just tore a flannel shirt off one of the costume racks and pulled it on.

"I'm going back out. See you in the mornin'."

He left.

I glared at the back of the door. Had the con failed? How much longer did we have to stay in Luisonn? I worked my fingers into my palms. Sometimes cinching a deal took days, even weeks, of negotiating with our marks. Maybe he just hadn't completed it yet.

The questions sat like coals on my chest.

If I stayed here in silence, they'd burn a hole through me.

I kicked open the bedroom door, shimmied into a dress, and dabbed a lemon oil perfume—the kind Labor-class women wore—on my wrists. Then I propped my pocket mirror on the kitchen table and tamed my hair into a smooth braid. Once finished, I surveyed myself: a linen Gwyn-style dress, a thin brown sweater, an orange wristband.

Firin, the Labor girl.

Shivering, I clicked the mirror shut.

I felt my way down the pitch-black tenement steps and out into the evening. The Bilge should have been buzzing, but in the aftermath of last night's shoe-factory strike, the streets were eerily silent. No children played. No revelers cackled. The few people winding home kept their frowns fixed on the ground. A dog bolted across the street.

A soft rain fell as I set off down the muddy, winding path to the Labor District. I had to hurry if I wanted to meet Bregan before the play started. The closer I got to the border, the thicker the quiet grew. It curdled my stomach. Reform strikes usually lasted days. This one had ended before it could start.

"Hey." The word was a rock thrown from the shadows. I froze as a lanky Stav soldier materialized from the smoke. Wet hair stuck to his cheeks. "Where do you think you're going?"

I'd reached the district border checkpoint.

I ripped my fake Labor-class papers from my sweater pocket. He barely glanced at them. "What's a Labor girl doing in the Zed?" His gaze raked from my braid to my boots.

I glanced down the street, but we were entirely alone. Rain dripped off my chin. "I got lost."

The soldier grunted. "Did you, now?"

When he stepped forward, I lurched back, and with the shift in perspective, I saw them: dozens of bodies, swaying in front of the shoe factory, so close together they touched. The Stav had hung the rioters.

"My father is waiting for me," I blurted, as if that would help me.

I was so transfixed by the corpses that I didn't see the soldier move until it was too late. Until his fingers clamped around my throat.

"Your father might have to wait a bit," he said, thrusting me into a brick wall. The weight of him bore down, the scent of whiskey poured into my mouth, rough fingers groped at my dress collar, and before I even fully registered what was happening, I popped my knife out of my sleeve like a cat with claws.

I stabbed blindly.

He roared as the blade slid through fabric and skin. Again and again. When his grip loosened, I ran. My boots splashed in puddles as I raced for the nearest street corner, trying to outpace my heart. I ran without thought or direction, turning and turning, until I realized I'd headed farther uphill. I should turn around and go home, but I didn't dare risk passing the same soldier again. Moving forward was safer.

When I reached the square where Bregan had told me to meet him, I could barely think. I stumbled over slippery cobblestones, searching wildly for him, but the streets were empty. Factories loomed like slumbering beasts from Gwyn folktales. Somewhere nearby, boots brushed stone. I tripped and fell into a building, slapping my hand on brick to stay upright.

My hand was red.

I swayed back, staring at my crimson palms. Rain made rivulets of the blood. I'd *stabbed* a Stav soldier. I wasn't even sure where I'd stabbed him. My knife was small, but with the right angles I could have done significant damage. I pulled off my sweater and scraped at the blood with jerky, frantic swipes.

Saints, I was smarter than this. There was a reason I never walked alone dressed as a Labor. I snarled, acid burning the back of my mouth. Like their emperor, the Stav took what they wanted, hurt anyone who tried to fight back. If that soldier hadn't been alone . . .

I hated this city.

A whistle shot from the shadows. A figure hopped down from a nearby roof, and I staggered away from it, until Bregan said, "Firin? I was starting to worry you— *Shit*, what happened?" He jogged over, staring at my bloodied sweater.

The sight of him broke a dam inside my bones, sending tremors rippling through my limbs. He looked different from before, with his hair freshly washed and his simple Labor-class clothes traded for a flowing yellow-and-blue-patterned tunic, its top laces undone.

Slowly, he raised his hands. "Are you hurt?"

I couldn't speak, so I shook my head.

"Was it a Stav?" he asked. I nodded. "*Bastards.* Come here." When he gently touched my arm, my ribs unclenched, reopening my lungs to air.

He led me to one of the buildings, the hulking shell of a match factory that had burned a few years back. Just through a side door, he sat me on a broken crate. The space smelled like old, wet ash, and I couldn't see more than a few feet in the dim moonlight spilling through the propped door.

"Let me get rid of that," Bregan said, taking my sweater as if he'd done this kind of thing countless times before.

When he started unlacing his tunic, I flinched. His fingers paused. "Your dress," he said quietly. I glanced down. Blood streaked my midriff. I'd have to get rid of the costume somehow, in a way Father wouldn't notice.

When Bregan handed me his shirt, my chest caved. I shrugged into the worn, colorful fabric, and the smoky-sweet scent of him burned my eyes. When buttoned, the shirt completely covered the bloodstain. He returned a moment later with a wet handkerchief.

"You sure you're not hurt?" he asked, crouching.

"Yes," I managed to say. I took the cloth and wiped the remaining blood off my hands, then cleaned my knife and slipped it back up my sleeve. Bregan watched. I waited for him to ask more questions, but he didn't. In the dim light, his short-sleeve undershirt revealed lean, muscled arms covered in freckles. He kneaded knuckles into his thighs, as if unsure what to do with his hands. They were shaking. For the first time, I wondered if he knew any of the people hanging outside the shoe factory.

"I'm so sorry," he said quietly. "I should've come and gotten you myself."

I blinked at him. "It's not your fault." His throat bobbed, as if he disagreed. If Father had seen me like this, he'd have screamed and blamed and accused. It was *my* fault that I'd wandered right into the checkpoint at night, and yet Bregan was blaming himself. "Really," I pressed, "if I hadn't—"

"Tonight, I'll show you the route using roofs," he cut in. "It's safest."

I hesitated, teasing the ends of my dress sleeves between my fingers. "All right. Has the show started?"

"Not yet. You still want to go in?"

I nodded, and a dimple appeared in his cheek. He rose to his feet and held out his hand. When I took it, his calluses tickled my palm.

Hand in hand, we went into the factory ruins. I couldn't see my nose in front of my face, but he moved with memorized precision. Soon, a hum shook the floorboards.

"Up here," he said. Steps creaked.

We emerged on a brightly lit mezzanine stuffed with people.

"'Scuse me," Bregan repeated, elbowing a path between bodies. He slipped a loose arm around my waist to guide me, and I angled toward his chest. I'd never worn my own face where so many people could see it. Without an illusion, I felt alert, alive, and exposed, like I was standing naked on the shore.

We wove through to the railing and looked down on an old production floor that was also crowded, except for a rectangle of space in the middle where a roughly hewn castle turret threw shadows over part of the audience.

"Now wait just a moment," someone said in a heavy Vorstav'n accent. A peppered beard filled my vision. "Who is this?"

My mind tumbled off a cliff. "Vota, sir," I blurted. The name on the fake papers I'd brought with me.

The massive man's bushy brows pinched together; then he erupted in laughter. I jumped as the hearty sound drew the attention of everyone on the mezzanine. The severe lines of him melted. "New friends," he said, engulfing my hand with his own. "Would you look at that. I am Tez. Is so nice to meet you, little Aza."

I flushed at his use of the Vorstav'n honorific for higher-class women. He wasn't a Stav soldier; he was just Vorstav'n. In Vorstav, the number of syllables in your name denoted your class. That meant he was Zed. He wasn't a threat. I tried to exhale.

"Your parents are from Vorstav?" he asked, smiling with his eyes.

I swallowed. Vota was Vorstav'n, Labor class.

A detail is truth once presented. "Yes."

When I looked over, Bregan was watching me, that question divot gouging deep in his forehead. I'd told him my name was Firin. *Please don't say anything,* I prayed.

A half second passed; then he turned to Tez. "She's never seen a play."

Tez gasped. "No? Well, you are in for a treat. I must go backstage, but your ma wants to see you after the show, Bregan, yes?"

The moment he disappeared, Bregan's questioning look burned the back of my neck. I knew I should say something. Explain.

"C'mon," he said, swinging his legs between the bars of the railing and dangling them over the audience below. He reached up and touched my orange Labor-class wristband. "You can take that off. No one wears them here. It's a class-free space."

Class-free? I pictured the bodies hanging outside the shoe factory, then felt the checkpoint soldier's fingers around my neck. Bumps raced up my arms, but I stuck the band in my pocket. Dangerous as it was, standing out would be worse.

"Vota?" Bregan asked, watching my face.

I threaded my legs through the bars. "I got nervous. He sounded like . . ."

"A Stav soldier?" He hung his arms loosely around the rail. "Tez is one of our best actors. Been around since Mezua started the troupe."

"Oh," I said. I held my breath, again expecting him to pry, but he just jostled my elbow and pointed down at the set castle.

"I helped build that," he said. "It's one of the biggest pieces we've been able to make since we move locations a lot. Look, they're dimming the lights."

The factory plummeted into darkness. Bregan's leg pressed against mine; then a circle of light flared in the middle of the room. A violin crooned. Two identical dancers vaulted into the light. The rivers of the women's obsidian hair wove around the thick, voluptuous curves of their golden-brown bodies as they twirled and writhed in ways I'd never seen serdzat dancers move. They looked like flames, flickering and seductive.

"Shasta, dear sister, have you heard the news?" A stunning woman stepped onstage with elegant poise and sharp, deep-brown cheekbones.

"That's Mezua," Bregan whispered, hot against my ear, "and that's my ma."

Another woman stepped up to join the first, her sun-kissed freckled skin and mahogany hair just like his. I shifted to get a better view, and Bregan's hand knocked into mine.

My breath caught. When I didn't move, his fingers slid tentatively over the back of my hand. We'd held hands before, as he'd led me places, but this felt different. Something heady rushed over me, and I turned my palm upright, tangling my fingers with his over the top of his thigh.

"I cannot imagine any better chance," Bregan's mother purred, just loud enough for her voice to carry, head angled for her madness to catch the light. "The gods have dealt us true."

In the clutch of revenge, heartbreak, and satisfying tragedy, I came alive. I couldn't tear my eyes from the actresses, from the way their masks were both obvious and believable. They positioned themselves in strange, inauthentic positions so the audience could see them best. Their voices were too loud, but that was so they carried.

It wasn't like how Father transformed. It wasn't like illusion. There was a truth in the acknowledgment of the falsity. The audience knew they wore masks. The knowing *was* the magic. It was the most beautiful thing I'd ever seen.

Bregan watched me more than the show. He grinned every time I jumped, and whispered facts about the actors and the play's production, all while rubbing his thumb over the back of my hand, sending sparks up my arm.

Long before I was ready, the audience was clapping. Gaslights flared. I tore my focus from the stage and glanced up. Over the course of the show, we'd folded together. Half of my back nestled against his chest. Bregan's eyes were as dark as the sky between the stars. They dipped to my mouth, then back up.

"You liked it?" he asked, running a finger down the inside of my palm. Heat tightened deep in my core.

"Liked it?" I breathed. I felt like I'd been parched my whole life and had only just gotten my first taste of water. When I smiled, he did too, like he couldn't keep my joy from spreading to his own face. My heart swelled, filling with something like hunger.

This was something I could do—something I'd be *good* at.

I wanted to be an actress.

The clapping crescendoed, tugging our attention back to the stage. The cast stepped out one at a time, bowing in turn as an announcer named them. The star actresses—"Mezua Bentea!" and "Esmai Nimsayrth!"—curtsied last.

As they straightened, they transformed. It wasn't the shedding of an illusion, but it might as well have been. Mezua's shoulders loosened, Esmai's smile softened; their postures curved. Then, with a grin as sharp as a cackle, Esmai engulfed Mezua in a hug.

The audience's adoration surged, broken with laughter, like waves crashing against a rocky shore, pulling with the force of a rising tide.

Mezua gracefully extricated herself from Esmai's hold. "Thank you!" she said, now with a Kirru accent. "We are so grateful."

When the applause began to fade and cheers morphed into chatter, I stared at my fingers in Bregan's, at the freckles on his forearm. I felt alive in the dizzying way I only ever did when a con went sideways, as if my next move had the power to change the course of my life. Except for once, my life wasn't on the line, and I wasn't scheming. Was this what life would feel like in Iakirru?

"Better than the Grande, wouldn't you say?" Bregan's body shifted away from mine.

I spun to face him. "Are you . . . are you going backstage?"

He tilted his head. "Why? You want to come?"

"Yes." Desperately.

His dimple winked as he helped me stand. With his hand on my back, we threaded through the bustling mezzanine to an exit different from the one we'd entered.

"Thank you, thank you," Mezua said onstage as we ducked out into a hallway. "Now, please, we'd like to take a moment of silence in honor of the men and women we lost in yesterday's efforts . . ."

Bregan's touch slipped a little, and I realized I'd halted.

"What?" he said, just an outline in the dark. The theater was part of the Reform movement. I should have guessed that. His grip pulsed. "Shit. I should have told you last night, in the chaos I—"

"It's fine."

"It's not. You deserved to know what you were risking coming here."

"Really, it's fine." I was already taking a risk being at an illegal play. I just had to be careful with my persona—more careful than I'd been earlier tonight.

The audience faded with every step, and new voices filled the air ahead. Gleeful laughs reached high and low octaves. Easy, ecstatic voices skittered over my skin, drawing me in. Then Bregan pushed through a swinging door into a maelstrom of sensory overload.

Costumes hung wall-to-wall, in colors so bright they couldn't be dulled by the cigarette smoke and puffs of makeup. A dozen people bustled around half a dozen mirrors. The twin dancers sat nearest us, their open robes revealing red chemises that glowed against their bare skin. My whole body lit on fire as Bregan dragged me inside.

"Bregan! Vota!" Tez boomed. His unbuttoned costume hung over a hairy white stomach.

"Have you seen Ma?" Bregan asked.

"Well, hello there."

Bregan spun, gripping my hand. "Ma, this is—"

"Vota," I said.

Esmai Nimsayrth beamed so bright I had to blink. If Bregan was a hearth fire, she was a sunrise over a sea. "Nice to meet you, Vota." She adjusted the scant robe draped over her shoulders, and her eyes flicked from Bregan's shirt—which I still wore—to her son. "What's your story, darling?"

"My pa's in textiles." The lie slipped out like honey, brewed in the back of my mind since my misstep with Tez. The cotton mills were close to where Bregan had dropped me off the night before.

"I see. Well, what did you think?"

"It was amazing. Your acting, I mean. The way you pretended to befriend the queen, even though you were just using her to get to the king."

Her brows rose. "How observant. What about the queen, though? Don't you think she was using me a bit too?"

"C'mon, Ma. Don't test her." Bregan touched my elbow. "Let's go."

But Esmai had pinned me with sea-glass eyes. There was a curiosity, and a challenge, in her sudden focus. As if the world weren't swirling around us in a hurricane of sound and color. She cared about my answer.

I groped for something smart. "Well, I . . ."

"Esmai, Esmai, Esmai," Tez chanted. The big Vorstav'n man's jubilation was gone. "The shipyard baron is here to talk to the leaders."

"W-what?" Esmai stammered. All the color leached away behind her freckles.

"Shit," Bregan breathed, as if he'd been caught in something. His mother's gaze snapped to his. He swallowed.

"Where?" Esmai spun around, but it was obvious. The entire room was looking toward a second exit, where the other actress and director, Mezua, stood in the half darkness beside a man with slicked straw-colored hair, an immaculate suit, and a top hat in his hands.

Baron Hulei.

Suddenly the room's colors were blinding. The scents suffocated. There were too many people. Too many eyes.

Father had conned the baron last night, and *I'd* helped him do it.

"Hey," Bregan murmured, "you all right? You look a little—"

I shoved my way to the opposite door and veered into the hall. My face burned, as if to remind me it was exposed, real. I wasn't wearing my illusion; the baron couldn't possibly recognize me, but a hummingbird panicked in my chest anyway.

"Fir—I mean, Vota," Bregan called down the hall. "Wait."

Panic is the enemy. The rule slowed my feet, my pulse. This wasn't a con, I wasn't conning Bregan, but the training soothed me nonetheless.

Breathe. I wasn't wearing the same face. I was fine.

"What's wrong?" he pressed, catching up.

Grinning took immense effort. "Nothing, it's just hot in there." In the dark it was hard to make out Bregan's expression. Hopefully it was hard to see mine too.

After a moment he said, "C'mon, we can get to the roof here."

He led me to a window and we climbed out. A damp breeze teased the loose strands of my hair, blowing east, toward the Zed. We sat down on a dry patch beneath an overhang and hugged our knees, shoulders touching.

"Why's the shipyard baron here?" I asked. I needed to know how involved Baron Hulei was with the theater, with Bregan.

Bregan didn't respond immediately, staring out over the city, and for a moment I regretted asking, but then he sighed. "To meet with the Reform leaders. My pa and the others are trying to get his support." I blanched. I'd guessed Bregan was in the Reform movement, but if his pa was a leader, he was at the *center* of it. "My pa thinks that if we can get upper-class buy-in, we could defeat the Stav," Bregan added.

"Defeat? I thought they were striking for wages?"

He leaned into a palm, arm stretched out behind my back. The bakery scent of him curled up my nose and cinched around my heart. "They are, but my pa and a few other Reformist leaders want to overthrow the Stav altogether. Get rid of classes and districts so we can live freely."

A shiver ran down my spine. I fixed my gaze on a stubborn star and tried to picture a Luisonn without the Stav Regime, without checkpoints, food lines, and Nodtacht on every corner. It was the dream I had for a life on the continent—a place where Father and I could stop stealing and get any jobs we wanted—but not a life I'd ever imagined here, on the Iket Isles. I glanced down at Bregan's shirt, which still covered the blood now dried on my dress.

It sounded treasonous, dangerous to even dream.

"You think that's possible?" I asked.

"My pa does."

I looked back out over the city with a strange, bad taste in my mouth. Bregan and his father were trying to build a better future for all Labors, despite the risk, while Father and I were cheating our way to an escape.

Bregan coughed softly. "I, uh, brought you something." He reached into his back pocket and pulled out a worn, rolled-up booklet. When I uncurled it, moonlight illuminated an illustration of a man and woman wrapped in a kiss. *Qoyn & Insei*, it read. "It's a script of my favorite play."

It became very hard to breathe. "It's yours?" I ran a finger down the well-loved pages. The Stav would hang him if they knew he had this.

He reclined onto both his hands. "Yeah. It's about two lovers who accidentally get lost in time. They impersonate people throughout history while they search for one another. In Qunsii they say it's so difficult the Sage King cursed it. I'll need it back eventually to practice, but I thought you'd like to read it."

Something cracked behind my ribs. The chaos of backstage clung to my skin in a haze of perfume and cigarette smoke. Bregan's warmth wrapped around me. I looked up and found him staring at me again, brow slightly pinched, as if he were trying to see through all the layers of me, as if he thought he would like what he found.

But how would he look at me if he knew the truth? If he knew what Father and I did every day to people like the baron?

I swallowed. Did it matter?

Bregan didn't need to know I was a thief. Father and I were leaving soon, regardless of how the Baron Hulei con had gone last night. Until then, maybe I could be this persona, just a Labor-class girl with a factory-working father. The beginning of a story, like a blank page I could fill. A chance to experiment with who I wanted to be across the sea.

"Is there another show soon?" I asked.

"Not until next month. But if you want, you could come by my place sometime. Ma and I rehearse during the day."

I sat up. "Really?"

"I can show you how to get there using roofs."

"All right," I said. Sneaking out again would be risky, but I'd find a way.

When he smiled, I hoped for the first time in my life that Mr. Finweint wouldn't show.

TEN

Bregan

Now

Blood coated everything. Bregan's hands slipped in it as shots reverberated in every corner of Luisonn.

"Shit," Cidd groaned. The fighter's torso dripped crimson onto Bregan's pants and Jaq's boots as they carried him across the street. They'd been storming the Stav's central headquarters when the bullet sliced through Cidd's side.

"You're fine," Jaq promised, but his eyes were pinched beneath his circular glasses.

Bregan glanced over his shoulder. A few more yards until they reached the office building where the Reformists had stationed medics. "Just gotta get you patched up," he said, praying Suri wouldn't be inside yet. They were supposed to meet her here before heading to the prison, but if she saw Cidd like this, she'd lose her mind.

That was, if she showed at all. Earlier tonight she hadn't been at the docks, where she'd been ordered—she'd been at the temple.

The medics' door flung open, and a watch boy scampered aside to let them through. The putrid scent of mixed bodily fluids billowed with cries of pain and shouts of orders.

"Here!" Someone pointed them to a bare piece of floor.

They set Cidd down, and Bregan started pulling the man's coat off. "Don't forget that tomorrow you have—" He blanched.

The bullet hadn't just grazed the surface.

Bregan blinked, and Cidd's brown shirt became his cousin's yellow one, the red stain near his heart growing, spreading, flowing—

Cidd shifted, wrenching Bregan out of the memory. He snatched the other man's chin before he could see the dire wound. "You have to play Seorsus," Bregan said. "I hate that fucking role, and if you can't do it, Mezua will make me." It was a miracle his voice didn't crack.

Cidd tried to laugh. "She'd never let you."

"Oh, fuck off."

A medic appeared with a band of white wrapped around her arm. "We need to get the bullet out," she declared, waving another medic over to hold him down.

Bregan rocked back into a squat, and Cidd moaned again. The fighter hadn't even been with the Reformists for a year, but there was a bond that forged unnaturally fast when you fought for freedom side by side. A few weeks ago, Cidd had even joined the Veiled Players as an actor.

Even when Bregan thought he had nothing and no one left to lose, the Stav always found more to take.

At the thought, the iron curtains he'd locked the past behind parted, and Firin's face burst through. He pushed the heels of his hands into his eyes, willing her away.

Firin had died on Bloody Fifthday with everything else.

Four years ago, Stav soldiers had raided the Players' performance of *Skarnti's Revenge*. They'd flooded the audience, guns blazing, and shattered the Reformist movement like glass. A dozen people died; dozens more were wounded, arrested, or disappeared. Five of the movement's leaders, including Bregan's father, were locked up in a high-security prison.

Bregan had never seen Firin again.

After that, Bregan had gone underground with the rest of the rebels. They'd spent four years rebuilding the movement in secret. A month ago, they finally secured the foreign support they needed for an insurrection. If this didn't work, Bregan wasn't sure anything would.

With the pain of nailing shut a wound, he shoved out thoughts of Firin. He had to get to the prison before the Stav decided to kill Pa and the other old Reform leaders out of spite. After squeezing Cidd's arm, he headed for the exit.

Jaq followed, brushing ash from the short, dark twists of his hair. "Breg, don't you think we—"

"Cidd?" Suri's voice cut through the din.

On the other side of the room, she stepped inside. Bregan lurched into a run, weaving through writhing bodies of medics and injured fighters, to cut her off.

"Bregan. Jaq. There you are," she gasped. "Where's Cidd? We have to go." She held a shotgun that was nearly as tall as she was. A pistol hung from the belt of her pants. Bregan scanned her again. When he'd seen her on the roof of the temple earlier, she'd been in a dress.

"What were you doing at the temple?" he asked.

"What? I've been at the Landings with Mezua."

That wasn't true. He'd seen her hours after Mezua left. "You were there. When the Stav arrived."

Her nose wrinkled. "No, I wasn't. Listen—"

"I saw you. We talked on the roof."

Small hands snatched his shoulders. "Listen to me. The barracks fell." Her grin shoved all the air from Bregan's lungs. "The Qunsiian navy has the harbor. Taidd and the Kirrus infiltrated Central. It's only a matter of time until the Stav governor is dead."

Bregan stared at her. If the governor fell, the Stav soldiers—who were all from the Vorstav'n mainland—would likely surrender.

"It worked," Suri breathed.

Bregan squinted against smoke.

Forty years.

Four decades had passed since the Vorstav'n Empire conquered the pirate Iket Isles. Bregan's great-grandfather had lost his head in the First Rebellion. His uncle had been executed in the Second. Then his pa had taken up arms. Four generations of fighting had cost Bregan his cousin, a mother, four years with his father, and a lifetime with Firin. The chaos of the makeshift clinic pressed in, choking his senses. He gripped the barrel of his gun.

Today it all ended, one way or another, but his father wasn't free until he walked through the prison's gates.

"We should find the others," he said. "It's time to—"

Cidd bellowed. The whites of Suri's eyes flared.

"Suri—"

She bolted, skidding to her knees beside the injured man. They had joined the Reform movement together, closer than family, closer than lovers—the way the Veiled Players had become his family: bound in blood, heartbreak, and abandonment. As she took in the severity of Cidd's wound, Suri let out a cry that Bregan knew all too well. The wrenching, splitting sound of a piece of one's heart severing from the rest. It harmonized with the clinic's symphony of loss, then stabbed into the Firin-shaped hole in Bregan's chest.

Bregan shook himself. There was no time to waste. They'd have to free the prisoners without Suri and Cidd. He hoisted his gun and headed for the door.

His father *had* to be alive.

He refused to lose another person to this saints-damned regime.

ELEVEN

Firin

Now

The chaos of the insurrection was deafening. As I raced back toward the Landings, nearby shots shook my bones. Screams raked over my skin. Distant cannon strikes shook the cobblestones. My lungs strained but I pushed onward. If that ship left without me, I'd be stuck on this island forever, running in circles to escape the Stav.

Beneath a smoke-filled, starless sky, I wove through throngs of terrified citizens, forced to take side route after side route, until I tasted the ocean. Around the next corner, I ran into a mother holding a screaming child, and the solid wall of bodies beyond them. A stampede of desperate people undulated toward the Landings.

If I hadn't gone all the way to Sovest Square, if I hadn't gone to see the Players, I would have been on the docks already, taking advantage of the madness to leave. If I hadn't gone, I wouldn't have seen . . .

I shook my head. I couldn't think about who I'd just left behind.

The ship was all that mattered.

I shoved a dead-eyed old man, tried to push past the sobbing mother, but there was no use; I'd never make it to the harbor like this. As I backed away, I hoisted my bag, only to find the strap had broken.

All my stuff was gone, devoured by the mob. Swearing, I found the nearest fire escape and swung myself up. My boots left footprints in ash as I raced to the roof.

At the top, I had a perfect view of the sea. Sunrise stained the horizon like a bruise, casting gray light over the battleships that crowded the hazy harbor. Plumes of smoke billowed from buildings and ships where cannons had made their marks.

Luisonn sagged against her own weight. Pillaged, burned, and shattered. I scanned the docks, praying to the Gwyn saints and the Kirru gods, to anyone that might hear me. But it was no use.

The ship was gone.

A scream clawed its way out of me, a ragged sound that I couldn't hear past the storm of the city's raging, terrified grief. After years of preparation, I'd lost everything in one go.

A sudden, deep urge to *move* hammered at the inside of my skull, pushing me to my feet, away from the harbor. I stumbled, then jogged, and then I was running from building to building until I couldn't take in air.

Until I realized I had nowhere to go.

Leaning against a chimney, I tried to center myself, but brutal reality swept in. No room, alley, or corner in Luisonn had ever been safe from the Stav, not for me. For the briefest moment, my heart ached for Father's old apartment. I growled.

Even in that life, I'd never been safe. Not truly.

Then laughter rippled through the night.

The sound was pure glee, too clean for this nightmare. Heaving ragged breaths, I peered over the side of the roof. The street below was thick with people, but no one shoved or shouted. Instead, they were cheering around a fire that spit embers into the already smoggy sky.

A pile of burning wristbands.

A Labor-class man howled. People poured in from adjacent streets, stumbling through steps and laughter. In the distance, on Regents' Hill, the Stav's central buildings glowed with ravenous flames.

I swayed. The Reformists had won.

Whoops of glee from the north clashed with the terror of the people trying to escape to the south. The news hadn't yet spread, hadn't seeped into the city's bedrock, but it would thicken with the sunrise, it would dawn with the day.

A Luisonn where we can live freely, Bregan had once said.

It had always seemed like a child's dream: naive, intangible.

In the square below, a white-haired, tight-jawed old woman removed her Labor-class wristband and identity papers with a shaking grip. As she tossed them into the bonfire, I pulled out the weaver's stolen identity papers, then looked toward the harbor and to the horizon beyond it.

My whole life, I'd danced from shadow to shadow, face to face, trying to outrun Father's crimes and the Stav's noose. I'd yearned for a fresh start across the sea, for a life where I wouldn't have to use my illusion, where I could bury all the terrible things I'd been forced to do, the person I'd become, and finally *live.* But if the Reformists had won, if the Stav Regime had truly toppled . . .

An ache nearly split me in half.

"They're draggin' 'em to the Corners." A horde of children poured into the square, screeching at the top of their lungs. "They're hangin' the Stav!" They swept the celebrating Labors with them like fish in a net, moving everyone in the same direction.

I followed from above until we reached the canal; then I fell into a crouch on the clock-tower roof.

The packed Corners roared with a vicious kind of righteousness. People swarmed around the massive statue of Emperor Dreznor'proska'ed'nov. Some even sat on his shoulders and hung from his crossed arms. Beyond them, a wall of Labors blocked the entrances to every canal bridge, corralling captured Stav *onto* the bridges like sheep into pens. They stuffed black-clad Nodtacht in with uniformed military soldiers, suited officials, and even normal citizens.

On the one empty bridge, a handful of Labors fashioned ropes for what looked like makeshift gallows.

Then a man emerged from the wall of soldiers and raised an ash-stained top hat, revealing a head of thick straw hair. Ice spread under my skin as Baron Hulei shouted, "Today, we take back what is ours."

With a flick of his wrist, he signaled a group of Labor-class guards. They shuffled forward, leading a massive prisoner to the gallows: a man with a beard split by a hook-shaped scar.

The Nodtacht who had hunted me.

TWELVE

Firin

Then

The bar of gold felt like ice in my palm.

My knees pressed against the floor as I stared into the hole where Father stashed our money. Fifty *bars* of gold, the kind the bank gave away, shone inside a thick leather bag. It was more than we'd ever managed to save, more than a Merchant saw in years—and more than most Labors made in a lifetime.

After days of silence and slammed doors, the money had just appeared beneath the floorboard. I hadn't seen him put it there. He hadn't said anything. Yet it was the kind of money that could only have come from Baron Hulei.

Father had finished the con without telling me.

I dropped the bar back into the bag, my blood humming. After conning and striving for so many years, we finally had enough. We could sail to Iakirru tomorrow and start over. So why had he left this morning without a word? Why weren't we planning?

Why were we still *here*?

Had Father changed his mind about wanting to leave?

I glanced at the Labor-class dress I'd worn to the theater, the one I'd planned to wear today to sneak out to Bregan's apartment. It hung from the costume rack, beckoning me like a question. I shoved the floorboard in place. If Father was going to keep sneaking off to saints-knew-where without a word, then why shouldn't I?

An hour later, I was scrambling over rooftops in the Labor District. The sun beat down from a rare cerulean sky, a tease of the summer that had yet to arrive. I followed the directions Bregan had given me. As I drew close, massive steamships blocked the view of half the horizon. I swallowed, realizing that these were Shipyard apartments, the ones Baron Hulei owned. Bregan's father wasn't just collaborating with the baron—he worked for him.

I inhaled deeply. The baron didn't know my real face. I was safe.

I heard them before I saw them. Esmai's laugh sparkled like sunlight. Bregan's groans were laced with good-natured irritation.

I ducked behind a chimney. My fingers were slick against the bricks, betraying the kind of nerves I felt before a difficult con. This wasn't a con, though.

On a tattered quilt, Esmai sat cross-legged, swatting at Bregan with a shoe. He'd rolled his stained trousers up at the bottom, and his half-buttoned shirt revealed swaths of freckles. His feet were bare. In full sunlight, he almost seemed more real, like a dream manifested.

"You're not *using* the accent right," Esmai said.

Bregan rolled his eyes. If I acted with such flippant disregard toward Father, I'd find myself bruised and hungry, but Esmai only raised an eyebrow.

"Try it again," she said.

Bregan exhaled and moved back. "Well, now, I must point out," he recited, throwing out a finger, "that it was me who boarded the Dread Skarnti's ship first. There is—"

"Tha-*t*," Esmai interrupted. "And it's '*I* who boarded.'"

Bregan groaned. "I sound ridiculous." He wasn't wrong. The Kirrus highly articulated their consonants, but he was overdoing it so much he sounded like he was making fun of it.

I stepped out into the light. "It's the emphasis."

They turned.

"Vota!" Esmai said.

Bregan met me at the edge of the roof, beaming, and when he helped me across, the scent of him made me lightheaded. The sun danced in his curls like flame through embers. His hands lingered on my waist. "You actually came."

"Sorry it took me a few days," I said.

Behind him, Esmai squinted up at us from the blanket. I flushed and shifted out of his grip. Without her makeup, her eyes were more hollow and her skin a bit pallid, but her smile was genuine. "She's right, Breg," she said. "It *is* the emphasis."

"It's the line," he insisted.

I bit back a smile. "It's a weird sentence, but only because you're not stressing the right parts."

Draw them in with emphasis, Father used to croon in the harsh, bitter voices of his training personas. *Show them what to pay attention to.*

"Huh." Bregan sucked his teeth. "All right, *Vota.* Let's see you do it, then."

I stilled. No one had ever watched me act except Father, and he didn't call it *acting.* But Bregan glowed with a kind of curiosity, and I wanted to learn, so I wiped my hands on my skirts. I inhaled, as he had done, then threw my shoulders back and wrinkled my nose.

"Well, now, I must point out," I said, hitting every *t*, "that it was *I* who boarded the Dread Skarnti's ship *first.*" Bregan shook his head, dimple wrinkling. My insides did a weird, unfamiliar dance.

"Brilliant! See how she used the pomposity?" Esmai laughed.

Attention still on me, Bregan attempted the line again, then again. He and his mother cycled through a set of sentences, then scenes, and with each try, Esmai asked me what I thought. Warmth beat down from the sky and emanated from the roof as minutes turned into hours. They taught me about projecting, showed me how to block, and shared tales about the playwright. All the while, Bregan's gaze bored into me, almost molten in the sunlight, as if I held some kind of wonder.

It was a day unlike any I'd ever experienced. Easy, simple. On the roofs of Luisonn, there was no Reform movement. Neither the Stav nor Father could reach me. Every moment was an improvisation I didn't have to overthink.

Eventually, the sun dipped an edge over the horizon. Esmai stood. "I should go get dinner started. Vota, I think you got through that thick skull of his. Tomorrow, when he shows Mezua, she won't chastise me."

"I could come back," I said.

The hands she was brushing on her simple Gwyn-style skirts went still. "Do you not have work?"

My heartbeat quickened. "I sew for a tailor in our apartment build-ing," I lied. "But she doesn't need me every day."

After only a moment's pause, she smiled. "That would be lovely, then. Tomorrow you could even come to the theater. I'm sure Mezua—"

Bregan coughed, cutting her off. Their eyes met. "I told Mezua I would come on Secondday," he said. Turning to me, he added, "But you could come back tomorrow? Stay for dinner, maybe?"

Esmai gave her son an assessing look, and my fingers twisted together. Did she not want me to come for dinner? I'd never been to a dinner at a table, with a family. None of Father's personas cooked. But when Esmai looked back to me, she beamed again. The chill of the strange moment vanished so fast I wondered if I'd imagined it.

"Yes, you must come to dinner tomorrow. I'll make a stew." As she headed for the fire escape, she added, "I'll see you in a bit, Breg." Then she disappeared over the edge.

Bregan snatched me by the waist. I shrieked, and the world blurred as he spun me.

"*Where* did you learn how to act?" he demanded.

My cheeks caught on fire. "I didn't."

"You're just naturally *that* good?"

"Am I good?"

"Are you kidding me?" He set me down, lips parting with another question.

I pulled his copy of *Qoyn & Insei* from my sweater and shoved it into the space between us. "I brought this back."

I'd read the script a hundred times over the last few days. The sweeping epic painted a kind of relationship I'd never seen before—not in the nighttime escapades of the Zeds in my tenement, not in the chaste touches of upper-class couples, and not even in the dances I'd seen at the Grande. *Love* burned through the very ink of the lines. I'd blazed through hours of lamp oil losing myself in the Qunsii couple's heart-wrenching travels through time, again and again, imagining it onstage.

I wanted to see it performed. I wanted to *be* Insei.

And if Bregan, someone who watched Esmai and Mezua act all the time, thought *I* had talent, then maybe I actually had a chance.

"You sure you don't want to keep it longer?" he asked.

I wanted to keep it forever, but it was clear he adored it, and I was afraid of Father—or the Stav—finding it. "I don't need to. I memorized it."

"You . . . memorized it?"

I hesitated. Was that strange?

He laughed, pulling me to his chest. When I looked up, his lashes dipped, the corners of his mouth softened. Suddenly we were so close I couldn't see him clearly. His curls tickled my forehead. The world slowed, narrowing to the hitch in my breath and his quick, soft inhale. Our noses brushed, and a sharpness coiled in my stomach.

"Firin," he murmured, "can I kiss you?"

I froze. *Kiss me?*

Bregan was the first person I'd ever told my name, ever spent time with, ever really known—and he wanted to *kiss* me. Dizziness rushed from my toes to my head, and maybe I swayed, because his grip around my waist tightened.

"I'm sorry," he coughed, face flaring red. "If you don't—"

I cut him off with my lips.

The kiss was soft, almost curious. I wondered if he'd done this before, if he expected that I had. When I put my hand on his chest, his heart raced beneath my touch. I gripped the fabric of his shirt and rose on my toes, easing closer, exploring the shape of his lips with my own. He tasted like a rare cloudless horizon, like an adventure I could find myself in. His body softened, shaping to mine, and he slipped his hand into my hair. Every bit of my awareness shot to the spot where he brushed a thumb across my collarbone.

When he pulled back, I had the strange urge to cling to him, and when he pressed a smile to my forehead, something inside me fractured—because for the first time in my life, there was something in Luisonn that I didn't want to let go.

THIRTEEN

Bregan

Now

Luisonn's prison appeared on the horizon, shrouded in smoke from all corners of the city, looming over the southwestern cliffs to the sea. Bregan's thighs burned as he and Jaq climbed the low sloping streets.

Near the top, they ducked down an alley where the other fighters who had volunteered for the prison break huddled out of sight, collars pulled up over their mouths. They squinted at him and Jaq. Without Suri and Cidd, they numbered eight.

Thom Draifey, a middle-aged Labor-class man, lumbered forward. A cigarette dangled from his lips, below the burn scar that covered half his weathered face. "Where's the orphans?" he asked.

"Injured," Bregan said. Draifey sniffed, but before he could start posturing, Bregan turned to the others. "I think Jaq and I should enter the tower alone. The rest—"

"We're down four fighters." Draifey hacked a watery cough. "We'll have to reevaluate. If you and Jaq go in the tower, we can post outside in the courtyard, drawing the guards' focus."

Bregan gritted his teeth. That's exactly what he'd been about to say.

He didn't like Thom Draifey. The Labor-class man had joined the Reformists two years ago, and was arrogant and unpredictable. From the beginning, he questioned and countered the movement's new leaders at every turn, riling up the rebels most eager for blood and sowing division during a time when consensus was critical to their success. But he was an excellent shot and a strategic fighter, so Bregan had accepted his offer to help tonight. The other fighters were newer recruits, people who tended to flock around Draifey. They'd volunteered because he had.

"Agreed," Bregan said. They didn't have time to waste. "Let's go." He yanked his shirt up over his mouth and headed back out to the main street.

Pirates had originally built the prison, but the Stav had reinforced it during their occupation. Three sets of concentric walls held convicts in by level of crime. Cells for minor offenses lined the outside layers, while major prisoners were kept in a separate tower at the center—the tower where Bregan's father had been locked up since Bloody Fifthday.

He clutched his gun. Pa was alive. He had to be.

A block away from the entrance, Draifey's whistle split the darkness. He raised an arm. They all halted. When he dropped it, they separated. Bregan trailed Jaq along the edge of the street until the front gates of the prison loomed through the smoke. Jaq looked back, then signaled, and they ducked into the refuge of an overturned market cart.

Pop, pop, pop.

The cart shook against the barrage of bullets.

As soon as the Stav stopped shooting, Bregan and Jaq spun, bracing their weapons on the side of the cart. Shapes moved at the top of the prison wall. Bregan pulled his trigger. Jaq pulled his. The shapes vanished.

"I think we got 'em," Jaq rasped, swiping at the panes of his glasses.

Bregan nodded.

Draifey emerged from the smoke across the street. He motioned them forward. As they approached the gates, Bregan raised his gun, prepared for another round of defense, but none came.

The night remained silent as they fashioned a scaling rope, climbed to the top, and dropped down inside. A massive open archway led into the prison. Nothing moved.

"It worked," one of the other fighters spit. "Bastards all left to protect Central."

Bregan led the others past open entrances to endless hallways of cells. The prison was as wet, frigid, and dark as the bottom of the sea. Prisoners' shouts echoed down the windowless corridors, but he ignored them, picking up his pace.

There were no guards. Not a single soul who wasn't behind bars.

Bregan's chest tightened when dim light finally appeared at the end of the hallway, signaling the inner courtyard. He jogged back out into a night lit by distant fires. The high-security tower loomed over the open space like a king, disconnected from the rest of the prison, framed by an ocean horizon.

Bang.

The bullet hit the outer wall, showering Bregan with pieces of stone. He slammed to the ground, his body a vibrating shell, as shots erupted from everywhere, all at once.

His gun spun ahead on the hard-packed gravel. He looked up. Perched atop the courtyard's outer wall, a sandy-haired Stav soldier stared down the barrel of a rifle. His nose was crooked, as if it had broken and healed wrong.

A trap. The Stav guards had known Reformists would come to the tower to free the Five. They'd led them here and trapped them in the courtyard.

The world stilled as Bregan waited for the man to pull his trigger.

Then Draifey exploded into the courtyard in a stream of gunfire. The Reformists rained bullets at the walls, and the sandy-haired Stav disappeared.

"Inside!" Draifey bellowed, reloading.

Bregan snatched up his gun and raced toward the tower. Jaq shot the lock, spraying shards of wood and metal. They slammed into the door, and it opened into a dank, dark entry.

"Pa!" Bregan shouted, flying up the only staircase.

When he reached the fourth floor, his own name reverberated back. "Bregan!" Hoarse, but undeniable.

Bregan tripped on a step, then leaned into the wall to steady himself. His father was alive. For once, the saints were watching. For once, he didn't have to lose someone else.

At the top of the steps, he emerged in a hall lined with barred windows. Faces peered out, shocked voices filled the air, but he zeroed in on the set of dark eyes that matched his own and launched for the door they were locked behind.

"Keys!" Jaq shouted. Metal jangled from his hand. Bregan snatched them, trembling as he shoved them into the lock, one after another.

"You did it," Pa muttered through the bars.

The lock clicked. Bregan tossed the keys back to Jaq so he could free the other prisoners, then threw open the door and wrapped his arms around his father's chest. Pa's bones pressed through his shirt.

"What happened?" Pa asked. "How did you get in? The guards left, and then we heard the cannons and smelled the smoke, but—"

"We got help from the continent," Bregan choked, struggling to keep his voice level as he faced his father head-on. "The others are toppling Central now. How . . ."

Flesh hung off Pa's too-thin limbs. Scars mottled his sunken face, some older than others, some deeper. Thin, straight cuts made by blades. A few stretched into his skull, drawing lines through his shorn hair. Bile burned Bregan's throat. "What did they—"

Pa shook his head. "It doesn't matter. I'm fine. How . . . Where is your mother?"

A new chill doused the moment.

"We need to get you out," Bregan said, backing toward the door. "Get you behind our own lines until we're sure—"

"Tell me." Pa's bony fingers dug into his forearm. One was missing. Bregan didn't want to do this here, now. "Pa . . ."

"Where is she, son?"

"She's gone."

Pa's lashes quivered. "What do you mean?"

Bregan thought about saying she'd died, but his father would find out eventually. Lying now would only compound the pain later. "She's the reason you're here. She betrayed us."

"No." Pa's nose wrinkled.

"Yes."

Four years ago, on Bloody Fifthday, Ma had given in to her cowardice. In exchange for protections, she'd betrayed the Reformists to the Stav. She was the reason the Stav had found the factory theater, the reason the movement had imploded, the reason Pa and the others had been captured and so many had died. The reason he'd lost Firin.

Pa shook his head. "The Stav said . . . but I didn't—"

"It's *true*. She told me everything before she packed her bags, got on a ship, and fled to Qunsii."

A sound came out of Pa, a moaning rush of wind, as if he were deflating. He backed up, deeper into the cell. Bregan grabbed his arm. "We need to go," he snapped, harsher than he meant to. He had given *everything* the last four years to get here, into this cell. He wasn't about to risk their lives arguing about his mother. Not when this was her fault.

"The shooting stopped," Jaq said.

He and the other prisoners stood just outside the cell, watching Bregan and his father. The Five—what people had called the old Reformist leaders since their arrest—were ghosts of the fearless rebels Bregan had once revered. Stained uniforms, scars, and gaunt faces.

He swallowed. They'd left Draifey and the others in the courtyard.

"Let's go," he said, handing his pistol to Pa.

They descended in heavy silence. Bregan led with his rifle, his father a step behind him. A drumbeat battered against his skull as he approached a gun hole that looked north. He signaled for the others to stop, then threw his weapon through the opening and squinted out.

Draifey stood in the middle of the gravel courtyard, alive. He was gripping the crooked-nosed Stav's arm. Another Stav soldier, with blinding-white hair, stood beside him. Bregan blinked, waiting for a gunshot, for a punch—but then Draifey shifted, and let go.

The Stav nodded at the Reformists, then jogged out of the courtyard with his companion, right past where his bullet had almost hit Bregan in the face. Atop the wall, two more figures rushed south.

Four Stav guards. Draifey was letting them go.

Bregan pounded down the stairwell and flew into the courtyard, gun pumping at his side. "Where are they going?"

Draifey wiped at his chin. "They surrendered."

"Surrendered?" The other fighters—Draifey's people—glanced between them. A shiver slid down Bregan's spine.

"They didn't actually shoot anyone." Draifey spit on the courtyard sand. "Stopped fighting when you went inside. Said they disobeyed orders to leave them alive." He jerked his chin at the Five. "It's an honor to meet you all. I'm Thom Draifey, one of the new government's councilmen."

Bregan could barely speak. "Just because they left the prisoners alive to save their own asses doesn't erase their crimes. It doesn't make them *innocent*." He glanced at the newest puckered scar that traversed Pa's skull, and his vision flared red.

"No one else needs to die tonight, son," Draifey said. He was too calm, collected.

"Since when were the options *freedom* or *death*? We should have arrested them, investigated—"

"It's over," Draifey said, with the weight of an adult trying to placate a child.

Bregan bristled. This didn't make sense. The Stav guards had occupied the high ground. They could have run and disappeared in the chaos, escaping capture on their own. Why had they come down off the parapets to *shake* Draifey's hand? Why surrender if you didn't need to? The rest of Draifey's fighters squirmed, eyes on their boots.

"Did I miss something?" Bregan asked.

"No, son. A runner just came from Regents' to confirm it," Draifey said, blatantly misconstruing the question. He motioned to a boy who was chugging water from another fighter's flask. "The governor's dead. We've officially won."

The Five looked at one another, lips parted in shock, but Bregan couldn't shift past his fury. Draifey was lying—and the other Reformist fighters knew it.

Bregan stepped forward, but a hand fell like a steady weight on his back. He looked up into Pa's tired face. "Let it go, Breg."

The prisoners and fighters watched him. Weariness weighed them down. Eagerness glinted in their eyes. They wanted to be done. They wanted to go home.

Bregan exhaled, eyeing his father's hand on his shoulder, his missing finger.

Fine. But this would not go unaddressed.

FOURTEEN

Firin

Now

The sun rose on a new Luisonn.

Before a crimson sky, the Reformists executed every Nodtacht and Stav who wanted me dead. As they announced convictions for crimes against peace, humanity, and freedom, the accused were led onto the canal bridges in groups of five. Black bags were yanked over their heads. Nooses snaked around their necks.

Baron Hulei, Luisonn's new interim president, orchestrated the deaths like a conductor. Sunlight gilded his hair until he gleamed like the gold bars Father and I had once stolen from him—the theft that had condemned everything, the first snip in the unraveling of my reality. I'd been *sure* he'd abandoned the Reform movement after Bloody Fifthday, and yet here he was, leading them.

I watched from the clock-tower roof as the baron ordered the Nodtacht pushed over the side, as their bodies hit the canal boats waiting beneath. He would kill me just as quickly, for everything I'd done to him.

But he didn't know my real face.

Only the Nodtacht in Luisonn had ever discovered my illusion, and they were dying before my eyes.

By the time the carnage ended, I felt hollowed out, emptied. Thoughts skimmed the surface of my shock like snowflakes on a frozen pond. The world slowed. The sound of rebellion dulled. The shattered pieces of my past floated around me, waiting for me to decide which shards I'd pick up. Which parts I'd keep.

Sailing to Qunsii, reinventing myself, was a half-formed dream crafted from desperation, just like all the imaginings of my youth. But I hadn't really wanted to board that ship. There was only one life I had ever *truly* wanted—among the Veiled Players, onstage with Bregan at my side. I thought those dreams had died on Bloody Fifthday, but maybe today they, like this city, could resurrect with the dawn.

When I closed my eyes, I saw Bregan hoisting a gun on the roof at Sovest Square. My heart panged. That summer, he hadn't wanted any part of the Reformists' violence, but Bloody Fifthday had clearly changed everything, for both of us. It seemed that he had sacrificed pieces of himself to survive, just as I had.

In the last four years, trapped inside Father's poisonous legacy, I'd done terrible things—things Bregan would hate me for, the troupe would reject me over, and Hulei would kill me because of. But now that the Stav Regime had toppled, maybe no one ever needed to know.

I stood. I dusted off my dress.

My pocket mirror, my hidden knife, and the dress on my back were all I had to my name. Even if I still wanted to, I didn't have the money to leave. But I didn't want to. Not anymore. With steady hands, I ripped off the weaver's bracelet, crumpled her identity papers, and sent both tumbling off the roof.

Blood splattered the surface of my old mirror. I smeared it with my thumb—this one last piece of my childhood—then clicked it open.

Suri, the blonde Reformist girl, peered up at me. I glanced at the baron and hesitated for a heartbeat. As long as he never figured me out, it might work.

I dropped my illusion cord. Relief barreled into me and I braced on all fours, breathing against the sudden absence of years of tension. When my vision stopped flaring, I raised the mirror again.

My own face stared back at me.

FIFTEEN

Bregan

Now

The entire city clogged Luisonn's streets.

Draifey and his fighters headed for Regents' Hill to check in with Addym Taidd, but Bregan and Jaq took the Five back to the temple at Sovest Square. As they walked, black curls of ash danced with wisps of fog against the backdrop of a deep, victorious sunrise. For once, people's gazes affixed to the cityscape rather than the horizon. Bregan wanted to relax with them, but he couldn't stop seeing the Stav prison guards, walking free.

Draifey had let them go, then lied about why. Bregan was sure of it. He couldn't fathom what Draifey had to gain from freeing four Stav guards, but the usually agitated man had acted too nonchalant. He and his fighters had refused to meet Bregan's eye. They were hiding something, and the interim president needed to know.

As they neared Sovest Square, whispers rose like a wind.

Look, there they are.

The Five are alive.

Eyes followed the still-uniformed prisoners as they passed, faces haggard and bones thin. Bregan twitched at each new murmur, watching his father. Pa stared blankly at the back of Jaq's boots, and Bregan doubted that he felt heroic. Bregan certainly didn't. Neither of them had joined the Reform movement for notoriety. No one in their family had. They'd joined the rebellion out of desperation and a need to write their own futures, a chance to live in a world where they could speak their minds and do what they desired without condemning their loved ones to death.

Now that they'd succeeded, Bregan felt merely hollowed out.

"We won," he said quietly, to his father as much as himself. Pa looked up, blinked a few times. Bregan didn't look away. He'd lost Firin, and they'd lost Ma. Over the years they'd done things they weren't proud of, things that would haunt Bregan forever, but at least they'd ensured that his great-grandfather, uncle, cousin, and countless others hadn't died in vain. That was something. Maybe it could be enough.

After a long, heavy moment, Pa nodded. "What's this about a council?"

"The movement voted on an interim government last month," Bregan said. "We needed some leadership in place to secure stability when we won." They'd agreed on a structure: a president who served on a council of five members—one each from the Baron, Manager, and Merchant districts, and two from the Labor District. One Labor to represent the District in Luisonn, including the Zed District, and another to represent the outlying Iket Isles, which were overwhelmingly populated by Labor-class citizens. Eventually they would rename and redefine the Districts altogether, but they couldn't do everything at once. "We're going to hold a presidential election in a couple of months," he added, "and then another election to appoint the council after that. Draifey and the others are just serving as leadership until then."

"You're not on it?" Pa asked.

"No. I didn't run." Bregan didn't want to be a politician. He'd never even wanted to be a Reformist.

Shouts bit into the morning as they turned into Sovest Square. A bonfire crackled in front of the abandoned temple where the Veiled

Players lived. A dozen young Labors perched on a toppled statue of the Vorstav'n emperor, trading drinks and pointing people toward a fire of burning identity bracelets and papers.

"What will you do then?" Pa asked.

Bregan stared into the licking flames. Leather smoked and paper curled.

The future had always felt elusive. Whenever he allowed himself to envision it, the Stav tore it apart. For the last four years, living underground and hiding from the Stav, he'd focused solely on getting Pa out of prison. Anything beyond that was impossible to imagine. A large part of him hadn't expected to make it this far, and now that he had? He honestly didn't know what he would do.

Firin's face swam in the tired corners of his vision. He rubbed her away and, instead of answering his father, searched the square for a sign of Baron Hulei. He didn't see him. In fact, none of the Reformists' councilmen appeared to be present.

Someone grabbed his shoulder. When Bregan turned, Tez's bright smile was like a punch to his chest. The actor seized him in a bone-breaking hug, and Bregan gripped him back. He hadn't realized, until that moment, just how much he'd been trying not to think about who had and hadn't made it through the night. Most of the troupe had volunteered to help the injured during the insurrection, and when Tez pulled back, his linen shirt was streaked with blood that wasn't his.

"Bless the ancestors that you are all right," Tez said, swiping at red eyes.

"You too," Bregan said. He wanted to ask about the other Players, but the question wouldn't form. Instead, he asked, "Do you know where Baron Hulei is?"

"Not here that I've seen. Might ask Mezua."

After squeezing Tez's shoulder one more time, Bregan climbed the temple's front steps alongside volunteers leading the injured, and when he stepped into the entryway, the world shifted like a winter wind.

Corpses lined the walls, covered in blankets. Beyond the inner door, groaning patients littered the temple's nave. They sprawled on pews, curled in aisles, perched in every corner. Bregan halted, surrounded by the dead. A strange sensation unfurled in his core, weighing him down.

This was the price they had traded for their freedom.

No. This was the price the Stav had forced them to pay.

"You've got to be kidding me," Pa snarled, right behind him. The shift in his despair was so sudden that it took a moment for Bregan to realize he was glaring at the Veiled Players' director, Mezua, as she helped an injured woman lie down in a pew.

Bregan's stomach dropped. "Pa—"

His father marched past him. "It was you, wasn't it?" His shout echoed, drawing the focus of everyone in the nave. Pa and Mezua had never gotten along, not even when they were both with the Reformists. Pa had never forgiven Mezua for recruiting Ma into the illegal troupe, and Mezua had begrudged him for his lack of support.

But Ma was gone. The revolution was over. People lay dead at their feet.

Mezua set the injured woman down, then stepped out of the pew, wiping blood on her already ruined skirts. Dust and ash clung to her jacket, streaked her cheeks, and coated the tight curls that haloed her head, making her look far older than she was.

"Hello, Dech." Her stare was steel.

"I swear to the saints, if you're the one who convinced her to—"

Bregan stepped in front of his father. "Pa, lower your voice."

"If your ma betrayed us to the Stav, then *she* had something to do with it."

"No, she didn't."

"I never trusted her." Pa jabbed a finger at the director, voice breaking as it rose. "I told your ma she always looked out for herself. I told her she—"

"Stop it, Pa," Bregan said, taking his father by the shoulders. "I have been underground with Mezua and the rest of the Reformists since you were arrested. What Ma did isn't her fault."

"You've been *living* with her?"

"Where else was I supposed to go?" It's not like Ma had left him many choices when she sailed for Qunsii, abandoning him with a father in prison and a price on his head.

Something died in his father's eyes, and Bregan felt sick. He just wanted to put the last four bloody years behind him.

"Why don't you get some food, get changed, take a breath," he said. Then he turned to the entryway, where Tez stood frowning between Pa and Mezua. "Tez? Can you get him some clean clothes?"

Pa's eyes didn't leave Mezua as Tez led him away.

Wiping ash from his face, Bregan turned to the Players' director. "I'm sorry about—"

Mezua placed a hand on his cheek. "Don't. You're not responsible for your father's actions any more than your mother's. Praise the gods you're safe."

Throat tightening, Bregan nodded. "Where's the baron?"

"They moved the victory meeting to the Trade building. He left for the Corners hours ago. But Bregan, we need to talk about Cidd."

"Why?"

She didn't meet his eyes. "He's in the left wing, with Suri. But since he can't . . . play the Sage King, I need you to pick up the role. I know it's not your favorite."

"What?" The word came out hoarse, covered in barbed wire.

"*Seorsus.* I need you to take Cidd's role."

The words tore something in Bregan. Suddenly, he wanted nothing more than to retreat to the temple's kitchen and collapse with the other troupe members, to forget the violence and lose himself in the lines of a play. But even that respite wasn't possible, not with their loved ones at death's door.

"I can't think about a play right now," he forced out.

Mezua squeezed his forearm. "We have to remind people that tonight's tragedies bought us a better world."

He shook his head. "I can't."

The *tragedies* were exactly why. Bregan had taken lives, failed to save lives, and ruined lives to get here. Not just tonight, but over the last four years. Maybe Mezua could enjoy today, but he couldn't stand here and talk about *Seorsus* with suspicion about Draifey racing up his spine. They had sacrificed too much to risk their success on anything. The interim president needed to know about the escaped Stav guards and Bregan's fear that Draifey was hiding something. Then, maybe, Bregan could think about what came next.

He found Pa with the medics at the back of the room, picking through a pile of clean shirts with shaking fingers. His father didn't look up.

"I need to go to the Corners," Bregan said. "If that's where Baron Hulei's moved the victory meeting, he'll want you and the others there too. Will you come?"

Pa's jaw worked; then he nodded.

SIXTEEN

Bregan

Now

The Corners reeked of death.

The bridges over the Centre Canal were supposed to serve as temporary holding cells, but they'd been turned into gallows. Bodies hung from every rail. The boats in the canal were stacked high with corpses. Hundreds of them. Some uniformed, many not. The dispersing mob thrummed with electricity. Bregan stared from the edge of it all, a buzz swarming his ears.

The Reformists had *killed* every Stav they'd captured.

"Well, damn, you actually made it." Addym Taidd sauntered over, his broad shoulders at ease, as if this level of violence were an everyday occurrence. Over the years Addym had become as impulsive and bitter as his father. Bregan wanted to punch through his smug grin.

"What the fuck is this?" He led Addym away from Pa and the rest of the Five.

Addym sniffed. "We caught every Stav soldier and official, all the Nodtacht, and most of their spies too."

"What happened to giving people trials?" Bregan asked. Addym laughed under his breath. The sound crawled up Bregan's spine. "Does the baron know about this?"

"Of course."

"Where is he?"

Addym ignored him, turning to the Five. "The council's waiting to greet you. They're in the eastern receiving room." He gestured toward the smoldering shell of the Trade headquarters. Bregan didn't miss the way he wiped his palms on his pants, not quite looking any of the Five in the eye. Addym's own father hadn't survived the Bloody Fifthday raid long enough to be captured with the other leaders. Bregan swallowed a pang of pity. Right now, Addym didn't deserve it.

He headed for the Trade building, Pa a half step behind him. Blood rushed in his ears as they entered a gilded, wallpapered lobby stuffed full of Reformist soldiers waiting for the council's victory speech. He wove his way to a door beyond them.

When Bregan entered the small side room, half a dozen heads swiveled in his direction. All the interim council members lounged on embroidered chairs and chaises. At a bar cart, Draifey poured himself a glass of whiskey. With his scarred, weathered face and bloody, ashen clothes, he clashed with the room, but when he turned and raised a brow at Bregan, every line of him stood at ease.

"Dech Nimsayrth, how fantastic to see you well." Baron Hulei rose as Pa appeared at Bregan's side. The clothes Tez had given him hung off his bones. The two men clasped arms. They'd been allies before Pa's arrest. Pa was the one who'd brought the baron into the Reformists' fold. "Bregan, I'm so glad you made it through." The interim president looked as if he'd aged a decade overnight, but despite his tired eyes and mussed yellow hair, his suit was clean and straight.

"What's going on?" Bregan demanded.

"What do you mean?"

Draifey grunted as he lowered into a gold-stitched armchair. "Isn't it obvious? He's upset about the executions."

"Those people deserved trials," Bregan said.

The baron sighed. "In a perfect world, yes. But we had to make a tough decision."

"We?"

"The council. We voted last night."

All the council members examined their fingernails or boots, except Draifey. He threw an arm over the back of his chair, clinked the ice in his glass, and met Bregan's glare with a clear challenge. Bregan's fury popped. Draifey had known about the planned executions all night, yet had said nothing.

"I need a private word," Bregan said to the baron.

Hulei nodded. "Excuse me, everyone. I figure we can get the meeting started. If you'll head out, I'll be right behind you." He gestured to the entrance hall, where Reformist fighters waited. The council members and former prisoners glanced between Bregan and the baron, then rose to their feet. Voices swelled as the doors opened.

"All right, I'm listening," the baron said.

"We agreed: no executions without trials." The Reformists, drunk on victory and fueled by revenge, had undoubtedly swept up innocents in their wake.

"I know." The baron fixed him with a tired but steel-sharp look. "That's what we're working toward, but there won't *be* anything to work toward if we don't secure this transfer of power. Leaving the Stav alive was a risk we couldn't take."

"So you rounded up everyone suspicious and executed them?"

"We couldn't risk Nodtacht slipping through the cracks," the baron said. "We had to catch and eliminate as many of them as possible, as fast as possible."

Bregan hated the Stav's secret police more than most. They'd hung his great-grandfather and kicked his grandfather out of his home. He'd watched them drag his cousin—a *child*—from his bed and shoot him point-blank. They'd corrupted his ma into a spy and killed countless Reformists Bregan cared about. In all likelihood, they had killed Firin.

They deserved to die for the terror and heartbreak they caused; the world would be better without them, but this wasn't how it was supposed to happen.

If citizens in this country couldn't trust the new government to uncover the truth before condemning them to death, how were they any better than the Stav? Weren't they *worse*? At least the Stav were honest when they killed innocent people.

"You can't know all those people were guilty," Bregan said quietly, "and even if they had been, whether or not their crimes were worthy of execution."

"I know," the baron repeated. "But we don't have a justice system in place yet. We haven't fully taken hold of the prisons or the court. Without organized manpower, how were we supposed to keep all the Stav locked up? How could we ensure they didn't launch a counterattack?"

"We have support from the continent." The bay was full of ships from the north.

Hulei spun his top hat between his fingers. "The Kirrus and Qunsiians only agreed to stay for a fortnight. The Gwyns agreed to patrol the waters for a few months, but we can't rely on them. For long-term stability, we need to be able to stand on our own."

"What about the constabulary?"

"Last night we lost three of the men who agreed to serve leadership positions. The commissioner's still in place, but we're going to have to rebuild the rest of it."

"He's right, Breg," Pa said, making Bregan jump. He hadn't known his father was behind him. "To keep the Stav alive, to risk Nodtacht escaping, would risk a backslide."

"How many innocent people did we just kill to ensure that?" Bregan asked.

Pa's throat bobbed. Hulei dropped his gaze.

Bregan's fingers wrapped into fists. A naive part of him had hoped the revolution would end in a single night, but the Reformists had lit a bonfire yesterday, and now they had to deal with the embers and put out the coals.

Draifey's booming laugh echoed out in the lobby. Half a dozen unfamiliar faces huddled around him as he punctuated his speech with a cigarette.

"If you're worried about retaliation," Bregan said, "then you should prioritize finding the prison guards Draifey let escape."

The baron's eyes flashed. "Draifey did what?"

"He says they surrendered, but he's lying about something."

"Shit," the baron murmured. He wiped at his face and turned to Pa. "Dech, I know you never wanted to, but the constabulary could really use—"

"No," Bregan said. Absolutely not. Pa had sacrificed enough.

Pa shifted. "Son . . ."

"*I'll* do it. I'll find them," Bregan said. In the process, he'd figure out what Draifey was hiding. "But once I do, they *will* stand trial."

SEVENTEEN

Firin

Now

The temple clinic housed its own kind of war. The tang of blood and bile blew through the open doors. As I climbed the front steps, side-stepping hordes of volunteers carrying bodies and patients, I thought I'd choke on my fear. Seeing Bregan mere hours ago had shown me that my love for him was still the air I breathed. If, after *everything*, he hadn't survived the night, I didn't know if I would either.

When I stepped into the entry, I scanned for his curls, and for every second I failed to spot them, the hook lodged in my sternum pulled tighter.

Just inside the main door to the nave, a curvy, dark-haired woman stared out over the suffering. A pile of blankets teetered in her arms.

"Excuse me?" I said in a scratch of a voice.

When she turned, her heavily lashed eyes were achingly familiar. She was one of the Veiled Players' dancers. Nyfe—it had to be, because the Stav had killed her sister in a raid before Bloody Fifthday. She looked unmoored without the mirror of her twin.

"Can I help you, love?" She shifted the pile of blankets to her other hip, brows pinched. She was trying to place me.

"I'm looking for Bregan."

She gasped softly in recognition. "Oh, of course. He's back there." My knees nearly gave out. I spun, following her finger as she pointed to the right wing of the temple, where Bregan stood with Tez. He'd lost his flatcap. Dried blood stiffened the front of his shirt, and ash was smeared on his old olive-colored jacket, but he gesticulated to Tez in some kind of frustrated conversation without any signs of pain. I stumbled toward them on shaking legs.

Tez saw me first. His pale eyes flared behind his thick hair and beard, which were more gray than black now. He snatched Bregan's elbow, said something. Bregan turned. I halted in the middle of the aisle.

For a moment, neither of us moved.

Then Bregan's lips parted, his lashes fluttered, and he was walking toward me without blinking, as if floating by the pull of his own shock. Bruises indented the skin beneath his eyes, which seemed darker than they used to, like a night sky without stars. I white-knuckled the side of a pew, my heart barely beating, as it occurred to me for the first time that maybe he'd changed *too* much.

He halted a good two arms' lengths away.

"Hey," I whispered.

His bloodshot eyes scraped down my body, tracing my shape, bringing every inch of me back to life. I wondered what he saw, if he, too, was searching my contours for traces of who I had been. I wondered if he could see her there, that old version of me. His fingers shot into his hair. "W-what . . . what are you—I thought you were . . ." *Dead.*

There, in the pained crack of his voice, lay my answer.

Everything and nothing had changed.

When a sheen fell over his eyes, a hurricane of grief blew through me. I'd left him. I'd vanished. I'd had to for his own sake, but that didn't erase the fact that he thought I'd died, that he'd lived four years with the loss I'd feared on the way here tonight.

"I'm sorry," I managed to say.

A ragged sound burst from his lips, a sob that could have been a laugh. "Firin?" The name struck me in the gut like a beautiful, ornamented blade.

"Bregan . . ." My voice broke.

In one smooth movement, he tugged me to his chest. When his fingers nestled in my hair, I wrapped my arms around the hardened planes of his back in an embrace that was altogether foreign and familiar. Beneath the layers of blood, sweat, and smoke, he still smelled the same. When I closed my eyes, I could almost believe that no time had passed at all.

"How is this possible?" He ran calloused palms down my neck, then my arms, landing on my hips, as if trying to reassure himself that I existed. I clutched at the familiar stiff wool of his jacket, my lips salting with tears.

When he leaned back, he towered over me, all broad shoulders and lean muscle. The moment our eyes met, his gaze pierced through the layers of me, flaying me open, as if he could see every bruise on my broken soul.

He couldn't, of course.

He had no idea what the last four years had wrought of me.

And yet, Bloody Fifthday had forced us both underground. I didn't need to know what he'd been through to understand that we'd both suppressed our true selves, our desires and values, to stay alive. Heat intensified, filling every corner of me with the blistering hope that maybe we could climb out of this together, that *maybe* the broken pieces of me could be forged into something new, something Bregan could still love.

"You're real?" he murmured.

"I'm real."

As he drank me in, I placed a palm on his bloodied shirt, feeling his heartbeat, the proof he was reeling as much as I was, that he still cared. Shoring up my courage, I asked the questions that scared me the most.

"Is your pa okay?"

Bregan nodded. "We got him and the rest of the Five out last night."

I exhaled slowly. "And your ma?"

He stiffened. "She's . . . gone."

Dread pooled in my gut. "What do you mean?"

"She was a spy, for the Stav." Short sentences, like factual nails. "She's in Qunsii now."

"W-what?" I breathed.

"It's a long story." The words were steel.

I wanted to press him for details, to make sense of how Esmai could have committed such a betrayal, but the rage suddenly roaring in Bregan's eyes was cleaving open the ground beneath my feet. I understood the lengths to which a person would go to survive, to keep their loved ones alive—but if Bregan understood what his mother had done, he harbored little empathy and absolutely no forgiveness.

I should have known that even Bloody Fifthday couldn't have swayed him from his principles. Bregan's heart made him who he was.

And that person would never forgive the things I'd done.

I drew my hands out from the folds of his jacket. "Is Mezua here?" I asked.

He looked down at the space I'd put between us. "No, she's helping transfer the injured to the Enlightened Hospital. Why?"

"I want to audition."

Bregan's lips pressed together, and for one awful moment I thought he would attempt to dissuade me, as he had so many times before. But then he said, "She won't be back until morning." He paused. "Firin . . . I searched for you. What happened?"

On the walk here, I had arranged the pieces of a logical story. But, as Bregan held me in a gaze both desperate and expectant, it tangled like fishing line. "I just, I—"

"Aza Vota!" Tez appeared behind Bregan, his arms full of bandages.

I snapped my teeth shut. *Always think before you speak,* Father whispered in the back of my mind. "Tez," I said, smiling weakly.

Bregan guided me into one of the pews to let him pass, hands still on my waist. Near the temple's entrance, Nyfe whispered something to a woman with dark hair. They were pointing at us. People all around the temple were sneaking glances. During our summer together, I hadn't spent much time with the Players, but clearly they knew who I was. My cheeks heated.

"Is good to see you." Tez winked.

Once he passed us, Bregan released me. Cold slid into the temple like a storm cloud. "Vota?" he said quietly.

"It's what everyone here knows me as," I said, my pulse quickening. Bregan had always allowed me to pose as Vota around others, calling me Firin only when we were alone.

He scrubbed a palm down his face. "Where were you, Firin?"

"I tried to find you," I lied, "but I didn't know where you'd gone or if you were even alive. I assumed you went underground, but then today I heard the Five were here, and I thought if you were anywhere, you'd be with your pa."

Bregan squinted, as if trying to read the truth in the angles of my face. "Right," he said, clearly finding my explanation lacking. He pulled out his great-grandfather's old wristwatch, and I felt him slipping away. When he looked at the watch face, my heart strained. It worked now. He'd fixed it. One of so many unknown pieces of his life that had changed. "Look, I have to go uptown for a meeting," he said. "I'll be gone for a bit, so why don't you take my cot? It's in the basement."

"What about Mezua?" I asked.

"I'll talk to her in the morning." He ran a finger lightly down my cheek. "My cot, okay? I'll come find you."

As he stepped out of the pew, the distance between us stretched, and I wanted to pull him back, but I forced my fingers to release. With a small smile, he flipped his coat collar, turned, and left—and all I could think was that the old Bregan never would have let me go.

EIGHTEEN

Bregan

Now

Firin was *alive*.

As Bregan climbed the sloping streets to Regents' Hill, he tugged his jacket against a sharp wind off the shore, and her lingering scent suffocated him.

He'd tried to find her.

After she'd disappeared during the Bloody Fifthday raid and the movement was forced underground, he had risked his life to search for her against Mezua's orders, against common sense. But there'd been no sign of her. For months he'd asked around everywhere but found only dead ends: apartment building owners who'd never seen her, Labor-class workers who'd never heard of her father. It was like she'd never existed. Finally, he accepted that she must have died in the raid, another casualty of his mother's betrayal. But all this time she'd been out there, somewhere.

Each night he'd grieved her, she'd been alive.

A stone burned in the pit of his gut and another in his chest as he rounded the final corner. The insurrection had been a wretched montage of violence and death, and then she'd walked into the temple, backlit by the evening sun pouring through the open doors like a gift from the damn saints themselves. Every bone in his body wanted to turn around and run back, to hold her and make sure she wasn't some kind of hallucination. Maybe he should.

The last time he left her, she had disappeared for four years.

But after the bloody battle, and Draifey's lies, and the new council's endless executions, his bones already wanted to rattle out his skin. When Tez had called her *Vota* and she hadn't corrected him, Bregan watched the familiar gleam of lies forming in her eyes, and something fraying inside him had snapped.

Bregan wrung his shaking hands together. He could face Firin—and everything her return meant—after this meeting with Draifey was over.

The Nodtacht headquarters cut a black rectangle against the twilit sky, filling his steps with lead. Unimaginable suffering had occurred behind those walls. Lives ended. Spirits broken. He pictured his mother, climbing the steps to receive orders, then blinked the image away. It was just a building.

Stuffing his hands in his pockets, he trotted inside. The entry held a maelstrom of activity. Military soldiers in colorful Gwyn and Qunsiian uniforms wove around the building, moving furniture and carrying boxes. A few cleaned bloodstains from the marble floor.

"Mr. Nimsayrth." A man appeared, beefy hand outstretched. "It's great to meet you."

"Commissioner," Bregan said in surprise, taking in the newcomer's badge. He had a genial smile and imposing bulk. Several Reformists, including Addym Taidd, had clamored for his position, but the interim council had appointed the Qunsiian man instead. He wasn't from the Iket Isles, so he didn't carry the class biases that men like Addym did.

"We lost a lot of our leadership yesterday," the commissioner continued in an accent like ocean-smoothed stones, "so I want to thank you for helping us while we're short-staffed. Here's your badge." He held out a metal badge that said INSPECTOR above FREE ISLES OF IKET. It was heavier than Bregan expected. "You'll report directly to me, as we're postponing the official creation of the Investigations branch for now. I'll show you to the room you can use." The commissioner led him down a freezing stone hallway lined with barred cells.

When he opened the last door, a wave of excrement and mold shoved Bregan's center of gravity off-kilter. He stood in the interrogation room's entrance, vision adjusting to a dark stain that marred the back wall. The commissioner placed a candle lantern atop a small table framed by two simple chairs. Its light danced over his shaved head. "This one's the cleanest, believe it or not," he said apologetically. "I'll send the councilman down when he arrives."

When he left, Bregan lowered into one of the chairs. For a few minutes, he just massaged his temples. How had he ended up here?

"Well, this is a surprise." Draifey appeared in the open doorway.

Bregan stood. "Councilman."

Draifey surveyed the rank cell with a faint frown. He, like Bregan, still wore his bloodstained clothes from that morning. "I thought you weren't joining the constabulary."

"I'm not, just helping while the force gets on its feet." Bregan swept an arm toward the second chair. "I apologize for the state of the room. I have a couple of questions about the guards you released. It shouldn't take long."

Draifey didn't move. "You could have been commissioner, you know."

"I didn't put my name in for it."

"Then why are you here?"

Bregan gritted his teeth. "Because those escaped guards are a threat."

"To whom?"

"They could be Nodtacht, they could be planning a retaliation, they—"

Draifey grunted. "You're wasting your time, kid."

It took a lifetime of acting training for Bregan to keep his expression calm, impassive. Those were the soldiers who'd kept his pa and the Five locked behind bars for simply wanting to be free. Without questioning them, there was no telling what atrocities they had committed. They could have been the soldiers who'd tortured his father, or the ones who'd dragged his cousin from his home and shot his uncle's entire family.

"Why did you let them go?" Bregan asked.

The councilman leaned against the doorframe. "They left your father and the rest of the Five alive against orders. They surrendered."

Bullshit, Bregan thought. Did Draifey know one of them personally? Had the guards blackmailed him? Promised him something?

"You still could have arrested them," he said.

"Would you rather they were dead?"

"It's not either-or."

"You know it was."

Silence scraped at the edges of their shared glare, but Draifey didn't get to use yesterday's executions as an excuse. If he hadn't agreed with the council's plan to execute every damn Stav, he shouldn't have voted for it.

"I need to speak to the other fighters who were with you that night," Bregan finally said.

Draifey raised an eyebrow. "You're what, twenty-three? Four?"

"With all due respect, sir, I'm the one asking the questions."

"If you think finding four Stav soldiers will solidify this regime so you can go relax with a clean conscience, then you're more naive than I thought."

Bregan's calm investigator mask slipped. "Excuse me?"

"You know how I got this burn?" Draifey gestured vaguely to his face, then stepped inside the room. Exhaustion pulsed at the edge of Bregan's vision. "I was a few years younger than you, working at one of the steel mills in the Factory Block. I was good with the equipment, but the floor boys didn't get to engineer."

Draifey examined the stain on the back wall. "Our supervisors were nasty. Labor class, like us, but in charge. It was on their heads when we didn't make our quota, and they took that out on us. Liked to push us to the brink. One day, one of the boilers broke a couple hours before we were supposed to finish. We didn't have time to let the boiler cool, fix it, and get it back up and running in time to stay on schedule, so I made my supervisor a bet: if I could fix the boiler *without* taking it offline, he'd ask the factory Manager to promote me."

Spinning back around, Draifey splayed his hands theatrically on the table. "He didn't think I could do it, figured I was just trying to prove something. But I didn't want his respect. I needed his *rank*. I saw the opportunity that, while underestimating me, he didn't think twice about. Nearly burned off half my face to get that promotion, but then I had the *power* I needed to protect myself. From him and the other supervisors, at least."

A shiver ran down the back of Bregan's neck. As impressive as Draifey's audacity was, he didn't like the self-righteous slant to his smile. "That's what the revolution was," Bregan said carefully. "We *have* the power now."

Draifey snorted. "No, Bregan. Last night was just the beginning."

"It was supposed to be the end."

"The Stav aren't a threat anymore. Their empire was already crumbling, and we just cut off their only reliable trade route, not to mention executed most of their seasoned manpower. If you're worried about the success of this regime, you should focus on future threats, not past ones."

"What is that supposed to mean?"

Draifey bent over the table. "Son, as long as that baron is in power, *you* aren't. No Labors are."

Bregan couldn't speak. This was the same classist rhetoric that had turned Qunsii's People's Republic into tyranny, complete with a years-long massacre of anyone with royal blood or money. It was the same hot-blooded, vengeful hatred that had failed previous attempts to overthrow the Stav. Hatred was a poor foundation for a free nation.

"Well"—Draifey straightened—"you're wasting your time, but here's the fighters who were with us that night." He tossed a piece of paper onto the table, then paused in the doorway. "And, Bregan, if and when you're ready to face the next stage, come find me."

The list of names curled in Bregan's fist. He stared at the now-empty doorway, blood pulsing in his skull. Then he headed for the lobby, where Baron Hulei was reviewing papers with the commissioner at the front desk.

"Ah, Nimsayrth." Since that morning, the interim president had scrubbed himself back into something that looked intact. Suit pressed. Hair combed. The only sign of the last few days' strain was laced in purple beneath his eyes. He gave Bregan a once-over, lingering on his new badge. "You should really get cleaned up, Inspector. We want to show the public strength and stability."

"Sir, I believe Thom Draifey is organizing a campaign against you."

The baron flushed. "Do you?" He tugged at his tie, loosening it. "He has every right to run, of course, but—"

"His rhetoric, sir; it's downright classist." The last thing they needed, in the dawn of freedom, was an unnecessary class war.

The baron clapped his back. "Thank you, Bregan, but finding the guards should be your main concern. Stay focused. We can't be certain about what happened until you find them. And please, do get some sleep. You look as if a summer breeze could blow you over."

———— ❧~⧉ ————

By the time Bregan reached Sovest Square, he truly felt a breath away from toppling. He wanted to find Firin and bury himself in the feel of her, the proof of her existence, but as he approached the temple, he slowed at the sight of Jaq, holding his four-year-old daughter on the temple's moonlit steps.

One of the troupe's musicians, Jaari, sat with an arm slung around him. "Where the hell have you been?" she demanded.

When Jaq looked up, Bregan halted. Tears sparkled in tracks on his friend's brown cheeks, a sight Bregan hadn't seen since his wife, Taira's, death four years ago. He wasn't wearing his glasses.

"What happened?" Bregan asked. The child's spindly limbs curled around her father's torso, but she looked fine. Sound asleep.

"Cidd is gone," Jaq said.

Bregan braced himself for a wave of grief, maybe tears, but nothing happened. Two days ago, Cidd had danced through the temple, whiskey fueling unsteady steps and bright laughs as he butchered a scene from *Seorsus* to ward off the troupe's anxieties about the pending insurrection. They had let him sweep them away from the taut, endless agony of waiting, and Bregan had looked at each smiling face, knowing they wouldn't all make it.

Then, fear had roared like fire under his skin, but now he only felt a bone-deep, hollow exhaustion, as if the battle had siphoned the very blood from his veins.

"Jaq," he said, "I think Thom Draifey's going to run for president."

Jaari snorted. "That bastard? He goes through women like cigarettes. I wouldn't touch him with a long oar."

Bregan ignored her. Jaq had been there when Draifey let the guards go. Maybe he'd picked up on something Bregan hadn't. "I don't trust him. I can't shake the feeling that he lied about why he let those Stav guards go. Do you think—"

"You're still on about that?" Jaq said, gripping his daughter like he'd lost her.

"Yeah, I am. He's a councilman. I want to know why he protected Stav soldiers."

"We won, Breg. It's over."

Bregan bristled. Was it?

Jaari stood. "C'mon, now's not the time." When she reached out a placating hand, Bregan shrugged her off and headed inside. He couldn't blame Jaq for wanting it to all be over, but he didn't control whether it was or wasn't.

"Wait." Jaari followed him. "We need to talk."

He pulled open the front door, but her fingers clamped on his forearm.

"Who is she?" The Qunsiian musician, who'd been in the Veiled Players almost as long as he had, looked nothing like her usual primped self. Her messy bun spit like static around her circular face. Dark strands stuck to a shallow cut on her pale forehead. Her wide, slim eyes were red, and stained linens hung off her bones. "She's that girl, isn't she? The one you used to hang out with?"

"Yeah, she is."

"Why is she here?"

"Why does it matter?"

"You don't think it's odd she shows up on the exact day of the insurrection?"

Bregan sighed. He didn't have the energy for Jaari's conspiracies. "We were underground, remember? How was she supposed to find us until now?"

"Don't bullshit me. I remember how you used to look for her. You can't honestly—"

"What? Are you jealous?"

"Seriously? Don't deflect. You can't just bring a stranger into the troupe, especially not *right* after a damn revolution. We have to be careful who we—"

"Not everyone is a villain, Jaar."

Before she could protest, he escaped inside. The moans of the injured in the nave intensified, fueling a pounding in his head. He ducked down a side corridor, passing bodies without looking too closely at them. As he descended the steps to the basement, his heart rose into his throat. Wooden curtains and boxes partitioned the massive room into living quarters separated by tight makeshift corridors. By the time he reached his space in the back corner, he couldn't breathe.

Light from a tiny ground-level window near the ceiling pooled over his cot. His mother's old quilt tangled with Firin's skirts between her legs. Bregan's knees almost gave out. He leaned against his dresser, heart racing.

She was still here.

Four years of dreaming couldn't have conjured the way she looked in real life: a woman who'd grown into all her awkward, youthful edges. A glint on the floor caught his eye. Bregan lowered to his knees beside the bed and ran his thumb over the cover of a silver pocket mirror: the one she had always carried.

On the bed, Firin sighed in her sleep. Bregan looked up and found himself a hand's width from her sleeping face, peaceful and *alive*. Something hot burst behind his ribs. He shifted into a seat and pressed the back of his hand against his mouth. Gripping the mirror, he watched her fingers twitch.

He'd thought she was dead.

He'd blamed himself.

Yet now, she was here, and the Stav were gone. He wanted to crawl into bed with her, untangle the quilt from her legs, and kiss down the new contours of her body. He wanted to wake her, to shake her and demand every detail about where she'd been.

But he couldn't move, afraid doing so might curse her to disappear. For a long time, he just watched her breathe. Eventually, his inhales slowed to match hers, and he prayed to every saint that it would all be worth it in the end.

NINETEEN

Firin

Then

Father's pocket watch ticked on the café table. I shifted to try to read it, but at this angle it wasn't clear. After weeks of silent punishment, I had woken that morning to Mr. Finweint. For the first time ever, he'd taken me out to the Manager District for no reason. We weren't doing a con. We weren't celebrating one. We were just . . . *having tea.*

Baron Hulei's gold was still under our floorboard.

We still hadn't talked about it.

At this point I was sure something had gone wrong. There was no other explanation for why we weren't already across the sea, or why Father was being so damn secretive.

Teacups clinked around us as Father turned a page of the *Stav Observer*, brow furrowed. I sliced a piece of sugar bun with a knife and clenched my questions between my teeth. Was this some kind of apology for weeks of ignoring me? Because if it was, I would have rather been with Bregan.

I'd been sneaking out to see him for weeks now. He hadn't brought me back to the theater or introduced me to anyone but Esmai, but we spent our days acting and kissing on rooftops, as if we were a living version of *Qoyn & Insei.*

Father hadn't noticed me missing.

Behind him, two young Manager-class men sat at a window table, hands clasped beside their teacups. I distracted myself from my frustrations by watching them drink each other in, touching in the chaste way all Managers showed affection: a thumb stroking the back of a hand, a knowing smile, a kiss to the temple. I thought of Bregan, kissing down the edge of my ear, and a shiver shot to my core.

"I'm glad you're hungry."

My spine snapped straight. "What?"

Across the table, Mr. Finweint folded his paper. "You didn't eat dinner."

I almost dropped my fork. Yesterday, Esmai had fed me. I completely forgot to check what food Father had left me. I stuffed down my shock, shrouded it in the veneer of Afyn. "I wasn't feeling well."

"No?" He raised a piece of sugar bun to his lips.

I held his stare. If I'd been sick, it wasn't like he would have noticed. Since the Baron con, he rarely came home. Under the table, my hands started to shake.

"Well, I'm glad you're eating now."

"How did your dinner with the baron go?" The question shot out of me.

Father's smile thinned. "It was fine. Atzuie's has improved the quality of its menu."

"The baron's from Qunsii, right?" I leaned forward, a strange heat coursing through my veins. He wouldn't punish me in public, but that didn't mean he wouldn't later. Even still, I added, "I've heard it's nice there this time of year. Perhaps we should visit, since we have the money."

Father's eyes flashed. He set down his fork. "We should be going. I've got a meeting this afternoon." He stood. Maybe I should have been frightened, but I wasn't.

I felt the knife in my sleeve, the one I'd used to stab the Stav soldier. A shiver slid down my spine. "We need to talk," I said, not rising.

He grabbed my bicep and yanked me to my feet. "Don't make a scene, darling," he murmured, steering me through the line of customers at the counter, leaving our expensive sugar buns behind, half-eaten.

Just as we reached it, the café door opened, filling with black.

Father and I stared up at the leather-clad Nodtacht agent: the same bearded man with the hook-shaped scar who had checked our papers during the Baron Hulei con. Sugar bun lodged up my throat.

"Ah." The man's top lip curled. "Othan Finweint, is it?"

My heart seized. How did he remember Father's fake name?

"Greetings," Father said, clawing my shoulder.

"Heard you were here," the Nodtacht said. "Wondered if I might have a word."

Father's grip turned from sharp to bruising. When he looked at me, something unnerving burned behind Mr. Finweint's pleasant smile. Father *never* let his emotions break through, but in that split second, he brimmed with one I'd never seen. Something sharp and agonizing. It iced over my blood.

"Of course," he said. "Head home for your lessons, Afyn."

"But—"

"Now." As soon as his grip loosened, there was nothing left to indicate he'd been shaken at all. He gestured amicably to the Nodtacht and asked him something mundane as they stepped outside. I headed in the opposite direction, my insides thrashing. At the edge of the square, I paused and looked back. Father and the Nodtacht had disappeared.

I raced home.

Back at the apartment, I locked the door and paced the kitchen. Twice, I checked under the floorboard; both times, the count was the same.

Fifty bars of gold.

If the Nodtacht arrested Father, what would happen? Would they come here? I stared at the gold. I could take it, buy a ticket, and leave by myself, disappear before the Nodtacht knew to look for me. I should.

But I couldn't make myself pick up the bag.

The Nodtacht had questions. That didn't necessarily mean he'd arrested Father. But what if he had? What did they know? Was it possible they'd discovered our illusion? It seemed unlikely, unless they'd caught Father in the act of changing. Had they caught on to our thefts?

If they had, Father wouldn't give me up. He wouldn't.

The sun fell, then set.

I pulled a chair to the kitchen window and watched the streets around the canal for Father or any Nodtacht, but no one appeared.

Eventually, one of the women who worked in the brothel next door sauntered down the alley just beneath my window. A few minutes later, her lover arrived. They folded into one another, and I watched, as I often did, as he untied the wraps of her dress, kissing over her collarbone and farther, eliciting moans.

I bit the inside of my cheek. If Father didn't come back, maybe I could stay with Bregan. As long as I stopped conning and stuck to my Vota story, as long as Father didn't tell the Stav about me, surely it would be safe?

The moon rose, then set.

Next I knew, the door rattled with the force of a battering ram.

I fell out of my chair, hitting my chin on the windowsill in my delirious half-sleep haze. The horizon was stained purple with the first hint of sunrise. When someone knocked again, I remembered Father—and the Nodtacht—and my stomach fell through the floor.

"Open up," they bellowed. The voice was familiar. *Restuv.* One of Father's personas. My knees wobbled. "Let me in!"

I unlocked the latch, shaking from head to toe. Restuv was a vicious Stav soldier, and he usually only appeared when I'd done something terribly wrong. Why would Father wear him now? Had he worn Restuv to get us out of trouble?

When I slid the latch, the door flew open. Father strode inside in full Stav uniform, looming over six feet tall.

"Sit," he demanded.

I obeyed.

He poured a glass of whiskey, then threw something on the table. A rag, with dried blood on it. No, not a rag. My dress. The Labor-class dress I'd worn the first time I sneaked out to see Bregan. The dress with the Stav soldier's blood on it. The dress I'd thrown in the brothel's garbage heap.

"I found *this* weeks ago, but I didn't know what it meant until now."

I couldn't breathe.

"What were you thinking?" he growled, the words so low and shaken they almost weren't audible. "You *stabbed* a Stav soldier?"

I shivered. "He attacked me."

What did this have to do with the Nodtacht at the café?

The whites of Restuv's eyes flashed. "At night, in the Labor district, and wearing your own saints-damned face? They have *illustrations* of you, Firin. He described you in detail. Down to that freckle on your cheek." He brandished his whiskey. "Where were you going? To see the fucking *Debutante*?"

He didn't know about Bregan.

The realization hit me like a dead spot at sea, pouring calm into my limbs. When I spoke, my half truth was steady. "You cut me out of the Baron con, so I went to see *The Debutante* by myself."

"I hope it was worth it," he snarled. "We have to abandon your personas. No more jobs. No more cons."

"Well, it's a good thing we have the money now, isn't it? We don't have to do them anymore."

Father froze. "The Stav know your *face*, Firin."

"So?" My voice rose. The Stav had known about my face for weeks, and nothing had happened. "I thought we were going to *leave*. When were you going to—"

He slammed the glass on the table. Liquor sprayed the wood, my sleeve. "You compromised *everything*." He leaned in, one hand white-knuckled on the glass, the other fisting the back of my chair. I'd gone too far. But my fear sizzled like water droplets on a bed of coals, evaporating before it could take root.

My whole life, Father had been all I had. But that wasn't true anymore. Knowing *someone* else out there knew my name and my face—even cared about me—was enough to put steel in a spine that was tired of bending.

"Did I?" I sneered. "Is this actually about the Stav I stabbed? Or is it about the con with the baron that *you* messed up? Because it seems like you stopped planning to leave weeks ago. What happened? What did you—"

The whiskey glass shattered on the wall.

I collapsed to the floor, arms over my head.

"You have *no* idea what you're talking about," Restuv growled, kicking my chair so hard it toppled. He loomed over me, cheeks scarlet.

"Because you don't tell me anything!" I scrambled to my feet, wanting to attack him, to chase Restuv out of his body, but it was no use.

The door slammed, and he was gone.

I sank to my knees, chest pumping. Digging half-moons into my palms, I breathed sharply through my nose. I wouldn't sob. I wouldn't roll over like a kicked street dog. I glared at the pieces of glass scattered across the rug like tiny stars. Whiskey slid down the wall above the small hearth we never lit.

If Father wanted to live in fear, fine. I wasn't joining him.

Knees quaking, I stumbled out of the tenement. The sun hadn't yet risen. Black night swathed every line of the Bilge. Arms hugged around myself, I sidled from roof to roof until I reached the Labor District.

On the fire escape of Bregan's apartment, I found the right window and rapped my knuckles on the glass. Bregan rolled over on his mattress, spotted me, then threw off the same tattered quilt we used when we rehearsed on the roof. He glanced to where two dark shapes slept on a larger mattress. His parents' chests rose and fell slowly.

Bregan opened the window with expert silence, climbing out onto the fire escape. Instantly, my breathing evened. "Firin? Are you . . . crying?"

"No."

"Firin—"

"Come on," I said, grabbing his hand.

I led him to the roof. The tumultuous, lightening horizon promised a storm.

On the top step, he halted, blinking away sleep. "Wait, Firin . . ."

I caught his question with my lips. We fit together with a familiarity birthed in stolen moments over the past few weeks. As he folded into me, I slid my hands up his back into his hair, then pushed him down on the steps, straddling his lap.

When his palms found my hips, easing me closer, my throat tightened. How long would he put up with my half-truths? If he knew what I'd done to the baron, what I'd done to innocent people my whole life, he'd hate me. I shut my eyes, willing the thoughts away, and tilted my head, exposing my neck. But his lips didn't find my skin.

Instead, he pulled back, panting. The air hung thick with moisture. "Are you sure you're all right?"

"Yes," I whispered. I didn't have the words to explain that, despite everything, I *was*; that the sight of him filled me like a bright, humid summer day, heavy and soaring at the same time. I knew, deep in my bones, that he was the only reason Father's sudden silence and abandonment hadn't broken me.

I reached for the ties on the back of my dress. Bregan stiffened, transfixed, as I pulled the first, then the second, working down one by one. When the neckline slipped over my shoulders, sunrise fell across my exposed torso. Bumps shivered over my skin. Slowly, I placed his hand on my rib cage. For a heartbeat, our heavy inhales were the morning's only sound; then he brushed his calloused palm upward, feeling the shape of me, and a soft gasp escaped my lips.

His eyes shot up, meeting mine. I smiled.

When I checked the next morning, the baron's gold was gone.

TWENTY

Bregan

Then

The sun wasn't rising fast enough.

Bregan leaned against his apartment's window, foot tapping the fire escape step. The streets below were quiet. The work bells wouldn't ring for another couple of hours, but the days were longest this time of year, so the sky was already brightening. As soon as the sun cleared the horizon, he would head for Firin's apartment. He didn't dare leave while it was still dark—as the Stav patrols were worse than ever, and Labors were going missing left and right—but he wanted to get there before she left for work.

He hadn't seen her in three weeks.

Three.

Before that, she had visited every few days. She'd been tight-lipped about her life at home, but Bregan gathered, in bits and pieces, that she was afraid of her father. Whenever he tried to ask about him, she shut down. The last time he saw her, she'd been crying, but she yet again avoided his questions. Then she vanished.

At first, Bregan worried they'd taken things too far and maybe she regretted it. Then he wondered if she was upset that he had yet again come up with an excuse to keep her away from the Players. But then a week had passed, and another. He couldn't sleep. Every time he closed his eyes, he saw her outside the factory theater, covered in blood. When he did manage to drift off, he dreamed of her morphing into his cousin, their lives bleeding out through bullet wounds.

At the theater last night, Jaari had called him out. *You look a wreck,* she'd said. *That girl you're keeping from us break your heart?*

Bregan rubbed the leather band of his great-grandfather's old wristwatch between his fingers, a piece he'd stolen in the old pirate days. The tarnished watch face didn't work, but the leather band was imbued with a prayer to the minor Gwyn saint Siag, protector of the seas—the saint his pirate ancestors had worshipped. Bregan flipped it and ran a finger over the engraved words, hidden from the Stav on the inside of the band, faded with time and wear.

Whether Firin wanted to see him or not, he needed to know she was safe.

When the fire escape shook beneath someone else's steps, Bregan's heart leaped. He half expected to see her. But it wasn't Firin; it was Pa.

"Thought you'd be out here," Pa said, taking a seat beside him.

Bregan had barely seen his father in the last few days. He never came home right after work. Some nights, he didn't come home at all. Bregan knew he was out mobilizing—meeting with potential supporters, raising money and awareness, debating with opposition—but the virtue of it didn't dull the edge of his annoyance.

"Is your ma in bed?" Pa asked.

Bregan didn't bother answering. They both knew she hadn't left her bed in days. When she'd found out that Pa was trying to convince the shipyard baron to help the Reformists overthrow the Stav in a true revolution, she lost her mind. Ma had been through the revolution in Qunsii. She'd left her home country for Gwynythaid because of it, and gotten stranded on Luisonn instead. She rarely talked about her life there, but it was the source of her fear. She'd screamed and sobbed for days, but Pa refused to back down. Eventually, she'd disappeared into the worst bout of malaise they'd seen in years.

"Where were you?" Bregan asked. He couldn't remember the last time he and his father had talked together for more than thirty seconds.

"At a meeting," Pa sighed. His thumb rubbed across his knee, over and over. He glanced at the old watch Bregan was still holding, then said, "The baron finally committed his support."

Bregan stopped breathing. His father's smile was thin. Despite his parents' arguments, and Pa's determination, Bregan hadn't believed he would succeed. He assumed the baron would measure the potential risk to his own luxurious life and deny them his support.

This would change everything.

"When?" he stammered.

"Not sure," Pa said. "Some of the others are resisting. They don't trust him because of his class." He coughed. "Have you seen Addym lately?"

Bregan stiffened. "Why? Is his father resisting?"

"Gauf resists anything that isn't his idea." Pa's pointed look made his intentions clear: he wanted Bregan to talk to Addym, maybe get to his father through him. Bregan almost laughed. He and Pa hadn't had a conversation in *months*. Of course he only needed something for the movement.

"I don't think Addym would listen to me," Bregan said.

Pa shifted, facing him more directly. "This is a big opportunity, son. This could be the turning point, maybe our one big chance. We could really use—"

"Have you lost your mind?" Ma snarled.

They both jumped, twisting to the window Bregan had left cracked open. Ma's hair was as frazzled as the glare she pinned on Pa. In her rage, she looked more alive than she had in weeks. "Even your brother wasn't selfish enough to drag his *son* into the movement." The mention of his cousin tweaked a thorn in Bregan's chest. Maybe his uncle hadn't included his family in his rebel schemes, but they'd paid the price anyway.

Ma spun, vanishing into the dark apartment, but not before Bregan saw her toss the old Saint Chyira prayer bracelet he'd made her into the clothes trunk. His heart clenched. She'd been upset with him since she learned that he knew about Pa's plans with the baron and hadn't told her.

"He's not a child." Pa yanked the window fully open. As he dropped inside, his eyes locked on to Bregan's. "It's *your* future, Bregan. If you want to fight for it, you're allowed to."

"He won't *have* a future if you drag him into your shit," Ma spit. "You can't trust the baron, Dech. What do I have to do to make you *see*?"

Bregan stood. He clasped his grandfather's watch around his wrist.

"I thought you were above classism." Pa's whisper rose to a low shout.

"It has nothing to *do* with classism," Ma growled.

Bregan snapped the window shut, praying the neighbors wouldn't hear more than they should, then raced up the fire escape. The argument faded with distance, but continued to writhe under his skin. The pull to fight. The desperation to stay safe. They were both right, and they were both wrong, and the tension of it was enough to rip him open.

The sun still hadn't fully risen, but Bregan headed for the cotton mills anyway. A *war*. That's what Pa was proposing. A full-out affront against the Stav, fueled by upper-class money and lower-class blood.

He only made it a couple of roofs before he spotted Firin.

At first, she was just a gray silhouette against the brightening sky. But by now he knew the shape of her, how she moved. He halted, half-sure he was dreaming, until she glanced up and broke into a smile brighter than midday.

She burst into a run, and when she wrapped her arms around him, she knocked all the remaining air from his lungs. He buried his hands in her hair, ruining her braid.

"Where are you going?" she asked, almost giddy.

"To find you," he sputtered. "Where have you *been*?" The question broke at the end. She recoiled from it.

"I had a lot of work." All the warmth left her voice.

Bregan didn't believe her. "You could have told me."

She tucked loose strands of hair behind her ear. "I'm sorry, it just got hectic."

"Did your father—"

"*Work* got crazy," she interjected, too harshly. Bregan's hands curled into fists. What had her father done to make her so afraid to even speak of him? He wanted to press, but as she squinted out at the sunset, picking at her skirts, she looked like a bird one scare away from taking flight.

Bregan's exhale shook. "I was worried about you," he said.

When he reached for her, she curled back into his chest. "I'm sorry," she said. She glanced up, and her expression softened. "Are you all right?"

He wrapped one of the ribbons on her back around his thumb. The shape of her against him was a balm to his nerves. "I don't know," he admitted. At least with Firin, he didn't have to pretend. For once, he had someone he could be honest with, who didn't push him to feel something he didn't. "Pa convinced Baron Hulei to support a revolution," he said, getting the words out in the air where he could see them clearly.

Firin stared at the sunrise, her squint unreadable. "Isn't that . . . a good thing?"

It was good for the Reformists' chances of success. With the baron's help, they could secure resources and foreign support. But what if those chances were just chances? What if they didn't succeed? When he closed his eyes, sunlight burned through the back of his eyelids, darkening to the color of blood.

"Luisonn without classes. Can you imagine it?" Firin whispered. When he looked down, her temple rested against his collarbone, and there was no tension in her face. "Us onstage. We'd be such famous actors and make so much money that we could snag an apartment in the Trade District, one of those Merchant-class ones with two rooms and the big windows facing the bay."

She said it so easily, as if it were possible, as if it were already true.

"We could perform all night and sleep all day," he said quietly.

"And wake up without *worrying*." She grinned. "Saints, it sounds beautiful."

Bregan tucked her under his chin, trying not to grip her too tightly, and something painful swelled in his chest. He would give almost anything to make that vision a reality, for her. To get her away from her father, to build a life together.

But what if, in the battle to do so, he lost her before it came true?

He gripped his own wrist around Firin's back, clasping over his old wristwatch. *You migh' not be able to read the prayer,* his grandfather had told him when he passed the broken heirloom to Bregan as a child, *but it says, "For horizons unknown, may the seas be calm."*

It's your future, Bregan, he heard Pa say.

For the first time, he could see it. He could picture what his life might look like, what he *wanted* it to look like.

It terrified him more than anything.

TWENTY-ONE

Firin

Now

I woke with a gasp, like a drowned person coming back to life.

"Firin, you're all right."

I'd always been plagued by terrible dreams—ones where I relived my worst decisions, or my childhood, or Bloody Fifthday—but the worst ones were the warm ones, filled with light and Bregan. At the sound of his voice, my heart fell off a cliff because I always lost him on the precipice of waking.

Except this time, when I opened my eyes, he was still there.

He perched on the edge of the cot, palm cupping my side. In clean Labor-style linens, with his hair still wet, he looked like his old self. The smoky, sugar-laced scent of him wrapped around me, and pressure swelled behind my eyes.

"What time is it?" I rasped, my voice raw from disuse.

"Midday," he said, running a thumb down the front of my rib cage. The touch chased away the remaining fog of sleep, and the events of the last few days gushed over me.

I sat up, and his hand slid to my waist. He left it there. All the heat in my body pooled to where the quilt was cinched between us. I stiffened, remembering the flare of his fury as he'd spoken of Esmai, but I didn't pull away. "Is Mezua back?"

"I already talked to her." He rubbed my hip bone absentmindedly. Every stroke burned. "She's not auditioning right now, but she said you can stay for a few days."

A lurching sensation seized me.

"Hey . . ." He lifted my chin. "What's wrong?"

"I just . . . I have nowhere else to go." The admission slipped out. As much as I wanted to join the Players, I *needed* to more. I had no money, no connections except Bregan, and no skills outside deception and acting.

"We'll figure it out." He squeezed my hip. "I just found you. I'm not going to lose you again."

I wanted to soak up his surety, but the knot in my chest didn't ease. Bregan searched my expression, and his own was so familiar: adoration and worry wrinkled the skin around his eyes. No one else had ever looked at me like that, like they truly *cared* about me. I ran a finger over the back of the hand he'd rested on my hip, my throat tightening.

"What about your father?" he asked.

I flinched. "He's dead."

I could feel Bregan's gaze on my face, heavy and expectant. I couldn't meet it. I was afraid of what I'd admit if I did. Down the street, a church bell clanged out the late hour. When it stopped, laughter floated down from upstairs.

"I looked everywhere for you after the raid," he said. "What happened? Where did you go?"

"I was with my father for a while," I said, trying and failing not to sound like I was seven years old again, reciting a script. "Then I worked for a tailor in the Trade Market."

He pulled back slightly. "I looked for you in the Trade Market."

"We must have missed each other."

The light in Bregan's eyes flickered. "Maybe."

My pulse stuttered. I touched a half-moon-shaped scar on his temple, drawing his attention elsewhere. "What happened here?"

The lines of his jaw tensed. "Missed a bullet a few years ago."

I dropped my hand. Before Bloody Fifthday, he had stayed as far from the Reformists' violence as he could. What had happened when he'd learned of his mother's betrayal? What had he seen in the years since then? What had he done? The questions crouched, uncertain in my chest. Once, I'd known all of him. I didn't know how to bridge this new chasm between us without condemning myself.

"I've got to get to another meeting on Regents'," he said, brushing a finger down the side of my face. When it caught on the edge of my lip, my breath hitched. He glanced at my mouth, and the pull of him became a riptide, a current I might drown in if I leaned in any closer.

"A meeting?" I said breathlessly.

"There's a situation. I told Hulei I'd manage it."

Not *Baron Hulei*—just *Hulei*.

Ice slid down my spine. I shifted back, breaking all the places where we touched. "You're . . . you're working for the president?"

"For now. Short term."

"On what?" I smoothed my hands on my skirts, trying not to reveal the panic writhing under my skin.

"An investigation," he said slowly, watching my every twitch. "I've been questioning witnesses all day, but they're all giving me the exact same story, word for word."

"If their stories are that alike, they're hiding something," I said.

"I know."

The air in the room shifted.

Bregan's face drew taut along strange, suspicious lines, and he looked so much like his father that it took my breath away. Suddenly, I realized just how risky coming here was.

Before, Bregan had never questioned my lies. Never pried. We'd lived in our own world, one of warm rooftops, soft skin, and careful diversion. We'd hidden ourselves from the realities of Reform and my father, dancing around the hurt to find delight.

But then reality had swallowed us both whole.

Before me sat a man who'd lost more than I could fathom, who'd fought in a war, and whose mother had betrayed him. I had nearly succumbed to the dark waters of my father's lies, committing atrocities to survive. The kids we'd been were gone. However much I wished to go back in time, those versions of us weren't salvageable. I was a criminal, and Bregan was a revolutionary with the new president's ear—the president, who would execute me if he knew who I was and what I'd done. The only thing that hadn't changed was Bregan's ability to see right through me.

Years ago, my love for him had kept me alive.

Now it might be the thing that could end me.

When he stood, I didn't move to stop him. "You dropped this last night," he said, holding out Father's pocket mirror.

I stiffened, but took it. The cold metal bit into my palm. "Thanks."

He waited, as if hoping I'd say more. I didn't, so he stuffed his hands into his pockets. "I'll be back later," he said. Then he left.

When I swung my legs out from under the quilt, they trembled. The empty basement throbbed around me. Stains splattered the front of my dress: dried blood and ash. Poisonous thoughts of the night before lapped in the distance of my mind. I pushed them away.

Digging my nails into my knees, I refocused. As long as Bregan was close to Baron Hulei, getting close to him would be dangerous, but I could work around it. I had to. The Veiled Players were my best option for a new life in this city's new world.

I needed to find Mezua.

If I could prove myself a worthy investment, she might change her mind.

I pocketed my mirror and headed down a hall made of crates and wooden folding curtains. At the bottom of the basement steps, eight waist-high stone statues lay discarded in a pile—the eight Kirru gods.

Before the Stav had arrived and outlawed all the northern religions, the statues would have lined the front of the temple. Their empty faces stared up at me. No eyes, no mouths, just stone. I hurried past them and emerged on the main floor with the eerie sensation of stepping off a boat onto unknown shores.

Beyond the arched doors that led into the nave, thin beams of light streamed through the cracks of boarded-up stained glass windows, slicing over the insurrection's remains. Bloodied rags hung off almost every pew. Blankets and medical supplies were piled in every aisle. A dozen people scattered throughout the room, picking up items, mopping and cleaning.

I didn't see Mezua among them, but a head of messy blonde hair crouched in a pew near the front. Suri. The woman I'd impersonated the night before, the actress Bregan said Mezua had recently hired. If I could learn more about how, when, and why Mezua had hired her, I might glean insight into what the director wanted.

I moved toward her. She was tiny, curled over herself on her knees. "Excuse me?" I said, stepping into the pew.

Suri whirled so fast she blurred. "You can't take him."

I froze against the knife tip she'd pressed between my ribs. A pale, shirtless young man lay still on the bench of the pew. Copious soaked bandages were wrapped around his torso. Two green leather boots lay tipped on their sides, sprayed with blood. He wasn't breathing.

Slowly, I raised my hands. "I was just looking for Mezua."

Suri blinked wet lashes. The knife vanished up her sleeve. "I haven't seen her," she choked out. In the space of a finger snap, her feral panic morphed into a wide-eyed, childlike distress—as if she were masking her true personality. She glanced at the body, then away. "Would you help me put his shirt back on?"

I glanced at the body again. I'd seen plenty of dead and dying people, and this man had been dead for hours. I stepped into the pew. The corpse's skin was slick, cold. I slid a hand under his back and lifted as Suri drew a clean shirt over his head, tears streaming down her face.

"You're new to the Players?" I asked.

She started to shake as she tugged the shirt down.

"Are you all right?" I reached for her shoulder.

The touch broke her like a boot to beach grass. She collapsed in a heap. "I just . . . H-he's all I have." Her helpless innocence might have been a facade, but there was no falsity to her grief.

Her sobs yanked at something in my chest, as if she were drowning and dragging me with her. The body grew somehow heavier in my arms. I blinked, and the executed Stav hung on the back of my eyelids. Right now, Reformists were collecting them in canal boats. Sinking them at sea.

I rose, dropping the body to the bench. "I'll go get more help."

When I backed away, Suri didn't seem to notice. Swallowing a rise of bile, I rushed for the western corridor. In the cool, dark hall, I wiped my lips. What was wrong with me? Death wasn't anything new. Resting the back of my head on the wall, I inhaled deeply.

Mezua's new talent was a *mess*. Suri's unchecked grief was a weakness, which could be an opportunity for me if it impeded her ability to act. First, I needed to know more about Suri: her relationships with the dead man and Mezua, her role in the troupe.

"Aza Vota, are you all right?" Tez asked in a low rumble. He stood in half shadow, a yellow apron tied around his girth, wooden spoon in his fist.

"I'm fine," I said. "I don't think she is, though."

He frowned into the nave, where Suri sobbed over the body. "She is not taking this well."

"Doesn't seem like she will be for a while."

Tez gave me a curious look. "There is soup. Why don't you come eat." A statement, not a question. I couldn't remember the last time I'd eaten, so I followed him down the hall.

"Were the two of them close?" I asked.

"Suri and Cidd? Ah, yes. Always together. Kind of like how you and Bregan used to be." He waved me through a door.

The old Kirru temple may have sagged like a wounded, exhausted soldier, but the kitchen beckoned with loving, open arms. A luxurious warmth hugged around me as I stepped inside. Lanterns cast a soft golden glow over a wall-to-wall table, lined with empty benches, its wood smooth from time and use. Boots piled on the floor. Jackets layered atop one another on hooks by an outside door. Mismatched dishes stacked haphazardly on sagging shelves above a huge wrought iron stove, where Nyfe stirred a pot of something herbal and meaty. My stomach growled, and she turned around as if she could hear it.

"By all the saints, Vota," she gasped, eyes flashing at the sight of my stained and shredded dress. "You cannot keep wearing that. I'll go get you a new one." She disappeared.

"Sit," Tez said, pulling out a bench at the table. He spooned up a bowl of stew, then set it in front of me. The simple act sent a shiver up my arms. I couldn't remember the last time someone had served me food. Probably not since dinners at Bregan's house. At the thought of the hazy, warm air, his smiles, and Esmai's laughter, my eyes burned.

Tez sat across from me, and even though we barely knew each other, there was concern in the tilt of his head. His mustache twitched. Before he could ask any questions I would have to lie to answer, I said, "Now that the revolution is over, do you know which play you'll do?"

His inhale expanded his broad chest. "Well, it seems—"

"*Tez,*" someone hissed in the hallway. "Have you heard this bullshit?"

A petite, vaguely familiar woman burst in from the hall. Underneath her apron, she wore a silk Qunsiian-style pantsuit that looked utterly out of place in the well-loved kitchen. She halted at the sight of me, and her angular, furious eyes thinned. "*You.*"

My spoon froze halfway to my mouth.

"Jaari," Tez said. "This is Vota."

"I know who she is," Jaari said. A half-healed cut was slashed across her forehead, just visible beneath her sleekly styled bun. "Did you make him do it?"

"Excuse me?" I asked.

"Bregan."

She paused dramatically, as if I was supposed to know what she was talking about. I held her sneer as my pulse thundered. She was very pretty, even while angry. Was Bregan *with* her? If he was, surely he wouldn't have touched me the way he had this morning? The thoughts were an axe, ready to cleave the island open beneath my feet.

"He isn't doing *Seorsus*," Jaari said. "Which means we don't have a damn show anymore. You let him think you were *dead* for years, then waltzed back in here as soon as it was *safe* again, and now you're taking—"

"That's enough," Tez said calmly.

Goose bumps swept up my arms. Bregan wasn't acting?

"Did you know?" Jaari asked Tez. He shook his head. "Well, apparently he told Mezua this morning, and now she's changing our performance again, to something that Suri can star in."

I shifted in my seat. Mezua couldn't possibly place *all* her faith in Suri, not right after she'd lost someone she clearly loved.

"Do you think she'll be up for that?" I asked. Tez frowned.

"She'll have to be." Jaari looked back to Tez, and her fury wilted. Her next words trembled. "If this show doesn't do well, we're screwed."

"Mezua will figure it out," Tez said firmly.

"Will she?" Jaari said. "The Grande just announced they're doing a play next. Of course, Veska can't just stick to dances; she *has* to compete with us."

"Yes, well, that was to be expected," Tez said.

"What do you mean?" I asked.

He sighed. "Mezua and Veska have a . . . history."

"A history?" I had no idea that the Grande's Manager-class owner even knew about the illegal underground troupe, let alone who Mezua was.

Tez cracked his knuckles on the top of the table. "They used to work together, back when they first—"

"Did you know Jaq got an engineering offer at the new steel mill?" Jaari interjected. Tez paled. "Yeah, I didn't either. People are making *contingency* plans, Tez."

I stared between them. After years underground, fighting for the right for their shows to be legal, the Veiled Players deserved to thrive in this new Luisonn. The idea that they might go under from a simple lack of funds was so unjust and terrifying that it made my head spin. If the Players dissolved, where would I go? Would Bregan keep working for Hulei?

"Have any of you seen Suri?" Nyfe reappeared, face drawn with worry. "She's not in the nave. I can't find her anywhere."

"Shit," Jaari said under her breath. She ripped off her apron and threw it on the table. "I'll go look for her." With a scowl at me, as if Suri's disappearance were my fault, she disappeared through the door that led outside.

Tez turned to me. "I apologize for Jaar—"

"It's not a problem," I insisted. I turned to Nyfe. "How can I help?" Relying on Suri was a risk the Players couldn't afford.

I had to find a way to replace her.

TWENTY-TWO

Bregan

Now

The owner of the woolen mill had a blue cravat tucked into his jacket the same shade as a Stav Manager-class band. Bregan had hoped to deal with the floor controller, but he'd arrived just as the Manager—well, technically *former* Manager—who oversaw the factory was leaving. The man glared down his nose at Bregan's Inspector badge with classist scrutiny. He was posturing. Bregan didn't think he would dare to challenge the new regime's authority directly, but it still grated his nerves.

Machinery ground and clanked below the mezzanine. Despite the cold outside, the air was hot and acrid. Memories crawled up his skin like spiders. He had only worked in a factory for a few months when he was twelve, but the haggard faces and scratch of dust were as familiar as if he'd been there yesterday. Those had been the dark days, before his mother found theater and he found Firin. Every part of him wanted to walk out and never come back.

In fact, he almost hadn't come.

That morning he'd questioned most of the Reformists who'd been at the prison break, but he'd only gotten half answers and vague, obvious lies out of them. At midday, he'd gone back to the theater to check on

Firin, and the moment her eyes opened, he decided to give up on the interrogations and stay with her. He didn't think the last Reformist on Draifey's list would give him any new information anyway.

But then Firin had lied to his face.

After Bloody Fifthday, he'd searched *everywhere* for her, including the Trade Market. He had gone there over and over, for years, just to see if anyone had heard anything new. If Firin had worked there, he would have found her.

Bregan was used to Firin's secrecy. That summer, she'd always resisted talking about her father and her life at home, but she had been the only bright spot in a storm of continuous violence, so he'd let it slide. If her father was dead now, though, what reason did she have to keep holding back from him?

The factory owner sniffed. Without deigning to speak, he motioned Bregan to the stairs, apparently deciding that his badge was legitimate.

As they descended to the production floor, Bregan felt the ghosts of wounds on his hands, the kind his mother had wrapped every evening, and which broke open before the sun rose. Even in sleep his hands had moved in phantom patterns, the sound of the machines haunting his dreams. Despair had settled over him like snowfall—a soft, slow buildup that sought to bury and freeze him over time.

He followed the Manager past table after table of bent-backed workers, and the weight on his shoulders seemed to shift, settling anew. A battle had been fought for these workers' freedoms, and yet, other than their bare wrists, nothing in this room had changed.

Maybe Draifey was right about one thing: the revolution was only a beginning.

The beginning of *what* remained to be proven.

The factory Manager halted. Up the aisle, one of the Reformists who'd helped free the Five worked deftly at a power loom.

"Espurra?" Bregan shouted her name over the noise. "I need to speak with you." The middle-aged, dark-haired woman pulled a lever, and the machine's frame shivered to a stop. Her mouth pinched, pulling her age lines like an anchor to a net.

"I can spare her for five minutes." The factory owner pointed to the floor clock.

"Can we use a closed room?" Bregan asked.

The man's lip curled. "*Five* minutes."

Bregan didn't have time to knock the man's ego down a notch, so he let the bastard walk away. He turned back to Espurra, who had joined the Reformists about six months ago and was one of those who crowded around Draifey. During the insurrection, she'd stormed the Stav prison with a gun strapped to her back. She'd been one of the movement's best snipers. Something about the sight of her now, twisting her fingers in the folds of her regulation aprons, curdled Bregan's gut. There was still so much to change.

"I have a few questions about the prison break," he said. "Can you tell me what happened with the guards after I went into the tower?"

"There were four of them," she said, sharp enough to carry over the din. "Three men, one woman. They stopped shooting; then the one with the broken nose"—she gestured across her face—"and the young one with pale hair came down alone, hands up. Talked to Mr. Draifey."

"What did they say?"

She shrugged. "They left the prisoners alive and just wanted to be left alone."

It was the story Bregan had heard from the other fighters, almost word for word. He didn't buy it. "I know Draifey is planning a campaign for president," he said, taking a new tactic.

She blinked. "What's that have to do with the prison guards?"

"That's what I want to know."

"I'm sorry. I can't help you." Bregan read her lips more than heard the words as her machine whirred back to life.

"Espurra!" he shouted.

She yanked on the lever again, then looked at him straight on. "They kept your father alive, Bregan. They just wanted to live. Would you punish them for that?"

"I'm not trying to punish anyone."

She jerked her chin toward the clock that hung from the rail of the mezzanine, where the factory Manager was watching them, then slid out the loom's shuttle and rethreaded it.

"Can we talk when you get off?" Bregan asked.

"Can't. Don't know anything else."

The Manager sauntered toward the stairs. Bregan growled under his breath. He could ask Espurra to come to the constabulary tomorrow for more questions, but would she give him anything? If he let her go and she *was* conspiring with the others, they would likely craft another cover-up story overnight.

Bregan intercepted the factory owner. "When does her shift end?" The man wrinkled his nose but answered.

When the clock struck the hour, Bregan stood in the shadows of a shuttered grocer's market across the street. Espurra flowed with the other workers toward the squat, gray factory housing unit around the corner. When she went inside, he followed.

Blending in with the waves of Labors, he wound up to the fifth floor. When she entered a room, he pressed an ear to the door but could only make out the giggles and shrieks of small children. Nothing suspicious. Noting her apartment's location in the building, he found the nearest exit and posted up on a nearby stoop to see if anyone came in or out. The shapes of Espurra's family danced on the other side of the curtains for a while; then the room went dark.

Bregan had almost given up when Espurra stepped out the back door of the building. Her chin swiveled as she adjusted the strap of a heavy bag and headed down the street.

He followed.

She went straight to the Centre Canal and caught a flatboat upstream. Bregan flagged a gondolier and paid the woman to follow her. When Espurra hopped off at the western edge of the Labor District, Bregan trailed her to a back-alley building and watched her vanish down a set of cellar steps. Bregan peered over the edge of the rail, glimpsing the back of her head as she knocked five times. The door opened, and just before Bregan leaned out of sight, he caught a flash of white-blond hair.

One of the prison guards.

TWENTY-THREE

Firin

Now

Nyfe and I searched the temple top to bottom, but Suri was nowhere to be found. Hours later, she still hadn't returned.

"Have Cidd and Suri been with the theater for long?" I asked as we folded linens in the back pews. Ominous brown stains still marred many of them. The linen dress Nyfe had given me—one of her own—hung a bit too large off my bones. It smelled like the same lavender perfume Esmai had always worn, and though it was soft and clean, my skin itched.

"They were with the Reformists before they joined us," she said. "Wasn't much of a point, since we couldn't put on plays, but Cidd got curious and approached Mezua. She agreed to an audition, and they moved in downstairs maybe three weeks ago?"

With a tired sigh, she scanned the empty temple. Volunteers had moved the last of the dead and dying to funeral ships and the hospital. The nave now seemed larger than it had the night before. "It almost feels like a bad dream, doesn't it?" she asked quietly.

"It does," I said.

She patted my arm. "Well, I'm glad you're here. Especially for Bregan's sake."

"I'm glad too," I said, setting the last linen on the pile. I'd never been part of the troupe, but they all seemed to know who I was and who I'd been to Bregan. It was strange, being remembered, as if people saw an old version of myself when they looked at me, like an illusion I couldn't take off. I wasn't sure how I felt about it.

Nyfe picked up the pile of linens. "These should go to the basement."

"I can do it," I offered.

If I wanted to find a smooth way to take Suri's place, I needed to know more about her—and people always left pieces of their true selves where they slept.

After storing the linens in a closet, as instructed, I wandered down the aisles between the makeshift bedrooms, searching for Suri's. Small memories filled every corner of the basement: drawings pinned to walls, broken instruments, worn leather books. I ran my fingers along a wooden divider painted with a depiction of the Great Cataclysm—an event featured in every religion. This one had flames that burst from a core, like a sun, with its rays twisting at the ends, curving into rivers, hills, and flowers, like a love note to fresh beginnings. The Qunsiian version of the story.

On the opposite side of the basement from Bregan's room, I found Suri's. Two lumpy straw mattresses sat side by side on the floor. At the foot of the left one, green leather boots lay toppled, as if thrown. Dark speckles tarnished the toes. Men's clothing scattered Cidd's bed, thrown in a heap with his blankets as if he'd left in a hurry. A collection of stones lined a small box at the head of the bed, arranged with the kind of care someone took when they wanted to make a place a home. A book was open on a page he would never read.

The second mattress was bare. A pillow and neatly folded blanket perched on the end of it. I picked up the pillow. Surely if they'd been as close as Tez claimed, Suri and Cidd would have shared a room.

Maybe she wasn't missing.

Maybe she'd left.

My foot was halfway back in the aisle when I noticed the strap peeking out from where the bare mattress met the wall. I yanked it, and a bag slid out. The patched, worn leather sack was ancient. I pulled out a sweater first, old and threadbare, the exact right size for Suri. She hadn't left then, not without her stuff. But if she'd lived here for three weeks, why did her bed look so unused? And why pack a hidden bag? Unless she thought she might *need* to leave.

Rummaging deeper, I found a wooden ball, the kind children batted around with sticks in the streets. I held it to the swiftly fading light and ran my thumb over a worn emblem that could have been a hammer, or a horse. SAINT HEKET's was carved beneath it. The major Gwyn saint of labor and dedication. Maybe a temple? Or a shop? I frowned. *Suri* wasn't a Gwyn name.

The only other object was a tiny journal. It was empty. No sketches. No entries. Just blank, stained papers. I tossed it to the bed—and two things fell out: a pressed flower and an old pamphlet.

"Shit," I muttered. Wildflowers didn't grow on any of the Iket Isles. This was a rarity from the continent. If it broke, Suri would know someone had been in her stuff. I carefully pinched the fragile flower and placed it back into the book.

The pamphlet was an advertisement for a serdzat performance at the Grande, *The Haunting of Pervo'tok*, dated a month back. On the back, in smeared ink, was an address I recognized from sniffing around the Grande years ago—the address for Veska'nora's house in Cliff Manors. I flipped it over three times.

Tez had implied that the burgeoning competition between the Grande and the Veiled Players in this new world was personal. If that was true, why did Suri have the Grande's owner's *home* address?

Footsteps echoed down the stairwell like gunshots. I shoved the pamphlet and journal back into the bag, my heart in my windpipe, and wedged the whole thing back between the mattress and the wall.

As the footsteps grew louder, I jumped into the aisle—and collided with Nyfe.

The dancer gasped. "Vota, there you are. They found Suri."

Upstairs, Nyfe and I couldn't have squeezed into the kitchen if we'd wanted to. The entire troupe was there except for Bregan, hovering around Suri like moths to a flame. Slouched at the table next to Jaari, she looked like death. Cidd's blood blotched every inch of her tunic and trousers. Her cheeks were gaunt, and her greasy hair was slicked to her forehead.

In the back corner of the room, Mezua watched her, arms crossed. In my years around the troupe, I'd seen the director many times, but we'd never spoken. When she caught my eye, however, her lips thinned. She knew exactly who I was. Hopefully, she remembered my acting talent.

"For the Sage King's sake, *where* have you been?" Jaari asked, pulling Suri into a hug she didn't seem to want.

For a moment so fleeting I could have imagined it, Suri's gaze met mine; then she shrugged from Jaari's grip and took the bowl of stew Tez handed her. "Just had to walk for a bit," she said. Her fingers twitched on her spoon.

"Well, we're glad you're back," Mezua said. Everyone turned to her. "Now, we all lost people last night. We are all reeling. I know none of you want to think about a show right now, but we must. For the first time in half a century, we can put on a play without threat of execution. Sitting here today, having survived this fight, is a privilege. We make the most of it by claiming our new freedoms."

"Is the Grande really doing *The Pirate Widow*?" someone asked.

"Yes," Mezua said calmly. "But we expected Veska'nora to branch out from serdzat dance and into theater if the Stav were overthrown. All we can do is outperform her. Unfortunately, we won't be able to move forward with *Seorsus*."

Worried murmurs rippled through the kitchen.

"What are we doing instead?" Jaari asked.

"We're going to put on *Sweet Winter's Eve*," Mezua said. "Tez will play the father, I'll play the queen, and Suri will play Gaydra. The rest of you will cycle through the minor roles."

As she spoke, Suri ate mechanically, as if lost in a cloud of grief, but gears turned behind her innocent facade. My neck tingled. Clearly she wasn't invested in this job. Was she planning to leave the Players? Or was it worse than that? Was she planning to betray them? I thought of the pamphlet, the address. Could she be spying for the Grande? What kind of money might Veska offer for information about Mezua's plans?

"Suri?" Mezua asked.

Suri nearly jumped out of her skin. "What?"

"You're going to play Gaydra."

"Right."

Mezua frowned. "Well, then, that's that. We'll start tomorrow."

Voices exploded in the kitchen, punctuated with benches screeching and spoons clanging. In the chaos of everyone lining up for dinner, Suri put down her spoon, wiped her chin, and slipped through the bodies like a ghost. She passed me, and into the hall, without so much as a glance. Mezua watched her go.

She was leaving again, in the middle of dinner.

I stepped after her, then heard Nyfe say, "Are you sure she can do this?" The dancer approached the director in the growing food line.

"She has to," Mezua answered.

Except she didn't. My pulse pounded, but Father's voice whispered in the back of my mind: *Never leave anything to chance.* Another rule that had kept me alive this long.

I could offer to cover Suri while she was grieving, and I might gain a temporary spot with the Veiled Players, but then what? I needed security, a spot among them that I could depend on. Without the Players, I had nowhere else to go.

If Suri *was* planning to betray the Players, then I needed to prove it. If there was any chance that I could get rid of her for good, I had to take it.

I headed down the hall. Just as I rounded the corner, a shape bounded up from the basement. I sank into the shadows and just made out Suri's outline. She was holding her bag. She strode into the temple's nave, stalked down the aisle, and trotted out the front entrance.

When she reached the far edge of Sovest Square, she glanced over her shoulder, then ducked into an alley. I rushed after her.

TWENTY-FOUR

Firin

Now

Suri wove a nonsensical northwest route through the Merchant District. I followed flashes of her blonde hair through alleys full of rubble and down boulevards strewn with glass and debris from the insurrection. Just when I started to wonder if she suspected my pursuit, she strode into the Commerce Block down the street from the Grande.

But she didn't head toward the dance hall. Instead, she jogged over to a small huddle of people outside the Crow's Nest, an establishment well known for its private luncheon rooms. Even without wristbands, I could tell the lurkers were mostly Labor and Zed, not the usual Merchant-class clients. When they headed inside, Suri joined.

I pulled on my illusion cord, lengthening my nose and adding fullness to my cheeks. By the time I reached the entrance, I was just another factory worker in Nyfe's too-big dress and multi-patched sweater. A Labor-class man leaned against the building as if guarding the entrance, but he gave me no more than a once-over as I stepped inside.

The tavern's tables had been shoved to the side to make space for the crowd of all classes, mostly lower ones. The people painted a mottled tapestry against the polished surfaces of the room. The air was hazy with cigarette smoke.

Suri stood at the bar with several young men, knuckles clenched around her bag strap. I positioned myself behind a tall man with coal streaking an olive moleskin jacket that closely resembled Bregan's.

"We were sorry to hear about Cidd," the man said. Suri's response was muffled against someone's chest. "He was a good fighter," the man added. It didn't seem like he knew her well.

I chanced a glance and caught Suri swiping at her face with her wrist. "Thank you. I know he wanted to be here tonight. He thought you all—"

"Do you think there's a chance he'll win?" another man asked, speaking over her head.

The man next to me scoffed. "He has to. Otherwise, what was it all for?"

"They're saying the vote might be rigged."

Suri's chin trembled, but no one noticed. They moved on from her grief to some kind of political discussion. One even pushed in front of her. I turned and waved to the bartender. On a gust of night wind, more Labors spilled inside, debating loudly. Was this why Suri had been cagey all day? Because she planned to attend a political meeting? Suri picked at her sleeve before backing out of the group. The bartender handed me a glass of ale.

I almost went after her, then thought better of it. Wrapping my palm around the glass, I slid down the bar and bumped into the man nearest me instead. A bit of ale sloshed onto his side.

"Oh, excuse me," I said in a singsong Gwyn accent. "I'm so sorry."

He turned, leaving little space between us. "No worries." When I didn't withdraw, he smiled. He smelled like brine.

"That girl you were just talking to," I said. "I *know* I know her, but I can't place her name."

"Suri?"

I squinted. "Are you sure that's it?"

"Suri Saains. She's Zed."

"I can't figure out why she's so familiar."

He shrugged, more interested in my face than my words. "She was attached at the hip to another Zed boy, Cidd. Both runaways from the Cradle, I think."

The marking on the ball in her bag.

The Cradle was the nickname for a block of factory orphanages. Saint Heket's was one of them. *That's* how I knew it. Suri was an orphan.

"Are you headed upstairs?" the man asked.

I drained my drink. "Might be."

He shifted back, and his jacket fell open, revealing half of the shiny badge pinned to his shirt:

CHIEF CONSTABLE

FREE ISLES OF IKET

The hair on my arms rose. He was one of Baron Hulei's new constables.

Lifting my chin, I winked, then backed into the growing throng of Labors. Thanking the saints it was so crowded, I searched for the wealthiest woman I could find: a Merchant laughing with her husband and a group of Labors. I nicked her nice wool jacket off the back of her chair.

Suri was an orphan and a rebel, which implied that she probably had as little to her name as I did. If that was the case, she wasn't likely to voluntarily leave the Players.

Shrugging into the stolen jacket and lifting the hood, I pulled on my illusion cord. As I followed Suri to the back of the room, warmth flushed out from my rib cage, sending a tingle over my skin as my complexion darkened slightly. My bones ached as they stretched, and my view of the room changed as I grew taller. My hair lengthened, sliding farther down my back beneath the jacket.

"Suri Saains?" I called out.

She turned, saw my face, and blinked rapidly. Her cheeks were wet with tears. "Aza Sochya'tov?"

"Yes," I said in the Grande's star dancer's haughty Vorstav'n accent.

"Can I . . . help you?" Suri stammered.

I glanced around the room from beneath the jacket's hood with my nose wrinkled. Sochya'tov wouldn't be caught dead in a place like this, surrounded by Labors. Not unless she had a vital reason to. "Aza Veska'nora wondered when she'd see you next," I said.

Suri flashed a hysterical smile, like a knife drawn in defense. "She won't. Tell her I got the message; so did Cidd." Her voice broke. "We found employment elsewhere."

I hid my shock beneath a conceited scoff. "Fine."

"Oh, and Sochya?" she added, cleaving the Merchant-class woman's name in half with disrespect. "Tell her I don't want to work in such a classist cesspit anyway."

She turned and disappeared deeper into the crowd.

I bit my lip as the truth clicked into place. Suri was a Cradle orphan. Cidd, also an orphan, had been her person, probably her sole person. They'd both gone to Veska for jobs, been denied, and ended up at Mezua's. Based on her bare bed, she wasn't used to having a home. She likely kept her packed bag on her to protect it.

I glanced over at the group of men by the bar. It didn't seem like Suri had come here tonight because she cared about politics. My bet was that she'd come to be near people who had known Cidd and fought alongside him. People who, unlike those at the theater, didn't put pressure on her shoulders. As well meaning as they were, the Players needed her performance to shine, despite her grief.

Pulling off the expensive jacket, I replaced it with one from the back of another woman's chair. As I made for the hall to the water closet, I stole a scarf from a young Labor-class man for good measure. Out of sight of the main room, I shrugged the new clothes on, both thick and woolen, practical but ugly.

Your mark's deepest desire is the key to getting what you want.

Suri yearned for connection. If Veska had denied her a job, then she wasn't likely to let go of her role with the Players regardless of how distraught she was—not when they were the closest thing to family she had left after Cidd's death.

Not unless I offered her something better.

TWENTY-FIVE

Bregan

Now

With each passing second, it became harder to stand still. Bregan leaned against the cellar steps' wooden railing, close enough that he could see the lights glowing behind the single window's thin curtains, but far enough that he could disappear around the corner if anyone emerged.

As soon as Espurra had gone into the cellar, he found a messenger boy and sent him to find the nearest constable. The cellar only had one entrance, so they were still inside, but he didn't want to confront them outnumbered.

Bregan reached toward his hip, and his fingers closed on thin air. After four years spent yearning for the day when he wouldn't have to wear a hidden firearm, here he was, two days in, already reaching for his pistol. In its absence, he pulled out his new government-issued club and spun the polished wood against his palm.

Gravel crunched under boots. The messenger boy reappeared at the end of the alley, followed by a familiar figure. Addym Taidd. Bregan swore internally. The rash, violent man was the last person he wanted to see, but he wasn't the worst person to have on a raid. The Stav had killed even more of Addym's family than Bregan's.

Addym bent to say something to the messenger boy, who then scampered off. Addym straightened. "Bregan, what's this about?"

"Keep it down." Bregan got a heady whiff of ale. "Are you even on duty?"

In the regime change, Addym had been appointed chief constable of the eastern Labor District—on the other side of the island. This wasn't his territory.

"Are you?" Addym countered. "I thought you weren't joining the force."

Bregan flashed his Inspector badge. "I followed Espurra Bespe here. She's in the cellar with one of the Stav prison guards that escaped. I want to question them."

Addym looked toward the building. "But Espurra's a Reformist."

"Well, she's harboring a fugitive."

"I thought those guards left the Five alive."

Bregan almost laughed. Addym hadn't questioned the guilt of the Stav he'd executed in droves the other night. "Are you going to help me or not?"

"Did the baron put you up to this?"

Since Addym had been denied the role of commissioner, he'd held a ridiculous personal vendetta against Baron Hulei, as if it hadn't been an entire council vote. "No one *put me up* to anything," Bregan said. "They're orders. Now, let's go."

When he headed for the cellar, Addym followed. He muttered something with the words *boots* and *licker* before stomping down the stairs. Bregan grabbed his elbow, but Addym was already knocking, five times in quick succession. "Open up."

Bregan could have strangled him. The door cracked open on a hazy room barely larger than a closet, lit by the dying embers of a fire without a chimney.

"Addym?" Espurra's line-drawn face peered out. When she noticed Bregan, her watery eyes went as wide as coins. Behind her, a sharp-faced, white-haired man backed away like a cornered animal—the second Stav who had shaken Draifey's hand at the prison. A bag lay open next to a pile of blankets on the floor, full of food and various supplies.

Bregan stepped around Addym. "In the Free Isles of Iket, withholding information and harboring criminals is a punishable offense."

Espurra's hands flew up. "We can explain."

"What he means to say," Addym interjected, "is that we just have a few questions."

Both accused looked at Addym, and something unspoken pulsed through the room. Bregan's heart stopped. The last few minutes clicked into place: the way Addym had defended the Stav guards, how he'd knocked first, the not-so-subtle way he was now leading the interrogation.

Did Addym know something?

"No, actually," Bregan said, pulling out handcuffs, "you're both under arrest for treason."

"Please," Espurra gasped. Behind her, the prison guard eyed the exit.

"Cuff him." Bregan tossed a second pair of handcuffs at Addym.

"Bregan," Espurra said, trying to tuck her hands behind her back, "please just let us explain. I must go home; my girls are alone, please . . ."

Bregan tried not to think about the giggles behind the door of her apartment. He needed the full, unadulterated story, and he had a feeling he wasn't going to get it with Addym in the room. "Wrists, Espurra," he said.

Firin

Now

In the hall outside the Crow's Nest's water closet, I held my mirror up. I sharpened the angles of my face and lightened my hair until I was nearly Suri, but distorted, as if through a rippled reflection on water.

"All right, everyone," a voice boomed inside the tavern. "Whoever's here for the meeting, c'mon up and give your name at the door. Invite only."

I ducked into the packed main room and made my way for the open stairwell at the back. I had reached the base when Suri was halfway up.

"Suri?" I called out, this time in a coarse outer–Iket Isles accent. She halted, bent over the rail, then went as white as a ghost. People hurried up behind her, curiously watching us. "Can I . . . can I have a word with you?"

"Who are you?" she demanded.

"My name is Neera . . . Neera Saains."

"W-what?" Suri rushed down against the flow of patrons, then scanned my illusioned features, which looked so much like hers. "That's impossible," she said. Red lines spiderwebbed across her eyes.

I twisted the end of the stolen scarf. "You look just like her. Our ma."

"My ma died birthing me," she said with an edge.

A knot cinched in the center of my rib cage, but I ignored it. "Or that's just what Mother Jehmah told you. She didn't exactly seem like an honest woman."

"You know Mother Jehmah?"

I didn't, but I knew *of* the infamous Mother of Saint Heket's Industrial School. "I met her while I was looking for you. Came over from Nusias." At the mention of the neighboring Iket Isle, a couple of days' boat trip from Luisonn, Suri gripped the cuffs of her coat. She recognized my fake accent. "But I couldn't find heads or tails of you," I added. "Even after talking to Mother Jehmah . . ."

"I've been underground," she said, "with the Reformist movement."

I nodded. "Someone told me there was a Suri in a Veiled Players' troupe, that you were living in a Kirru temple. I . . . I saw you leave the temple and followed you here. I'm sorry if I startled you."

We stared at each other, the chaos of the tavern billowing around us. Then the clock chimed the late hour.

I jumped. "Oh, I must go."

"What? Why?"

"My ship leaves at first light. I have to get back to the Landings." I grabbed her hands, thin and bony, and felt my touch shiver through her. "I hadn't thought it'd take so long to find you, and I promised Ma I'd get back. She didn't . . . she didn't wanna give you up. The Stav, they took you."

A common-enough story. Though the practice was never sanctioned, everyone knew the Stav stocked the Cradle orphanages with stolen children—especially from the outer Iket Isles. A sheen fell into place over Suri's eyes as her grief for Cidd dissolved into something molten. It turned my stomach, but I forced myself not to look away.

Maybe it was terrible, conning her while she was suffering, but I'd done worse for less. Suri wasn't a spy or a schemer, but she also wasn't stable right now. I had to do this, for the Players, for myself. *Sweet Winter's Eve* had to succeed.

"I can't believe I found you," I whispered.

"I'll come with you," she said, gripping my fingers.

I shook my head. "You can't. The ship's full. But there's another one tomorrow. I'd wait, but I already paid, and Ma's been sick. I promised her . . ." I choked off. "Will you come?"

If Suri went to Nusias, it would take her almost a week to get there, discover the story was false, and return. She'd miss more than half the time the troupe had to prepare for *Sweet Winter's Eve*. I'd prove myself in the role of Gaydra, then worry about a long-term plan after she returned. It wasn't ideal, but it would have to work.

Suri's brow wrinkled. I lifted her hands and pulled her closer, letting her drink in my very real desperation. "Ma came herself, to look, a few times. But she's too weak now. I can wait for you at the port in Nusias for a day. Please come."

Suri bit her lip, then nodded. "Of course."

I released a shaky exhale.

Dropping her hands, I darted into the crowd. When she called, "Wait!" I pretended not to hear her. By the time she reached the front door, I'd disappeared into an alley. As my boots pounded cobblestones, I glanced back, just to make sure she hadn't followed me, then tripped straight into a group of people.

A chorus of curses scattered in the air. Someone caught my shoulders. Familiar freckles swirled in my vision, and I went rigid as a board.

"Bregan?" I sputtered.

"What . . . Suri?"

I was still wearing Neera Saains's face.

"Let me go," I snarled.

He dropped his hands like hot stones, and I swayed back, catching sight of the three people behind him. Two were handcuffed prisoners, the other was a constable in an olive-colored jacket. The man from the bar.

Saints above.

I ran.

TWENTY-SIX

Bregan

Now

The cell door thudded shut, blocking out the fearful white of the Stav prison guard's eyes and echoing with Espurra's cries farther down the hall. Bregan turned the key over in his palm. Why had Suri been in the Commerce Block tonight? Why had she *run* from him?

Espurra's cries cut off, pulling him from his thoughts. A few cells down, Addym whispered something in the woman's ear before shutting her inside.

"What was that?" Bregan demanded.

"What was what?"

"You just said something to her."

"No, I didn't."

Bregan had known Addym since they were children. He had played enough cards with the man to know when he was lying. Addym knew something about Espurra and the guards. Bregan would have bet money he was in on Draifey's campaign plans. It made sense. Addym always looked for a fight, and his hatred for Baron Hulei made him an easy mark for Draifey's classist rhetoric.

Bregan hesitated, wanting to wring the truth out of him, but then headed for the lobby instead. He needed to get rid of Addym, not argue with him.

In the middle of the night, headquarters drank up the sound of their boots. "What is your plan?" Addym asked. "Are you going to give them lawyers? A trial?"

Bregan halted. "How dare you pretend to give a shit about people's rights. After Bakuit? After the executions the other day?"

"That's why your dick's in a knot? *Bakuit?* That was two years ago."

"You murdered him in cold blood." Bregan blinked and saw an old man's pain. A gun. A room sprayed with blood. Two years ago, his grandfather's old friend had betrayed the Reformists the first time they tried to free the Five. Addym had shot the man point-blank without consulting anyone else.

"Bakuit was a liability, don't you fucking—" Addym choked off, spotting something over Bregan's shoulder.

Bregan turned and found himself nose-to-nose with his own father. "Pa?"

Pa stared at Addym. Color drained from his gaunt face. Bregan hadn't yet told him their old family friend was dead, or that Bakuit had been executed as a spy. "What are you doing here?" Bregan asked. It was the middle of the night.

"Was looking for you." Pa watched Addym stomp to the front desk. He looked like he hadn't slept since the insurrection. "How's the investigation?"

Bregan had dropped his father off at his new government-sanctioned apartment two days ago. When he'd tried to stop in the day before, Pa hadn't been there. "I'm sorry I've been busy."

"Don't apologize. I'm fine. How's the case going?"

Bregan sighed, the gravity of his huge lead finally sinking in. "I caught a Reformist with one of the Stav prison guards tonight—one of the Reformists that hangs around Draifey." He suddenly felt very, very tired.

"That's good. What's next?"

"Questioning. But I need Addym out of the way."

Pa squinted. "You think he knows something?"

"Yes."

"Based on what?"

"Gut instinct," Bregan admitted.

Addym's voice bounced off the walls of the polished lobby, rising in tenor as he gesticulated to the commissioner, who had just appeared from the opposite corridor.

"Trust it," Pa said. "The Taidds have always been loyal, but they haven't always been trustworthy."

Bregan hated that he was right. Four years ago, Addym's father had gone rogue and blown up a Stav official's personal ship with his entire family on it, women and children included. The attack had sparked a month of brutal retaliation from the Stav, culminating in Bloody Fifthday. Bregan had hoped that becoming a father himself would calm Addym, but his son was a year old now, and Addym was, if anything, more antagonistic than ever. Just like Thom Draifey.

"Did you separate the prisoners?" Pa asked.

Bregan nodded. "There's just two of them."

"When we were first locked up, the Stav isolated us for over a week before they started questioning," Pa said, staring toward the hallway of prison cells. "The isolation was almost worse than the questioning."

Bregan tried not to look at the puckered scar on his father's skull, tasting the acid of disgust. How did you talk to a man about his torture? "That's terrible," he said insufficiently.

"It was effective."

Bregan's heart skipped a beat. "You think I should *isolate* them?"

"You think Draifey is up to something and they're in on it?" Pa stood as rigid as ever, his emotions locked behind a sense of purpose.

"Well, yes, but—"

"You have no proof."

"Not yet." Bregan wiped a hand down his face, as if he could scrub away the heaviness of what his father was implying. But Pa was right. He needed to loosen the prisoners' tongues, and isolating them would be an opportunity to test Addym's loyalty.

Bregan headed for Addym and the commissioner. "We should question them while the shock is still fresh," Addym was arguing. "It would be—"

"Well done, Nimsayrth." The commissioner sidestepped Addym to offer Bregan a firm handshake. "One out of four, and an accomplice."

Bregan rolled his shoulders. "Sir, I'd like to keep the prisoners in isolation until tomorrow. With rations, but no contact."

"*What?*" Addym's glare swiveled to Bregan like the barrel of a gun. Bregan stared it down. This was his case.

"Go home, Taidd," the commissioner said. "Your shift is over."

Addym hesitated, then stalked off. The entrance doors slammed. In the sudden quiet, Bregan's head throbbed. He turned to the commissioner. "I have questions about Taidd's motivations."

The man's massive chest rose, then fell. "That's a heavy accusation, Inspector."

"It's not an accusation, sir. Just a concern. While the prisoners are in isolation, I'd like to keep visitation records and note if anyone tries to enter their cells."

"Very well. I'll give the orders."

When Bregan strode back to Pa, it felt like a building had settled on his back. Pa watched him with his hands in his pockets. Bregan managed half a smile.

"You have a badge," Pa said.

Bregan's smile vanished. He closed his jacket over the offending piece of metal. "The job is temporary."

"I heard about the need for job openings. Surely he'll make you chief inspe—"

"No."

Pa stared at him. "You're going back to the troupe."

Bregan said nothing. Of course he was going back.

Shadows contorted Pa's face. He had never understood Ma's love of theater, nor approved of Bregan's involvement. He had wanted Bregan to support the Reform efforts, and eventually Bregan had, but he was done with it now. He just wanted to enjoy their hard-won freedoms, but he didn't know how to explain that in a way Pa would understand. In the wake of the night's events, he was plunging into exhaustion's embrace.

"This is because of the girl, isn't it?"

Bregan tensed. "What?"

"The one you used to hang around with. I heard she's back. Are you willing to throw this opportunity away on a distraction?"

"Is that what Ma was to you?" The blade-sharp accusation shot out unintentionally—and struck Pa dead center in the chest.

Bregan slid back, fists trembling, heat burning up his neck. Pa had gone to prison because Ma had put him there, but that didn't erase the fact that for most of Bregan's childhood, the Reformists had always won more of Pa's attention and loyalty than his family was allowed. It didn't erase the years of absence, half-truths, and fear for their lives. Years ago, Bregan had vowed to never do that to Firin.

The devastation on Pa's face was harder to look at than a midday sun, but Bregan couldn't find it in himself to apologize. He walked away.

Firin

Now

When I got back to the temple, I tossed and turned on Bregan's cot, listening past waves of soft snores for Suri's footsteps. Eventually, I gave up on sleep and swiped a wrinkled copy of *Sweet Winter's Eve* from someone's small bookshelf. But even memorizing the lines by candlelight was difficult with anticipation itching up my spine.

Deep in the night, familiar footsteps finally sounded—far too heavy to be Suri's. I slid beneath Bregan's old quilt and closed my eyes just before he stopped outside his bedroom. Fabric whispered as he crossed to me.

I slowed my breath as he knelt, blanketing me in his scent. When he brushed hair from my neck, I fought every instinct to keep from rolling over. But then he pulled the quilt up and pressed a featherlight kiss to my forehead. My heart fractured.

He'd arrested people tonight. I'd *seen* him with one of the new constables. I couldn't afford to be alone with him right now. Not while he worked for Baron Hulei. Not with his power to see right through me. And yet, everything about the distance between us was wrong.

He pulled away, and I heard him settle on the floor. Eventually, his breathing evened out, and I risked a look. He lay just inside the room, resting on a pack as a pillow. His dark lashes were stark against his pale skin. One arm folded under his head. A pang ripped through me.

Somewhere in the basement, someone stirred.

I raised my head, listening for Suri, but the sounds didn't come from the stairs. Clothes rustled. Flesh grazed against flesh. Breaths quickened, then turned into muffled moans. My core tightened as the unmistakable sounds of lovemaking trickled through the cellar.

With a soft sigh, Bregan shifted. The hem of his shirt rode up, exposing a strip of freckled flesh I had once intimately known. My breaths grew heavy. I traced him with my eyes as his chest rose and fell in deep sleep, and imagined lying down beside him. Would his touch feel the same? Would we fold together easily, as we once had? Or would there be a newness, maybe even a boldness, in the space where we'd grown? I twisted beneath the quilt, squirming inside my own skin. After four years of imagining him, pretending others' bodies were his, yearning in every possible way, he was *right there*, his scent lingering in the room like a drug.

Somewhere in the distance, the lovers' tryst crescendoed. I pressed my face into Bregan's pillow. I couldn't maintain this. Bregan wasn't something I could resist.

I had to get him away from the baron.

TWENTY-SEVEN

Firin

Then

I dedicated myself to conning Father.

After discovering I'd stabbed a Stav soldier, he became more paranoid than ever. For the first few weeks, he watched me like a hawk, but then he grew distant again, bit by bit, until he was disappearing for days at a time. I tracked his schedules and patterns, learned which personas took him to which parts of the city, and perfected feigning despair upon his returns. Soon he seemed more ghost than human. Months passed, and I didn't hear a whiff about Baron Hulei or the Stav looking for me, but I was careful to stay away from the checkpoints, just in case.

In the depths of night, staring at the tenement ceiling, I hated myself for not taking the baron's money when I had the chance. I wondered if Father's promises of a new life across the sea had always been a lie. But when daylight came, and I escaped to the Labor District, my anger always faded in Bregan's arms.

"Watch my feet," he said one summer evening on the rooftop of his apartment building. "I go forward, you go back—like this. We're like a mirror of each other."

"Do it again," I said, memorizing his steps.

For weeks we had practiced a tap dance for the Veiled Players' upcoming production of *Skarnti's Revenge*, which he would star in. I savored the single-minded focus of it. Sweat beaded at the edges of my hair, and my muscles ached in the best possible way. Light-gray clouds blanketed the swiftly darkening night sky. In the distant harbor, Baron Hulei's half-built ships loomed like beached whales.

After the third demonstration, I said, "Okay, I've got it."

"You sure?"

"Yes," I hissed with a grin.

We transformed into sets of tapping feet, floating across the rooftop in perfect unison. When we finished, claps sounded behind us.

"I think we could call you master *and* professor, Bregan," Taira said. The dancer sat cross-legged, cradling a baby to her breast on the quilt beside a lounging Esmai. Thick hair poured over Taira's exposed golden-brown shoulder and curled around her hips. She was one of the few members of the Veiled Players I'd met.

"It's beautiful choreography," I said. "Who wrote it again?"

Taira beamed. "My sister, Nyfe. I still can't believe you haven't met her. We should really have you perform for her and Mezua."

I glanced at Bregan, who stared at his boots.

"Let's try the set again," he deflected.

My cheeks heated. Despite my hinting repeatedly that I yearned to meet the rest of the troupe, he always kept me at the edges of his life. I didn't understand why.

As we positioned ourselves for the dance, Taira's baby let out a cry.

"Hello, Phinnin," Esmai crooned, tapping the tiny bundle on the nose. "Here, let me take her; she'll need a change. We're almost out of light, anyway." Taira smiled gratefully, and my insides tightened. The love between the troupe members shone like the sun, so bright you couldn't look right at it. I wanted so badly to bask in it, to be part of it.

Bregan hugged me from behind. I stiffened, but he didn't seem to notice. "Can you stay out later?" he murmured. I nodded. Father was gone until tomorrow. As he nuzzled his face beside my ear, my stomach sank. Why wasn't he letting me in?

Hurried footsteps shook the fire escape.

A man vaulted over the edge of the roof. "Esmai?"

Although I'd never met him, I instantly knew he was Bregan's father. Circles painted a bruised expression beneath a mess of curls the same color as the sky between the stars. His dark eyes were coals that had long gone out. A need to disappear thrummed through me. He *worked* for Baron Hulei at his shipyard.

Esmai rose. "Is everything all right?"

"We found Quan's body," Dech said.

Taira gasped. Bregan went as white as a cloud. *Quan?* Did I know that name?

"The Stav had him this whole time. Somehow, someone figured out he was part of the movement. They tortured . . ." He noticed me. "Who are you?"

"She's a friend, Pa," Bregan said, shifting in front of me. My cheeks burned. He hadn't told his father about me?

Dech crossed to us in three short strides. "What's your class, girl?"

"Labor, sir," I said.

"What industry?"

Esmai grabbed her husband's arm. "Calm down."

He rounded on her. "How could you bring a *stranger* here? How much does she know?" I blinked at Bregan. Was he keeping me at arm's length because he didn't *trust* me?

"I'm going to go," Taira muttered, rubbing Phinnin's back. She vanished over the edge of the roof, leaving me alone with Bregan's family. I considered bolting after her, but if I did that, everyone would suspect me.

I stepped around Bregan. "My name is Vota, sir. My pa works in textiles. I've just been helping with—"

"Textiles? What factory?"

"Cotton."

"Which mill? Who's your pa?"

"Dech," Esmai said.

My hands shook. A story. I just needed a story. I should have already had one, but I'd been living in the vague boundaries of the initial story I'd told Bregan, reluctant to commit to details I might forget. He stared at me now, waiting for me to answer his father, and the lies all tangled together. *Focus, Firin.* We'd just moved here? Or maybe—

Dech stepped forward. "Who is your pa?"

Faces burst through my thoughts.

Sniq. Restuv. Mizak. Mr. Finweint.

"Answer me."

I don't know.

"This is absurd," Esmai snapped.

"Seriously, Pa. She's fine," Bregan said.

Dech's lip pulled back, reminding me of a cornered street dog. More terrified than angry. He whirled back to Esmai. "I know you don't believe in this movement, but you could at least try not to get us killed."

"Please," I stammered. "I'm just . . ."

"Let's go." Bregan's fingers found mine, but I had to convince his father he could trust me.

"My pa shifted from the Landings a couple months ago, sir," I said. "Got fired by the Manager there. He's new to textiles."

Dech frowned, but Father had trained me well in Luisonn's politics, even Labor politics. The western-docks Manager was known for his ruthlessness. He hired and fired as often as he drank. Dech couldn't know all the new cotton workers. For now, he couldn't prove me wrong.

"Bregan, take Vota home," Esmai said, an order and a warning.

Bregan glared at his father, then dragged me to the edge of the roof. When we were a good four buildings away, he released me, a hand flying into his curls. "I'm sorry, I should have told him about you."

I watched the last trace of the sun fall over the horizon, turning the ships in the Shipyard into two-dimensional silhouettes. My hands shook. For the first time, improvisation had nearly failed me.

"Why didn't you?" I asked. "Do you not want me in your life?"

He spun to face me. "What?"

My hands shook. The idea that he might get angry, might leave, seized my bones, but I'd already asked the question. "You hold me at the edge of it," I said quietly. "Do you not trust me?"

He blinked. "No, Firin. That's not . . ." He closed the distance between us, took my face in his cool palms. "It's nothing like that, I'm just . . . I'm terrified." He pulled me to him, and his next words rumbled through his chest. "When I was a kid, my uncle joined the Second Rebellion. They tried to bomb Central, but their gunpowder was faulty. It failed, the Stav caught him, and . . ." His voice broke. "I was there when the Nodtacht dragged my aunt and my cousin—a *kid* who had nothing to do with it—to the execution wall. The Stav shot them in front of him, before killing him too."

My skin crawled. I knew he'd lost family to the Stav, but murdering a child out of spite was a special kind of evil. "Saints, Bregan . . ."

When I leaned back, he didn't meet my eyes. "When Pa joined the new wave of Reformists, he promised it wouldn't be like that. He said they'd pressure the Stav without provocation this time, fight for incremental change." He laughed. "Obviously, that's bullshit, as they're now planning a full insurrection with Baron Hulei."

My fingers twisted in his shirt. Every time he mentioned Baron Hulei's involvement with the Reformists, my blood ran cold. I still didn't know what had happened between the baron and Father, or what Father had done with his money, but right now, Hulei was less of a threat to me than the Stav. They knew my real face. He didn't.

Bregan cleared his throat. "For years, I swore to myself that I wouldn't bring anyone else into the Reformists' orbit. I refused to give the Stav anything else they could take from me. But then I met you." My heart tumbled. "I'm not trying to keep you out, Firin. I'm trying to protect you."

Heat flared behind my eyes. Bregan had a family, a community, people who depended on and cared about him. When he met me on the roof of the Grande, he hadn't needed me the way I needed him. Yet he'd still broken his promise to himself to let *me* in. I pulled him closer.

Bregan leaned back. "You didn't tell me your pa used to be a dockworker."

Internally, I recoiled, but externally I slid my fingers into his hair. "I didn't think it mattered," I said, running my nails against his skull in the way that always made him close his eyes—but he kept them open, holding my gaze.

"Of course it matters. I want to know everything about you. What your day is like, what you wish for, what you're afraid of . . ." He brushed his thumb over the top of my cheek, where my freckle sat. "I want to know *you*, Firin, who you really are."

I was trained in improv; I knew every accent in Luisonn; I had pockets full of faces, but I had no idea how to respond. I wasn't who his father thought I was, and I wasn't a thief anymore, but what did a half-life of stolen days with him make me? When I looked up, Bregan's eyes were so dark I could see myself reflected in them—the person he thought I was.

Something shifted inside me, like bedrock settling beneath the isles. For the first time in my life, I knew exactly where I wanted to be. I didn't want to sail to Qunsii or Iakirru. I didn't want to start over. I wanted to be here, with him.

He'd become my new horizon.

"I'm yours," I said, "and you're not going to lose me."

His mouth met mine with a firmness, a claiming. We backed into a chimney, fire sparking between our bodies.

"Firin," he moaned under his breath, tugging the ribbons on my dress. I let him undo them. During the day, I was careful to keep my X-shaped illusion scar hidden under fabric—I didn't want to have to explain it with another lie—but at night I forwent the caution. His kisses trailed lower, drawing sighs from me.

In the last few months, I had come to know desire. I'd worn faces to learn about it from the women at the brothel beside our tenement, then explored almost every facet with Bregan.

All but one.

When he reached down to draw his hand up my skirts, I stopped him. Holding his gaze, I slid out of my dress completely.

I wanted all of him.

I wanted to be his.

TWENTY-EIGHT

Firin

Now

When I woke, Bregan was gone.

Rubbing away my fatigue—and the slight sting of his absence—I sneaked to the other side of the basement. Suri's bed was empty, and her pack was missing. Either she'd already left for Nusias or she hadn't come back, but I needed to be sure she was gone.

On the ground floor, light flickered beneath the kitchen door. Inside, Nyfe and Tez stood before the stove, assembling a soup in their nightclothes. Thick heat from the stove blanketed the room. When I stepped over the threshold, a flurry of brown curls charged at me from the corner. I leaped out of the way as a little girl in trousers and a too-big leather jacket brandished a wooden sword at me.

"On guard!"

"Shhhh, Phinnin," Nyfe said. "Everyone is sleeping."

My knees locked as I stared at the little pirate costume. Taira's child. The baby. Phinnin turned her big brown eyes on me, and the last four years gaped like a lifetime. I rubbed my arms.

"Who are you?" She tugged at my skirts.

I crouched and winked. "You can call me Vota, but my real name is Starkey."

"No, *I'm* the Dread Starkey!"

"Phinnin," someone else shushed, "we can be pirates later." A man I didn't recognize bent over a washtub at the back of the room. His billowing nightshirt was tucked into a pair of Labor-issue trousers. As he scrubbed at his exposed neck and chest, I hugged my elbows around Nyfe's dress. The troupe members, like Bregan, were so at ease with their intimacy, as if they were all blood relatives.

"Will you play pirates with me?" Phinnin asked me, lowering her voice. "I like your freckle." Light as a feather, she touched my cheek with her finger. My skin burned.

The man patted his dark skin dry, then donned circular glasses. Even after he'd cleaned them, ink stained his hands. "Sorry about her," he said, peeling Phinnin off me. "I'm Jaq."

"Jaq's our set designer," Tez said from the stove.

"He's my pa," Phinnin added seriously as her father stuffed her on the bench beside him at the table, in front of a pile of *Sweet Winter's Eve* posters. So far, they'd only been printed with the background image of a child at a piano. There was still time to change the lead actress's name.

"I'm Vota," I offered.

"I know," he said.

To hide yet another blush, I turned to Nyfe. "Figured I could make myself useful."

With a grateful smile, Tez tossed a bag of potatoes on the table. Nyfe placed a knife next to it. "Wash up first?" she said. "The water's still warm."

Given the nonchalant looks on everyone's faces, it was clear that Suri hadn't told them she was leaving, but if she was going to make the next ship to Nusias, she'd have to leave soon. Hopefully I hadn't misread her.

"Have you seen Suri?" I asked, crossing to the washbasin and picking up the cloth Jaq had hung on the side of it. The damp fabric was warm to the touch.

"She just returned a few minutes ago," Nyfe said.

"From where?"

"Not sure," she said.

Tez's eyes flicked to me, then back to the stove. I bit back the rest of my questions, so as to not sound suspiciously concerned about a girl I'd just met. As I submerged the cloth, my knuckles soaked in the warm water, and my very bones sighed. I couldn't remember the last time I'd washed in water that wasn't ice cold; it was rarely worth the fuel. But here, where the stove was almost always lit, heating water seemed to be an afterthought.

Although my scar was hidden beneath my dress sleeves, I positioned the offending arm out of view of the others as I squeezed out the rag and wiped my neck and face. When I finished, I sat before the bag of potatoes. Before I could figure out how to ask where Suri was now, the front door flung open.

A lanky person with unkempt blond hair and kohl-smudged eyes strode in with a newspaper folded under the arm of their red velvet overcoat.

"Luka!" Nyfe said brightly. "Have you met Vota?"

Luka shoved the newspaper into Tez's chest. "Look at this," they said in a harshly articulated accent native to rural Iakirru.

"*Luisonn Daily?*" Tez frowned. "There's already a new newspaper?"

"*Look.*" Luka jabbed a finger at a section of the front page.

Tez gasped. "Oh no . . ."

Jaq set down his printing block. "What?"

"They're opening the same day as us."

"Who?"

"The Grande."

Nyfe gasped. My knife froze mid-slice. If the Veiled Players and the Grande opened on the same night, they'd be competing for audience members and patrons. If Veska and Mezua's competition was personal, she'd likely done this on purpose, and she probably knew exactly which patrons to target. I turned to ask Tez what he knew about the two directors.

"I know you don't want to," Nyfe blurted, giving Jaq a devastated look, "but maybe you should accept the offer."

"No." Tez turned around, his age lines drawn uncharacteristically tight as he glared at Jaq. "We need you. If you start at the steel mill, they'll keep you all day and night. *She* needs you." He glanced at Phinnin, who was scraping a charcoal nub against a discarded poster.

"She needs food, too, Tez. Clothes. A house over her head." Jaq glanced at the open rations bin beside the stove. It was almost empty. "If Mezua can't turn this around, then I have to put a plan in place, *for* her." He glanced again at his daughter, and there was a sharpness to his love for her—his *need* to keep her safe—that I had to look away from.

I stared at the potatoes. If the Players were going to compete with the Grande for Luisonn's wealthiest patrons, they'd have to move up their premiere date.

A voice shot down the inside hall, clearer than a bell. "Suri, be reasonable," Mezua said. "We have less than *three* weeks until this play goes up. We need you." The door swung open, and Suri barreled through with the director on her heels. "How long will you be?"

"I don't know," Suri said, rounding the table, not meeting anyone's eyes.

Nearly a week, I thought. It would take at least that long for Suri to discover that her long-lost sister didn't exist. By the time she returned, rehearsals would be well underway, especially if Mezua had to move up the date. Perhaps I should have felt some guilt, but the Players' conversation weighed me down, anchoring me in surety. If their finances were truly this bad, Suri had to go.

"Suri, please," Mezua begged, arms wrapped around her nightgown. "Surely whatever it is can wait until next month?"

"It can't. I just . . ." With a tremor in her lip, Suri left.

The whole kitchen stared after her.

"Where's Suri going?" Jaari stood in the hall, eyes bleary and lips swollen. When she looked right at Luka, I took in their mussed hair and makeup again, and thought of the lovemaking I'd heard the night before. I shifted on the bench.

"I don't know," Mezua admitted.

"What do you mean you don't know?" Jaari snapped.

"What are we going to do?" Nyfe said.

Mezua held a shaking fist to her forehead. "Maybe we can push opening night."

"You might actually want to move it up," I said. Everyone's eyes snapped to me. I handed Mezua the newspaper. As she read the date of the Grande's premiere, the light drained from her face.

"But we can't do *Sweet Winter's Eve* without Suri," Tez said.

"I'll go get her," Jaari said, heading for the door.

"I could do it," I said.

"What?" Jaari halted. Luka noticed me for the first time.

"You'd play Gaydra?" Mezua asked.

I nodded.

Jaari snorted. "We don't even know you."

"I studied under Esmai."

All the warmth fled the room. There was a thud as someone dropped something. I bristled. Esmai had betrayed them, but she also had extraordinary talent.

"How special for you," Jaari sneered.

"Relax," Luka said, trying to put an arm around her waist.

Jaari shook them off and rounded on Mezua. "She hasn't even auditioned."

But the director was staring at me.

"Do you have a choice?" I asked quietly.

Mezua's jaw tightened. "Vota will stand in for Suri. We'll move up the premiere to Fourthday." She nodded pointedly at Jaq's half-finished posters. "Make sure you reflect that. That means we have two weeks to pull this together. Everyone meet in the nave after breakfast so we can get started."

When the director headed into the hall, I dropped my knife and followed her. Conversation exploded in the kitchen behind me.

"Mezua?"

She paused outside her office. "Yes?"

"What patrons are you targeting?"

"Excuse me?"

"Which patrons do you hope to secure on opening night?" She needed to make sure she had a few outside of Veska's regular orbit.

She scrutinized me for a long moment, then stepped inside, leaving the door open. Silence thickened as she lowered into her desk chair.

"Esmai told me a lot about you," she finally said. "Went on and on about the talent of a Labor-class girl who was friends with Bregan. Tell me, Vota, what does a Labor girl know about securing patronage in Luisonn?"

I froze. What did Mezua know about me? Exactly how much had Esmai told her? Her gaze flicked over my face, assessing my reaction, and a small part of me thawed. She was testing me, weighing if I was hiding something. If she knew—or had even guessed—the truth, I wouldn't be here.

"Nothing," I lied. I had spent the last few years weaving in and out of the upper echelons of Luisonn's society. I knew the names of all the art lovers in the city, whom they gave patronage to—here and abroad—and whom they scorned. But to say so would reveal far, far too much. "I apologize," I added, scratching at my elbow.

She folded her hands in her lap. "I appreciate your eagerness, but without a stellar production, it won't matter who attends on opening night. Focus on Gaydra. I'll do the rest."

The order held no room for argument, so I backed out of the office. Maybe I couldn't directly advise Mezua on whom to target, but there were other ways to seed that kind of information.

TWENTY-NINE

Bregan

Now

Onstage, Firin glowed. Bregan adjusted his shoulder against the entry doorframe. His back was still stiff from sleeping on the floor. Earlier, when he'd left for the constabulary, he'd forgotten his badge, so once rehearsal started, he slipped back inside to snag it. He'd been on his way out when he heard Firin onstage.

Her delivery was masterful, her accent perfect, but there was a tentativeness to her performance, as if she were skating along the surface of the show's emotions. The Firin he'd once known had flitted around questions like a bird afraid to land, but she hadn't been guarded—not like this. The last four years had changed her.

In the front pew, Mezua watched Firin's performance with her arms crossed like a gate over her thoughts. Just yesterday she had refused to audition her. He wondered what had changed.

The scene ended, and Mezua called for a break. Bregan straightened. So far he had avoided prying questions from the troupe about why he couldn't act, and he didn't have time for them now. But before he could duck out, Firin noticed him and swept down the aisle.

"You're back," she said.

A dozen accusatory stares pierced him from every corner of the room. He ignored them, focused only on her. "Had to grab something. That was impressive."

"It's hard to tell if Mezua thinks so."

"She knows talent when she sees it." A tiny smile danced over her mouth. "Where's Suri?" he asked. The other woman wasn't in sight.

Firin shrugged. "She left."

"Left? Where?"

"Didn't say. She just packed a bag this morning. I told Mezua I'd help with Gaydra."

Suri had been gunning for a role in the troupe for months. Bregan's heart panged. He hoped she wasn't making rash decisions in the wake of Cidd's death, as he'd done after he thought Firin had died. Did her absence have something to do with why she'd been at the Commerce Block last night? Bregan rubbed a hand down his face. The last few days were a blur. He hadn't had time to ask Suri why she'd been at the temple during the insurrection, let alone support her in her grief.

"How do Mezua and Veska'nora know each other?" Firin asked.

Bregan frowned. "They did theater together, years ago. When Mezua first came to Luisonn, I think. She doesn't talk about it." Veska was a topic the troupe knew to avoid around the director. His best guess was that they'd worked underground together and Veska had somehow sold Mezua out to climb the Stav's class ladder.

"What do you know about her patrons?" Firin asked.

"Mezua's?" he asked. "Nothing. Why?"

"Do you know if she's talked to the Trade Market Board?"

"Not sure." Mezua had always kept her financial backers' identities close and private, to protect them from the Stav Regime. "Why?"

Firin crossed her arms. "Bregan, the theater's financial situation isn't good."

"Of course it isn't. We've been underground."

"The troupe is worried you won't come back."

He bristled. "What, so the finances are *my* fault?" It wasn't like he didn't *want* to be here, onstage with the rest of them. He'd stayed away from the temple mostly to avoid questioning, but he couldn't pretend it didn't hurt to see them up there playing, truly at ease for once in their lives, without him. But the mystery of Draifey's lies was getting fishier by the day. He couldn't just abandon his investigation.

"Of course not, but they need you. Here."

"Well, I'm needed elsewhere too." The fate of the Veiled Players wasn't his responsibility. At least they were free to perform now. Mezua would have to figure out the rest. Bregan checked his watch. He needed to get to the constabulary before Addym did.

"You don't owe your father anything," Firin said.

He barked a laugh. "This has nothing to do with him."

She raised an eyebrow. The air grew taut. Suddenly, music trilled to life up on the balcony, a desperate, yearning tune. Luka was leading the troupe's small orchestra, their velvet coat flaring with each graceful movement of their hands. Jaari glared down at Bregan over her violin, fingers never faltering. He resisted the urge to roll his eyes.

"Jaari doesn't like me," Firin said.

Bregan snorted. "Jaari doesn't like anyone."

Firin bit her lip. "Is she . . . Are you two . . ."

"Me and Jaari? Oh saints, no." Bregan exhaled a half laugh. He and Jaari were like oil and water. They'd found that out the hard way, deep underground, shrouded from the world with little hope. But those nights had been filled with desperation and despair, haunted by the loss of Firin. He stuffed his hands in his pockets. "She's with Luka, the conductor. They're probably the only person in the world with enough patience for her." A faint blush painted Firin's cheeks. It warmed every part of him to know that she cared.

"I'm sorry if she's been hard on you," he added. Firin glanced sideways at him, then kept watching the musicians. "Jaari was in Qunsii when the People's Rebellion turned to tyranny. They beheaded her entire family just because they had royal blood. She doesn't trust easily. She just—"

Firin grabbed his wrist, flashing a catlike smile. "Dance with me." She yanked him into the entryway. "They're playing 'The Queen's Dance,' right? Teach me the steps."

A sting itched down Bregan's spine. Avoidance, again. This was the game she'd played years ago: rarely outright lies, always diversion. If she wanted to play now, so be it. He knew every move.

Without warning, Bregan pulled their bodies flush. She gasped in surprise as he spun her deeper into the entry. When she tripped, he lifted her into the dance steps, and their bodies clicked together with a familiarity that set him ablaze. Her curves fit into his palms exactly as he remembered, as if she were made for him, and yet the flesh beneath was firmer—stronger, even—than before, reminding him how little he knew about where she'd been.

"You're rusty," he said.

She stepped on him on purpose.

He laughed softly into her neck, trying not to lose himself in the citrusy scent that had haunted him for years. Her breath caught. Good. "It's a Gwynythaid three-step," he explained against her ear. "Not unlike that number we made Taira teach us from *Qoyn & Insei*."

"That dance was a pain in the ass."

He slid a palm lower, cupping the curve of her hip, and a wave of memories pushed him closer. It took everything in him not to mold to her entirely. "Relax," he whispered, to himself as much as her. "It's similar steps, but it's not as stiff as the Qunsii version. It's more intimate."

String music bounced around the stone walls, filling the entry with levity, but with each step, it grew harder and harder for Bregan to concentrate on anything except the shape of her. Just when he thought he might shatter from the pressure of resisting her closeness, her chin jutted up. "There's a twirl, isn't there? Toward the end?"

"Yeah, it's—"

A smile licked her lips; then she spun out on her own, completely out of rhythm and yet full of grace. Bregan tripped to a halt and just caught her as she spun back in with a laugh that could have melted entire winters.

She looked up, her back pressed against his chest, and Bregan froze. *This* was the Firin he remembered, with pink cheeks and the ghost of mischief on her lips. She'd always been steel wrapped in sunlight. Darkness shrouded in joy.

This was the woman he'd fallen in love with.

The woman who had shown him how to live.

She was really *here*.

That inescapable truth seeped through the pessimistic glacier he'd become, and a part of himself that he'd buried years ago surfaced, taking its first breath.

Bregan tilted toward her. She went as still as stone as he brushed his thumb down the side of her face, her neck, her collarbone. She was as beautiful as she was frustrating, as transparent as she was unknowable. When she bit her lip, it threatened to undo him—exactly, he knew, as she intended—but suddenly, Bregan didn't want to play games.

"Firin . . . ," he breathed, lips hovering over hers, "whatever happened with your father, whatever you're trying to avoid, you know you can talk—"

She dropped his hand like a stone. "There's nothing to talk about." He could all but hear the locks of her armor thudding back into place.

An ache tore through him. He grabbed her hand. "Firin."

"You should go. You have work to do." She shoved her hurt behind an iron mask, just as his mother always had when his father demonstrated, yet again, that the Reform movement took precedence over her.

"Wait," he called as her skirts disappeared around the corner.

He took a step after her, but then, somewhere in the city, bells marked another hour. Right now, Espurra Bespe was separated from her daughters, locked in a lightless cell, awaiting his interrogation.

All while he danced a three-step.

Back at the constabulary, the lobby bustled with business. Bregan checked the secretary's list of visitation requests and found Addym's name right in the middle.

Officer Addym Taidd, requested a visit to Cell 13, 7:00. Denied. With a bitter laugh, he pocketed the paper to show the commissioner and checked the chalkboard of active-duty assignments. Addym was in the Factory Block for the morning. He wouldn't be back for a few hours. Bregan headed straight for the prison cells.

Espurra blinked against the sun when he entered, then scrambled to her feet. "My girls? Please. Are they all right?"

"Cuffs," Bregan said, waving in one of the hall guards. He had sent someone to watch her children last night, but he needed her to talk.

Espurra sputtered as metal bit around her wrists. They led her to the interrogation room, which was just as rank and disgusting as it'd been the night he'd questioned Draifey. Bregan signaled to the guard to seat Espurra at the table while he lit the lantern on the wall. The flame threw more shadow than light. When the Reformist saw the stain on the back wall, her whole body trembled. The door closed.

Bregan braced his palms on the table. "Those missing prison guards are an issue of national security. I will find the rest of them, with or without your help, but you were caught harboring a known criminal. You will receive a trial, and whatever happens in this room today will determine what that trial looks like."

Espurra wrung her fingers together in her lap. "Vorkot isn't dangerous."

"Who is he?"

"M-my brother by marriage."

"You were covering for him, then?"

She lifted her cuffed hands to wipe at her nose. "He got in over his head. I was trying to help him. I just . . ."

"You just what?"

Her chest strained, as if unable to suck in air.

Bregan pushed off the table. "Bring the other prisoner in!" he shouted. Distant chains and locks clanged; then rich light poured in. Espurra and the Stav guard's eyes bounced off one another, then back to Bregan. He sat on the corner of the table. "Vorkot, your sister is on the line for protecting you. The longer she is in here, the longer your nieces are without a mother."

The guard drew himself up. "I will give you what you want, but leave them out of this." His broken Iaqun was thick with a mainland Vorstav accent. Bregan jerked his chin to the hall guard, and when Espurra was gone, Vorkot collapsed into the chair and held his face in his handcuffed hands.

"My brother came here from Ketchzta," he said. "He thought it would be different, so far from the emperor, but it is worse. The emperor sends his worst soldiers and Nodtacht here. But when my brother got sick, he wrote to me for help. So I came. I joined the prison guard one year ago, after he died, because I needed the money for the girls. But then, when I started the work, we realized the danger. If the Reformists won, then you would kill all of us who worked at the prison, whether we liked the emperor or not."

Bregan wanted to deny it, but he couldn't. If Vorkot had been captured that night, he'd be dead. "Who's 'we'?" he asked.

"Me and three other guards; we made a plan to survive. We got word through Espurra to the Reformists—to Thom Draifey—that if you told us when the insurrection would happen, we would make sure to be on duty at the tower and keep the Five alive in exchange for our freedom."

Bregan's heart skipped a beat. "Draifey told you when we planned to attack?"

"Yes, but I didn't know until later that one of the other guards was actually a Nodtacht."

"What? Are you *sure*?"

"Absolutely," Vorkot said. "I overheard him talking to Draifey, after we met to confirm the plan. Draifey said, 'And the other Nodtacht?' and the guard said, 'I am working on my superiors.'"

"Draifey *knew* the guard was a Nodtacht?"

"Yes."

Bregan's palms against the table were all that held him upright. Draifey had told a *Nodtacht* about the Reformists' plans. If Stav officials had known the insurrection was coming, there was no telling how many had escaped justice. Had the Reformists won *despite* the Stav knowing, or had the Stav let them? Had they chosen to support Draifey's election campaign rather than fight to win?

"Which one is the Nodtacht?" Bregan asked.

"He's got brown hair and—"

"A broken nose?"

"Yes."

The Stav who had shot at Bregan. The one who had shaken Draifey's hand. "I need you to tell me everything you know," Bregan said. "Names, safe house locations, meetings—any pieces of information you might have overheard."

Vorkot sighed. "It won't do any good."

"Why?"

"Because they will have moved. The other constable, Addym Taidd—he's one of Draifey's. I am sure he told them that I am here."

Bregan slammed his fist into the table. That bastard.

"Draifey held a meeting," Vorkot continued breathlessly, clearly relieved that Bregan believed him. "Last night, at that Crow's Nest tavern. Espurra was trying to help me escape to Qunsii while they were distracted."

"How many people were there?"

"I don't know; invitations were spread from person to person, to keep the—"

Heavy footsteps thundered outside the cell. After years of working with him, Bregan would know Addym's cadence anywhere. Vorkot's eyes widened.

"Say nothing," Bregan ordered.

Metal groaned, then screeched. "What's this?" Addym demanded.

"A finished interrogation." Bregan waved for the hall guard to take Vorkot, then sat on the edge of the table.

"What'd he say?" Addym asked.

"He was tight-lipped." Bregan called on his acting training to keep his shoulders loose and his expression blank, but a bonfire licked at his composure like flames against glass. "This isn't your case, Addym. Why are you so interested in it?"

Addym laughed. "You suspect me, then? Of what, exactly?"

Bregan stared. He and Addym had never seen eye to eye on anything. Just like their fathers. But Addym had always been predictable, a violent man driven by a thirst for vengeance against the Stav. At least they'd been on the same team. Until now.

The Crow's Nest wasn't far from where they had arrested Vorkot and Espurra last night. Addym must have responded to Bregan's call for help so quickly because he had been down the street at the meeting for Draifey's campaign.

Addym couldn't know that Draifey was working with Nodtacht, could he? He had a son, for saints' sake. The Nodtacht had murdered his father. But even if he didn't know, he was lying on Draifey's behalf. He was hiding something.

Accusations laced Bregan's tongue. He wanted to throw them just to see how Addym reacted, but he couldn't rely on Addym to be honest. He stood. "Can you have someone go back to the cellar where we found them and collect evidence?"

Addym's eyes fell into slits. After shoving him to the side, Bregan was suddenly offering him responsibility—and an opportunity to cover Draifey's tracks. Addym sniffed, and left.

As soon as his hands stopped shaking, Bregan headed straight to the commissioner's office.

"He's not here, sir," the secretary blurted as he passed.

"Can you send for him?"

"I'm afraid that's not possible. He's with the president on the *East Etherea* for a private meeting out in the bay. Won't be back until tomorrow evening."

"Can we get a message to the ship?"

"It's a confidential meeting; their location is unknown."

Bregan bit back a stream of curses.

THIRTY

Firin

Then

Bregan learned how to touch me in all the right ways.

A late-summer sunset painted a wildfire of the clouds above us. He bent over me, spread beneath him on the quilt atop his apartment. With each circle he drew between my legs, he drank my moans with his mouth. I grew tighter and tighter, almost desperate, but it was too soon. We hadn't been alone in a while, and I wanted to consume him.

I reached blindly for the waist of his pants. As I fumbled with his buttons, he withdrew his hand and kissed down my neck, unbuttoning the front of my dress.

"Take it off," he murmured, pulling at my sleeves.

I tensed. It was still too light out. "I'm cold."

"You weren't cold last time," he said. Last time, it had been the middle of the night. If I took my dress off now, he might see my illusion scar. *It's fine,* a small part of me whispered, urging me to release this last piece of Father's paranoia.

Footsteps broke the evening, rattling the fire escape.

We sprang apart like startled gulls.

Bregan staggered upright, pulling me with him as he fumbled with his pants. I straightened my skirts and threw my sweater back over the undone front of my dress. We barely managed to cover ourselves before Esmai appeared at the edge of the roof, the brown creases of her dress molded with the bricks of the low wall.

Her eyes slid from our mussed hair to our flushed cheeks, and my throat cinched. We'd told her we were practicing for Bregan's opening night of *Skarnti's Revenge*, which was tomorrow. Her frown wasn't new—Esmai had smiled less and less over the past few weeks as the Reformists spiraled into disarray—but I couldn't have her upset with me. Not now.

"It's almost time for dinner," she said.

I resisted looking at Bregan. Esmai never came to find us for meals.

"What is it?" Bregan asked. "What's wrong?"

"Nothing. Can you run down to Okena's? We're having soup, and I want bread with it. Vota can help me finish up." The fire escape creaked as she disappeared.

"What's this about?" Bregan asked, smoothing his hair.

I tried to shrug as I buttoned my dress back up, but my pulse was thundering. Just three days ago, after months of patiently waiting for Bregan to ease up on his worries, I'd finally told Esmai I wanted to join the troupe. She had stared at me with a knifelike look, then agreed to talk to Mezua. I had no clue what I would do about Father, but that was a problem for after I officially got in. We hadn't talked about it since.

I hadn't told Bregan.

I understood his fear. The troupe was deeply connected to the Reform movement, which had gotten more reckless lately, their strikes turning bloody and their requests turning into threats. Bregan's father was still trying to convince the other Reformists to partner with Hulei and some other upper-class parties, but the Labors were resistant to the idea of working with the men who owned the factories that mistreated them, even if they weren't Stav. For a while I'd been careful to stay away from Baron Hulei, but I still hadn't heard any hint that he was looking for me, and I wasn't sure how much longer I could handle living in the chasm of Father's neglect.

I needed this new life, wholly and fully. It was time.

"I'll be quick," Bregan promised, kissing me before hurrying down the fire-escape steps.

I descended to their open apartment window, fingers tangled in my skirts. The room was sparse but clean. Two mattresses lined one wall. A rickety table leaned against the other. Meat-scented smoke poured out of a pot steaming over coals in a small hearth. Warmth slipped lazily from the window, beckoning me inside.

"Come in," Esmai said. "I want to talk to you." She lowered herself gingerly into a chair at the table, as if the simple act drained her.

I dropped in through the window but hovered by the sill. "Is this about Mezua?"

"Yes." She peered at my face. "Does Bregan know you asked me?"

I swallowed. "No. I wanted to audition first."

After a long moment, she nodded to herself. "Well, Mezua's agreed to see you. I told her you're incredible, that I've not seen anyone with your natural talent since I left Osiv City, and I meant it."

Even if I'd been able to speak, I had no idea what to say. *Thank you* thickened in my mouth, but it didn't seem remotely strong enough. I fell into the chair next to her.

She continued, leaning closer to me. "If Mezua takes you on—and she will—you'll get food, a bed, and a stipend. But, Vota . . ." Her expression shifted like an evening shadow. "If you're running away from something, I need to know what it is."

When she took my hand, I couldn't move. Esmai thought I was a Labor-class girl without a mother, who feared her father. Simple. Innocent. Savable. Never in a thousand years could she imagine my real life. "I'm not running."

"Does your father—"

I yanked my hand from hers.

"Vota."

201

The door flew open. Bregan trotted in with his father on his heels. I stood. Over the summer, Dech had come to tolerate my presence, but I generally tried to avoid him.

"What happened?" Esmai's voice broke.

Coal streaked her husband from head to foot, amplifying the whites of his terrified eyes. "Gauf Taidd went rogue. He blew up a Stav official's ship, with his wife and kids on it."

My heart tumbled. I hadn't seen Father in three days, but if there was an attack, he might come home early.

"Both of you, leave us," Esmai said.

I stepped toward the window to the fire escape, but Bregan didn't move. When I reached for his hand, he jerked away.

"I want to know what's happening," he said.

"You already do," Esmai said bitterly.

"I want to know *all* of it. If there's going to be an attack, I need to—"

"Bregan, leave now," Dech echoed.

"But—"

"C'mon," I urged.

Bregan flinched from my touch, glared at his parents, then vaulted onto the fire escape. I scrambled out after him. I couldn't give Father any reason to suspect me, not if I was planning to run away soon. I could get home in half an hour if I left now.

Bregan stopped so fast in his descent that I tripped on a step, almost falling into him. "They're going to assume Taidd killed that Stav family on behalf of all the Reformists," he said. "None of the other Reformists wanted it, but they'll blame it on us anyway."

"You think the Stav will strike back?" I breathed.

"I know they will." His dark eyes flickered like flame through coals. "Pa thinks they'll move tonight, use this to wipe us out. Yet Ma won't let him tell me anything." He sat on the steps, head in his hands. "I get that she's scared, but ignorance is dangerous."

The gears of my brain stuck on the words *wipe us out*.

"What did Ma want with you, anyway?" he asked.

"Nothing," I said, too quickly.

He snorted. "Right."

I placed a hand on his shoulder. "Really, it was—"

"You should stay here tonight," he said with steely severity.

I stared at his knee. "I can't. My father is expecting me."

"And?"

"If I'm late, he'll . . ."

Bregan stood back up and took my chin. "He'll what?"

I couldn't risk raising Father's suspicions. If he discovered I wasn't home, there was no telling what he'd do. I had to be careful until I was sure the Players would take me in; then I could plan a successful escape.

I twisted out of Bregan's touch. "I'll see you tomorrow, at opening night."

"I don't know if *Skarnti's* will still happen."

"I'll meet you at the factory anyway."

His jaw clenched. I could tell he wanted to argue, but he just drank in my face. "Promise?"

"Promise." The word hung in the air as I left.

The streets channeled rivers of people, parting around Stav soldiers like water around rocks. Despite the day's heat and the pressing sea of bodies, I couldn't stop shaking. I ducked down an alley, then another, racing toward the Bilge as if I could outrun fate. If Father got home before me, I might never see Bregan or the theater again. My chance at a life with the Veiled Players, the one life I finally knew I *wanted*, would be gone.

Somewhere deep in the Factory Block, a group of Labor-class women accidentally elbowed me into a wall. I stared at the pistols strapped to their hips and fought a wave of nausea. Would Bregan join the fighting? He would stay home with Esmai, wouldn't he?

I shoved the thoughts aside. I just had to get home before Father did. Bregan would survive this, the Players would survive it, and when everything was calm again, I would run away and join them.

I was so deep in my worry that I didn't see them until it was too late. I veered around a corner and halted. At the end of the alley, swathed in twilight, stood Father in his dockworker persona, Mizak.

He was talking to Esmai.

I hurtled out of sight, my back slamming against a brick wall. *Father is talking to Esmai.*

A shot sounded in the distance; then the city exploded in gunfire and piercing screams. I bolted. Father hadn't seen me. He couldn't have. I just had to get home before he did.

But he'd been talking to Esmai.

Bregan's family didn't have any money. *I* was the only reason Father would have to talk to Esmai. In smoke so thick I couldn't see an arm's length in front of my face, I skidded into the Bilge and used years of muscle memory to find our tenement and race up the steps. *Please, please, pl—*

The apartment was empty.

I staggered into the table. With shaking fingers, I ripped my smoke-laden top layers off. I needed to appear normal. Calm. Maybe confused.

Wood creaked.

I stopped breathing. When I turned, Father stood in the doorway, fists clenched at his side. Not as Mizak, but as the Stav soldier, Restuv. "What the fuck were you thinking?" he asked in the most dangerously quiet voice I'd ever heard.

With spiraling horror, I realized how stupid I'd been to come home. He'd talked to Esmai. He probably knew everything.

My lips parted, but my mind could only stutter. The day Esmai finally offered me a different life, he had found me out. The door slammed shut. My bones rattled. Outside, gunshots popped. Like a cornered animal, I tried to back away, but Father grabbed the front of my dress. There was a wildness in his eyes.

"You have no idea what I've done for you. What you've risked."

"I didn't risk anything," I cried. "I just want a *life*. I want to be an actress."

"A what?"

"An *actress*. I just want—"

He shoved me into the bedroom so hard I tripped into the costume racks. The door shut, shrouding me in darkness. A heavy grinding sound shook the floor as he dragged something in the kitchen. My lungs seized. I launched for the latch, but when I shoved it open, it hit the chest we stored our coal in. I couldn't move it.

"You can't lock me in here!" I screamed.

He had always left me in the kitchen. The window. The light.

Boots thudded. The front door creaked, then clicked shut. The darkness pressed in as tears poured down my cheeks, pulling me into a heap on the floor, yanking my heart deep through the building until I was falling endlessly into a cavern of hopeless hate.

THIRTY-ONE

Firin

Now

"All right, stop there," Mezua said yet again. She leaned on the back of the first pew, arms wound tight around her torso, as if holding in everything she wanted to say. Her script lay at her feet.

I was rehearsing a scene from the end of *Sweet Winter's Eve*, a pivotal moment when Gaydra's fear about playing the piano for the queen gets so bad she can barely do so. We'd been at it for hours, and Mezua had rejected my every approach. My nerves were fraying. I had no idea what I was doing wrong.

At breakfast she'd told us she was going uptown to talk to patrons, but then she spent the morning training me instead. What opportunities was she squandering because I couldn't get this scene right?

She sighed. "I need to *believe* you. Try it again, with less dramatics. Gaydra's not putting on a show for her father. She's not pretending to be afraid; she *is* afraid."

I ignored the other troupe members watching, weighing, waiting, and shook out my arms. Maybe the memory of the petty, anxious Manager-class girl I was pulling from wasn't right. If she wanted me to act *afraid*, I could try the memory of my first con—of the Labor-class man's terror when the Stav had arrested him.

Pulling from the memory was as familiar as donning an old coat. With two breaths, adrenaline rushed through my limbs. "Please, Father," I recited, hoarse and desperate, "you don't understand. It's as if . . . as if the more I play, the more my fingers p-panic."

"All right, all right." Mezua flapped a hand. "That was good fear, but it's too much now. She's not being abducted."

I inhaled sharply through my nose, then spotted Bregan. He was lounging in one of the last pews, watching me with a flat, unreadable expression that made me want to shrink offstage and disappear. "Can we break?" I asked.

Mezua checked her watch. "Fine. Sit with Gaydra's emotions. Do the thought exercises we talked about. We'll pick up here again in the morning."

When I reached Bregan at the back of the room, he had an ankle propped on one knee and an arm slung over the back of the pew, but he looked anything but relaxed.

"Mezua's meeting with some patrons today," I said. "Do you know who?" The director had already vanished.

"Why don't you just ask her?" Even his voice was rigid.

"I tried. She told me to stay out of it."

"Then stay out of it."

It shouldn't have bothered me, how he kept pushing me away. I should have been relieved. Getting close to him while he worked for Baron Hulei was dangerous. This was for the best. But once in a while, his face would shift, and I'd see a flash of the adoration he'd once poured on me, and I couldn't dam the hurt when it disappeared again.

"What's the matter?" I asked.

He picked at the sock on his propped foot. "Nothing. But you should be focused on Gaydra. It won't matter if the right people are there if you don't put on a good performance."

My nose wrinkled. "It also won't matter if I perform well if the right people *aren't* there."

"Mezua can deal with the patrons. The only person who can improve this role is you."

"Yesterday, Mezua said I'm doing fine. It's just this one—"

"*Fine* is Mezua speak for 'you're not where I want you, but now's not the time to dig into it.'"

"How would *you* do it, then?" I snapped.

He assessed me, then made some kind of decision. "I'll show you, but I want to watch you again first." He glanced around the nave, which was sprinkled with troupe members, then jerked his chin at the door to the bell-tower ladder.

I hesitated. I needed help, but being alone with him was risky. "Don't you have work or something?"

"I can't do anything until the president gets back."

"From where?"

"Stop evading," he said, by way of evasion.

I wanted to push, if only to understand the source of his foul mood, but the less I asked him, the less he could question me in return. "Fine."

Up on the flat, square roof of the bell tower, before a singular, moody audience under an equally gloomy sky, I performed the scene for the hundredth time. I tried to channel the memory of the Labor's panic, toning it down as Mezua suggested, but it still didn't feel right.

"Please don't make me do this," I finished, my voice wavering at the end of Gaydra's final-breakdown plea.

Bregan leaned back on a palm and shielded his eyes against the overcast late-afternoon light with his elbow. "You're not getting deep enough. The emotion is too stiff."

I groaned. He sounded exactly like Mezua.

"The scenes that come easily—what's your process for those?" he asked.

"I don't know."

"What about *Qoyn & Insei*? You used to love the scene where they meet for the first time. What was your process for getting into that one?"

My heart tipped, pouring molten memories. We'd spent so many hours with his favorite "impossible, cursed" play. I still knew every line, but those days had been different. I wasn't even sure I'd had a process.

"Let's do it," I blurted. "That *Qoyn & Insei* scene." If I could still do it well, maybe I could figure out what wasn't working with Gaydra.

He stared at me, still vexed by whatever had his trousers in a knot. Then he sighed and got to his feet, dark-red curls clashing against the gray sky.

I spun away, and the lines bubbled up with ease. "There must be more to this life than duty," I recited, becoming Insei as she lamented her position as heir. "Why am I enlightened with dreams and longings if I'm not meant to seek them?"

"What's a duchess got to wish for?"

I whirled—as Insei would, in shock at being overheard—but a real surprise stabbed into my ribs as Bregan's accent thickened. His icy annoyance vanished as he melted into a stable boy with precarious dreams in his eyes.

"Excuse me?" I breathed. "Who are you?"

He tipped an imaginary hat. "Just Qoyn, milady. Stable boy on your estate." He hovered at the edge of proper distance, fingers tapping his leg. "What's wrong? If you don't mind me askin'."

I drew myself up. "The world is just so unfair. We're all placed in roles, bound by rules, but no one ever *asks* us what we want, what yearnings hold our hearts."

"The age-old conundrum."

"What do you mean?" I stepped sideways, chin tilted.

He leaned the opposite direction, following my lead until we were slowly circling one another. "To bemoan one's place is the most basic of bemoanin's. But rules are just rules for a reason." He edged closer.

"What reason's that?"

"To be broke." A grin split his face, brighter than the sun, more mischievous than a child's. It sliced through me like a knife.

"You can't mean that." I wasn't sure if my racing pulse was Insei's or mine.

"Oh, I do. I promise you, milady, I'm gonna break all the rules. I'm not gonna let no world keep me from becoming who I'm meant to be."

"And what's that?"

"I'm not sure yet."

We were a pace away now.

"I'm envious," I sighed. "Of your ability to choose."

With one stride, he closed the distance between us. He drank me in as if I were a sunset or a painting, and a heat swept up the back of my neck that wasn't intentional. I didn't want to blink. Somehow, in becoming Qoyn and Insei, we'd conjured up that summer, and I wanted to bask in it forever.

"You can choose too," he murmured.

"I'm not sure that's true."

"Well," he said, too soft for any audience to hear, "would you at least choose to meet me again?"

"Yes."

Our breaths mingled, and when his lashes dipped, I lit on fire. The ground beneath my feet pitched, urging me toward him, and I knew, without a doubt, that this was it. I couldn't stop myself. Until, with a single harsh inhale, he stepped back and wrenched the heat from the day.

"See?" He turned on his heel, grayness sweeping back in, as if the moment hadn't affected him at all.

I swayed. "Bregan—"

"*That* felt real."

"That scene's different," I said, failing to quench the tremor in my voice.

"No, it's not. What were you pulling from? What memory?"

I blinked and saw the night I'd met him. The curious Labor boy atop the Grande.

The corner of his mouth curled. "That's what I thought. That scene in *Qoyn & Insei* works because you're pulling from real emotion; you're fully empathizing with Insei. You need to find a way to do that with Gaydra. What's she feeling in that breakdown scene?"

"Fear," I said flatly. I wasn't interested in repeating my debate with Mezua.

"Why is she afraid?"

"She's afraid of failing at the concert."

"You don't sound convinced."

"To be honest, I don't get it. She's incredible at piano, so what is there to worry about?"

He laughed. The grate of it made my teeth ache. "Then there's your problem. I can *tell* you're not convinced. Why is she afraid?"

"She doesn't want to fail."

"Why?"

"Because her parents will be upset if she fails."

"*Why* does she believe that?"

I threw up my hands. "Because that's what they show her?"

"*Exactly.*" He closed the distance between us in three long strides. Above us, the sun fought to escape the clouds. "Now, think of a time when you felt that same fear of losing someone because you failed."

Restuv, looming over me in the kitchen.

"There. Whatever you were just thinking about—*that* is it."

My chin jerked to the side. "No."

"There must be *one* memory you could pull from. Maybe one about your father?"

My vision flared black, then red. "You know nothing about my father."

"Of course I don't, and whose fault is that?"

I staggered back. "Excuse me?"

"You're hiding, Firin," he said, so close I had to look up. "As long as you're hiding from yourself, you'll never master the stage."

An ache shot through my bones. "How can you know that? You haven't even been here."

"You think I haven't noticed? All your half-truths and evasions. You and everyone else."

This was ridiculous. I didn't deserve to be the brunt of his anger or frustration or whatever this was. He was wrong, anyway. There was nothing in my memories that compared to Gaydra. Her parents loved her. Their worst crime was supporting her, urging her to do her best. *Her* worst crime was messing up on piano. How was I supposed to empathize with that? My knees threatened to buckle, so I yanked open the hatch.

"Saints, what's the point?" He clutched at his hair. "You clearly don't want to let me in. I don't know why I'm even trying."

"I never asked you to," I spit. Then I dropped down next to the bell.

"Wait, Firin."

The words echoed as I climbed through the second hatch and back into the temple. I ran into the nave, following the smell of dinner to the kitchen, my whole body shaking because, despite the years and everything unspoken between us, I *knew* him. I knew exactly what his problem was, why he was avoiding me, and why he was so upset—the reason he seemed so changed from the boy I'd known.

Bregan had always feared losing what he loved: his mother, me, the theater. It was hard not to, when the Stav kept killing people you cared about. The fear had paralyzed him back then, and now, after he'd lost me and Esmai, his father, and countless others, he was afraid to *stop* fearing, afraid to reopen his heart, because he was terrified that if he did, it would just get broken again.

The problem was, I couldn't guarantee that it wouldn't.

I was halfway across the kitchen when I realized the troupe stood circled around someone at the table. My heart stopped dead in my chest.

"Vota, look who's back!" Nyfe squealed.

"Suri?" Bregan said behind me.

THIRTY-TWO

Firin

Now

I moved like a marionette on the strings of Father's training.

"Suri," I gasped, elbowing my way through the packed kitchen to where she sat hunched at the table, "thank the saints you're back."

Everything about her was travel-worn—tangled, stained, and soot-smeared. Had she failed to get a ship to Nusias? If so, where had she been instead?

"Are you staying?" Phinnin asked from Nyfe's hip.

"Of course," Suri said, with a strained smile that was more concern-ing than placating. "Someone has to play Gaydra."

Everyone glanced at me.

I sat backward on the bench beside her. "We were so worried. It's good you're back so soon; now *Sweet Winter's Eve* can go as planned."

The tension in the room disintegrated like an exhale. Suri didn't seem to notice.

"Thanks," she said, rising.

I joined her in the food line. Jaari slid into place behind us, her ears practically perked like a dog's. "Luka's pulled some gorgeous Gwyn pieces for Gaydra to play," I told Suri. "It's fun pretending to play the piano when someone else is actually doing it offstage."

The ladle paused halfway into the pot. For the first time, Suri looked straight at me. "You've been playing Gaydra?"

"Oh . . . I thought you knew. We weren't sure when you'd be back."

She stared, gears turning. Then she slopped stew into her bowl and headed back to the table. I followed without serving myself. Troupe members shot us nervous glances.

"Now that you're back, of course it's yours," I said, sliding onto the bench. Leaning in, I whispered, "Except it won't be you up there on opening night."

Suri's spoon clattered against her bowl. "Excuse me?"

I smoothed my braid. "I just said I'd love to show you what I've been working on, to catch you up."

"What are you playing at?"

"Nothing. I'm just trying to help."

"If you think you can just—"

The kitchen fell silent. Everyone looked between us, measuring the scale of our jealousy. Suri's chest heaved as she stood. "I'm going to wash up." Chins swiveled as she left. Her bowl of stew steamed, untouched.

I turned to Nyfe, aghast. "I was just trying to help . . ."

"Of course you were. She's a bit of a mess after Cidd, that's all."

"I don't give a shit how much of a mess she is," Luka said at the stove, serving themself. "That was unnecessary."

Jaari's eyes narrowed, this time at the door instead of me. I gripped my empty bowl underneath the table. Since Suri had come back so early and I'd embarrassed myself onstage today, Mezua would certainly give her the role back. But that would be a mistake. Suri looked half-dead, but I knew *I* could do it; practicing the *Qoyn & Insei* scene had reaffirmed that.

Since she hadn't left on her own, my only other option was to get her kicked out.

I waited until the depths of the night to make my next move. Once Phinnin had been put to bed, Tez left the kitchen, and Jaari and Luka retired, I rose from Bregan's cot—he hadn't returned, which hurt more than it should have—and slid through the basement on bare feet.

When I passed the cordoned-off space that belonged to Jaari, a floorboard creaked under my foot. I froze. Something rustled behind the folding screen. Someone whispered.

I bolted past the forgotten statues up the steps, trying not to imagine that the faceless gods were judging me. Snagging a lantern from the hallway sconce, I rushed into the nave. Glancing back every few steps, I headed for the stage.

Atop it, Jaq had scaffolded the inside of a set castle, complete with a balcony and turret. I ducked under the balcony and peered up at the intricate woodwork, which was held together with several metal pins. As I reached for one of the pins, a strange lurch stayed my hand. I worked my fingers into my palm.

I didn't have another option.

Everything would have been so much easier if Suri had left for Nusias, but she hadn't. I pried at two of the pins securing the wooden beams beneath the stage, and after some effort, they slid free. I held my breath for one heartbeat, then another, but the structure held. For now. I pocketed the pins and ducked back into the hall like a ghost.

"Who's there?" Jaari appeared, wrapped in a blanket that did nothing to soothe the chill of her frown. At the sight of me, her eyes widened. "What are you doing up here?"

"Couldn't sleep," I muttered, racing back down the stairs. My pulse pounded in my ears, but I didn't hear her follow me. With a massive exhale, I ducked into Bregan's bedroom.

Suri glared at me from Bregan's cot.

I lurched to a halt.

"It was you, wasn't it?" She uncurled to her feet.

"What?"

"I couldn't figure out who would have done it, or why. But you sent her to me somehow. To get rid of me. Didn't you?"

Neera. "I have no idea what you're talking about."

She closed the space between us without a whisper of sound. Her good-girl persona distorted into the vicious thing I'd glimpsed beneath the surface. "You should be careful." Her fingers pulled at the end of her sweater sleeve. The sleeve that hid her knife.

I almost sneered at her to try it. "I think we've had a misunderstanding," I said instead with a nervous smile.

She snorted. "Good night, Vota."

You too, I thought. It would be her last in the temple.

THIRTY-THREE

Firin

Now

The next morning, I woke before sunrise and helped Nyfe and Tez make breakfast. While the cast ate, I kept Phinnin busy with one of Father's coin tricks. When Jaq requested help mixing paint for the castle walls, I volunteered. By the time the day's work actually started, Mezua found me splattered and sweating in the back of the nave, helping Tez haul boxes of costumes and props from the dressing room for Nyfe to rummage through.

With professional sincerity, Mezua thanked me for standing in and offered to host me for a few more days. Not even a week. "We *are* very grateful," she insisted.

"I understand," I said. Her tight nod revealed little, but the hands clasped behind her back loosened. "Can I help with anything? I'd be happy to show Suri what we worked on. Perhaps the balcony dance?"

Mezua's brows rose. "That's very generous, thank you." She waved Suri over from where Nyfe was knee deep in a pile of costumes. "Vota's offered to show you the balcony dance."

"Did she?" Suri had washed up and changed into a clean pair of trousers, hair tied back. Skepticism bled from her pores. "Why don't I start with the monologue that leads into the dance?"

I stiffened. I hadn't planned for Suri to take the stage first, but when Mezua waved her up, I couldn't do anything except sit in the front pew to watch. The half-constructed castle dwarfed her as she climbed to the balcony bracketed by mock towers and turrets.

The construct groaned.

At the director's cue, she began. "What is wrong with me?" she moaned. "Why c-can't I play? Please, Father. You don't understand." She shook out her hands, gaping at them as if they didn't belong on her body. "It's as if . . . as if the more I play, the more my fingers p-panic."

She was good.

I gripped the pins in my pocket. Once I got onstage, her skill wouldn't matter. While everyone's full focus was on Suri, I pulled the pins out and slid them into the folds of her jacket on the bench next to me.

When Suri finished the monologue, someone whistled. She stood, and the set creaked. I clapped with everyone else. As she hopped off-stage, she tossed me a wry, triumphant grin, and when Mezua finished giving her notes, she turned to me. "It's tight up there; want to show me the dance before I try it?"

I gave her a bright smile. "Gladly."

Suri settled in the front pew, her eyes never leaving me. With careful, deliberate steps, I ascended and took my place on the balcony. Wood groaned. The hair on my arms rose, but it was too late to change my mind. I was committed.

"Ready," I called to the musicians.

They put bow to string. Notes rang clear and true. I tapped out the pattern Nyfe had bored into me. I twirled and leaped—and slammed my heel into the balcony floor's center seam.

It cracked open.

Wood popped, then fractured, and I was falling, scrambling, just barely managing to get my arms beneath me as I crashed through the center of the splintered set. My lungs collapsed, screaming for air as I tried to turn over.

Seconds later, my breath returned in a flood, and with it came searing pain. Set pieces protruded from my left arm, between the shreds of my sleeve, covered in blood. A small part of me screeched that I might have overdone it, but I pulled my focus to the warm feel of my illusion cord and used my breath to dull my awareness of the pain, as I'd learned to do over the last few years. This con wasn't over.

"Vota! Vota! Are you all right?" Tez threw aside debris, digging to get to me. "Oh, saints, you're bleeding." Jaq appeared behind him, a hand to his mouth.

"I'm okay," I lied, staggering out of the wreckage with Tez's help. The whole troupe gaped at me. My ears rang.

"What happened?" Mezua cried.

Jaq emerged, gripping the twists of his hair. "Some of the structural pins are missing. I swear I put them in there."

Jaari abandoned her violin and raced down from the temple balcony. She shot straight for Suri in the front row. "Did you do this?"

Suri recoiled. "What?"

"Is that why you were creeping around up here last night?" Jaari's voice rose an octave. "Were you *pulling the pins?*"

"I wasn't up here last night."

"I saw you," Jaari shrieked.

It was working. Just as I planned. I had worn Suri's face last night to sabotage the stage, and Jaari had bought it.

Suri stood. "If anyone did this, it was her." She jabbed a finger toward me.

I backed into Tez. "What? I didn't do anything."

"*Clearly* it was her," Suri snapped. But no one looked convinced. After all, my arm was pouring blood. Who would believe I'd done this to myself? It was almost laughable, if tears of pain weren't burning my eyes.

"Everyone calm down," Mezua said. "Let's not throw accusations."

Nyfe appeared out of nowhere with a basket of medical supplies. "Come here," she whispered, guiding me into a crouch. She pressed a thick cloth to my main wound. I gritted my teeth as she pulled splinters from my flesh.

"I didn't do anything." Suri snatched her jacket.

The pins clanged to the floor.

Jaari's chin disappeared. "Oh really?"

"*She* must have put them there. You can't seriously—"

The front doors groaned. Bootsteps thundered. Sunlight flooded down the center aisle, as none other than interim President Hulei strode into the temple, followed by a handful of constables with shiny badges, including Bregan.

My whole body seized.

"Good evening," the president said to the shocked room.

I tried to stand, but Tez clamped down, holding me in place as Nyfe wrapped a bandage around my arm.

The president scanned the broken set, and me. Then he spun to Suri. She froze.

"Suri Saains," Bregan said, "you're under arrest."

ACT III

THIRTY-FOUR

Firin

Then

It took me thirty-four days to break out of my bedroom.

Thirty-four days since I'd seen Father with Esmai and he'd locked me up. Thirty-four days of listening to the Reformists warring with the Stav outside. I hammered, again and again, at the floorboard I'd managed to splinter and wedge between the door and the frame. *Please,* I prayed. Father was gone, but I didn't know for how long.

Crack. The padlock he'd installed finally ripped free. The crash echoed as I fell into the kitchen, blinking in the dim light. Sunset burned beyond the window. After so long in the dark—broken only by Father's daily delivery of food and a clean chamber pot—my mind spun with half thoughts and half-delirious desires, all tangled in a web of stewed fury.

Clean. I needed to clean up.

Stumbling to Father's wash bin, I dunked my hands in the frigid refuse water. My fingernails, which I'd chewed to their stubs, burned, but I scrubbed away crusted sweat and tears. Wiping the cold, dirty water from my chin with the sleeve of my sweater, I forced myself to take a breath.

I needed to make sure Bregan was still alive.

For a month, gunshots and screams had been my only companions. I'd spent night after night haunted by the image of him hanging from a canal bridge. But the Reformists still rioted from dusk to dawn, which meant they were holding on. They hadn't been defeated. There was hope.

He's alive, I chanted to myself. *He has to be alive.*

But I had no idea what Father might've done to Esmai.

I backed away from the evidence of my escape and flew down the tenement steps. My legs trembled from disuse. If Bregan was anywhere, he'd be at the ruins of the factory theater. That's where the Reformists gathered during strikes.

As I raced out of the Bilge, smoke poured into my throat, yanking coughs from my chest. Sunset stained a blanket of fumes, making everything glow orange. But the streets were empty. No rioters, no Stav, no citizens.

When I reached the silent, vacant match factory, the knot of my stomach was so tight I could have vomited. I entered the dark maw of the ruins, listening as hard as I could past my own wheezing breaths. Then laughter bounced down the hall, hitting me like a tidal wave, so beautiful I had to brace against the wall, tears springing to my eyes.

The troupe was okay.

Which meant Bregan might be okay.

I followed the voices to doors spilling bright light and shadows. The dressing rooms. I hesitated. All I'd thought about for thirty-four days was getting to Bregan, not what I'd do once I had. What was I supposed to say?

A boot scuffed behind me. I jumped.

"Aza Vota? Are you all right?" Tez peered down. A lump formed in my throat. He remembered my name, all these months later. "You are looking for Bregan? I'll get him. Wait here."

I sagged against the wall. Despite my exhaustion, pins pricked my veins. Father would be home eventually. Could he find me here?

"Firin?" Bregan's whisper struck the remains of my tattered heart. Framed by the glow of the dressing room, with his costume half-buttoned and his hair askew, he looked like home.

My knees shook. Then he was there, pressing kisses to my forehead, then my eyes. He wiped tears from my cheeks. "Firin." His voice broke. "Where have you been? You didn't come to my show, and then I couldn't find you. I went to your apartment, but you weren't there. I even checked the cotton mills, but I couldn't find your pa. What happened?" In the dim hall, he seemed thinner, his edges sharpened.

"Is your ma all right?" I asked. "Your pa?"

His chin quivered. "They're fine. But so many people are dead. Taira . . . they killed her."

I gripped his shirtsleeves. "W-what?"

"They got her in Fisherman's Wharf, with a dozen other women from the soap factory."

Sweet, kind Taira. I pictured her on the roof, glowing in the sunlight, patient as she taught us dance, loving as she held her daughter. She was *dead*. The word bounced in my skull. I'd seen a lot of death in Luisonn, but I'd never *known* anyone who died, never cared about them. My heart clenched. "What about Phinnin?"

"She's all right; she was with her father." He wiped at his face. "But it's been awful. After the Stav burned down that apartment building, all anyone wants is blood, but no one can agree to what end."

"Apartment building?" I stammered.

"The hat-factory apartments?" When I stared at him, he blinked. "Firin, where have you been?"

"Places!" Mezua's deep voice shot down the hall. "Two minutes. Bregan? Where's Bregan?"

"You're still doing the play?" I asked. It seemed impossible that a play could still happen.

"It's closing night," he said, pressing his forehead to mine. "Just the final act is left. But I don't have to—"

"You need to go," I said. His fingers dug deeper into my sides, as if he might drag me onstage with him. Half of me wanted to let him. But I couldn't ask Mezua to take me in if he ruined this show because of me. "They need you," I made myself say. "I'll be up on the mezzanine. I'll find you after." I pried his fingers from my waist. "I won't leave," I promised.

The mezzanine was so crowded I could barely cram through to the railing. I slotted my legs through the bars. The lights went out. The audience fell silent. But when the spotlight flared, it wasn't on a play.

Mezua stood center stage, in a sleek modern dress. "Good evening," she said. "We're excited to continue our production of *Skarnti's Revenge*, but before we do, it is my great pleasure to introduce Baron Ihan Hulei to the stage."

My hand flew to my mouth as the elegant, ocean-eyed baron brandished his top hat to the room. Had the Reformists finally agreed to work with him? My skin prickled. If they were going to officially try to overthrow the Stav, would Bregan get involved?

"Good evening, ladies and gentlemen," the baron said. Labors and Zeds glared, tense as sheep in the presence of a wolf. "Friends, we are different, you and I. I will not deny it. But we are also the same. We all know the sting of loss, but still we fight. These are our islands. We've dedicated our lives to the Iket Isles while the Vorstav'n emperor sits on his throne, thousands of miles across the sea, with his Stav's leash around our throat. Out there"—he swept his hat to the side—"hundreds of Labors who have worked to the bone for this city's success are dying in simple demand for fairer wages and taxes. But it's not working. It's not *big enough*."

Murmurs crackled like the air before a storm. I leaned into the bars.

"I propose a partnership—between you and me." Spinning slowly on his heel, Baron Hulei took in every audience member. "When rights are not freely given, they must be taken back. You cannot demand of a captain what he is not willing to give. You must remove him. And this ship"—he jabbed his hat into space—"Luisonn is our ship to—"

A shot broke the night open.

Baron Hulei flew sideways, crashing to the stage. My forehead bounced off the railing. A heartbeat later, he moved, swaying to his feet, one arm bent like a shield. Crimson blossomed between the folds of his blue jacket, painting his white shirt red.

Stav soldiers burst from the shadows.

They swarmed the production floor. Another shot rang out, then screaming billowed, and everyone ran, pushed, scrambled for the exits. I jumped to my feet. I had to find Bregan. Somebody shoved me against the railing, and I looked down.

My heart stopped beating.

Father, as Restuv in Stav uniform, looked up at me from the heart of the chaos. His gaze locked on mine, and the barrel of his gun dropped. His lip curled. Everything in me flew back, up, away, horror pumping through my veins.

No, no, no. How was Father here?

I joined the fleeing crowd and bolted down a hallway, tripping over unseen obstacles in the dark, whacking into walls, bumping corners. People scrambled everywhere, their terror echoing as the Stav bore down. Around a corner, a row of windows shimmered. I yanked one open and swung my legs out, reaching my toes for the ground.

Somewhere nearby, someone screamed.

Then Nodtacht black engulfed my vision. Fingers dug into my waist.

"Smoking out the rebel rats," a deep Stav voice said.

Lightning struck my bones. "Let me go!" I screeched as I clawed and kicked against thick, impenetrable leather.

With a heave, the man spun me, smacking my head on brick. Sparks flashed in my vision. I slithered sideways. As I strained to escape, he snatched my sweater sleeve, tearing the neckline wide open. A night breeze curled around my shoulders, stole the warmth from my arms.

A hand clamped around my bare bicep. Over my illusion mark. "Well now," he grunted, snatching my chin. It was the Nodtacht with the hook-shaped scar. "What the fuck are you running—"

"Firin!" Father's shout strained with an emotion I had never heard before.

The Nodtacht's eyes blew wide open. He looked toward Father's voice, then back at me. When Father screamed my name again, the man's sneer could have frozen oceans. "No way," he grunted, and I had no idea what he was talking about.

Until, inches from my face, the whole of him rippled. His hair bled white, his facial hair vanished. Then, without moving a muscle, his cheeks rounded, and his hair turned brown. Again and again, he transformed.

Illusion.

I collapsed in his hold. The Nodtacht had illusion.

"Firin, where are you?" Father rounded the corner to the alley.

The Nodtacht flung me around and trapped me with a muscled arm. Father skidded to a halt. "You," the Nodtacht spit at him, shaking me. "You have been hiding something that belongs to us."

Restuv's lips parted. I searched his soft-brown eyes, the one constant in my life, desperate for some sign I was wrong. But his gaze was a sky of glittering despair. It was the scariest thing I'd ever seen.

When the butt of the man's gun flew toward my temple, I didn't fight. I couldn't. Because I couldn't feel my limbs.

Father was a Nodtacht.

THIRTY-FIVE

Firin

Then

Nausea wrenched me awake.

Vomit burned up my throat, then spewed onto a wet stone floor that smelled like piss. My mind clutched for shore like a half drowned man in a tide. Where was I?

"Bregan," I groaned, trying to sit up. My temple throbbed, yanking me off-kilter. But I fought it, blinking. One side of the room was all bars. A prison cell.

The theater had been raided.

I had to get out of here. Find Bregan.

"Please," a familiar voice echoed. Restuv. "Let me talk to her."

"After hiding her from us all these years?" The Nodtacht who'd caught me. "You said she was *dead*. The only reason you're not hanging from a bridge right now is—"

"I can convince her," Father insisted.

Gagging over the floor, I tried to think past the pain to where new facts whirled like seabirds in a storm. Father was a Nodtacht. One of the undercover ones. Was I supposed to be one too? Was that why I had illusion? *You have no idea what I've done for you,* he'd said. A chill dug needles into my bones.

I squeezed my eyes shut against the pain. Had they locked Bregan and the other rebels in this prison too?

"Five minutes," the Nodtacht said.

Metal rattled. Restuv sauntered in. My whole body shook with rage. I scrambled back until I hit the wall, clenching and unclenching my ruined skirts, desperate to rip into his face. To tear out those eyes. I hated him for locking me up. For lying to me. For being the reason I was in this cell. For working for the Stav and never telling me. For aiding the people who'd raided the Reformists and killed Taira. For making my whole life one massive con.

"What happened to everyone?" I snapped. "All the people in the theater?"

"So you've been sneaking off to that Reformist theater this whole time?" he said. "Did you fancy yourself an actress?"

"What did they do to them?"

Restuv crouched in front of me. "There's no 'they,' Firin. You're a Nodtacht too."

"Tell me where they are." I tried to crawl around him. If Bregan was in here, I'd have to get him out.

Father yanked me back. "The Reformists aren't here."

"Then where? I swear I'm going to—"

His nails pierced my chin. "What? What are you gonna do? Those Reformists would kill you if they knew what you are."

"I'm not a Nodtacht," I spit.

"You were born a Nodtacht. You'll die one. This mark means they own you." He glanced at the X-shaped scar poking through the rips in my sweater. He'd told me it just meant illusion. Another lie. "I tried," he said, lowering to a whisper. "I tried to save you from this fate. We were *so* close to leaving, but then you had to get their attention during the Baron job, then again when you stabbed a Stav soldier. I tried to clean up your mess, but you couldn't just stay put, could you? You let them find you. Now you have to live with that."

"Let go of me," I snarled. He didn't get to blame me for this. He didn't get to pretend it was my fault.

"The Stav are upset you hid from them so long," Father said, "but give me something useful about the Reformist leadership or their plans and we might see sunrise."

Upset that *I* hid? No. The Stav were mad at Father, not me.

"What did you tell Esmai? To get her to trust you?" I demanded. He must have been conning her for information.

A cruel grin slithered across Father's face. "Oh, child, I've taught you better than that. She didn't need convincing."

I sneered at him. No. Esmai would never help the Stav. "You're lying."

"I assure you, I'm not. Now, you can hate me, you can pretend you're different, but deep down you know you're not. We're the same, Firin, you and I."

"We're not."

He yanked me to him so hard the world spun, and held my chin firmly, inches from his own. "What about Quan?" Father's hair bled black, his nose lengthened, the angle of his sneer tilted. He became Kenkitu, the trader who had brought his daughter to dine with a kind Merchant-class man from Iakirru. The man who'd told me all about Kirru-style dances. "He was tortured for weeks, you know," Father said, "about his involvement with the rebels."

A memory dislodged like a stone in a riverbed.

We found Quan's body, Bregan's father had said. *They had him this whole time.* I'd recognized the name, but I hadn't connected it. My gut lurched again, but there was nothing left to excise, so I gagged against Father's shirt.

His face changed once more.

"Or Shistae?" He became Unduik, the Labor-class fisherman.

"Or Zukst?" He became Ohero, the Gwyn refugee.

"Or Hoithyn?" He became Lust'tovn, the Merchant-class jeweler.

"Stop," I groaned, as each face stabbed into me, bleeding memories of the people we'd conned while Father had worn them.

"Each of those marks was a traitor to the Stav," he said.

He'd told me the cons were for money. To survive. How many of those marks were people Bregan had known? How much loss had I brought to his life, to the lives of all the other Reformists?

"Why did you bring me?" I sobbed. If he'd been hiding me from the Stav, why would he use me in their missions?

"Because you were *good* at it," Father said, shifting into Mr. Finweint's honeyed Gwyn accent. "Together, we got more money than I could have alone. Money we could have used to escape. But that's not possible anymore." He cupped my cheek. When I blinked up, the stiff but loving persona I'd clung to my whole life beamed down. "Give the Stav what they want, and we can walk out of here; refuse, and they'll hang you. I don't want to see you hanged, Firi."

The nickname curled around my heart like a collar. Years ago I would have melted, letting Mr. Finweint wrap me up in stories, paint over realities, and spin me a bed of lies. But now I had seen behind the curtain. Now he could never manipulate me again.

"That won't work," I breathed. "Afyn's dead, remember?"

The slap sent me reeling, my cheek burning, but I couldn't feel it past the inferno of rage incinerating my every other emotion.

Your mark's deepest desire is the key to getting what you want.

I was Father's mark. He'd begged to come in here and "convince" me to save his own hide. Which meant two things: the Stav wanted something from me, and Father didn't have the power to get me out. If I wanted to find Bregan, Father wasn't my mark. He was just in my way.

"Guard!" I screamed. The Nodtacht swam into view, a shark in midnight waters. "I want to talk to someone."

"Firin," Father said, "don't do this."

Everyone else is out for themselves; you should be too. His own rule.

If I was going to get out of here, I had to do it on my own.

The Nodtacht motioned me forward. A Stav guard twisted my arms behind my back. She led me into a cramped, dark hall. Between one breath and the next, I was shaking. I dug my nails into my palms and took in my surroundings.

A stone corridor lined with cells, most with solid doors. The Nodtacht jingled keys in the lock of the last one. If there was an exit, it was at the other end of the hall. Slipping away wasn't an option. I needed leverage. Maybe information.

The interrogation room smelled like rotting death. A small table and two chairs sat in the center, ringed by dim candlelight. The guard stuffed me in one of the chairs, then left me alone with the massive Nodtacht. He sat.

"What do you want?" I demanded.

He stared down his illusioned beard at me, unreadable. His hooked scar gleamed. Silence stretched, drawing taut. "You can call me Eznur," he said.

A false name, probably. Did the Nodtacht even have real names? I searched his pocked face. I'd always been able to read people; even Father had tics. But this man was stone.

"You want information about the Reformists," I guessed.

"Oh, no, we don't need that."

I twisted sweaty fingers together. "Then what do you want?"

"You."

ACT IV

THIRTY-SIX

Firin

Now

Bregan was arresting the wrong person.

"You're under arrest for acting against the Free Isles of Iket as a Nodtacht agent of the Stav Regime," he said, not meeting anyone's eyes as he took Suri's arms behind her back.

I swayed in my crouch beside Nyfe, the word *Nodtacht* reverberating through my skull. Baron Hulei said something to Mezua. They disappeared into the hallway. She only looked back at Suri once.

"I'm not a fucking Nodtacht!" Suri screeched. "I swear I didn't touch the set."

Bregan's focus shot up to the ruined balcony, seeing it for the first time, then found me. He shoved Suri into a constable's arms. "Take her to the carriage." Leaping onstage, he said, "What happened?"

I jerked away from his touch. Suri's shouts echoed through the temple.

"Suri broke the set," Nyfe murmured.

Bregan's entire face contorted into something ugly as he took in my wounds, as he falsely attributed them to Suri.

"How do you know she's a Nodtacht?" I asked.

"We'll confirm it soon enough."

The scar. That was the only way to confirm it. He had to know about the scar: what it meant, how horrible it would reveal me to be. Somehow the constables had put two and two together. With all the Nodtacht they'd executed after the insurrection, I suppose it wouldn't have been difficult.

"Excuse me," I blurted. Wrenching out of Nyfe's grip, I fled into the temple corridor. Agony radiated from the shoulder she'd barely managed to bandage, but that pain was nothing compared to the butcher's knife lodged in my stomach, ripping into my rib cage, flaying me open.

Suri wasn't a Nodtacht.

Bregan only thought she was because *I* had impersonated her. I was sure of it. He had seen me wearing her face in two suspicious locations: on the roof of the temple during the insurrection and at the Crow's Nest the other night. As soon as he checked her for the brand and realized she was innocent, he'd resume his search.

I had to ensure that if he turned to me, he wouldn't find any evidence.

If he did, he'd never understand. He'd never forgive me.

"Vota?" Nyfe called down the dark hallway.

My knife shook in my blood-soaked hand like a tiny, useless sword. There was no privacy in this whole damn building. I could run for the square and disappear again, but I was done scrambling for a hold on the cliff's edge of discovery, only to get pushed back over the edge.

I shoved through the closest door.

The lit hearth in Mezua's office cast eerie light over her desk. She was somewhere else, speaking with Baron Hulei, and the others were still in the nave. Kneeling before the fire, I pulled my dress up over my head. I winced at the throb of my injuries, but I'd endured worse. The Nodtacht had seen to that.

Blood seeped through Nyfe's bandage, blotching my slip, but I lifted my knife to my other, unharmed arm.

To the Nodtacht brand that glowed in the firelight.

My chest squeezed like a pair of wringing hands. Finally, I had secured the life *I* wanted, but to keep it I had to cut the past away, and I had to do it now, while I could still blame the injury on the set disaster. I gritted my teeth and pressed the tip of the knife to my flesh. But when blood bubbled above the scar, my hand stilled.

This scar gave me my illusion. If I removed it, I'd be stuck with my own face forever. Flames shivered and blurred in front of me. My hand refused to move.

Then the office door burst open.

"Vota?" Mezua jerked to a halt.

My knife clattered to the floor.

I slapped a hand over my bicep, but it was too late. She'd seen my scar. We stared at each other, for three heartbeats or an eternity. Only her chest moved, rising and falling, but the revelation blooming in her eyes was unmistakable.

She knew what my scar meant too. Somehow, impossibly, she knew.

Her foot slipped backward.

"Touch that door and you'll regret it," I snarled. I couldn't let her leave.

"You're the one they're looking for," she said.

I lunged for my knife. "The president would kill you for housing me. The whole troupe would go down if he found out."

"Listen to me. We can—"

Her spine hit the door as my knife met her throat.

"We will do nothing," I growled, grip shaking. "You *saw* nothing."

Mezua slowly raised her palms, holding my glare with a severity that felt like an icy hand against the back of my neck. "What's your plan, Vota? To cut away your powers?"

I blinked. I'd never met a soul outside the Nodtacht headquarters who knew about the face-changing powers our scars gave us. Was *Mezua* a Nodtacht? She couldn't be. I'd have known.

"I had a friend once," she explained, "who could change her face. But not when she tried to remove that mark. Are you *sure* this is what you want? The woman I knew, she suffered when she—"

My hand trembled so violently that my knife broke the director's skin. She flinched.

"You have no idea what I want," I spit.

"Yes, Vota, I think I do." Blood trickled down her throat. "Esmai always feared your background was dark, but this is beyond what I imagined."

"Shut up." I would not be seduced to the gallows with niceties like a fly to a web. "I know what you did. I know you helped Esmai spy for the Stav."

Mezua's entire body tensed beneath my hold.

Years ago, Eznur told me that Esmai and Mezua had conspired against the Reformists to protect the theater. The Bloody Fifthday raid had been both their faults. I'd written him off as a liar trying to twist my love for them into something he could control, but Mezua's pupils flared.

Her throat bobbed against my blade. "You have no idea what you're—"

"I will tell the president," I said, pressing closer. "He's right out there, and I will tell him everything if you don't swear to forget this ever happened."

"It doesn't have to be this way, Vota," she said softly.

Suddenly, her slate eyes became a mirror, reflecting how she saw me: a feral woman with a criminal past who was threatening to bring down everything and everyone she wanted to love.

What was I doing? Blackmailing, betraying, and conning my way into the world I wanted to be part of? Threatening to bring it down in order to be allowed to stay? This was what Father would have done. This was what I'd sworn I'd leave behind in that sunrise over Luisonn's burning corpse. I'd come here to start over, to build a life where I could be a better person—and I had failed from the start.

I staggered back.

Mezua wiped at the blood on her neck, a slight tremble in her elegant fingers. I dropped my knife onto her desk, and the clatter rang through the room like a settling defeat. I turned to the hearth and wrapped my arms around my torso.

"I can help you save the theater," I said into the flames. The tension between us curved into a question mark.

"Can you?" she asked tentatively.

"You need to reach higher. You need the president to patron you."

"That will never happen." Her words were flat, bitter. "He made it clear that he has no intention of supporting us, even after we helped him overthrow the Stav."

"Ihan Hulei isn't a man who deals in favors. He only deals in merit." I had tailed the baron for years under Nodtacht command. I had spied on him at balls and meetings, on ships and in bars. Of every soul in this city—perhaps in the world—I likely knew him best.

"Ihan Hulei is one of the biggest patrons in Qunsii," I explained. "He thirsts for art more than politics, but in his mind there is no art in Luisonn that parallels Qunsii's. If you prove otherwise, he will shower you with money."

"I already invited him to patron *Sweet Winter's Eve*. He declined."

"Because it's not flashy enough."

Mezua eyed the blood sliding down both of my arms. "I promised the troupe that we wouldn't get involved in any more political schemes. The last time almost destroyed us."

I sniffed. "Everything is political. Look at the Grande. Aza Veska'nora has all of the resources and all of the power right now. You can't compete with her—not for the richest patrons, not without Baron Hulei's help. With his word, the rest of the city will fall in line. You'll have more money than you know what to do with."

"What are you proposing?"

"Let me figure out what he wants. Then we give it to him."

She stared at me for a long moment, weighing the threat I posed. I could turn her in to Hulei and reveal what she and Esmai had done to save myself, but I was tired of scheming. I was tired of destruction. I wanted to create something beautiful. I wanted to work *with* people instead of against them, to *earn* my place among the Veiled Players, not steal it.

Everyone is out for themselves, I heard Father whisper.

I ignored him.

"This isn't blackmail," I said quietly. "What do you have to lose by trying?"

Finally, she nodded.

I grabbed my knife and shrugged back into my ruined dress, wincing as the sleeves brushed the edges of my wound.

"You should let Nyfe stitch that up," Mezua said, settling at her desk chair and raising a handkerchief to the cut I'd made on her throat.

"And, Vota?" I hesitated at the door. "I know a man who can cover up that scar—a tattooist. He's discreet, and he's expensive, but if you can make this work, we can get rid of it. Safely."

When I glanced back, her eyes were warm, if wary, as though she genuinely wanted to help me. I'd learned long ago that people's generosity only stretched as far as your usefulness to them; to believe otherwise would spell your own heartbreak. But as I pushed out of the room, something warm and dangerous stirred between my ribs. Something that felt an awful lot like hope.

THIRTY-SEVEN

Firin

Then

On Bloody Fifthday, Eznur offered me a choice: I could work for the Nodtacht or I could die.

He gave me a night to decide, and I spent the entirety of it zigzagging through the streets of Luisonn, as if I could outrun the starless sky expanding inside me. But the new knowledge of what I was, and all the terrible things I had done, was an oil I couldn't wipe from my skin.

Eyes trailed me everywhere. They shone in shadowed alleys, tavern stoops, and curtained windows. No matter where I went, no matter how many different faces I wore, I couldn't shake the Nodtacht agents following me.

When twilight arrived, plumes of smoke rose from the Labor District, staining the eastern sky. The old factory remains burned like a warning, bright with finality. An awful weight sat on my chest.

The Reformists were ruined. The theater was gone.

There was no avoiding what I had to do next.

As the sun appeared over the horizon, I returned to the Nodtacht headquarters. The monstrous building swallowed the sunlight whole, and as I stepped into its shadow, a shiver slid down my spine. Father had made his choice to pander to the Stav a long time ago, but I wouldn't roll over like he had. I would work for them, for a time, but eventually I would escape.

I dragged myself up the front steps.

Inside the lobby, a thin, severe-looking woman leaned against a bare reception desk with a steel frown, aged hands stiff behind her back. "Hello," she said in Vorstav'n. "Eznur is waiting for you." Her heels clicked as she led me down the hallway opposite the cells where they had locked up Father and me. I kept my chin high.

We entered a brightly lit office. Eznur leaned back in a chair at a polished wooden desk, probably shipped over from the Vorstav'n mainland. He nodded to the woman. "General Skavka'tor."

Her sharp chin slid toward me. "This is the one?"

"Yes," Eznur said.

Her lips twitched in a sneer. "How are we supposed to control her?"

"The ambassadors cleared it."

"Your father should be swinging over the canal," the woman said to me.

"I agree," I said coldly, in perfect Vorstav'n.

Skavka'tor raised one perfectly manicured eyebrow, then turned back to Eznur. "If you're smart, you'll get rid of her." She disappeared in a flapping of skirts.

Eznur pulled a cigarette out of his pocket. As he lit it, emotions buzzed at the distant ends of my consciousness, held at bay by a numbness that weighed down all my bones. I squared my shoulders. Escaping the Nodtacht would require knowledge: what they wanted, who served them, how their surveillance worked—and I could only get that information one way.

I let my chair screech over the stone floor as I drew it out. "I'll do it."

Eznur took a drag of his cigarette. "I told you to come with your father."

I sat. "I'll work for you, but I won't work with him."

"Why the change of heart?"

"He lied to me my whole life." I didn't have to fake the venom in my voice. "I've never known who or what I am, or why I can do what I can do. But you do."

"What about the Reformists?"

"There's nothing left of them, so there's nothing left for me."

We stared at one another, seconds stretching. A more convincing argument would include stating that I supported the Vorstav'n Empire, that I *wanted* to serve their government. But the words burned like acid. I couldn't make myself say them.

"Very well," he said. "You will join the Vtor, the Nodtacht's trainees."

I blinked. That was it?

Eznur set his elbows on the desk and waved his cigarette. "Once you've proven your worth and loyalty, you will be promoted to an Iket Isles division. There are three that focus on surveillance. The First does foreign operations on the northern continent; the Second does public control here. The Third Division focuses *internally*. Do you understand?"

I gripped my knees beneath the table. If the Nodtacht had an entire division devoted to sniffing out dissenters within their own ranks, I could never seek out Bregan again, not without risking his life.

"Yes, sir," I said. Escaping would be near impossible, but I had to try.

"Good. If, at any moment, we question your worth or your loyalty, you will be disposed of. Now, what should we refer to you as?"

I hesitated. Surely he knew the name my father had given me?

"Afyn," I finally said. "Afyn Wainrite."

"Well, Afyn, let's get started." He stood.

As I followed him into the hall, my head spun. "What will I—"

"No questions." Two heavy, final words. He flipped up his coat collar and quickened his pace to the lobby. He led me past a glaring

Skavka'tor, back to the hallway of prison cells, and all the way to the end.

As he pushed open the door to the same cell where we'd spoken the night before, sweat broke out on my brow. Stains and chains still decorated the back wall. The lamp and table were perched in the middle of the room, now adorned with a notebook and inkwell.

Eznur held the door open, his smile sharpening the curve of his hook-shaped scar. "First, we must determine what you can do."

With my heart in my throat, I stepped inside. If he wanted skill and unquestioning obedience, I'd give him both.

I'd earn his trust so I could break it.

THIRTY-EIGHT

Bregan

Now

Suri had done this to herself.

The moment Bregan saw her back in the temple kitchen, he had connected all the dots. The night of the insurrection, she'd been on the roof of the temple right when the Stav attacked. Then, when she ran from him in the Commerce Block, they'd been right down the alley from the Crow's Nest, where Draifey's people were meeting. Bregan had known something wasn't right.

If Draifey had one Nodtacht working for him, it was likely he had others.

As soon as the *East Etherea* had disembarked, he told the president his suspicions about Suri's involvement with the Stav. When Hulei asked if he was sure he wanted to lead the arrest and interrogation, Bregan hadn't hesitated. Whatever her transgressions, they were not on his shoulders, even if it had been impossible to face Tez's shock or Jaari's disgust. If he was right, the troupe would understand soon enough.

The chill in headquarters could freeze bone marrow. Bregan pulled his jacket tighter as he made for the interrogation office. Inside, Suri writhed and spit curses as several constables worked to chain her to a chair.

"Stop," Bregan barked. "I'll take it from here."

The guards snapped to attention, then left. In the echo of their exit, Bregan stared down at the girl he'd thought was his ally. A little less than a year ago, he had caught her and Cidd raiding the stores of a Merchant who had worked underground for the Reformists. Half-starved and lethal, the two Zeds had nearly killed him, until Bregan offered them a different path. They'd joined the Reformists and been vital to the planning and success of the insurrection. He'd thought he could trust them.

Suri tucked her handcuffed wrists to her chest with a sneer, and the jagged edges of the broken set flared red at the edges of Bregan's vision, painted in Firin's blood. If Suri was working for the Stav, why hurt Firin? Theater jealousy, or something else?

"I'm not a saints-damned Nodtacht," Suri snapped. The static tangles of her blonde hair burned in the lantern light.

"I need to see your arms."

"Why?"

"Take your sweater off, or I'll call them back to do it."

After overthrowing the Stav, the Reformists had discovered that the Stav branded their Nodtacht with an X-shaped scar on the inside of one of their biceps. It seemed asinine to brand undercover agents so clearly, but it was exactly the kind of thing arrogant Vorstav'n would miscalculate. Bregan had waited until now to check Suri—alone—as they'd kept the revelation within the higher ranks of the constabulary, not wanting to alert any Nodtacht who might still be hiding in the city, or who might try to sneak in from the Vorstav'n mainland, that they were onto them.

"Fine." Suri pulled her sweater awkwardly over her head with her cuffed hands. When Bregan reached to check both her biceps, she shivered but didn't pull away.

Her pale skin was bare.

Bregan dropped her arm. His conscience squirmed, but he buried it. The absence of a scar only meant she wasn't a Nodtacht. His mother hadn't had a scar, but she had still spied for the Stav. He sat down. "You can put it back on."

Suri slid back into her sweater. "What the fuck is going on?"

"Where were you the night of the insurrection?"

"At the Landings."

"What were you doing at the temple?"

"I was only there until we left to meet the Gwyn soldiers at the docks."

Bregan folded his hands in his lap. "But you didn't go to the docks."

"Yes, I *did*."

"What about the other night?"

"What about it?"

"You met with Draifey's people at the Crow's Nest."

Blood drained from her cheeks. "I wasn't . . . I didn't go in."

"Which is it?" Her lips pinched, so Bregan leaned forward and shoved a finger into the table. "I've now seen you in two places you shouldn't have been. Then you just disappeared for days with no explanation."

"Bregan . . ."

"*I* want to know what the fuck is going on."

She swallowed once, twice. "You won't believe me."

"Try me."

Her hesitation stretched, then snapped. She lifted her chin to the ceiling. "Yes, I was at the Crow's Nest, but I only knew about the meeting because Cidd had planned to go. After he . . ." A sheen slid over her vacant stare. "Well, it didn't make sense to go without him, so I didn't plan to, but then the theater was like a saints-damned crypt. Everything smelled like death, and all anyone wanted to talk about was fucking *Sweet Winter's Eve*. So I went to the meeting. I thought I might feel better seeing others who'd been close with Cidd too."

Bregan's gut clenched. Addym *and* Cidd. How many other people had secretly known Draifey would turn on Hulei? Had Jaq? Did any of them know he was working with the Nodtacht?

"Did you know Draifey planned to let Stav prison guards go?" he asked.

"What? No. I just knew there'd be a meeting at the Crow's Nest if we won."

"Was Addym at the Crow's Nest?" he asked.

"Of course. He's the one who dragged Cidd into Draifey's shit in the first place."

Bregan drummed his fingers on the tabletop. "What happened at the meeting?"

"I don't know. I didn't go to it. When I got to the Crow's Nest, this girl came up to me . . ." She rubbed her palms down her thighs.

"Who?"

When Suri met his eyes, hers bled agony. "She . . . she said she was my sister. She looked *exactly* like me. Said that she came from Nusias to search for me because my ill mother wanted to meet me. She told me to meet her at the docks in Nusias, then rushed out of the tavern. I tried to follow her, but she disappeared."

"That's why you went to the ticket station?" Bregan asked.

She nodded. "But when I got there, something didn't feel right. She'd said that she had met Mother Jehmah, so I decided to go to Saint Heket's to confirm it . . . and she hadn't. I swear, that's all I know. Maybe she's the one you saw on the rooftop and at the tavern? Because I *didn't* see you either night."

Suri swiped at her face. Bregan stared at her. Claiming to have a doppelgänger was straight out of an Iakirru legend, a cover-up story so bizarre that it was hard not to believe her. But if she was telling the truth, who was the girl? And what did she want with Suri?

"I feel like I'm going crazy, Breg," she whispered.

He rocked back and ran a hand through his hair. "What do you know about Draifey?"

She shrugged. "Cidd kept me mostly in the dark. He'd sworn some kind of secrecy."

"Do you know when the next meeting is?"

"No."

"Do you know anything about Draifey working with the Nodtacht?"

Her eyes widened. "What?"

A sharp rap sounded on the door. "Sir? The president has requested an urgent audience." Bregan turned toward the guard's voice.

"Am I still under arrest?" Suri asked. She pressed her lips together as if holding back tears.

Bregan hesitated. She seemed earnest. The itch of not knowing crawled down the back of his neck, but he didn't have enough proof either way, and he couldn't keep the president waiting.

"You're free to go," he said, just barely catching himself before adding an apology. He'd done his job tonight. That was all.

A few minutes later, the commissioner ushered Bregan into his spacious office, where the interim president paced behind a wide, polished desk. His usually slick hair stood on end, and his tie hung askew. He looked even more distraught than he had a few hours earlier at the docks, when Bregan had briefed him about Draifey working with a Nodtacht and his suspicions about Suri.

At the creak of the door, the president halted. "What did you find out?"

"No evidence that she's guilty," Bregan said, "but her testimony supports Draifey's secrecy and Addym Taidd's involvement. She doesn't know if they're working with the Stav. We should question Addym as soon as . . ." The other two men exchanged a look. "What is it?"

The commissioner shifted his gun belt. "Taidd turned in his badge a few hours ago. We were all at the temple when it happened. He's gone. No one knows where."

"*What?*" Bregan said. Addym must have heard they were arresting Suri. He'd known Suri would betray him, so he ran.

Hulei braced his hands against the edge of the desk and lowered his head. An uncomfortable silence thickened in the room, and an eternity seemed to pass before he straightened again. A sea roiled behind his glare. "I owe you an apology, Bregan. I should have taken your concerns about Draifey more seriously."

"It wasn't your fault, sir."

"It doesn't matter whose fault it was. The reality now is that my opponent is working with the Nodtacht, and half the damn city is already supporting him."

Bregan straightened. "Did he announce?" He hadn't thought Draifey's campaign was public knowledge.

The baron slid a stained pamphlet across the desk. It declared Labor Is Luisonn above a drawing of Draifey and a crowd of aproned factory workers, all in the same shades of red and black that the Stav Regime had used in their own propaganda.

Bregan stared at the date and time. "He's holding a campaign rally? Tonight?"

"The entire saints-damned Labor district is there," the commissioner grunted, "buying into tyrannical lies painted over with classist promises."

"We should arrest him," Hulei declared.

"But we don't know anything for sure," Bregan said.

"I thought you said he's working with the Nodtacht?"

Bregan shifted his stance. "Based on the testimony of one man."

"Well, that's enough to bring him in and question him, is it not?"

"If we do that, his people will have time to hide the evidence we need to convict him. The Nodtacht are trained to disappear."

Hulei threw out his hands. "Then let's go to the papers. That new one, the *Luisonn Daily*, will print it."

"We don't have *proof*, sir."

Hulei slammed a fist on the desk, then pointed south. "There are thousands of people out there, *right now*, who are buying into that snake's lie that he understands them. That *he's* the man to represent their interests, not the rest of us who've fought for this island's freedom for decades. They have no idea he's working with the Stav. We have to expose him, or he'll win this election."

"Sir—"

"He will hand us right back to the Stav, and we will lose *everything*."

"If we're going to take him down," Bregan said, "we need to wait until we have enough to incriminate him without a doubt. We need to find out exactly what he's planning with the Stav."

"The boy's right." The commissioner crossed his arms. "We can't tell anyone, not until we find a smoking gun, something indisputable."

The president's chest heaved.

"I could tail him," Bregan offered.

"No," the commissioner said. "I'll put someone else on it. Someone Draifey won't expect. We need you searching for evidence."

Hulei ran a hand down his face. "Tomorrow Draifey will be at the first council meeting, as well as many of his staff. I want you to come and pay attention to what he does, who he talks to, what his people say. See what leads you can find."

"Yes, sir," Bregan said, holding back a sigh of relief.

Hulei donned his top hat. "In the meantime, I have an election I need to win. I'll be at the Grande this evening with some donors, if you need me." He crossed to the door with finality in the click of his expensive shoes. "There's proof, Bregan. You just need to *find* it."

THIRTY-NINE

Bregan

Now

As Bregan strode down the temple's center aisle, he felt blind and unsteady, like a fisherman on a pier in a storm. Jaq crouched before the ruins of the *Sweet Winter's Eve* set. Lamplight quivered in a circle around him, illuminating just the blueprints strewn on the floor. In the last four years since Bregan's mother's betrayal and Jaq's wife's death, they'd grown as close as brothers, linked together by grief and circumstances. Unlike some of the other troupe members, the Stav had known their names and likenesses, so they hadn't been able to work. They'd held one another upright through the darkest days of living underground.

Bregan couldn't bear to consider that Jaq, like Cidd and Addym, supported Draifey's schemes, but he also couldn't neglect the possibility.

"How bad is it?" he asked.

"It's not great," Jaq admitted. "We'll need new raw materials and more time, neither of which we have. It's just hard to believe that Suri would do this . . ." He glanced up. "She came back about an hour ago."

Bregan massaged the curve of his neck. "Our suspicions were wrong."

"That's good, at least." Jaq turned back to his blueprints.

In the silence that grew, Bregan wanted to collapse in the nearest pew and pour out his worries, but since the insurrection, Jaq had closed off in ways he wasn't quite sure what to do with. Instead, he stuffed his hands in his pockets. The rally pamphlet was inside.

"Did you know Draifey contacted those prison guards days before we attacked?" he asked.

Jaq looked up slowly. His glasses shimmered. "I didn't."

Bregan believed him. "Did you know that Cidd and Addym defected to Draifey?"

Jaq flipped over a blueprint. "Is it defection to support a different candidate?"

"You can't seriously think Draifey is a typical candidate?"

"What would make a 'typical' candidate?" Jaq set down his pen. "C'mon, Bregan. People are sick of the rich taking advantage of them. It wasn't just the Stav who oppressed us. The Barons and Managers willingly aided them. To some, Hulei is just as bad as the Vorstav'n emperor."

"Hulei risked *everything* for this regime." The man had even taken a damn bullet on Bloody Fifthday.

"I know. But when Labors look at him and Draifey, side by side, they only see class bands."

Blood pounded against Bregan's skull. Had Jaq started sympathizing with Draifey before or after the insurrection? Jaq wouldn't support him if he knew that Draifey was working with the Nodtacht, the people who'd *murdered* his wife.

But Jaq didn't know. No one did.

That was exactly the problem.

The pamphlet crinkled in Bregan's fist. For years, the Stav Regime had acquiesced to the whims of the Iket Isles' wealthiest, but they didn't really *need* Luisonn's Barons and Managers—they had only ever needed the island's workforce to support their homeland coffers. By using Draifey to turn poor against rich, the Vorstav could easily push out the wealthy, then sweep back in and regain control of their economic assets. Even more control than they'd had before.

Jaq sighed. "This is what we fought for, Bregan—the freedom to debate and disagree, to choose our own leadership, to break the conventions of class. Is that wrong?"

Bregan wanted to tell Jaq the truth and show him how wrong he was, but he could no more tell his friend what he suspected than he could the papers, not without risking Draifey discovering they were onto him.

Bregan tossed the paper into the nearest pew. "Do you know where Vota is?"

Jaq hesitated. "In bed, I think."

Bregan headed for the basement. Every step sent electricity skittering through him, as if he were lost in a haze of lightning. The corruption, the betrayals—it all pressed in, as stifling as his childhood beneath the Stav and the last four years underground. Halfway to the basement, he halted. He had headed for Firin without thinking. She had always been a breath of air in the suffocation, a light in the dark.

But right now, she was upset with him.

He paused on the steps, wringing his cap between his hands. Other than their brief exchange on the ruined stage, he hadn't seen her since they'd practiced the scene from *Qoyn & Insei* on the roof of the temple.

She'd come alive in the skin of Insei, and Bregan had been swept back in time to before Bloody Fifthday, to rehearsing with a bright-eyed girl on top of the world. By sinking into Qoyn's stupid, relentless optimism, he'd tasted an echo of the sweet tang of hope—and he hadn't known what to do with it. For the first time since Bloody Fifthday, Bregan *wanted* something that wasn't violence, revenge, or retribution, but the last time he had dared to hope, Firin had disappeared twice. She was here now, though, and lashing out had been a poor way of showing he cared. Firin might not wish to see him, but he had ruined things. It was up to him to fix it.

He found her on his cot, wrapped in bandages. Newspapers and scripts littered the quilt around her. At the sound of his arrival, her chin lifted.

"Hey," he said, hovering in the entry, "are you all right?"

She folded the newspaper. "Nyfe stitched me up." Bandages thickened her arms beneath her dress sleeves. An ugly bruise painted her collarbone. "What happened with Suri? Is she . . . a Nodtacht?"

"No," he said.

"Right . . . well, that's good." Her frown was a locked box.

"I can't believe she did that to you," he said, itching to check every part of her for damage.

"It's fine."

"It's not fine."

She sighed. "Bregan . . ."

"I'm sorry," he said. "You were right the other day. I haven't been here. I threw you in with the troupe and left. I had no right to snap at you like that." He'd chewed Pa out the other day for years of treating Ma like an afterthought. But that was all he'd done to Firin since she'd reappeared. He couldn't expect her to open up to him if he wasn't giving her the time of day.

"It's all right."

"No, it's not. I've acted like I don't even care that you're here, when it's all I think about."

Firin's small smile held a lifeline. "Are you . . . okay?"

He released his death grip on his cap. "I'm better now."

Her cheeks turned a delicate shade of pink. Saints, he'd missed her. In the chaos of the early revolution, he had leaned on her without fearing his weight would be too much, but she never let him do the same. He rested an arm atop his dresser. "I'm here for you," he said. "You know that, right?"

"I know," she said softly. "You always have been." The knot of her hair wrinkled as she set her skull against the wall, holding his gaze. "My father was . . . unpredictable and unreliable, afraid of everything. You were a light in that, and you can't understand what that meant to me."

Bregan grimaced. He didn't deserve the gratitude in her soft words. Whatever she felt he'd done, it hadn't been enough. He could have— *should* have—done more to protect her from her father. Maybe if he had, the last four years would have been different.

He sighed. "Firin . . ."

"Please, Bregan." His name broke in her throat. "It's hard to talk about."

Saints, he could feel it, that door cracked open, just out of reach. This was the closest she'd ever drawn to directly discussing her father. He wanted to throw that door open, but she would only slam it shut in his face. Maybe even lock it. "All right," he made himself say.

Her lips trembled. "How's the investigation?"

"It's . . . shit," he admitted. She cleared a pile of scripts and newspapers so he could sit on the cot beside her. As he settled, he could feel her next to him, just outside his touch. "I'm not sure the new government is as secure as we hoped. The baron *needs* to win this election."

"Do you think he can?"

"I hope so. He's at the Grande now, trying to secure some donors."

She sat straighter. "He's at the Grande? Is he considering sponsoring them?"

"I . . . don't know." Bregan cracked his knuckles on his thigh. He hadn't even considered that, if the president were to patron the Grande, many of the city's wealthiest would follow suit, draining the resources the Veiled Players could access. Firin pulled her knees to her chest and stared, unfocused, at the opposite wall. Bregan gently squeezed her thigh. "He's there for a meeting with potential donors. It doesn't necessarily mean he's patroning the Grande."

When she met his eyes, they swirled with gold from the lamplight. Her leg was warm beneath his palm, the air thickened with her floral-laced citrus scent. It would be so easy to close the distance, to lay her beneath him and lose his worries in her skin. Years ago, she'd have let him. She would already have done it herself. But everything felt different now, strained, and he didn't know why.

"Let's go out," he said.

She raised a brow. "Don't you need to get back to work?"

"No." The entire future of Luisonn loomed over him, but there was little he could do until the council meeting. He took her hand. "Let's do something fun."

She chewed her lip. "Let's sneak into the Grande."

Bregan blinked. "I'm a constable, Firin. The *president* is there."

"So?" She got to her feet and stood between his knees. "Come on. We used to do it all the time. I want to see what kind of competition Veska's stirring up."

Bregan ran a thumb down the back of her hand. She wasn't wrong. They'd sneaked into the Grande a thousand times before. They wouldn't get caught.

Her smile reflected his defeat before he could admit it. As she pulled him off the bed, she let out a rare summer's-day kind of laugh, and he wondered, distantly, if there was anything in the world he wouldn't do just to hear the sound of it.

FORTY

Firin

Now

The Grande's tiny window was still broken. I pried it open, parted the velvet curtains, and listened. After a few seconds of quiet, I glanced back. Behind Bregan, the city stretched down toward the coast in familiar black waves, constant and unyielding despite how much had changed. When our gazes caught, my grip spasmed on the edge of the window.

I shouldn't have brought him. It would be much more difficult to spy on Baron Hulei now, but Bregan was a current I couldn't fight.

He dropped inside first, hitting the carpet with a muffled thud. Then he grabbed my waist to help me through. When I landed, he didn't pull away. A sliver of moonlight danced between the curtains, tracing the curve of his freckled jaw. Suddenly, his palms felt like brands.

He'd arrested Suri without flinching. He could kill me for what I was, would *hate* me if he knew, and I still had to fight to pull myself away.

I know a man who can cover up that scar.

The hope Mezua had handed me felt like a knifepoint at my spine, ready to strike if I moved or even breathed. If I could find a way to convince Hulei to patron us, and cover up my scar, I could have everything. But until then, my brand was a death sentence. I couldn't let Bregan close enough to even risk seeing it.

I slipped the whiskey flask from Bregan's pocket and smirked. Downing a clarifying swig, I headed for the maintenance door. The familiar must of old wood and dusty carpet enveloped us as I pushed it open into darkness with a soft *pop*.

Bregan's warmth curled against my back as we looked out on the hall. Rafters stretched out over a stage void of color. Dancers in gloomy black and white silks twirled like smoke to an eerie symphony. At their center, Sochya'tov moved like grace itself.

As I eased out onto the rafter, I watched the dancer, thinking of the night I took her face to con Suri. My gut twisted. Bregan hadn't imprisoned Suri, and she couldn't prove the arrest was my fault, but she *did* know I was behind the set collapsing. I needed to find a way to patch things up with her before her anger had time to fester.

Bregan shrugged out of his jacket. He kept one hand braced against the ceiling as he slid out onto the rafter behind me. The sleeve of his shirt fell back, revealing a freckled bicep. I swallowed. The rafter felt smaller than I remembered.

Attendees sparsely populated the seats below. The Grande's Vorstav'n-style dance was clearly suffering in the wake of the insurrection, but as soon as *The Pirate's Widow* opened, Luisonn's citizens would be banging down Veska's doors to see a true theater performance. Unless the Veiled Players presented a more seductive option.

Unless I found one.

Directly across the dance hall, in an elevated private box, Baron Hulei sat among two dozen coiffed attendees. I strained against the distance and dark, searching his guests' faces for one I could use. I needed to find out if he had already pledged patronage to the Grande. As long as he didn't announce anything publicly, I still had a chance to sway him, but it would be easier if he hadn't already made promises.

The stage lights shifted, spotlighting the blonde woman tucked into his side. *Hekita Nittaru.* A grin tugged at my lips. Hekita had been one of the baron's consorts for years. She was the daughter of a wealthy oil tycoon out of Iakirru and spent months at a time traveling between Luisonn and the royal cities. She was as obtuse and clumsy as a baby bird. She was perfect.

"I still can't believe Veska is planning to do a play here," Bregan whispered, looking down at the stage. "It doesn't feel real." He shrank back, settling his weight into his shoulders, and I knew he wasn't just talking about theater at the Grande.

"But it is real," I said. "You made it happen."

"Me and a lot of other people, many who died."

I twisted a little to face him more directly. "And if you don't *live*, what were their deaths for?" He looked up, and the shimmer of his agony wrenched at my heart. "You're allowed to enjoy it," I said.

Without breaking eye contact, he brushed a piece of hair from my face. Then his hand fell, sliding around my back, brushing down my branded arm over my bandage—mere fabric stretched over my fatal secret, flimsier than my resolve. When his hand settled on my hip, tucking me into his side, my gut clenched.

"Do you think Veska will have Sochya act?" he asked in my ear.

"Saints, I hope not," I muttered, watching the dancer onstage. "She can dance serdzat, but she has the emotional range of a sheep."

He chuckled. With half his torso flush against mine, I could feel his pulse racing through his shirt. Mine leaped in tandem, as if trying to keep up in a race I couldn't win.

The music swelled. The dancers twirled. Eventually, his chin rested in the crook of my neck. He drew circles on my hip with his thumb, just like he always had. It felt desperately unnatural not to turn and face him, like trying to fight an ocean's tide. My bones grew brittle under the effort.

A while later, the dance crescendoed to an emotional peak I couldn't follow. My focus was in tatters.

"Hey," Bregan whispered.

Like a fool, I looked back.

The stage lights played in the freckles on his face, painting a constellation I wanted to lose myself in. When the corner of his mouth curled, the vitality of his affection wrapped around me like thorns. His gaze dropped to my lips. I stopped breathing.

The audience lights burst to life like an explosion.

Intermission. I reeled back, clutching for purchase. What was I doing? This couldn't happen. Not yet.

I found Baron Hulei again. Lamps lit up in his private box as he got to his feet, his donors rising with him, jostling one another to reach his side. *He* was the reason I was here. He was my ticket to a world where I could love Bregan without fear.

The baron's consort, Hekita, rose with grace and reached for a knee-length, fur-lined coat of the finest Qunsiian fashion. She said something to the baron, then headed for the back of the box. This was my chance.

"I need to get out," I blurted.

"What?" Bregan said.

"I just . . . Just get out." I nudged him until he relented. As soon as I was on my feet in the hall, I brushed the dust from my skirts. "I need to use the facilities."

"The whole dance hall is roaming around right now."

"Exactly. No one will look at me twice."

Before he could protest further, I rushed into the corridor's dark embrace. Once I'd taken Hekita's face, I'd have precious minutes, maybe. I hurtled down the nearest steps, reaching for my illusion cord. By the time I got to the first floor, I was a stranger. Nyfe's dress wasn't nice enough to mark me as a guest, but I passed as one of the dozen backstage hands. At the end of the hall, a few dancers came around the corner. They didn't look at me twice. Voices rose, loud and emphatic, from the right. Audience members poured into the marble lobby, where I'd come with Father so many times.

There. The baron's date walked down the hall toward the washroom, her heels clicking loudly. That long black coat draped over her arm. I wove through the growing crowd.

Then a serving girl ducked into the hall like a gift from the saints. Balancing a tray of wines, she headed in Hekita's direction. As they neared each other I slowed and counted—and when they drew even, I knocked into the girl's side.

Hekita shrieked, lurching back, but it didn't help anything, as the wines slopped over the front of her embroidered silk wrap dress. Glass shattered on the marble floor.

"Oh, Aza," the servant girl gasped, "I'm so sorry, I'm so—"

"Get away from me," Hekita snarled, holding her unmarred coat to the side.

"Here," I said. "Let me take that for you." Another servant dived in with towels, and I grabbed the coat. Hekita barely noticed.

My dress wasn't a Kirru wrap and certainly wasn't embroidered silk, but it *was* blue, and beneath the coat it would work well enough.

As Hekita lit into the poor servant girl, I raced up the steps to the private boxes. By the time I reached the second floor, I'd donned the knee-length coat, gained several inches of height, and become Hekita Nittaru.

Half a dozen wealthy men and women milled around in the hallway marking the entrance to the baron's box. I used every bit of my new height to glare down my nose as I stepped through the curtains, not deigning to acknowledge them.

"Ah, darling." Hulei's familiar baritone voice slithered over my skin right before a cold hand caressed the nape of my neck. Then the baron's fleshy lips were on my temple. "I got us more wine," he crooned, placing the stem of a glass in my hand. I hoped he couldn't feel my pulse stuttering.

I took a sip of the drink, which was exquisite, and scanned the rest of the box. Well-dressed people scattered among small tables and plush seats. Some had faces I recognized, tradesmen and factory owners.

Subtle hints of blue and white decorated their ties and dresses, marking them Manager and Baron, even without class bands.

I didn't dare look up at the baron, lest he notice the wrong shade of my eyes, but I leaned in to him to ensure he didn't sense a lack of affection. I had minutes before I'd have to craft an excuse to leave again. I needed to turn the conversation to theater, quickly.

"The halls are positively crawling with people," I said in Hekita's sharp, rhythmic Kirru accent. "What are we—"

"Like I was saying," he interjected, "Draifey is riling the workers up. He's feeding them lies and platitudes to push them toward violence. I fear a Draifey presidency will lead us into just another kind of tyranny."

"Yes, yes. Draifey's a brute. But how do *you* plan to secure support?" Everyone fell silent. With a jolt of surprise, I recognized the woman who had spoken from the Nodtacht's target papers. She was a Reformist, one of the new regime's interim council members, and Merchant class. She was dressed as nicely as every Manager in the box.

"I already have the people's support," Hulei said with quiet steel.

The councilwoman spun her wineglass. "Yes, well, Draifey is not the only one the public's whispers name as a tyrant." Hulei's arm stiffened around me.

"Well," I sighed, leaping in with a hostess's grace, "what does everyone think of tonight's performance? Have you heard that Veska'nora is opening *The Pirate's Widow* next weekend?"

Hulei snorted. "She'll attempt it."

"You can't teach an old dog new tricks," a large Manager-class man in the back said. "Veska should stick to dance."

"I suppose we'll see," I said, loosening my grip on my wine. With that much disdain, Hulei couldn't be patroning the Grande. "I'm personally excited for the Veiled Players' opening."

Hulei shifted to look at me. "How did you know about that?"

My heart tumbled. I kept my lashes downcast. "Well, I—"

"Mezua Bentea's crew?" The Manager-class man laughed. "What are they putting on?"

"*Sweet Winter's Eve*," Hulei said, still watching me. "It's pure utilitarian Gwyn horseshit. The Players have been impressive in the past, but Mezua's struggling with her talent, and the shows she's picking aren't helping."

My chest caved. Of course. Hulei was a cutthroat Qunsiian businessman who valued individual merit and competition. *Sweet Winter's Eve* was a Gwyn drama about community, about love over perfection. No wonder he had turned Mezua down. She should have foreseen it. *I* should have.

"Well, darling, you're difficult to please." I brushed at his chest.

"How difficult can it be?" he scoffed. "In Osiv City, actors put the likes of *Qoyn & Insei* together in a week. How much leniency should I give those who can't even string together some Gwyn propaganda?" Several others laughed, all of them Qunsiian.

My wine nearly sloshed out of my glass.

Qoyn & Insei was the answer.

The box curtains swished. "Mr. President?" The elegant Vorstav'n voice was one I'd only ever heard on a stage. I spun to find Aza Veska'nora herself, peering down her sharp nose at me.

Shit.

"Yes, Aza?" Hulei's eyes flicked between me and the dance-hall owner.

"I was just going to tell you about Hekita's accident, but it seems she beat me." Her eyes glinted like daggers. Her thick, graying braid curled to her waist like a snake preparing to strike.

I coughed. "I was just . . ."

Veska's gaze—and then the baron's—slid down Hekita's coat, past my chest and knees, toward the blue hem that peeked out near the floor.

The hem that was not silk.

FORTY-ONE

Firin

Now

I flew up onto my toes and kissed Hulei's cheek, dragging his attention to my face.

"Ms. Nittaru?" Veska said, a bite in the name. Already, Hulei's brow was pinching.

"I'll wrap things up with the Aza," I said to him.

I swept out of the room, and Veska fell into step behind me. Saints, she was tall. Her heels clicked like rounds on an empty gun.

"Ms. Nittaru," she repeated.

"Everything is under control," I said, trotting down the steps to the lobby. "Thank you for your help."

"Hekita, if you would please—"

I bolted. Slipping into the throng of people filtering back to their seats, I dropped the coat to the floor and transformed. My bones throbbed as I shrank several inches; my hair bled back to brown. By the time I was on the other side of the room, I'd lost her. When I reached the maintenance corridor, I thought I might rattle out of my skin.

"Firin?" Bregan pushed off the wall, no more than a silhouette.

"I was seen. We have to go." I didn't want to be here when Hulei and Veska located the real Hekita.

I yanked the window open and scrambled out. Nyfe's dress snagged on the frame's rough edges. As soon as I hit the roof, I ran. When Bregan's fingers found mine, I gripped him like a lifeline. We bolted from roof to roof, sprinting from the Grande as fast as our lungs would allow, as if we were rebel kids again.

Five blocks away, my knees nearly gave out. We collapsed against a chimney. At the sudden inertia, my chest caved in. Then my lips trembled, and a laugh bubbled out, filling every corner of me. Bregan's laughs, pure and unfettered, joined mine, and I pressed my forehead against his shirt to stop my head from spinning.

I knew what to do.

If we put on *Qoyn & Insei*, Hulei would back us forever.

"Damn," Bregan breathed. "I haven't felt that alive in forever." When he pulled back, our eyes met and his smile faltered. "Can we stop with the games?"

The night froze.

"Bregan . . . ," I said softly.

"I love you, Firin. I always have. Nothing can change that."

The words crashed over me like a storm wave. *Yes,* I thought, *something can.* He had that burn of adoration again, the one I didn't deserve. When Bregan looked at me, he didn't see *me.* He saw someone I wasn't. Someone decent. But as I stared into that reverence, with the echoes of laughter still rising and falling in my chest, an old dream resurfaced on a breeze.

What if I could *become* that person?

If I could get Hulei to patron *Qoyn & Insei*, setting the theater up for decades, I could get rid of my scar. I could erase my past and truly start over. I could have Bregan. I could have theater. The Veiled Players. I could have everything. I just had to get through the next couple of weeks.

Bregan brushed a thumb down my cheek, sending a shiver to my core, and I teetered on the cliff's edge of desire, with no visible bottom. My gut fluttered, caught between caution and abandon. Here, right now, I had one true shot at an unmasked life.

But there was no Insei without Qoyn.

I couldn't do this without him, and Bregan didn't do anything halfway. For this to work, I had to be all in. I had to jump.

With an ache that rippled from my head to my toes, I rose to meet his lips.

Bregan

Now

The universe shifted back into place.

When Firin met his inquiry with a fierce answer, Bregan was knocked breathless by the dissonance. The newness versus the familiarity. Bright and clashing, as if he were reawakening for the first time in four years. He inhaled, tasting her mouth, and when he slid a hand up the back of her neck, she shivered delicately, like a bird settling into place.

Her smile flashed like a stubborn hint of spring, shoving up through cracks of gray, and yanked him back in time. To a memory so old it was more image than story: Ma and Pa dancing to a forbidden violinist's tune in the Spires, twirling together like a flame against the night.

He pressed his lips to her forehead, then to the corner of her eye, the side of her throat. When she moaned softly, he drank in the sound, running his hands up her hips, her sides, her back, relearning the shape of her body. Her fingernails raked down his chest, hardening every part of him.

When her back hit the chimney, he wedged his leg between hers, wanting to consume the closeness of her until he was drunk on it. Saints, her thighs were as soft as he remembered, hot against his palms as he slid them up her skirts. Propped against the wall, she arched into him, igniting a fire that—

Firin hissed.

"Shit," he panted. He'd grabbed her arm, where bandages covered her injuries from falling through the set. Bregan pulled back and set her on her feet, his heart racing. "I'm sorry."

Firin shook her head, eyes pinched shut. "It's okay."

"Are you sure?" he asked, kissing her collarbone. Her arm stiffened across her chest like a barrier. "I forgot myself, but we can slow—"

"I know how we can save the theater."

Bregan looked up. "The . . . theater?"

She pushed off the wall, her skirts fell, and Bregan stared.

"We should put on *Qoyn & Insei*," she said.

He swallowed, adjusted his pants. "That's impossible." *Qoyn & Insei* was ridiculously difficult. Never-ending costume and set changes, endless actors, a tricky score and an insane script. In Qunsii they said it was cursed.

"Not if the president patrons it."

Bregan's brain, still in a haze of arousal, struggled to process her words. "You want Hulei to sponsor the Players?"

"If the *president* of the Iket Isles sponsored us, we'd have more patrons flooding our doors than we knew what to do with. With you and I up there, we'd—"

"No." A chill wind swept through the space between them, rustling his shirt, scattering the rest of his lust.

"Think about it. If the Players—"

"I *can't* act right now." The kiss they'd just shared—the one *she* had initiated—felt like a delusion, so distant he could have imagined it.

Firin's mouth set in a line. "It's not forgiveness, Bregan."

"What?"

"Acting. Going onstage like she wanted you to."

Bregan barked a laugh. "This has nothing to do with my mother."

"No? Then what? You *won*, Bregan. The Stav can't hurt you, or the theater, or me, ever again."

"If only it were that simple." He backed up a step. "I have a job to do. I can't go gallivanting onstage and ignore it."

Exasperation sharpened her sigh. "Well, what if you don't have to? Sponsoring *Qoyn & Insei* could *help* the baron. He's losing the public's support." Her lashes flicked toward the horizon; then she exhaled more softly and straightened. "All my life I've had to fight against everything. My father, my plight, the path laid for me." She placed a palm over his racing heart. "But when we were together, I had something to fight *for*. Through *Qoyn & Insei*, Hulei could show the city he's willing to do the same for us."

Bregan's throat constricted. For as long as he could remember, he'd been on the defensive, fighting off threats to his life, to his loved ones, to their regime. The only time he'd ever even tried to dream had been that summer, with Firin, when she'd given him something to dream about. He thought of Draifey's campaign-rally pamphlet, the Labors with fists to the sky. Maybe Firin was right.

The Iket Isles had spent so long defending against the Stav that the moment they had their freedom, they only knew how to search for the next threat. They'd turned on the upper classes out of habit. But to what end? What was the point of overthrowing the Stav or winning the election if the country just continued to fracture?

"All right," he said. "I'll talk to him about it."

She laughed, and it was the warmest thing he'd ever heard. Grabbing his face, she kissed him again—a deep, joyful thing. When he pulled back, the ocean swimming in her eyes was more beautiful than the one on the moonlit horizon. Slowly, he reached for her. This time, she didn't flinch away. When he lifted her to the roof railing, careful not to touch her injuries, she wrapped her arms and legs around his waist.

"Thank you," she whispered against his lips—and for some reason, as he tightened his hold on her, a hole opened in his chest, like an echo of loss, as if to remind him that wanting something, *having* something, meant he had more to lose.

FORTY-TWO

Bregan

Now

The crowd outside the old Stav courthouse throbbed like fish packed into a barrel. As Bregan nudged his way to the front, reporters yelled at the council members climbing the steps for the regime's first government convening. Questions and accusations swirled in an incoherent cacophony reminiscent of the docks on import days.

At the front of the mass, constables in new gray uniforms held the public back like a solid stone wall. They nodded Bregan through, and instantly he felt like he could breathe again.

The commissioner climbed the steps beside him. "Restful night off?"

"Something like that," he replied, gaze forward. He and Firin had finally spent the night together—on his cot, completely clothed. For the first time ever, he'd held her that close, for that long, without burying himself in her skin. The strangeness of it had kept him up all night, watching her dream, wondering what she was dreaming about. He was so tired of searching for answers and finding only closed doors—with Draifey and Addym, with her. But he hadn't wanted to ruin the night with questions he knew she wouldn't answer.

The marbled courthouse bled wealth from its gilded seams, oozing tax money that the Stav had stolen from the Iket Isles. Gaudy as it was, at least the building belonged to the people now as the big double doors thudded closed, replacing the noise from outside with the echoed murmurs of mingling council members and their staff.

"Is Draifey here?" he asked, lowering his voice.

"Not yet."

Bregan nodded. Good. "Where's the president?" He needed to ask Baron Hulei about *Qoyn & Insei* before the meeting started.

The commissioner sniffed, then pointed. "He's down the hall. I should warn you, he's a bit . . . rattled. There was an assassination attempt last night."

Bregan's heart stopped dead in his chest. "What? Where?"

"Someone attempted to enter his private box at the Grande. We believe it was a Nodtacht. He's fine, just irritated. He plans to inform the rest of the council today."

Rancid heat swept through Bregan. He and Firin must have *just* missed the chaos. He hadn't been on duty, but still. They shouldn't have been lurking in the shadows like thieves. "Does he think it was Draifey?"

"Or the Stav," the commissioner said. *Or both,* he didn't need to add. "He's in here."

Bregan hesitated outside the small side office. It seemed insensitive, asking the president to sponsor a play in the wake of an attempt on his life, but Firin was right. They couldn't bank their success solely on Draifey's demise. Hulei had to win this election.

When Bregan stepped inside, the president's chair screeched as he launched to his feet. "Have you seen this? Draifey's not coming today." Hulei brandished a freshly printed newspaper. Compared to his usual sleekness, he looked positively feral. His hair stood on end like mussed straw, and his wrinkled shirtsleeves were rolled up. Even his tie was askew.

The commissioner spread the *Luisonn Daily* atop the room's small desk.

FREE ISLES OF IKET NOT AS FREE AS PROMISED

As we stand on the ashes of our oppressors, it gives me no pleasure to announce that another tyranny has stirred beneath the belfries of gods and saints. Today I am boycotting the first meeting of our promised Council of the Free Isles of Iket because it is not as promised. It is not free. It is not of the people. It was never intended to be. Our new leaders have plotted to remove the very rights and freedoms they promised us. They sent government spies to tail Labor Party leaders and executed two party members in an attempt to set back any competition. It is clear they intend to win this election by any means necessary—at best, corruption; at worst, a use of force that I fear may rival the infamous Fifthday.

A true election is not to be relied upon. The sun has yet to set on Iket Isles that are free. For the baron who helms us may yet prove an emperor of just another name...

Bregan stared at the still-wet ink, his head spinning.

Draifey wasn't *wrong*, exactly. Yes, they had someone tailing him, but only as a precaution; and yes, they had made Vorkot and Espurra disappear, but only to protect them from retaliation in a high-security safe house in the West End. Draifey had taken the facts and skewed them to his advantage.

"Last night, and now this." Hulei jammed a finger into the paper, smearing the headline. "Makes sure I can't go public about the assassination attempt without it looking like a pathetic cry of innocence."

Bregan couldn't respond. He was right.

Hulei whirled on the commissioner. "Draifey may have no class or finesse, but he's clearly not stupid. He controls the narrative now." The baron glared like a trapped animal, lashing out at whatever was within its reach. Draifey had published this article to push him over the edge, and it was working.

"Draifey doesn't control the narrative," Bregan said quickly. "He's merely redirected it."

"What do you mean?" Hulei spit.

"He's banking on a response from you that further fuels violence. But people are *tired*; they want peace more than anything. You just need to feed them a different story."

"What do you propose?"

"*Deliver* on the promises of the revolution: Peace and prosperity for all classes. Show support for the lower classes. Pull together Barons to deliver charity to the Zed and Labor districts. Announce the plan for education. Sponsor arts the Stav would have killed us for. The Veiled Players are doing *Qoyn & Insei*; that would be a great place to start."

Hulei's nose wrinkled. "*Qoyn & Insei?*"

"If they can secure the funds, they can pull it off."

"With what talent?"

"They have a new actress."

Hulei shook his head. "I can talk to the trade Barons about a charity announcement and move up the proposed education policies, but *Qoyn & Insei* isn't logical. If Mezua still had you, perhaps she'd stand a chance. But we'll have to—"

"I'm playing Qoyn," Bregan said without thinking.

The president's entire brow knit. "You are?"

Bregan hesitated. He hadn't entirely committed to Firin last night. Rehearsing would distract from his investigation. But there was nothing saying he *couldn't* take a stage role, and if that was what it took to pique the baron's interest, then so be it. "Yes, sir. *Qoyn & Insei* can remind the public of what you earned for them. Pour money into a theater that suffered under the Stav. Highlight the Reformist heroes onstage and the play that, just a month ago, we would have been murdered for. Open the ground floor to former-Labor attendees. Prove to people that you're not the villain Draifey claims by *giving* them a different future."

Hulei rubbed the heel of his palm into his forehead. "I'll think about it."

A knock sounded. A secretary entered. "Excuse me, Mr. President, the council would like a private meeting before we start the session."

With a quick tug on his jacket and a hand through his hair, the baron's frustration vanished in a flash of smile. "Of course."

"The play, sir?" Bregan pressed. To pull it off, the Players would need money soon.

"We'll circle up later," Hulei said, leaving with the commissioner on his heels.

"Mr. Nimsayrth?" the secretary added, still in the doorway. "There is a messenger in the lobby for you."

In the lobby a Labor-class boy hovered near the wall, fingers twitching at his sides. When he saw Bregan, his face lit up with relief. "Sir, I've a message from 89 Steeple Street. They ask to see you right away."

The address was where Bregan had hidden Vorkot and Espurra's family. He wondered what they could possibly need so urgently. After thanking and dismissing the boy, he glanced toward the council room. Without Draifey there, his presence was no longer necessary. It would be tight, making it back to the theater in time for Firin's planned troupe meeting, but it would have to work. He set off across town.

An hour later he climbed the few steps of 89 Steeple Street and banged on the door. The housekeeper he had hired poked his head out. "Right this way, sir."

They wove down a dark, sagging hallway, past a room full of giggles, to a small kitchen in the back. Vorkot jumped to his feet, white hair swept to one side as if he'd been continually running his fingers through it. He brandished the day's paper at Bregan, the same one Hulei had just read.

"Sir," the prison guard gasped, "I know how you can find Draifey's people. They're meeting on Fifthday at sunset." He pointed to Draifey's article. "He used an old code that us prison guards used with him. *The belfries of gods and saints*—that's what we used to call the warehouses where we'd meet with Draifey."

"Why would he use an old code?" Bregan asked.

Vorkot shrugged. "He must assume I'm dead." He pointed at the article again. "He named *Fifthday* and *sunset* because that's when it'll happen. This article is a call for his followers. They're going to meet in the Spires in six days."

FORTY-THREE

Firin

Now

The nave crackled with anticipation as the troupe took their seats for our first meeting after the stage disaster. As they entered, everyone's eyes flicked from my bandaged arms—revealed by the sleeveless dress I'd borrowed from Nyfe—to Mezua beside me, to the decimated *Sweet Winter's Eve* balcony behind us. Everyone's except Jaq's. With Phinnin curled in his lap, he stared, hollow-eyed, at the ruins of his creation.

Suri trickled in at the back of the group, arms wrapped around herself like a shield. The others gave her a wide berth. When she met my gaze across the room, the contours of her wounded-child charade shifted, exposing a glare. A shiver ran down my spine.

"Where's Bregan?" Mezua asked under her breath.

"I don't know," I said, wiping sweaty palms on my skirts. He had promised he'd be back from the courthouse in time to help us announce our *Qoyn & Insei* plans to the troupe.

"You're sure he's committed?" she asked.

"Yes," I said, but my stomach twisted. He had promised to help, but I was just now realizing he hadn't *explicitly* agreed to play Qoyn. I kept my bandaged arms loose at my side and my shoulders set. For this

E.B. Golden

to work, the troupe needed to see unabashed confidence. We couldn't afford a breath of doubt. If I had to convince him, I would. Bregan wouldn't let the Veiled Players suffer, not if he alone could save them.

"We'll have to start without him," Mezua said, her words drowned by the troupe's amicable chattering. "Don't mention the president."

I tore my focus from the pews. "Why?" Our plan to get Hulei's patronage was the only reason we could consider putting on *Qoyn & Insei*.

"The play itself will be enough for them to swallow," she said.

Before I could protest, Jaari broke from the others, bounding toward me. "Vota," she exclaimed. Hovering slightly too close, she glanced at my bandages, then lightly touched my wrist. "How are you feeling? We were worried when you weren't at breakfast."

The brush of her fingers sent bumps up my arm. Without the dripping distrust she had harbored for days, she shone. Her smile broadened her round face and wrinkled her pretty nose as she blinked her ridiculously long lashes at me. It should have been harder to push down my irritation than it was, but her guilt was so painfully genuine.

"I'll be fine," I said, taking her hand. When she squeezed my fingers, I felt my place in the troupe shift like settling sand.

Easing closer, she murmured, "The constabulary released Suri last night. I told Mezua we should let her go. I don't know why she's still here."

"I'm sure it was an accident," I said.

Jaari's frown said she disagreed, but at that moment, Mezua waved a hand at her, shooing her to sit down, and Jaari slid into a pew beside Luka. I stayed at the front as Mezua stepped forward. She opened her arms wide in welcome.

"Good morning, everyone. After yesterday's freakish mishaps, we're fortunate that no one was gravely injured." Troupe members glanced toward Suri, but she only had eyes for me. Her lips thinned. "Now, while this has set back our plans with *Sweet Winter's Eve*, I think it's also an opportunity to pivot."

Jaq tore his eyes from the ruins of the set. "Again?"

I stepped up beside Mezua. "The patronage we need will require performing something flashier, something that will make headlines."

"Like what?" Tez grunted.

"*Qoyn & Insei*," I said.

Gasps popped like firecrackers.

"You can't be serious."

"The dances are impossible."

"We don't have enough costumes."

"Just the *music score* is cursed."

"*Qoyn & Insei* is one of the world's most famous plays," I said, silencing the room. "The mere fact that we're attempting it will draw interest."

"I think it's a great idea," Jaari piped up. She winked at me. "Why not make a splash?"

"Because it's expensive," Tez said, "and there's not enough time. Even if we had the money and worked around the clock, we could never open before the Grande."

"We don't have to," I said. "As long as we *announce* our premiere before the Grande opens, all the city's biggest patrons will be too curious to commit to Veska'nora until they see how our performance pans out."

"Or they'll laugh at our hubris and reject us," Luka said, their feet propped on the wall of the pew in front of them. The mocking curve of their lips lit a spark in my chest. Doubt was a rot that would spread. We needed the troupe's full, unwavering faith if we were going to pull this off.

"They won't," I said, stepping forward without looking at Mezua. "Because we're going to get the president's patronage."

There was a long, shocked pause—then Luka dropped their boots to the floor with an echoing slap. "Hulei?" They turned to Mezua. "Absolutely not. You said no more politics."

"This isn't politics." Mezua sighed, sliding me a look that said, *This is what I was afraid of.*

"We need the favor of wealthy people," I said, "and those are people who will follow Baron Hulei's lead."

Luka pulled at their cropped hair. "We risked our lives for Hulei, we lived in hiding for four years because of him, and what do we have to show for it?"

"Our freedom," Jaq said quietly, bouncing a wide-eyed Phinnin on his knees.

"He already turned his back on us by not supporting *Sweet Winter's Eve*," Luka said. "I'm not on board with flashing *Qoyn & Insei* in his face like desperate children."

"Sit," Jaari snapped, pulling at the conductor's sleeve. "You're making a scene."

Luka ignored her. "The *Labors* won the rebellion, not Hulei."

"Stop it," Jaari said. But Luka had already left the pew. Their red-velvet coattails flared as they stalked down the center aisle, pulling my gut with them. Mezua had only agreed to *Qoyn & Insei* because she knew Luka could manage the tricky scores. We couldn't do this without them.

Then the temple's door creaked with a deluge of morning light.

Bregan stepped inside.

He intercepted Luka in the aisle. The conductor said something, Bregan responded; then he clapped Luka on the shoulder, turning them around. "Morning," he said. The troupe eyed him warily. Barely anyone had seen him over the last week. "I'm sorry I'm late. Have they told you I'm playing Qoyn yet?"

Cast members burst to their feet with overlapping variations of *Are you really?* and *Are you messing with us?* Relief nearly bowled me over. Luka looked like they'd swallowed a lemon, but they let Bregan lead them back to the front of the room. Mezua squeezed my wrist.

"Who will play the queen?" Nyfe asked, her voice rising above the din.

Mezua smiled. "I will. Vota will play Insei."

"Tez will play the Sage King," I added. "Suri, Insei's sister."

Suri's chin lifted. While Mezua continued listing off roles and responsibilities, I gave her a small smile. We needed her to pull this off. She didn't smile back.

The nave exploded with activity. People hurdled over pews, bounding for Bregan, descending on him like gulls on food. At his return, all the doubt disappeared like morning dew—and I felt strangely like a child again, watching the world from a tenement window.

"Hey," Bregan said, escaping the group to kiss me, chasing away the sensation.

"Where were you?" I asked, stepping into a pew to let a disgruntled Luka pass, Jaari chittering angrily in their ear. As Bregan ran a casual touch down my side, I resisted the urge to curl against him. Last night, with his body pressed against mine, I'd barely slept. At least a thousand times, I considered waking him with my lips. With my scar hidden beneath bandages, I could have, but then what? I had weeks to get through before it was truly safe.

"Had to go across town," he said, "but I got a lead on something else I can move on in a few days."

My heart leaped. "Can you stay and rehearse, then?"

"For today, at least."

I lowered my voice. "Did you talk to Hulei?"

"I did . . . he's going to be difficult to convince."

"Why?" *Qoyn & Insei* was everything Baron Hulei should drool over.

"Talent, I think, and he's worried it's a distraction from the campaign and investigation. I did what I could, but we might want to consider other patrons, just in case."

Talent concerns were easy to assuage. I just needed to get Hulei into the temple.

"Bregan?" Mezua appeared behind us like an apparition. "Can you help Jaq with some preliminary set-design ideas?" When he left, she took his place in the pew beside me. "What did he find out?" she asked quietly.

At the front of the room, Jaq waved his hands in arcs before the stage, painting a stage vision for Bregan. In the center aisle, Luka scratched their head, debating with the other musicians. Nyfe was dragging Suri from the nave to help her with costumes. I hesitated. They were excited, hopeful. They wanted to believe this was possible, and as long as they believed it, it was.

I could manage Hulei. There was no reason to sow doubt.

"The president is interested," I lied. "We just need to prepare for him."

Mezua exhaled. "Wonderful. Let's get you and Bregan onstage as soon as he finishes with Jaq."

"I'll help Nyfe with costumes in the meantime," I offered.

In the western corridor, boxes already spilled out of the costume room. Inside, racks stretched from wall to wall, a veritable treasure trove of sizes, origins, and time periods. Nyfe knelt in a pile on the floor, holding up various options.

"We'll need something for the Qunsiian fifth age that'll fit Vota," she shouted to Suri, who was somewhere among the rows, "and something from the seventh that'll work for Bregan. Oh, Vota! Can you see if there's a pirate costume that'll work for Iaqunsiad in the third age? In the back row there."

I found Suri sliding hanger after hanger to the side. "Suri?"

Without turning, she said, "What?"

"I hope there's no hard feelings about yesterday," I said. "With the accident and all." She raised one eyebrow. "We need you, for *Qoyn & Insei*. You're talented; you'll play the sister well. I think we can agree that we both have the troupe's best interests in mind. This could secure their future. *Our* future."

She stared blankly at my bandages, and I prayed she would choose reason. If what she wanted was a place in the Veiled Players, if she wanted the Players to *survive*, she had no option but to play along. We both knew that. But I'd seen people pick revenge against worse odds. Anger was often more powerful than reason.

I didn't want to have to get rid of her, even though arranging for her to stay—when she'd seen beneath my mask *and* resented me—went against all my rules of self-preservation. It was true that we needed someone to play Insei's sister, but it didn't *have* to be her. I couldn't deny that my motivations needled deeper, that some dangerous part of me wanted to prove that, moving forward, things could be different—*I* could be different.

"I'm glad you're not more hurt," she said wryly. "For the troupe's sake."

"The saints were generous," I said.

She snorted softly, pushing another costume down the rack. As I turned to leave, she added, "For what it's worth, I think it's a good idea, *Qoyn & Insei.*"

"Thanks," I said, careful not to reveal anything on my face, but as I slid back down the aisle, tension seeped out of me like fog in a morning breeze.

I ran my fingers over the various fabric textures, searching until my eyes snagged on exactly what I needed: a red-and-yellow-pinstripe suit. I smiled.

FORTY-FOUR

Firin

Then

Almost every table at Atzuie's was occupied. I scanned the restaurant, bumps dancing up my arms. My target, a Manager-class man who ran a carriage factory, sat at a front window table with a suited associate. Over the last few months, I'd unearthed that both of them were sourcing raw materials from the same black-market supplier out of Iakirru.

I needed the name of their supplier.

After spying in the lowest Nodtacht ranks for endless months, I'd been assigned to the Second Division a year ago, tasked with unearthing treason and dissent in Luisonn. Despite my official placement, it seemed like my Third Division tails—the Nodtacht tasked with sniffing out treason *within* the Stav's ranks—had increased in number.

Skavka'tor, my Nodtacht handler, never let me forget that she didn't trust me. No matter how hard I tried to identify and shake the spies she set to track me, she always knew more than she should. If I hoped to escape Luisonn, I needed to get out from under her heel. Which meant I needed a promotion.

If I could learn the identity of the black-market supplier, I might earn the attention of the higher-ups in my division and have a chance of snagging a higher-profile case that would finally earn me fewer tails and a longer leash.

Unfortunately, all the tables nearest my targets were occupied.

"Right this way," the hostess said, waving her arm toward the back of the restaurant.

I gripped my date's arm. "I'd like a seat by the window."

"We don't have any open seats at the window," the hostess said.

My date sneered down his pointed nose. Wealth oozed from the embroidered seams of his jacket and puffed-up posture. He was a Manager, and he wanted the world to know it. "Make one," he demanded.

The hostess paled but caved quickly. Wringing her hands, she headed toward a Merchant-class couple near my target. I looked away so I wouldn't have to see their disappointment, and spotted Baron Hulei.

I blinked several times, but it was definitely him. The former Reformist lounged in the very back of the restaurant with a man in a bright-red pin-striped suit. I hadn't seen Hulei since the Stav shot him on Bloody Fifthday. The *Stav Observer* had said he'd been exiled to Qunsii shortly after. My pulse quickened. Why was he back?

"Wait," I blurted. The hostess halted between tables. My date raised his eyebrows as I folded my trembling hands behind my back. "Actually, it's all right. We can sit in the back." There was an empty table next to the baron's. Gathering valuable intel on him could earn me attention from *all* the Nodtacht divisions.

The relieved hostess led us to the back. My date muttered under his breath that it was "really fine," as if taking the Merchants' table would inconvenience him, not them. I blocked him out, my head swimming.

This was a gamble. A risky one.

Skavka'tor would know that I'd abandoned my assignment. If I gathered something good on Hulei, she wouldn't punish me—but that was a big *if*.

We drew so close to the baron's table that I could have touched him. The man in the red suit looked up. When he caught me staring, he flashed a handsome, crooked smile. The brown of his eyes swept over me, the same shade and saturation of his golden-brown skin, and he leaned back, tugging at his blood-bright-striped jacket. A rope of dark hair curled over his shoulder.

"Ahem." My date coughed.

Baron Hulei broke off midsentence, noticing us. My date sniffed at them like a disgruntled schoolboy. The handsome stranger's grin widened.

"Excuse me," I said, half curtsying as I eased into the chair directly behind Hulei. Gazes always lingered when I wore this face—that of a Kirru businessman's beautiful daughter. The stranger's attention didn't mean anything, but my heart insisted on pounding anyway.

"Apologies, Mr. Diosi," a waitress said behind me. "We are out of that vintage." I cataloged his name. He was Qunsiian.

"So, your father is in minerals?" my date asked. He was fine looking, with dark hair and a close-cut beard. Sometimes when I wore this face, I let men take me home. I accepted their expensive courting gifts to pawn later, then lost myself in their touch. It warded away the hollowness that had consumed me since Bloody Fifthday, even if just for a few lustful moments. But my date tonight had an unsettling gleam in his eyes, as if I were a ship he might purchase. I would not be going home with him.

"Yes, he mines gold in Iakirru," I said.

He smirked. "Well, I've been talking with jewel traders out of Qunsii . . ." He filled the air with mindless, boastful rambling. I opened a menu.

"She starred in *The Witch's Heart* at the university," Mr. Diosi was saying. "Best performance I've seen in a decade. An absolute gem."

"Interesting," Hulei replied.

My palms were sweating. If I had abandoned my orders to listen in on a discussion about actresses, Skavka'tor would be furious. She would question my loyalty, considering the baron had once been a Reformist.

The edges of my vision blurred. The ghost of water pressed in on my ears, up my nose, burning my throat. I tasted the echo of salt and blood. Skavka's voice bounced through my skull, as it had off the walls of a Nodtacht cell: *You must know something.*

I dug my nails into my palms.

Focus, Firin.

"Have you been?" my date asked. I'd completely lost track of his soliloquy.

"Yes, of course," I lied. "My apologies, I just can't figure out what to eat."

He flashed a set of brilliant-white teeth. "I've had the oysters before; they're decent, though they're not from the North Shore . . ." As he dived into a new monologue, I made sure to keep a half-interested look on my face. At the front of the restaurant, my original targets leaned across the table toward one another, deep in a hushed conversation. There was still time to switch tables.

"Doesn't matter," Diosi said behind me. "I'm telling you, she is *incredible.*"

A chair creaked. Hulei sighed. "I just don't like to invest in what I haven't seen."

"Even if her father's the chair of J. Junsai & Co.?"

I leaned back. The Qunsiian steel baron, J. Junsai, had been all over the papers recently for his new inventions.

"That sleaze?" Hulei asked. "He all but told me he's evading the Stav's taxes in his partnerships with that Kirru mine. I don't need more trouble, Heynri. He's just a Reformist with a new face and lower morals."

"Ma'am?"

I nearly jumped out of my skin. Our waitress was back, poised to take my order.

"Oysters, please," I said faintly.

This I could use. J. Junsai evading taxes was nearly as juicy as my initial target's supplier's identity—and if Junsai *did* hold dissenting ideals, that was even better.

I nodded along with my date's winding story with one ear on the debate behind me. But as I broke into my oysters, it was difficult not to let my mind stray to what this information could do, the trust it would build. A rare heat stirred in my gut, flushing out some of the numbness that had long ago taken root.

In my years with the Stav, I'd put so much energy into the outer layers of myself—false faces and stories and desires—that I'd starved the part of me that was real. Firin had withered inside me until she vanished, leaving me an empty shell. The only thing that echoed inside the cavern I'd become was the promise of freedom, that when I left Luisonn, I could fill myself back up, become someone new. An actress, a farmer, a tradeswoman. I didn't care, as long as I was free.

When dinner finally ended, I was vibrating. I wanted to get to headquarters. My date pulled out my chair, slipped his arm into mine.

Then Heynri Diosi whispered, "Have they tried to contact you?"

My heart tripped.

"They have," Hulei replied just as quietly. "They've scattered, but they think they can regroup. I told them I'm not interested."

They were talking about the Reformists.

"Are you all right?" my date asked.

"Yes. I just . . ."

"I think most of them are in Fisherman's Wharf," Hulei continued, "hiding out in saints-damned basements, pretending they can bounce back."

A ringing filled every hollow corner of me, screeching and dissonant. Since Bloody Fifthday, the surviving Reformists had been mostly quiet. I had encountered them once, so I knew they were still out there, but I didn't know if Bregan was still among them. I didn't even know if he was alive. I shivered as a wound tweaked in my chest, a pain so old it had become part of me, like a bullet my skin had grown over.

"I need air," I said, leading my date outside before I heard anything from Hulei or Diosi that I couldn't *un*hear. The Nodtacht had questioned me about the Reformists before; they wouldn't hesitate to do it again.

Information about tax evaders and rebels was one thing, but intel on the Reformists' locations—even *vague* intel—would win the entire Nodtacht organization's attention. It could remove my leash completely. But what if Bregan was with them?

Everyone is out for themselves, I heard Father say. *You should be too.*

But I couldn't. I couldn't do it. Not if there was even a *chance* that Bregan was still alive, hiding with the Reformists.

In a daze, I let my date walk me "home" to an apartment on Regents'. I agreed to another dinner invitation I wouldn't attend. By the time I reached headquarters, I could barely breathe. When I burst into Skavka's office, wearing a new face, she looked up from paperwork.

"What is it?" she snapped in Vorstav'n.

"Baron Hulei is back."

"We know," a deep voice answered. I jumped. Eznur was lounging in one of the chairs near the door, his hook-shaped scar shining like a second smile. "We were just discussing it."

"He met with a man named Heynri Diosi," I said, spilling every word I'd heard about actresses, J. Junsai, and tax evasion.

I said nothing about the Reformists.

As I spoke, Eznur started to smile and Skavka began to scowl. When I finished, she asked, "What about your target?"

"I felt this was more important," I said. Her nostrils flared.

"Anything else?" Eznur's eyes flicked over my face.

"No." I hoped he couldn't see my pulse jumping at my throat.

"She can do it," he said.

"What?" Skavka snapped.

Eznur stood, filling the room. "I'm taking her. Have her file moved to my office." I stared as he waved a hand toward the hall. "You report to me now. I'm assigning you to tail Baron Hulei."

FORTY-FIVE

Bregan

Now

Salt winds ripped at Bregan's face as if the sea were angry he'd neglected her. Wet sand sank beneath his boots as he crouched behind a pile of fishing traps and signaled his unit of constables to do the same. For the first time since the insurrection, a pistol's smooth, cold barrel hung heavy in his grip, the weight like a promise.

Tonight, he would corner Draifey.

Between the ropes of the fishing traps, Bregan could just make out the Spires, columns of leaning wooden apartments set against Fisherman's Wharf's northern cliffs. Rocky beaches spread at their base, strewn with stone piers built in the time before the Stav by Pa's ancestors.

Bregan hadn't been in this part of the city for years. Lanterns flickered behind the Spires' hundreds of windows, and the soft-yellow light thawed a raw, wounded part of him. Once, back before everything, he'd known true happiness within the warm, unpolished walls of his grandparents' Spires home. It had been a haven of brine and bread, bony hugs and soft wrinkles, a place where he'd dreamed, wished, and believed. But then his uncle had joined the Reformists, and his entire family had been executed for it, and the Stav had taken the apartment when his grandparents were deemed "unfit" to qualify for Labor class due to the simple crime of old age.

It was hard to look at the Spires, even in the dark, and not think of his cousin: chasing cats, throwing rocks, and racing piers—and whenever he thought of his cousin, he saw that red stain blooming on his chest.

Clenching his jaw, Bregan tore his focus from the upper homes to the lowest levels of the precarious housing monstrosity, where wide, open market halls comprised the towers' foundations. During the day, the halls overflowed with fish, fishermen, and fishmongers. At night they sat empty, the perfect place to hide a secret meeting.

Since Vorkot uncovered the meeting in the *Daily* article, the constabulary had lain low, not wanting to give Draifey any indication that they were on his tail. Even though Bregan's days had been full of rehearsing *Qoyn & Insei*, the wait had nearly driven him mad. Well, that and Firin. He thought they had broken down the barrier between them at the Grande, had hoped she might finally open up, but whenever they got a moment alone, she always seemed to find an excuse to leave, as if she were still avoiding him.

The whites of eyes peered through the dark, waiting for Bregan's instructions. Most of the new constables were barely out of boyhood and straight from factories. None of them were Reformists. Bregan hoped that his training over the last six nights would prove enough to keep them in line if things turned for the worst.

The plan was to surround the warehouse and listen in on the meeting. Once they heard proof of Draifey's treason, they would bust in and arrest him. Since Draifey wouldn't expect them, Bregan hoped things wouldn't escalate.

Across the beach, a lamplight waved in an arc three times. The commissioner's signal. Their target was the third market hall from the east, based on Vorkot's intel. Its doors stood shut.

Bregan pointed his unit into the foggy night. They sauntered toward the Spires in their Labor-class disguises, trying to laugh and heckle as if they were just dock boys off shift, but their voices strained, their focus darted nervously. He led them toward the market hall adjacent to their target, which had its doors flung wide open. They slipped inside, boots splashing in fish blood and guts, and wound through stacks of crates waiting for the morning's haul.

When a circle of lamplight bounced ahead, Bregan halted. He raised a finger to his lips and motioned them into a crouch. Clipping his gun on the back of his belt, he eased forward alone.

A fisherman leaned against a side door, which Bregan guessed led into their target market hall. He held a lamp and a rusty handgun. Bregan recognized him instantly as one of his grandfather's old friends. With his heart thumping a slow, regretful beat, he stepped into view.

The fisherman pushed off the wall. His age lines were as familiar as a bedtime story, like the legends he'd once told Bregan on the steps of his grandparents' apartment building. "Bregan?" he said, eyes wide.

"Rocky. I was wondering if I'd see you here."

The man shook his hand. "Son, what are you doing here? You're not—"

With a sickening lurch, Bregan slammed the butt of his gun into Rocky's temple. When he collapsed, Bregan caught him. The old man groaned softly as Bregan propped him against the wall. He would be fine. He'd wake in a bit with a headache, but by then they'd be done. They'd have to be. At least Rocky would be safe out here if things did go sideways.

Raising the lamp, Bregan pressed his ear to the door. The rumble of voices on the other side was so loud he couldn't distinguish any single one. This was more than a small campaign meeting. With sweat beading on his brow, he eased the door open.

The market hall beyond was a bonfire of lamplight shining on hundreds of dirty, grim faces. Half the damn Labor District had to be here. Bregan shut the door, suddenly sweating, and waved the other constables out of hiding. They wouldn't hear anything from this side of the door.

"Go inside, spread out. Just blend in," he said. "You're here for the same reason as everyone else, understand? Don't do *anything* without my explicit signal." They were less likely to be recognized than he was, so he sent them in first.

When he followed, Bregan hunched his shoulders, eyes on the ground. Even though he'd been underground for years, people in here—people like Rocky—might still recognize him.

They'd emerged near the back of the hall. Not far away, on top of a stack of crates, Addym Taidd addressed the room in a booming voice. "This Luisonn is not what was promised. We will not be free until one of our *own* sits on Regents' Hill." Cheers split the night like firecrackers.

Pulling his cap lower, Bregan peeked up. Draifey leaned against the opposite wall, a cigarette dangling from his grin. Not far away, the commissioner stood in disguise, his own undercover unit spread out behind him.

They locked eyes, and Bregan shook his head. This wasn't the time or place for an arrest. There were too many people. If there was a shootout, innocents would get hurt. They were better off gathering intel and getting out of here.

To his relief, the commissioner nodded; then he jerked his chin toward a propped door on Bregan's side of the room. The market-hall office. If Draifey was using this as a meeting spot, it could also be his headquarters.

Bregan motioned his team to stand down—and found every one of them staring at him. For saints' sake. The boys were going to give themselves away. He slashed his hand, and they dropped their chins like he'd struck them, finally dispersing. Then he sauntered toward the receiving office with his hands in his pockets.

"And now," Addym said, "I'd like to invite Thom Draifey himself to speak with you."

The room exploded with cheers, and Bregan used the distraction to enter a dark office so small he could have touched all four walls without moving. Notes and receiving slips covered a desk without a chair. He flipped through them, heart racing, but found nothing of interest.

Then he noticed the crate of papers under the desk. He snagged the top one: a freight receipt. Beneath that, an accounting paper had *Campaign Expenses* scrawled across the top, followed by several clippings of Draifey's recent article and a couple about Hulei.

Bregan glanced again at the freight receipt and realized it wasn't a receipt—it was a promise to pay. It read SILISIA SALT TRADERS across the top, with a shipment date and location, and a request for payment to a Bank of Luisonn account. He stared at the astronomical fee. Draifey's campaign couldn't possibly need such a ridiculous amount of salt.

"Hey," a familiar voice called outside. Bregan dropped the receipt. "Who's in—"

He threw a satisfying fist into Addym's gut. The other man grunted, eyes widening, as Bregan shoved past him. Then Addym ripped out his gun.

Bregan leaped into the crowd, careening off the broad shoulders of fishermen and factory workers. Addym wouldn't shoot around so many innocent people. He pushed his way through the throng, aiming for what he hoped was another side door.

Bang.

The gunshot reverberated. Someone screamed.

Bregan turned. An old man toppled into Addym, red flowering on his chest. One of the young constables—who was *supposed* to have been lying low—gaped at the dying man with his shaking gun outstretched, smoke curling from its tip.

There was a hanging moment.

Then shots rang out everywhere. Labors shoved at one another like sheep pouring off a boat. Before Addym could extricate himself from the poor soul who'd taken the shot meant for him, Bregan disappeared into the panicked flow.

He was scanning for an exit when he saw him: the sandy-haired Stav with the broken nose, the prison guard Draifey had let go. The man Vorkot swore was a Nodtacht.

He ducked through a side door, heading into the next market hall. Bregan tore after him, back into a maze of crates that glowed silver in the moonlight pouring through the open front doors.

Gravel crunched to his right. Bregan raced after the sound, through stack after stack of crates, then skidded into the hall's wide center aisle, gun raised.

Bang. Fire ripped through Bregan's arm. He roared, tripped, and threw himself to the floor behind a pile of barrels, pressing a hand to his wounded bicep. The man's aim was impeccable, which meant he likely *had* spared Bregan's life at the prison—but had no intention to do so now.

The next shot skimmed the barrel above his head.

Bootsteps drew closer.

Bregan hoisted his pistol with bloodied fists. He had to finish this, immediately. He released a centering breath, then shot the ceiling. In the second's distraction, he threw himself to the ground, landed on his injured shoulder, and aimed right for the Stav's chest.

The bastard went down like a stone.

Bregan scrambled to his feet, weapon aimed. If the man was still alive, he might get proof that Draifey was working with the Nodtacht. Shaking with adrenaline, he eased closer and kicked the man's gun aside, listening past his pounding pulse for anyone nearby.

The guard made a horrible gurgling sound. In the moonlight pouring through the warehouse's front doors, his blood bubbled black at his lips. Bregan withdrew his knife and cut into the dying man's sleeve. An X marred his upper arm. The dying Nodtacht gasped. He met Bregan's eyes.

His broken nose healed.

Bregan froze.

In one breath, the Stav's hair was sandy colored; in the next, it was gray. His chin rounded, then squared. His nose was broken again, then it wasn't.

"Nimsayrth." The commissioner's voice sounded distant.

Bregan fell to his knees. The Nodtacht's bloodshot eyes were the only steady point in a face that flickered between two men so fast it made Bregan nauseous. Then the man gasped, twitched, and died.

The aged, square-jawed man on the floor was a stranger.

Thick hands shook Bregan's shoulders. The commissioner pulled him to his feet. Bregan caught a handful of words—*no proof . . . kids dead . . . have to run*—but he couldn't look away from the body.

Cold fingers gripped his chin. Bregan stared into his boss's blood-spattered face. "What happened?" the commissioner demanded.

But Bregan had no words.

FORTY-SIX

Firin

Now

The air in the Salted Crown was so thick I could have cut it with a knife. The polished, dark wood walls soaked up the golden lamplight with greed. In the corner nearest the door, I took a drag of my cigarette. Men coughed, bellowed, and boasted from every table and stool. Normally, they would stare at a woman in here who wasn't a waitress.

But tonight, I wasn't a waitress. I wasn't even a woman.

I exhaled and snagged a glimpse of myself in the clouded front window. Heynri Diosi's skin simmered copper in the tavern's dim light. The rope of his dark hair hung over the red suit I'd stolen from Nyfe's costume closet. The fabric wasn't anywhere rich enough for the real Diosi's taste, but it was the right color and style, and that would get me through tonight.

In the three years I'd spied on Baron Hulei for the Nodtacht, I'd tailed him like a burr whenever he was in Luisonn. I followed him from meeting to dance hall, from dinner to deal, and Heynri Diosi had been with him more often than not.

Diosi was more than an associate to the baron. The Qunsiian man was like a brother and business partner mixed up in one. They spent half their time discussing patronage opportunities in Osiv City, and the other half discussing business propositions in the Iket Isles. There wasn't a single person Hulei trusted more, especially in matters of art.

When the clock struck seven, Hulei's personal black carriage pulled up in front. He always came to the Salted Crown at the same time on Fifthdays to meet with a group of men from the Banking Quarter. Apparently, the insurrection and his new presidency hadn't changed that. The bankers were already here, in their usual back corner.

I drained half my glass. When the door opened, I spun on my stool. The baron wiped his boots on the mat.

"Ihan!" I exclaimed, my voice deepened by transformed vocal cords—a trick the Nodtacht had taught me. "What a surprise."

The baron flinched, then barreled toward me. "What? What is this?"

My fingers slipped on my glass. That wasn't the greeting I'd expected. "I'm in town for a stint before I head back for Osiv. Figured I'd find you here."

The baron hesitated, then shook his head. Precipitation beaded on the edge of his jacket. "Heynri!" he said, deflating. "Apologies. It's been a day. I just . . . wasn't expecting to see you."

He sidled up to the bar. The sweaty bartender poured him a whiskey.

"Just here for some unexpected negotiations," I said. "Have a meeting in a bit, but I couldn't risk the chance to congratulate you on your win"—I flashed Diosi's signature tilted smile and leaned closer—"and to ask if you've heard this news about *Qoyn & Insei* in Luisonn." Diosi could sniff out talent under a rock. It was entirely believable he'd know about the Veiled Players' plans. There was the small issue that Diosi wouldn't remember having this conversation, but the enigmatic, forgetful man didn't dwell long on any one thing.

Hulei accepted his drink. "I did hear about it, actually."

I straightened my jacket. "Well, I heard the troupe's got massive potential. Do you think they can pull it off?"

Sipping whiskey, he hesitated. "I'm not entirely sold. In fact—"

The door slapped open.

"Sir!" An achingly familiar voice silenced the room.

Bregan staggered inside with a man built like a boulder. Paler than the moon and trembling from head to toe, he looked as if he'd seen a ghost—and his jacket . . . His jacket was covered in blood.

I jumped to my feet at the same time Hulei did.

"Inspector? Commissioner?" he said.

Bregan glanced at the barkeep. "We need a private room. Now."

Then his terrified stare met mine, and it was devoid of all recognition. Because I wasn't Firin. I was Heynri Diosi.

I had no business still being here.

"This is where I take my leave," I blurted, flashing Diosi's grin. I granted the baron a small bow. "Do let me know if you hear anything."

"Sir, please," Bregan insisted, trying to pull Hulei aside. But the baron was staring at me. A heartbeat passed, then another. His gaze slid over my features, assessing my Diosi illusion, eyeing the cheap cut of my suit.

"Good evening," I said.

Then I stepped around the commissioner and out into the night.

Bregan

Now

"What is going on?" Hulei hissed. He and the commissioner stared after the man in the red suit.

"We need to talk, somewhere private," Bregan said, clenching his teeth against the white-hot pain zinging up his arm. The makeshift bandage tied around his gunshot wound struggled to hold back a heavy flow of blood. He needed stitches, but it had to wait.

The president said something to the bartender, then led them to the back of the tavern. Smoke poured into Bregan's lungs as if the place were trying to asphyxiate him. Hulei didn't seem to notice. The commissioner kept a heavy, questioning eye on Bregan's back.

They'd managed to escape the Spires with just over half their constables. Ten of the boys were missing; at least three were dead. It was possible others had escaped and would meet them back at headquarters, but Bregan was afraid to hope. The commissioner had wanted to go to Regents' Hill straightaway, but Bregan insisted on finding the president first. With what he'd just seen the Nodtacht do, the entire foundation of the world had shifted. He worried he would only be able to find the words to explain it once, so he had sought out Hulei. He'd tell them together.

The bartender ushered them into a cramped room. Benches lined the walls around a table that filled the space.

The moment the door clicked shut, Bregan said, "The raid was a disaster."

"Did you get Draifey?" Hulei asked, settling on a bench.

"No," the commissioner grunted, sitting across from him.

Bregan stayed standing. "It wasn't a meeting; it was a rally. There were hundreds of people, perhaps over a thousand. Ten constables are missing, three are dead. At least one civilian died in the gunfire."

"*What?*" Hulei turned to the commissioner. "I thought the plan was to *listen*, not shoot."

The commissioner crossed his arms over his Labor-class disguise. "It was—"

"I thought we expected a small group."

"We did."

"The *Daily* is going to have a field day with this," Hulei said. "If Draifey gets public sympathy because *you*—"

"I shot a Nodtacht," Bregan interrupted. Both men blinked. "The prison guard, the one who led the others' escape—he was Nodtacht. He had the brand."

Hulei straightened his tie. "Well, that's proof. Draifey's working with the Stav."

"*That's* what you couldn't tell me on the way here?" The commissioner's bushy eyebrows came together.

"No . . ." Bregan hesitated. The dying Nodtacht's shifting face burned his vision, as if he had stared straight into the sun. He knew what he had seen, but admitting it out loud? It would sound insane.

"What is it, Nimsayrth?" Hulei asked.

"I saw something impossible, sir."

Lamplight danced over both men's fleshy faces.

"What do you mean?"

"When the man died, his face . . . changed." Bregan braced for confusion or laughter or concern for his sanity. He did not expect their eyes to meet or their mouths to thin. His heart stumbled. "You already know."

Neither man denied it.

A thread of heat snaked into Bregan's veins. "Who else knows?" he asked.

"Just the people in this room," the commissioner said, "and perhaps some of Draifey's people. We questioned a few Nodtacht after the insurrection and discovered that the Stav have what they call 'illusion.' It's a kind of . . . magic, or curse, that they give their Nodtacht agents so they can shift identity. We're unsure how it works, but we think it has to do with their brands."

"At the Grande the other night," the baron added, "the assassin was using illusion."

The walls seemed to tilt inward. "You've known this since the *insurrection*?" Bregan said. "We have to do something."

The president braced his elbows on the table. "We are. We're exposing Draifey."

"We have to *tell* people." Bregan stared at the leaders of Luisonn, at the *president* and the *commissioner*. The Stav could be anyone, anywhere.

They could change their faces like saints-damned Kirru gods, and no one knew.

"Take a deep breath, son," the president said, eyeing Bregan's bloodied sleeve. "Do you really think it's smart to go to the papers and claim that the Stav have *magic?*"

"But it's true."

"We can't prove it."

"What about the Nodtacht you questioned?"

The commissioner shifted on the bench. "They didn't . . . make it."

"You were right to keep me from going to the papers before I had hard evidence on Draifey," Hulei said. "This is no different."

Bregan's lungs strained for air. Without visual proof of what he'd seen, taking this "illusion" to the papers would end in ridicule of the president's sanity and the collapse of his campaign. But Hulei and the commissioner had kept this crucial information even from *him*, details that would have changed his entire investigation, details that threw Vorkot's and Suri's testimonies into an entirely different light.

What else didn't they think he could handle?

"Son, are you feeling well?" Hulei asked.

Bregan wasn't sure. He pressed his palms into the table and leaned forward, bullet wound throbbing. A few drops of blood broke free of his bandage, splattering on the floor. *If* they had told him about this "illusion," would he have believed them? The president and commissioner had kept him apprised of everything else, proven themselves open with him at every other turn. He forced himself to inhale. These were exactly the divisions and suspicions that Draifey wanted to fuel.

He sat on the bench. "We can't just stay silent."

Hulei sighed. "We can't go to the papers with what you saw, but now we *can* prove Draifey's working with the Nodtacht. We should arrest him."

"We weren't able to extract the Nodtacht's body," the commissioner admitted. "We have enough suspicion to bring Draifey in, but not enough proof to charge him."

"For saints' sake," Hulei snarled, "what *did* you get?"

What had they gotten, other than as many as thirteen boys killed?

The freight receipt. Bregan had forgotten it.

"Sir, I did see something," he said. "In a pile of the Reformists' documents, I found a receipt for a shipment coming on Fourthday. Said it's for salt, but the fee is far too high."

The commissioner squinted. "Now that you mention it, I overheard one of Draifey's people talking about a shipment before the shooting started. Something expected at the south Landings docks?"

"Yes. That's what the receipt said. Which indicates it's likely some kind of contraband." The south Landings docks were known for tax evasion and black-market trade. "We should intercept it," he said.

"That's six days from now," Hulei said.

"Which could work to our benefit," Bregan said. For the first time since he'd pulled the trigger, the ground beneath his feet began to stabilize. "After tonight, Draifey will go underground. He'll expect us to try to find him right away. But if we lay low until Seventhday, we can goad him into a false sense of safety. Then we can intercept the shipment and—if the saints are good—it will lead us straight to him."

The commissioner grunted. "It's a good idea."

"Six days is a long time to do nothing," Hulei said.

"You don't have to do nothing," Bregan said. "You can focus on winning over the public through *Qoyn & Insei.*"

The president glanced at the commissioner. The back of Bregan's neck prickled. It was a good idea. If they could win the public's adoration *and* catch Draifey at the same time, they'd win the election without question, even if Draifey's trial dragged on too long to disqualify him from the run.

"Fine," the president finally said. "I'll talk to the *Daily* tonight, make it clear that you went to the meeting on suspicions of Stav infiltration. I won't name Draifey as a suspect, to help paint the image that we're backing off."

"And the play?" Bregan asked.

Hulei leaned back, entwined his hands in his lap. "If the Players can truly pull off *Qoyn & Insei*, then I will *consider* it. But I want a preview first."

FORTY-SEVEN

Firin

Now

"Vota?" Across the kitchen table, Tez peered out from behind his script pages.

"Right, sorry," I said, refocusing on my lines. "I see the wounds you carry. I see all the pain you have caused—*ah*." A sting lanced up my arm as Nyfe dabbed a wet cloth to my largest half-healed wound.

"Sorry, sorry," she said.

"The line is actually '*I see the pain they cause you,*'" Tez said softly.

Nyfe glanced up, then back to my wound. I shifted on the bench. At this point they knew that I never mixed up my lines, especially not the lines to *Qoyn & Insei*, but tonight I kept tripping over the words of the scene we were practicing like a drunk sailor on the familiar cobblestones that led from tavern to home. It was one of Insei's final moments, when she confronted her queen mother on her deathbed and refused to inherit her title, and for some reason it grated my nerves.

"Sorry," I said. "I'm a bit tired."

"Stop apologizing," Nyfe said, tapping my arm. I lifted it so she could wrap a fresh bandage on it. "It's been an awful week. I'm surprised you can remember any lines at all. You're allowed to rest, Vota."

Rest. I almost laughed. No one had ever told me to do *less* before. But even if I could lean into the comfort Nyfe was offering, no part of me was capable of unwinding. Hours ago, I'd left Bregan at the tavern, dripping in blood and terror, and he still hadn't come home. I wanted to go look for him, but that would reveal I knew something had happened. I could only wait and pray that whatever it was wouldn't ruin everything. He had *just* agreed to do *Qoyn & Insei*. I needed to make sure he didn't change his mind. I rooted my foot to the floor so it wouldn't bounce.

Tez set his script down. "Perhaps we should—"

"As if you haven't already picked a side." Luka's shout echoed down the hallway, followed by the clicking of boots. "Not everything has to do with you, Jaar."

"What does *that* mean?" Jaari's voice replied.

"Never mind," Luka said, with no small dose of exasperation.

"Never *mind?*" Jaari shrieked.

When I twisted in my seat, Nyfe gently touched my arm. "They fight like this at least once a week. Best to leave it alone."

"*Where* are you going?" Luka asked.

"Does it matter? I'm obviously not worth any effort."

"Are you serious right now?" Luka's angry voice faded as they headed away from the kitchen.

Tez grunted as he stood. "I'll go make sure they're not breaking things."

The door swung shut behind him, and Nyfe sighed. "Don't worry about them. Jaari loves with wild passion, but she doesn't trust easily. She likes to . . . test Luka's loyalty. Luka lets her because they can see through it. They'll be fine in an hour."

I wasn't sure what to say to that. The soft rustle as she organized her medical basket seemed to accentuate the sudden quiet rather than fill it. For the first time, I noticed a pendant hanging from a leather strap around her neck—a prayer token in the shape of Saint Aiddwyn, the

Gwyn saint of home and hearth. A token the Stav would have killed her for wearing.

When she finished what she was doing, she set the basket of supplies on the table. "It's terrifying, letting someone in."

I picked at a frayed thread on my skirt. "What do you mean?"

"You know, when Taira and I came here from Gwynythaid, we had nothing but each other. We'd lost everything in the rebellion there. We'd been through it all together. She understood me, and accepted me, in a way I didn't think anyone else could. When I fell in love with someone a few years later, I never really let her in. I was afraid she wouldn't accept me unconditionally, the way my sister had. I was afraid that if I let her in, she might not like what she saw. By the time I changed my mind, it was too late." She sighed, leaning back. "Bregan adores you, Vota. Whatever you—"

I gripped Nyfe's hand, my heart in my throat. "Thank you," I forced out. I doubted whatever she was ashamed of could hold a candle to my sins, and as much as I loved the idea of confiding in her, I never could.

The calluses she'd collected from washing, cooking, and caring for the troupe brushed my palm as she squeezed my hand back. "Do you want me to change the other bandage?"

"No. That one's healed," I said. I had removed the bandage from my branded arm the day before to keep her from continuing to ask.

A thud sounded on the outside door, making both of us jump. Then it swung open, and Bregan tumbled inside. His jacket hung stiff with both dried and fresh blood. His freckles stood stark against his cheeks. Too stark. How much blood had he lost?

"Oh, saints!" Nyfe gasped, grabbing at her Saint Aiddwyn charm.

He removed his cap, swiped it across his brow, and half collapsed against the counter.

"You're bleeding," I said, rushing over. He blinked at his ripped jacket sleeve. I took his face in my palms. "What happened?"

"A raid went badly," he said, out of breath.

"Let me see." Nyfe grabbed her basket of supplies.

"I can do it," I said, taking them.

She handed me a clean, damp cloth, and I led Bregan by the elbow to the basement. He stumbled down the steps as if in a daze, but he seemed more lost in thought than nearing unconsciousness. Something awful had happened, something that terrified him. Once I settled him on his cot, I helped him out of his coat, the same olive-colored one he'd worn for years. It was so stained I wasn't sure it could be salvaged, and the thought made my eyes burn. The ripped sleeve of his undershirt was soaked with blood.

"Are you dizzy?" I asked, sitting next to him. He shook his head.

With a pair of Nyfe's scissors, I cut the sleeve of the shirt off, revealing a slice across Bregan's inner bicep. A bullet wound. A near miss.

I could have lost him.

The thought sank talons into my flesh. When I placed the wet cloth against the wound to clear out debris, my hands shook.

"That fucking hurts," he said.

"Don't move."

He set the back of his head against the wall, eyes clamped shut.

When the wound was clean and my hands had stilled enough to thread a needle, I pulled one from the basket. I placed the tip to his skin. "What happened?" I asked, with more frustration than I intended.

"We raided a secret meeting. One of the new constables shot before he should have, and it turned into a bloodbath." Concise, succinct, evasive.

"The future we wanted is *here*," I said quietly. "Why are you still fighting?"

"Freedom isn't secured overnight, Firin."

"Haven't you done enough? Isn't it someone else's turn?"

"Whose?" His lashes fluttered open. "If this government crumbles, it was all for nothing."

"If you *die*, it was."

"It's not just about me."

For me it is, I thought. For me, he was all that had ever mattered. But just like the other night, when he'd told me he loved me, I couldn't make myself say what I couldn't take back—not yet. Maybe that made me a coward, but it was better for both of us.

I also wasn't the only one holding something back.

"If it was just a raid," I said, "why do you look like you've seen a Vorstav'n ghost?"

As I stitched him closed, he was silent for so long I feared he wouldn't answer, but when I cut the string, he said, "You wouldn't believe me."

"You'd be surprised what I can believe." I gently placed a new bandage over the stitches.

Instead of answering, he wound an escaped strand of my hair around his finger. When I finished wrapping his wound, the rest of him came into focus. Sweat lined his brow. New muscles rippled under the familiar freckled skin of his torso. As he gently tugged my hair, I leaned in, like a moth drawn to a flame dangerous enough to burn.

What if he hadn't come back tonight?

What if I'd squandered all the time we had left?

The thoughts hurt so much that I stopped breathing.

"Come here," he said, guiding me into his lap.

I didn't fight him.

The first kiss set off warning bells in my mind. He was avoiding my question, and Bregan never avoided difficult discussions. But then his tongue swept between my teeth, and his thumbs ran up my rib cage, then the sides of my breasts, and the screech of my desire drowned everything else out.

His kisses were laced with teeth. He smelled like sweat and blood but also *him.* Sweet and smoky at the same time. Intoxicating. When he shifted underneath me, I lit on fire. I scooched closer, burying my hands in his hair, in that scent.

"Firin." The vibration of his voice scraped down my insides, pulling me under the surface of reason.

With his good arm, he laid me on the cot, lips trailing down what was exposed of my chest as he tugged at the loose neckline of my dress. His rough hands slid up my skirts, and I arched into both touches.

I needed him. I had always needed him, and I had never needed him this much.

I ran my nails down his bare back, tearing through freckles I'd once memorized, and my heart swelled in a way that hurt. Because it was *him*. In our years apart, I'd lost myself in others' bodies, but whenever I'd closed my eyes, I'd always pictured they were him. This time, I didn't have to imagine.

My eyes were burning when his mouth found my thigh, his breath clouding between my legs, and I thought I'd go mad from the need. He eased off my undergarments and kissed up my flesh. Each touch was excruciatingly patient, drawing me so tight I thought I'd shatter without relief. Then his tongue slipped between my legs.

My eyes rolled back. "Bregan," I moaned as he painted circles only he knew how to do. The years melted away, and I became *her* again, a hopeful girl on a rooftop beneath a boy she loved with her entire heart. But it wasn't enough.

"Wait," I gasped, burying my fingers in his hair, guiding him back up to my mouth. I groped for the buttons on his pants, yanked them open. He growled as I straddled him, as I slipped my hand under his waistband. I leaned in, pressing his spine into the wall.

His fingers fumbled on my back. "Saints, Firin, I . . ."

I kissed him over the words, shifting, making room, needing him inside me. Then the back of my dress pulled. Cold air trickled over my shoulders, seeped down my arms.

He was taking my dress off.

I jerked back so fast I almost fell off the cot. "Stop."

Bregan caught me around the waist. "What? What is it?"

If I hadn't been so lust hazed, if I'd had another second to think, I would have found a way to keep going, even with my dress on. But in my moment's hesitation, any chance at masking shattered.

His eyes flashed. "No. Don't."

The thud of my heart threatened to break through my ribs. "Let me go."

"*Why?*" he demanded.

"Because . . . you're just using this as a distraction."

"Are you kidding me?"

I jumped to my feet, flattening my skirts, cheeks on fire. "What really happened tonight?"

When he slid forward on the cot, hair mussed and skin red, his eyes burned with an unfamiliar molten iron. "You want to know what happened?" he snapped. "I shot a Nodtacht tonight, and when he died, I watched his fucking face *change*. What's *your* excuse, Firin? Huh?"

I froze. "W-what?"

"Yeah, I thought I'd hallucinated. But *Hulei* said it's some kind of magic the Stav have, so excuse me if I don't want to think about it for a saints-damned second. We both know you've used me the same way. Or is now the time when you'll finally tell me what happened to you?"

A riptide pulled me under. Bregan's lips kept moving, but I couldn't hear him. I could only take in the ugly twist of his face, the haunted horror in his eyes.

He knew about illusion.

"*Firin.*"

I flinched. The tracks his fingers and lips had just traveled burned everywhere, all over my back, my arms, between my legs, as if I were unraveling along them, disintegrating. My flesh was suddenly so hot I feared I might combust.

If Bregan saw my brand, he wouldn't just know what I was.

He would know what I could *do*.

He would never so much as look at me again.

"Firin, wait. You can't just leave."

I fled the basement.

When I entered Mezua's office, she looked up from her desk in her bathrobe. "Bregan and Hulei know," I panted. "They know that the Nodtacht can change faces."

Mezua slowly stood. "Do they suspect you?"

"I—I don't know. Bregan doesn't, but Hulei . . ."

Saints, I had *just* used illusion to con the baron hours ago. Outside the Salted Crown, he had paused and assessed my Diosi facade. Something had flickered in his eyes. Had it been suspicion or confusion?

"You don't have to do this," Mezua said. "You can leave."

"What?"

"That's what you came to tell me, is it not?"

I stared at her. I hadn't come here to run. For once, I didn't want to. I finally had a place where, after I erased my past, I might truly belong. I thought of Nyfe's hand in mine, Tez's worried eyes, Phinnin's giggles. The whole troupe had slipped into the orbit of my schemes, and suddenly the stakes were so much larger than my life.

But what would happen to everyone if I didn't take this risk? Without Hulei, the troupe would shutter. We needed his money. I needed it to get rid of my Nodtacht scar.

"No," I said. "But we need to be more careful."

Bregan and Hulei knowing about illusion changed very little. Even if Hulei suspected someone had used illusion to impersonate Diosi, he would assume it was someone working for the Stav or Draifey, not a girl at a theater. As long as Bregan never saw my scar, I was still safe. The troupe was still safe.

I just had to get through this play.

FORTY-EIGHT

Firin

Now

Ribbons of morning light streamed into the temple through its newly uncovered stained glass windows, a colorful spotlight for a stage, upon which everything was going wrong.

"What's happened?" I gasped, pushing myself off the floor on shaking limbs. As Insei, I had just taken a persuasion draught with Qoyn, so we could convince my mother—the queen—to let me marry him. Upon drinking it, however, we'd fainted, and then I woke up on a beach, alone.

Nyfe sauntered over, portraying a time-traveling pirate. "Flash of light. Ground shook a li'l bit. Then you was on my beach."

"A man. Was there a man?" I searched the fake beach for any sign of Qoyn.

"No man," Nyfe said.

I scrambled to my feet, arranging my skirts the way a princess like Insei would. "Please, can you get me back to Resovia?"

"What is Resovia?" Nyfe asked.

I took a deep breath, readying myself to convey shock, but Mezua stood up in the front pew. "Stop, please. Vota, I want more guilt."

"But Insei doesn't know the witch tricked them until *after* the pirates tell her what year it is," I said.

"She took a persuasion potion but ended up on a beach," Mezua said. "She doesn't have to know she time traveled to realize the witch tricked her the moment she wakes up. We want a sinking sense of dread from the beginning, the seeds for her spiraling guilt later."

I groaned under my breath.

At the back of the temple, in a stream of dust-filled light, Bregan leaned against a wall with his arms crossed, talking with Suri. Both of them watched me, but neither had the right to judge. I wasn't the only one who'd struggled this morning.

Mezua sighed. "I need to work with Jaari and Tez, but go *practice*, Vota."

Afraid I might snap if I responded, I jumped offstage and headed down a side aisle. Around me, the pews were stuffed full of costumes, set pieces, and stage materials. Everything was half-done. Half-practiced, half-built, half-prepared. We'd taken a massive gamble announcing *Qoyn & Insei* in the paper a few days ago without Hulei's patronage secured, but I'd hoped the publicity would push the interim president through our doors. We didn't have enough musicians. We had none of the necessary set pieces and only half the costumes required. *Qoyn & Insei* was famous for its grandiosity; it wouldn't work as a skeleton show.

We had less than a week until the Grande opened *The Pirate's Widow*, and we *needed* to announce Hulei's patronage in the paper before then, or we'd lose out on all the city's wealthiest patrons. Even though Bregan had told me that he had voiced interest, the baron still hadn't come to preview us. At this point, Mezua was losing her patience for me in more than one way.

"She's right," Bregan said behind me.

I jumped and turned. Morning light danced between his freckles. Paint speckled his cheek near his ear. Even with tired circles beneath his eyes, everything about him was breathtaking. It made me want to scream.

We'd barely spoken offstage since I ran out on him. I had been careful not to let him corner me alone. After the second night I'd sneaked to bed first, I woke to find him on the floor again. I lay and watched him twitch in nightmares every night, too afraid to wake him, worried he was dreaming about the man he'd killed, the man whose face had changed. The distance between us felt like an ocean, with both of us on disparate shores.

I knew how to mask. I knew how to run. But this was different.

My whole life I'd hidden behind stories and faces, but my scar—now that Bregan truly knew what it meant—wasn't something I could cover up with anything other than fabric. Until the play was over and I could afford the tattooist, I couldn't do anything except keep him at arm's length.

I turned away, putting Bregan behind me. "What did Suri have to say?" I failed to keep the pettiness from my voice. She and I had been circling one another since our tentative truce. Her acting was more *good* than great, but at least it was stable. I was either fantastic or awful, depending on the scene.

"She was complimenting you. Said that when you're good, you're really good. But when you're not—"

"I guess I don't need to know." Onstage, Mezua was blocking a scene with Tez and Jaari. Nyfe had disappeared. Maybe she was in the costume room. I headed for the western corridor.

"I can tell you're still mimicking emotions," Bregan said, following. "You have to more than mimic Insei; you have to understand her so you can *feel* what she feels."

"I do understand her," I said flatly. "She wants to run away with Qoyn, but she doesn't want to upset her mother, so she tries to use a persuasion potion. Then, when it turns out the witch tricked them with a time-travel potion, she feels guilty because it was her idea." It was clear in the text.

"Why do you sound so annoyed?"

I rounded on him. "Because it's annoying!" The words echoed down the corridor. Luka and a few of the musicians glanced our way. I lowered my voice. "I love this play, Bregan, but the second quarter of Insei's story is so inactive. She wastes a ridiculous amount of time wallowing over a stupid mistake she never should have made in the first place while Qoyn spends that time *doing* things to try to get her back."

Bregan's laugh was barbed. "That's funny."

Shock zinged through me. Was he implying that I wasn't doing anything to get *him* back?

Before I could react, he moved on. "It doesn't matter whether you agree with her or would do what she does—all that matters is that you understand *why*."

I snorted. If only it were so easy.

When I headed for the costume room, he stayed at my heels. "Start with why she took the potion in the first place. Have you never made a mistake that affected people you loved?"

I froze with my hand on the latch. A nightmare memory stirred, covered in blood and ash, buried so deep that my flesh had grown around it. The pull of it promised to rip me to shreds, like he was peeling back the layers of me, exposing my chafing flesh.

Letting him corner me had been a mistake.

I threw open the door to the costume room. "You're awfully critical for someone who walked offstage this morning because *you* couldn't get a scene right."

"Yeah, because it's my mother leaving all over again."

I halted between two racks of costumes.

"The witch is like a mother to Qoyn," Bregan said, right behind me. "He loves and trusts her. To get his response to her betrayal right, I'll need to let myself *feel* Ma's betrayal again. I know I need to go there, I just couldn't do it this morning."

When I turned around, fractals of heartbreak floated in the dark pools of his eyes. The smell of him invaded all my senses. I hugged myself as if I could ward him off like a chill. Maybe his memories were painful, but mine were poison.

Bregan glanced around the dark costume room. It was empty.

We were alone.

"I'm going to find Nyfe," I blurted, bolting back into the hall.

I half expected him to grab my hand or shout my name, but he didn't. When I stepped back into the nave full of voices, hammering, and other people, I started to let out a relieved exhale . . . Until I saw Baron Hulei standing at the back of the room.

My whole body seized. He leaned against the last pew in a dark-blue suit and orange waistcoat, watching Tez and Jaari onstage with a slight frown. How long had he been there? Had he seen me floundering? As I gaped at him, he turned to leave.

"Mr. President!" I shouted, seizing the moment like a lifeline.

Hulei was the key to everything.

Tez fumbled mid-monologue. The entire temple fell silent. Every person spun to find the president. As I raced down the aisle, he turned back on one heel.

I sank into a curtsy. "Sir, we didn't realize you were watching."

"I prefer it that way," he said, checking his golden pocket watch.

Whatever he'd seen, he wasn't pleased. I glanced back, but Bregan was nowhere. He couldn't have gone far, though. "If you could just stay for a bit longer, we'd love to show you some scenes from the opening." The romance beats, at least, were solid. Usually.

"I don't think so," the baron said, heading back into the lobby, his leather shoes clicking on the wooden floor.

I followed him. "Please, sir. I'd love to tell you about—"

"Do you like Osiv cuisine?" he asked, pushing the front doors open.

"I'm sorry?" I blinked against the onslaught of sun.

"Lunch," he said, trotting down the front steps to a parked black carriage. The driver opened the door. Before getting inside, Hulei looked back, pinning me with those ocean-blue eyes. "Will you join me?"

My heart leaped. "Yes, that would be lovely."

We stepped inside the sleek, lavish walls of Atzuie's, and I shivered. In my time spying on Hulei, I'd been in here hundreds of times, but never without wearing an illusion, never *with* him.

The baron ordered a scotch. I ordered a wine.

When I asked for a more obscure but highly valued vintage, the corner of the baron's mouth lifted. To Qunsiians, the alcohol you picked was considered a sign of your intelligence, no matter your wealth. Hulei valued the image of ambition, and I meant to paint him one he couldn't look away from: a Labor-class girl clawing her way out of obscurity.

Around us, Luisonn's wealthiest wined and dined. The only signs of the revolution were the extra private security at the door and the lack of class bands on people's wrists. I made sure to glance surreptitiously around as if I were in awe but didn't want him to notice, the way a Labor girl would be had she never been inside before.

In all my years spying on Hulei, I knew he preferred when people didn't skirt their point. So I launched right in. "I believe this play is an opportunity you shouldn't miss out on."

He sipped his scotch. "Your beliefs are not in question."

"Bregan and I trained under Esmai Nimsayrth."

"A talented woman." Hulei swirled his liquor, watching me. I'd seen men flounder beneath his intensity. I didn't plan to join them.

"Luka, our conductor, was a renowned composer in Iakirru and Gwynythaid before they were arrested for their art during the Gwyn revolution. They've trained their own musicians, the star of which is Jaari Usenma, who began her career in the University of Osiv."

Hulei sniffed. "I know your troupe's qualifications. Esmai was talented, but she wasn't known for teaching. Luka taught themself and therefore lacks a fundamental understanding of theory, though I admit they have talent. But Jaari Usenma abandoned her training in Osiv as a child."

I fought the burn in my chest. If he'd done research on the troupe, he was at least considering patronage. But what had he found about me?

"You were born in the Factory Block, yes?" he continued, as if reading my mind. "Your father was a mill worker?" The opaque pages of the story I'd told the troupe years ago.

"Don't hold it against me," I said with a smile.

"On the contrary, it's impressive." He watched me over his glass. I clenched my fingers in my lap. If he had any inkling that I was a Nodtacht, I'd already be in another carriage, my scar exposed and my wrists in handcuffs.

I pivoted. "*Qoyn & Insei* is one of the most renowned stories in history. Everyone in Luisonn knows of it, even with years of the Stav's oppression. To put on this play—"

Hulei raised a hand. He set his scotch down and braced his elbows on the table. The blue of his eyes was a tad gray, almost thoughtful. "Vota, you are smart, that much is clear. I am sure it was you who fed this entire *Qoyn & Insei* idea to Bregan. It's clever, I'll admit. I do need to improve the way the city perceives me, and a play is a brilliant way to do it."

If he thought the play could help him, why were we here?

"There is nothing about your troupe's talents—or this play's ability to support my image—that you can tell me that I've not already considered. What I am not yet sure of is how you can help me."

I stiffened.

He sat back in his chair and propped his ankle on his thigh. "You hope to use my celebrity to fill your theater's pockets. I'd like to use yours to fill my ballot box."

Whatever Hulei's faults, he'd be a better leader than the Stav emperor had been. If support was his price, I'd pay it easily.

"I'm listening," I said.

"That man over there . . ." He pointed to the elegant bar in the corner, where a suited man sat with a briefcase at his feet. "He's a new reporter with the *Daily*. I'd like you to tell him your story . . . something the people can sink their teeth into."

The hair on the back of my neck rose. I'd suspected Hulei had the new *Luisonn Daily* paper in his pocket when a recent article about Bregan's raid blamed Draifey's Labor attendees for instigating the gunfight. When Bregan confronted him about it, Hulei had claimed that the newspaper published before they had all the information, but I wasn't so sure. The baron understood how to use public perception to his benefit—and this plan was smart. I glanced at the reporter. It would be a lie I could never reverse, but if I fed the public a saga worthy of gossip, they would chatter about the play, and tickets would sell.

"All right," I said. I'd figure it out.

"Good. After the interview, you'll publicly announce your support of my presidential campaign at my upcoming rally. A week from Fifthday."

I pinched my lips in a show of consideration, but the answer was easy. The rally would be a few days before opening night, just in time to stir the public's interest and flood our doors. Attending, and speaking, would work to the theater's benefit as well as his.

"Agreed," I said, leaning forward. "But in exchange, you will transfer the full amount of the Players' budget to Mezua today, and you'll announce your official patronage of *Qoyn & Insei* in the *Daily* tomorrow."

A vein in Hulei's forehead twitched. I waited.

"Fine, but one last thing." He pulled an envelope from inside his pocket. The air in the room seemed to shift, stretching thin. "I need you to deliver this letter to the Landings for me, as soon as possible. Here's the location and person I need it to go to." He placed the envelope and a folded slip of paper on the table.

I didn't take it.

"Why not use a messenger?" I asked. Draifey's people swarmed the docks. Who did Hulei want to talk with there? Was it some kind of top-secret or treasonous note?

Hulei drained his scotch. "Think of it as a way to prove I can trust you."

The envelope's parchment was thick, the seal blank. With a hot knife I could probably get inside it, but I rejected the idea as soon as it formed.

Whatever Hulei was up to didn't concern me.

Not as long as I had his patronage.

"Deal," I said.

FORTY-NINE

Bregan

Bloody Fifthday

The gunshot stopped time.

Bregan stood just offstage in full pirate's costume, waiting for the end of Baron Hulei's speech, when he would go back out to finish *Skarnti's Revenge*. But now Hulei was flat on his back, blood seeping through his shirt. Bregan blinked, and Hulei became his cousin, chained to an execution wall. He blinked again, and the theater erupted into madness.

Stav soldiers poured onto the stage like an infection, invading a space that had been safe for years. Someone grabbed Bregan's forearm—Mezua, pulling him toward the nearest exit.

"Wait!" Bregan shouted.

Firin was still here, up on the mezzanine. He knew exactly where she was sitting. But as Mezua's nails dug into his skin, he looked back, and Firin was gone.

A bullet thudded into the wall beside him.

He ran.

The ruined match factory was a pitch-dark maze of hallways and machinery, but Bregan knew it like the back of his hand. His breaths were ragged as he followed Mezua. Instinct urged him forward, but his heart was screaming at him to turn around.

He had just found Firin.

She'd gone missing a month ago, right after Gauf Taidd bombed the Stav official's personal ship and all hell broke loose. Bregan had gone to the cotton-mills apartments and asked around. There had been no sign of her. He'd beaten himself up over and over again for not asking more about her father, not demanding she stay with him, where it had to be safer. But then she'd come back tonight during intermission, tearstained and desolate.

He never should have let her out of his reach.

When Bregan and Mezua bolted up a stairwell and onto the factory's roof, the star-strewn night hit him like a slap in the face. His knees locked.

"I have to go back," he rasped.

"You can't. They will kill you," the director said, gripping his hand so tight he couldn't feel his fingers. The silk of her costume gown looked strange out in the fresh air, in the real world.

"But—"

"Someone betrayed us," Mezua said, and a strange crackle entered her always-steady voice. "The Stav will likely have your name, know your face. You need to hide."

"I need to *find* her," he said.

Mezua placed a cool palm against his jaw. "If Vota's alive, she's either already in a prison cart or somewhere safe. Where would she go?"

Bregan's ribs caved.

Mezua exhaled as if she knew exactly what he was thinking. "Go. Be careful. We'll meet at the backup safe house, all right?" The safe house only the Veiled Players knew about. The one Bregan had never thought they would actually use.

With one last pat against his cheek, Mezua headed north. Bregan spun on his heel and raced south, toward home. In the streets below, audience members, Reformists, actors, and musicians poured out of the match factory. Stav soldiers intercepted them, rounded them up. Bregan tried not to look down, tried not to think about Tez and Jaq, Phinnin and Nyfe. Jaari. His mother.

He thought only about Firin.

If she was captured tonight, it would be *his* fault. He was the reason she'd come. His feet tripped under the force of the thought, slipping on roof tiles. By the time he'd reached his apartment building, he couldn't breathe. When he saw the shape of a woman, he nearly choked on air—but when she turned around, it wasn't Firin.

"Ma," he gasped, capturing her in an airtight hug.

"Bregan," she sobbed, nails piercing his back.

"Why are you here?" he asked. She should have gone straight to the safe house.

"I saw Firin in the audience. I knew you'd come here to look for her."

He pulled back. "Is she—"

"She's not here." Ma's wet cheeks glowed. Her lip trembled. Like him, she was still wearing her costume from *Skarnti's Revenge*. "We have to go, Breg. We can't wait for her."

He shook his head. He couldn't. He wouldn't.

"Bregan . . ."

Ripping from his mother's hold, Bregan vaulted over the side of the roof and down the fire escape. Maybe Firin had gone to the apartment to look for him. If not, he would head back to the cotton mills. Whatever it took, he would find her.

"Bregan," Ma called after him, "we need to change clothes and head to the safe house." Bregan wrenched open their apartment window. When he dropped inside, it was empty. The belt around his heart tightened further.

Ma threw a change of clothes at him. He took them.

The front door flew open.

Pa stumbled inside like a soldier from a war. Blood splattered his front. A pistol shook in his fist. "What are you two doing here?

Mezua said—" Ma cut him off with a hug. He buried his face in her hair. "We have to go. The Players' safe house is the only one that's not compromised."

"I'm not going," Bregan said, slipping out of his costume coat.

"Yes, you are."

"No, I—"

Heavy boots echoed in the stairwell, a sound straight from Bregan's nightmares. All three of them froze. The whites of his parents' eyes grew, and the color drained from their faces.

Stav soldiers.

"The window," Pa growled, spinning his pistol to the door.

Bregan stepped in front of his mother, arms out at his sides. She pulled his wrist toward the fire escape, but Bregan couldn't move as the door broke off its hinges, as Pa's bullet hit the first Stav soldier in the chest. Another swung a club, hitting Pa in the back of the head. He stumbled. His pistol fell.

Ma screamed.

Bregan leaped for the gun. His knees hit the floor, but before his fingers could close around the pistol's grip, a Stav soldier kicked it across the room—then drove his boot into Bregan's gut. All the air punched out of his lungs as he landed on his shoulder.

They dragged Pa out.

Bregan clambered to his feet, still gasping for air. Ma snatched his waist, just as she had all those years ago, when he'd watched the Stav haul his cousin away by the throat.

"No," Ma sobbed, "you can't—"

Bregan wrenched out of her hold. He wasn't staying behind this time. He bolted down the stairwell, past cracked doors and curious eyes.

In the courtyard, the soldiers had Pa in handcuffs on his knees. "Pa!" Bregan screamed, running for him. Soldiers slid into his path, as immovable as glaciers. Bregan punched the first one in the jaw, but the second hit him in the stomach, right where he'd been kicked. His vision flared. He doubled over. His entire life was slipping through his fingers, like sand through a sieve.

"Stop!" Ma shrieked, flying out after him. She looked like love ablaze. Bregan's heart stretched to bursting. He couldn't lose her too.

As the soldiers stuffed Pa in a black carriage, she ran for the largest of the soldiers, a man in Nodtacht black who stood as wide and tall as the mast of a ship. A soldier grabbed her around the torso before she reached the Nodtacht, but she writhed and spit anyway. "Let him go!" she demanded.

The Nodtacht dropped his cigarette and flattened it with the heel of his boot. "You broke the terms of our deal."

Bregan stopped fighting, stopped breathing.

His saints-damned heart stopped beating.

"You promised." Ma's voice shook.

"Yes, well, you didn't tell us your *husband* was a leader of the movement."

The carriage driver snapped the reins.

Bregan lurched back to life. "No!" he bellowed, knuckles flaring as they connected with his captor's jaw. He slipped free and ran for the carriage, slamming his hand against the wooden door, as if he could break it down. But the driver spurred the horses, and the prison on wheels lurched into motion.

Bregan slipped on wet cobblestones. He landed on his back.

The carriage disappeared.

Boots slapped the street, splashing him with water, as the soldiers retreated. Bregan stared after them. His bruised ribs felt like splinters, piercing him all over, tearing him into pieces. This wasn't happening. It wasn't possible. His mother couldn't have—

Ma's soul-deep sob was a hook, tearing his heart from his body. He turned toward the sound and took in how the fractured lines of her face bled guilt. A fuse inside him erupted.

"Your fault," he rasped. "The theater . . ."

She had betrayed them.

"I didn't know they were going to attack tonight," she cried. "I swear. I did it for you, for the Players. I thought they would—"

"Stop," Bregan said. It didn't matter. Whatever she had to say was irrelevant. He gathered the broken shards of himself, strewn over the ground, and stumbled to his feet.

"Bregan, please." Ma's crimson hair hung in tangles; her red eyes gleamed. As she reached for him, her maroon dress pooled around her knees, like blood spilled over the cobblestones. The sight of the Saint Chyira prayer bracelet on her wrist severed the last tendon holding his heart in his body.

Protection for a family united in blood, heart, and soul, he heard his grandmother pray.

Ma had always feared the risks of the Reform movement. Bregan had known she feared losing him, so he stayed away. He understood that she feared for Pa's life, so he argued with his father, again and again, about the danger. Bregan understood her fear because he felt it too.

But fearing the revolution wasn't the same as working against it.

That was cowardice at an indefensible level.

"Please," she said, reaching for him.

Bregan recoiled. "I will never forgive you."

FIFTY

Bregan

Now

The gray, pregnant sky outside headquarters promised rain. Bregan flipped up the collar of his jacket—which Nyfe had miraculously cleaned and mended after the raid—and hurried down the steps. When he brushed absently at his hip and his fingers closed on air, he wiped his empty palm down his pant leg. He wouldn't need a gun tonight. Not if he stuck to his plan. A handful of constables waited at a tavern near where Draifcy's shipment was scheduled to dock. If he needed them, he could call them, but the goal was to follow whoever picked up the shipment, not attack them.

It felt good to finally *do* something.

For five days of lying low, he felt like he'd been standing in a tide, the sand beneath him sinking with every wave. He'd barely been able to focus on *Qoyn & Insei*, he hadn't slept well on the floor surrounded by the scents and sounds of Firin, and he was losing his mind to whatever game she was playing.

He thought that in choosing to do *Qoyn & Insei* and fighting for a better Luisonn, they were also fighting for each other. He had told her he *loved* her, for saints' sake. Instead of saying it back, she'd kissed him, convinced him to do *Qoyn & Insei*, then cut him out like none of it had ever happened. Part of him wondered if it was because of what he'd confided about the Nodtacht, that maybe she thought he was going crazy, but a larger part of him knew that wasn't it. Every morning, his heart stopped upon waking, sure that when he opened his eyes, she would be gone for good.

Bregan didn't recognize Pa until he'd almost run into him.

They halted halfway across the square in front of headquarters, breaths curling in the chill air. Bregan hadn't seen his father in nearly two weeks. Between constabulary work and rehearsing, he barely had time to sleep. Their argument in the lobby felt like a lifetime ago.

"I'm surprised to see you here," Pa grunted. "Thought you'd decided to frolic away your future."

"If this is about *Qoyn & Insei*, go ahead and say so," Bregan said. His father had likely heard about the play in the papers, just like everyone else. Hulei's decision to patron the Veiled Players was the talk of the city.

Somewhere in the distance, a thundercloud rumbled. Pa shifted on his feet. "You can't trust that woman."

"Who? Mezua?"

Prison had gouged worry lines in Pa's face. A new paranoia glinted in his eyes. "She'll ruin that girl of yours, just like she did your ma."

The words clamped like a hand on the back of Bregan's neck. "I'm not talking about this."

Pa stepped in front of him. "You're making a mistake, son. The *constabulary* is where your future waits." The same tired argument. "Can't you see that girl's already using you?"

Bregan stepped around his father. "I've got somewhere to be."

A carriage ride later, he wound through the meandering, nonsensical streets of the Fingers, a block of the Labor District that stretched along Luisonn's southern bay. Hundreds of docks and piers stretched into the twilit bay like the raised hands of a crowd, or a riot. He headed for the west side, where Draifey's shipment was expected.

Despite the downpour, the Fingers was as busy as ever. People marched up and down boardwalks, frequently halted in their paths by dockworkers lifting crates off ships and into storage units on the shore, breaths clouding in front of their faces.

At the address listed on the freight receipt, Bregan found a collection of storage cells arranged in low-lying rows like a regimented army prepared to charge the ocean. At their helm sat a skinny receiving office. Rain slid in buckets off its sloped roof.

Inside, a dim lamp shone on the quarters' receiving officer as he spoke through a small window to a sailor who stood with the ease of someone who barely noticed the rain anymore. Bregan couldn't hear them over the sound of the storm.

The sailor nodded, then shouted toward the docks. "Off-load to cell fifty-six!"

Draifey's shipment.

A set of sailors, all wearing the same generic commercial uniforms, lifted crates from tender boats. Bregan halted to let them pass and peered into the bay. He couldn't tell which ship they'd off-loaded from, but it likely didn't matter. Given their uniforms, they were just couriers for hire. If Draifey was smart, he wouldn't have told them what was inside.

Bregan hadn't even lurked long enough to look suspicious before the sailors finished. He ducked under the eaves of a shuttered storefront and waited. The freight receipt had said payment would happen *upon* unloading, so he watched the receiving officer's shack.

But no one came.

He waited until his fingers numbed and the rain let up. The fog thickened as the shore emptied. Dockworkers and sailors disappeared to find beds for the night. When the receiving officer finally put out the light in his shack, Bregan couldn't deny it anymore. No one was coming.

Unease made bumps of his frozen, already-pimpled flesh. Had Draifey abandoned the load? Had someone let slip that the constabulary knew about it?

Bregan wrung out his fingers and headed for the receiving office. When he rapped knuckles on the glass, the window flew open.

An old man's voice scraped through the night. "What?"

"I'm here about cell fifty-six."

"Abou' time. You got payment?" The oil lamp flared again, revealing a Merchant-class man's wrinkles, soft from years protected against the sea's wildness inside this shack. Under the Stav Regime, only Merchants had been allowed to own quarters of the docks; Labors were limited to loading and unloading shipments. Something else that could now change over time.

Bregan slid his constabulary papers out from his layers of clothes. Even wrapped in a leather wallet, they were damp. He handed them to the officer. "I'm here on behalf of the interim president. I need intel on that shipment."

The man squinted at the papers, his beady, watery eyes sharpening. "It's jus' salt from Silias."

"Who's it for?"

"Says a man named Oska."

Oska was the kind of Vorstav'n name that could be tracked to hundreds of men across every class. "Let me see the paperwork."

The man hesitated, then lifted his lamp. He sifted through a pile of papers before handing Bregan a slip. "Says tonight, but we've not seen 'em. Have to pay before they can receive it."

The order matched the freight receipt. Bregan's skin crawled. "Gather all the paperwork for this shipment. I'm confiscating it."

He left before the officer could protest and looked for a messenger. One materialized instantly. The Landings' boardwalk was a lucrative place to pass letters. Pressing a coin into the girl's palm, Bregan sent her to fetch the other constables at the tavern up the road. Then he followed the receiving officer around to the long, squat stone storage cells. The man's many keys jingled.

Without the rain, the night grew eerily quiet. For some reason Bregan kept picturing the cell empty, as if Draifey could have snatched his goods right out from under his nose. Keys rattled. Metal groaned. Then the receiving officer raised his lantern on cell fifty-six. The crates Bregan had watched unload sat in the middle of the room in a neat pile.

Half a dozen boots crunched on gravel as Bregan's backup constables materialized at attention behind him.

"What are your orders, sir?" one of them asked.

"We're going to confiscate these crates," Bregan said. "But first, I'm going to open them. You all stay out here; if something happens, go straight to the commissioner."

The whites of the young constable's eyes flashed. "Sir?"

Bregan grabbed a box pry from a hook on the wall and the lamp from the receiving officer. If Draifey knew they were coming, he could have set some kind of trap, and Bregan didn't need anyone else getting hurt.

He slowly entered the cell, waving his gun to every empty corner. No one was here. Setting his lamp down, he ran a gentle touch around the edges of the first box, then shoved the pry under the top flap and wrenched it open. A ringing filled his ears.

Brand-new pistols.

Dozens of them. In their newly freed Luisonn, there was only one reason Draifey would need weapons like this. If he didn't win the election—or maybe even regardless of it—the bastard planned to take the island by force.

"Open them," Bregan ordered.

The constables tore into the rest of the crates. More pistols. Shotguns.

Bregan's knuckles went white around the edge of the last crate. He stared down at rolled packets of powder he'd only heard about in stories from north continent rebels. Explosives. The kind used to mine on the mainland; the kind that could rip through rock and building foundations, that could shred a man to ribbons. The Reformists hadn't been able to get their hands on these, not even with Baron Hulei's influence.

Shit, Draifey, what are you doing?

"These belong to one of them politicians?"

Bregan jumped. The receiving officer had sneaked up behind him. Apparently, Bregan had spoken his thoughts aloud, because blood was draining from the man's face.

"We're handling it," Bregan promised, waving to the other constables. "Pack up every crate in this room. I want them tagged, counted, and locked up at headquarters in evidence." He turned back to the receiving officer. "The rest of the paperwork?"

The man squinted at him with the kind of fearful, morbid curiosity some might give the dead or dying, then offered him a small stack of receipts. "Here's the normal receipts, and I found this in the stack." He laid a small envelope on top. "Was supposed to be given to whoever paid."

The envelope's flat red seal was thin, unmarked. Someone had scribbled FOR PICKUP in the top corner. Otherwise, it was blank.

Bregan signaled for one of his constables' lanterns and tore into the letter with one hand. He scanned the contents, then instantly read it again. The third time through, understanding sank in, breaking the island's foundation beneath his feet.

The guns indicated an attack . . . but this?

This confirmed a coup.

FIFTY-ONE

Firin

Now

The temple buzzed with the sounds of metamorphosis. Hired tailors packed the western corridor. Cooks crowded the kitchen. Dozens of hammers echoed in the nave like a frantic heartbeat. Workers covered the stage, the pews, and the balconies like ants—fixing and polishing the entire building until it shone. At the center of it all, Luka and Jaari winced against the noise as they rehearsed with their new musicians.

The baron came through on his promises. After our lunch, he poured money into the Veiled Players' coffers, and a couple of other patrons followed suit. We now had enough money to transform not just the show and the stage but also the entire temple. If opening night went well, the troupe would have money flowing like this forever.

I wove through the aisles, searching for Bregan.

"Jaq?" I jumped onstage, where the set designer was adding the last coat of paint to a mock pirate ship. "Have you seen Bregan?" Nyfe needed him for a costume fitting, and I couldn't find him anywhere. He hadn't come back to his room last night, and outside rehearsing, we'd barely spoken over the last few days.

I could tell he didn't understand my silence. He was slipping away from me, receding like a night tide. But I didn't have a choice. In a few more days, I could cover up my scar, explain my behavior away as nerves about the play, and finally give myself to him the way he deserved.

Jaq shook his head, focused on the paint. Like Luka and some of the others, he had given me a slight cold shoulder since we announced *Qoyn & Insei*. They all seemed torn between accepting the blessing of Baron Hulei's patronage and blaming me for forcing them into a political stance they didn't agree with. But when it was all over, and they were swimming in long-term patronage, they would know we had done the right thing.

"Haven't seen him," Jaq finally said. "But he was quoted in the paper this morning." He pointed his chin to a *Luisonn Daily* folded in a pew.

I read the front page.

COUNCILMAN DRAIFEY ACCUSED OF TREASON

Late last night, Chief Inspector Bregan Nimsayrth reported that a shipment of contraband weapons and explosives was confiscated in the Fingers, originally slated for reception by members of Councilman Thom Draifey's presidential campaign. "We have evidence that Thom Draifey is conspiring with former Stav Regime leaders and Nodtacht agents," Nimsayrth said. "We fear we've just managed to snuff out an attempt at a coup to return power to their . . ."

"There he is," Jaq said.

I jumped. Bregan was stalking up the center aisle, hands deep in his pockets. I looked back at the paper. A *return* of the Stav Regime? All their leaders were dead. The Vorstav'n Empire was in shambles. This wasn't possible, was it? My stomach flipped, as if I'd been shoved off a cliff. How many other Iket Isles Nodtacht had escaped? I'd never worn my real face in front of any of them except Father and Eznur—and both were dead—but if Hulei launched a search for more of us, it would get harder to hide.

At the back of the temple, I caught eyes with Mezua. Her lips were thin as she glanced at the paper in my hand. My heart skipped a beat. She wouldn't turn me in, would she? She needed me. For now.

Bregan vaulted onstage.

I met him at the edge. "What happened last night?"

"Hey, can we talk?" he asked, crossing to Jaq as if I weren't there.

"What is this?" I brandished the paper. "Draifey's working with the Nodtacht?"

"We handled it." He still didn't look at me. "Jaq?"

Curious glances danced over us as the workers in the pews became our audience. Paint dropped from Jaq's brush to the protective cloth as he hesitated. "Maybe you two should—"

"Bregan," I said, stepping between them, "what happened?"

He ducked through a makeshift door that led backstage.

"Talk to me," I demanded, following.

"Why would I do that?"

"*What* is your problem?"

When he turned, the light from the now-distant door slashed over his face. Boxes, crates, and set pieces slumbered in the dark behind him.

"At the *Daily*'s office last night, they asked me if I wanted to comment on *this*." He whipped a rolled-up newspaper from his back pocket. The fresh ink shone. It wasn't today's paper. It was a draft of tomorrow's.

A FAMOUS LOVE STORY, PERFORMED WITH REAL LOVE

Next Seventhday, to mark the dawn of a new Luisonn, President Hulei is sponsoring a production of the infamously difficult *Qoyn & Insei*, starring two previously unknown actors. Bregan Nimsayrth and Vota, two

children from the Labor District, grew up in the shadows of rebellion, clinging to their love of art—and
each other. In this exclusive interview with Aza Vota,
we learn that the true love you will see onstage next
weekend is a symbol not just of our new freedoms but
also . . .

The interview Hulei asked me to give. I had avoided painting too
many lies by focusing on our past together rather than my childhood.
"It's just an article," I said.

Bregan laughed. Shook his head. "It's not even true. All the bullshit
you sold them. My father would say you're just using me for fame, just
like my ma."

"I am *not* your mother," I snapped.

"I don't have patience for this anymore." He stalked farther
backstage.

"Patience for what?" My knee hit a wooden crate.

"Everything. Look, after last night, I have a lot to do."

"It's just a publicity article. It will *help* Hulei win Labor votes. Isn't
that the whole point?"

"It's not *about* the article." He rounded on me so fast I backed
into the witch's house. The smell of the sea rolled off him, salty and
intoxicating.

"Then what?" I snapped. "You're mad I wouldn't have sex with
you?"

He blinked. "*What?* No. I'm mad that you won't tell me anything—
what happened to you, what the fuck is going on, what you *want*. I told
you I loved you, Firin, and now you won't talk to me? Was it all just a
ploy to get me to do *Qoyn & Insei?*"

His words knocked the wind out of me. "Of course not." I hadn't
treated him like a mark in a con, had I? The thought made me nause-
ated. Maybe using people was all I knew how to do.

With a single step, he closed the space between us, his leg slotting between mine, trapping me against the set house. "Then what are we doing, Firin? Because whatever it is, it's not what you told that reporter." He glared down as if I were a frustrating riddle he couldn't let go, and a traitorous heat trickled through my veins.

I wanted to mold myself to him, to prove I loved him, that he was the only thing I'd ever loved, but that would be the worst-possible move.

When he buried his fingers into my hair, the gentleness of his touch clashed with the fire in his eyes. "It's so obvious," he breathed. "It's so painfully obvious that there's something that happened to you—or something you did—that you're ashamed of. It's holding you back. It's stifling you."

My laugh strained. "Is this about us or my past?"

"Maybe it's about both. Maybe you can't—"

"Can you stop?" Something brittle inside me broke. I just needed a few more days. "Can you just be patient, for once?"

"Patient? Firin, I thought you were dead for *four* years."

"I don't owe you anything," I said, more breath than bite.

"No, you don't. But don't you owe it to yourself?"

The words snatched all speech right out of my throat.

He stepped back. "I can't do this."

My bones fractured. My mouth opened before I knew what to say, but then I saw it: the letter Baron Hulei had given me, peeking out from the inside pocket of Bregan's coat. I had dropped it off at the Landings days ago, wearing a messenger girl's face.

Why did *Bregan* have it?

"What happened last night?" I blurted.

"Seriously?" He threw up his hands. "I'm done."

I snatched his arm before he could leave. "You can't quit the play."

"Of course," he said hoarsely. "I'm here for the troupe and the president, though I'm not sure I can say the same for you."

As he turned and left, I swiped the letter from his coat.

Alone backstage, I held the envelope up to a sliver of light. The red seal was broken and the contents refolded. I took them out with shaking fingers.

The distant sounds of construction warped into a roar.

This wasn't a letter.

It was a list of names and locations.

The top line, which had been crossed out, read: *Skavka'tor—a.k.a. Cwci Ogwe, Prestup'ned, Iapia Kuon. Age in 50s. Last known location: Saint Fynwyth's.* Nails of fear raked down my spine, and with every subsequent pseudonym I recognized, the nails dug deeper.

This was a list of Nodtacht names.

I scraped over the paper until I landed on: *Restuv.* The list of aliases for Father went longer than most. I stared at each one. *Othan Finweint, Sniq Shiva, Mizak Osai, Bothwyk Perth . . .*

Like Skavka'tor's, Father's name had been crossed out. So had Eznur's.

Then I landed on: *Afyn Wainrite.*

The name I'd given Eznur on my first day.

A.k.a. Prit, Naemira, Jekita. Age in 20s. Last known location: 56 Ophil St., Trade Market. I backed into a set table. That was the address of my last tenement room, the one I'd abandoned in my attempt to escape Luisonn. My information had not been crossed out.

I was circled in red.

The paper whispered as it shook. Were the struck-out Nodtacht dead and the circled ones alive? Why had Baron Hulei given me this? Why had he wanted it planted at the Landings?

Bootsteps clacked on the stage. I stuffed the list back in the envelope at the exact moment Bregan reappeared.

"Have you seen—"

I held out the envelope. "This? You dropped it." He snatched it. "What is it?" I asked. Somehow my voice was even.

"Government business."

"Does it have to do with last night?"

"Yes. It's proof that Draifey was planning to arm his Stav allies."

I stared at him. Draifey?

This was his proof that Draifey was working with the Stav?

Excuses scrambled at the edge of my mind, but there was no reasonable explanation for this. That list was Hulei's, which meant the guns Bregan had confiscated were his as well.

Draifey wasn't working with the Stav.

There was no threat of a coup.

Hulei was framing him.

One heartbeat stretched into an endless, agonizing eon. A confession boiled behind the bars of my rib cage. I could tell Bregan about my deal with Hulei, the envelope, all of it. But then what? Bregan wouldn't understand why I'd done it. He would call me a liar and a schemer, just like his mother, and then he would confront Hulei and we would very likely lose his support of *Qoyn & Insei*.

"I'm heading out," Bregan said.

I let him go.

FIFTY-TWO

Bregan

Now

The temple yawned around Bregan in the quiet morning. The wooden pew dug into his hip as he blinked up at the ceiling. Beyond the freshly patched stained glass windows, the sky was still dark. With a sigh, he pushed himself to a seat. The nave swallowed the soft rustle of his blanket as he folded it. After a few nights of sleeping in the pews, and many more sleeping on the ground, his body ached. But he couldn't make himself go back downstairs.

Whatever Firin was holding back was festering and paralyzing her onstage, but she didn't want his help. At this point, she didn't seem to want *him*. For his own sanity, he couldn't stand to be so close to her while still feeling so far away.

Soft voices trickled in from the kitchen. Bregan rose with a stretch and slipped his flatcap on. While he had been explicitly ordered to attend the baron's campaign rally today as an actor, not a constable, he still wanted to get there early to discuss security with the commissioner. Draifey's weapons were locked up at headquarters, but they still hadn't *found* the politician, and he had plenty of supporters.

In the kitchen, Tez captained the stove. Luka and Jaq hunched over a pile of papers at the table. Upon his entry, the troupe's conductor straightened and left with a swish of their coat.

"Luka's still upset, then?" Bregan asked, heading for the washbasin. Now that they had proof of Draifey's plans, he'd hoped the conductor would come around. Steam curled above the water in a haze.

Tez sighed. "Mezua *did* promise we wouldn't get involved in any more politics."

"It's naive to think—"

Tez raised a hand. "I know, Bregan. We all know what we're gaining from this. I mean, just look at my stores." He glanced at the crates along the wall, overflowing with potatoes and squash from Gwynythaid.

"It's not just about the money," Bregan muttered, splashing water on his face. The searing liquid dispersed some of his mental fog. He patted his hands dry.

"Well, money is pouring in," Jaq said, frowning at some accounting papers. "Opening up the ground floor to the poor certainly worked in the president's favor."

Firin's romantic article had made them overnight darlings, living examples of what was now possible for the lower classes. When Hulei announced exclusive ticket sales for former Labors, people had lined up for blocks. When the Grande opened *The Pirate's Widow* over the weekend, rumor had it half the audience was empty. Attendees and patrons appeared to be hoarding their money for *Qoyn & Insei*.

"We've already sold out," Jaq said flatly. "Mezua wants to add more shows."

"Is that a bad thing?" Bregan asked, putting on his coat.

Since the article exposing Draifey's coup plans, tensions with Jaq had iced over. When Bregan asked him if he had known about Draifey's coup, Jaq hadn't even graced him with an answer. Bregan couldn't fault him, or anyone, for wanting a Labor as president. He couldn't even fault them for judging Hulei. The baron was shortsighted about classist issues. It had taken prodding for the baron to open the play to Labors, and he still didn't seem to understand why the *Luisonn Daily's* mistake in faulting Labors for the shoot-out at Draifey's rally was detrimental to their anti-classism cause—but Hulei was better than a return to the Stav, and right now that was their alternative.

"I'm heading to the rally," Bregan said. "Tell Vota that's where I am?"

"You're still not talking with her?" Tez leaned back against the warmth of the iron stove. "She's been worse up onstage, you know, with you two fighting."

"We're not fighting." You had to speak to one another to have a fight. Besides, it wasn't his fault Firin's acting had taken a dive. She'd locked her emotions in an iron box, and only she had the key. "I've done everything I can to reach her, but she won't let me."

"Can you blame her?" Jaq traced a finger over calculations.

"What does *that* mean?"

Jaq met his eyes behind his circular glasses. "We know you mean well, Breg, but sometimes you can be a bit . . . stubborn."

Bregan let out a grating laugh. If anyone was being stubborn, it was Firin. "I'll see you at the rally," he said, leaving before they could argue.

Chill morning air slapped Bregan's face, waking him up fully. He loved the troupe. They were his family. But sometimes, living in such close quarters with a dozen people who thought they knew everything about him was like being imprisoned on a saints-damned ship.

Firin

Now

"Chin up," Nyfe said.

I obeyed. As she came at my eyes with a thick liner pen, I stared at the kitchen ceiling and ran through the pillars of my speech. Hulei had seen the Veiled Players' potential. Just as he'd supported the Reformists, his generosity allowed the theater to thrive. *Hulei* was a candidate who demonstrated care for the Labor-class people, and I was a living example of that. None of it was technically untrue.

"Done," Nyfe said. I blinked watery eyes. "This paint from Iakirru is to die for." When my vision cleared, her sly smile lit up her whole face.

"Here's the suit the president sent you to wear," Suri said, entering with a bright-red Qunsiian-style two-piece draped over her arm.

Jumping off the bench, Nyfe ran her fingers over the fabric. "Saints, this is gorgeous."

"Did you find Bregan?" I asked Suri.

"No. Jaq said he left early this morning."

"He left?" Nyfe said. "But his suit is here."

I looked away from Suri's curious stare. This morning I'd woken, yet again, to an empty room. Since our latest fight, Bregan had made it abundantly clear that he wanted as little to do with me as possible. I couldn't exactly blame him, but I also couldn't do anything about it.

Once the election and *Qoyn & Insei* were over, the troupe would be secure, the political battles would be over, and I could deal with my scar. Safety lay at the end of this path, for everyone. I just had to stay the course.

Today, however, our estrangement was a liability. The public expected a fairy tale, not heartbreak. I needed to talk to him before we joined the president at the podium. "He probably went to check on security," I said, rising. "We can bring his suit with us."

I took the red suit from Suri and, refusing both women's offers for help, positioned my branded arm to the wall, yanked off my sweater, and slid into the black shirt that came with it. The silk cooled my skin. Over the years, I'd gotten well practiced at obscuring my Nodtacht mark in shadows and folds of hair. Still, I didn't breathe until the buttons were done.

After I'd pulled on the pants and jacket, Nyfe straightened my lapels. "Oh, Vota, you look incredible."

I glanced at the mirror propped on the table. Nyfe had piled my hair high in Qunsiian fashion and brushed delicate paints over my features. Beneath the makeup, you couldn't see my freckle. Even though I wasn't wearing an illusion, the sharp-eyed, straight-backed woman in the glass was a stranger. My throat closed up.

Vota the actress.

I was so *close* to everything I'd ever dreamed, so why did I feel so cold?

My gaze drifted to the door, just visible behind me in the mirror, and I wished, for one wild moment, that Bregan would walk through it, knowing he wouldn't.

Once Nyfe and Suri changed into their own outfits, we headed for the Corners with Jaq and Phinnin trailing behind us. Most of the troupe planned to meet at the rally in a show of gratitude for the president's support. Nyfe carried Bregan's suit in a bag over her arm.

The brisk morning warmed as people of all classes poured together like streams of water, eager to see the president who'd freed them. Over the past few days, every trace of the insurrection had been swept from the streets. The only remaining signs of the attack lingered in scattered bullet holes, the blackened walls of burned buildings, and the absence of the Corners' statue of Emperor Dreznor'proska'ed'nov.

As constables cleared a path for us to the speech platform, it took everything in me not to look at the canal bridges behind it, where the other Nodtacht had hung after the insurrection. I turned my back on the water and searched for Bregan.

He and the commissioner huddled behind the podium stage. Bregan gestured as he argued about something that didn't seem to faze his superior. When I approached, Bregan flinched, his chin slightly turning, as if he wanted to look away but couldn't. His gaze traced the curves of my custom-fitted suit. I suppressed the urge to smirk. The commissioner bowed and retreated.

"Everything seem safe?" I asked, with more bite than I intended.
Bregan scuffed his boot against the cobblestones.

"Is there something you want to say?" I lowered my voice.

He squinted at something across the canal. "There's nothing to say."

"Bregan—"

"Ah, Vota, you look exquisite." Hulei appeared in a black-and-yellow
pin-striped suit. From a distance, it seemed understated, but up close I
could tell the buttons were gold. The black of his top hat drank the sunlight.
"Nimsayrth, you're not wearing that, are you?"

"I brought his suit for him," I said.

"Good." He squeezed both our shoulders. "Well, let's talk about
your speeches. I think Vota can go first, and I know this is last minute,
but I'd love to build on that *wonderful* interview she gave. You're both
adept at improvising, yes?"

"The article?" I'd planned an entire speech about Hulei, not us.

"Well, yes. People adore you two—the love, the triumph. Let's sell
them more of what they want, yes?"

Bregan stared at his boots.

"Yes, of course," I forced out.

"Excellent." Hulei clapped his hands together, then headed for the
commissioner.

"Does Nyfe have my suit?" Bregan asked. "I'm going to change."

I slid in front of him. "Look, I know you're upset with me, but—"

"Don't worry. I understand my role."

My ribs cracked. "That's not what I was going to say."

"Isn't it?"

I watched him go, my hands in fists. Today, right now, we had
a chance to secure the Players' future forever, and he acted like *I* was
being selfish.

The next minutes, or hours, warped like an unsettling dream. Nyfe
touched up my makeup; Hulei introduced me to several businessmen
I couldn't retain the names of; and the whole time, the sound of the

distant crowd was drowned out by the clock inside my head, ticking closer and closer to the moment we'd get onstage.

When Hulei waved us over, I floated toward him on feet long ago trained by my father. Beside me, in the stiff and expensive suit Hulei had given him, Bregan didn't look like himself. As we climbed the steps of the platform, some part of me expected him to take my hand or put his arm around me. He didn't. But we still needed to win over the public, so when we were in full view of the crowd, I rose on my toes to kiss his cheek. The ocean of onlookers roared. They couldn't see him flinch.

Hulei said some words, then motioned me to the podium.

On the outside, I beamed as Vota, Luisonn's newest adoration.

On the inside, I couldn't feel anything at all.

My lips turned upward. I raised a hand. In the front row, a little girl with two brown braids lifted a bouquet toward me from her father's shoulders.

The sight of her clenched my windpipe like a fist, and I thought of another little girl, cross-legged before a mirror. Purpose settled in me like an anchor.

This was for her.

I knelt at the edge of the stage, took the flowers from the girl, and pulled playfully on one of her braids. The crowd went wild. Gripping the bouquet, I stepped back to the podium. The square quieted. New Luisonn flags snapped far above in a coastal wind that teased loose strands of my hair. The little girl gave me a toothy grin.

I took a deep breath . . .

And the stage exploded in a shower of fire and wood.

FIFTY-THREE

Bregan

Now

The back of Bregan's head hit something hard. The world plunged into silence. A single high-pitched note, like the screech of a violin, struck through the void, imbuing his every bone.

Firin.

Fleshy fingers—the president's fingers—reached to pull him back up, but he spun away, toward the podium, to the empty space where Firin had *just* stood, stunning and beautiful and infuriating. His still-empty lungs seized.

If she was hurt . . .

If the last thing he'd done was dismiss her . . .

Then he saw her. She had landed on her side; debris and soot sprinkled her red silk suit, her hair. When her eyes met his, full and alive, air pummeled into his rib cage with the burn of seawater. On shaking, failing knees, he crawled through the wreckage of the stage toward her, but then her face stretched in a moan. She pointed.

The explosion had taken a chunk out of the stage, just to the right of the podium, and in the middle of it lay *Pa*. Bregan stared at his father's parted lips, at the blood streaming down his face.

Pa was here. *How?*

Then reality broke through his shock, and a wail shot out of him. He half fell through the debris and crouched at his father's side. "Pa," he said, or mouthed.

The side of his father's face had been ravaged as if by the claws of a beast. His arm lay at an impossibly grotesque angle. Bile burned up Bregan's throat. After everything, after all of it, he could *not* lose Pa now. Otherwise, what had it all been for?

He screamed for help. Then people were there, hands pressing and pulling. As they lifted Pa, Bregan searched the crowd. Constables surrounded Firin and the president, but he couldn't see the commissioner anywhere in the smoke and dust and chaos. How had they missed this? Bregan had personally searched every crevice of the stage this morning.

Fingers wrapped around his arm. Bregan looked down into Pa's wide eyes. His body was strung between four different people but he refused to let go.

"Taidd," he choked, jerking his chin.

Addym Taidd hovered at the edge of the chaos in his gray constable uniform, observing the ruin with a bone-chilling, triumphant grin.

Their eyes locked. Then Addym ran.

Bregan scaled the wreckage with the frantic determination of a starving predator. He snatched up a broken piece of wood in lieu of a club, but when he cleared the destruction, Addym was nowhere to be found. The smoke had swallowed him whole.

Then Jaq appeared, covered in dust and blood, as if he'd stepped through time from the night of the insurrection. The horror on his face held a kind of weight, and Bregan knew, without a shadow of a doubt, that Jaq knew more than he had let on.

"Where is he?"

"Down the street," Jaq panted. "He'd go to Draifey's safe house."

They ran.

"Here," Jaq said, whipping around a corner. "He's just—"

At the row house Jaq pointed to, a young boy hammered on the door, shrieking a warning. When Addym stepped out, Bregan sprinted. The moment Addym spotted him, he bolted too, heading for an alley. In their days as kids, playing ball and racing through the streets, Addym had always been strong, but Bregan had been faster.

They tumbled to the ground in a mess of limbs.

"Bregan, what the—"

Pain burst up Bregan's forearm as he hit Addym's face. He felt, more than heard, Addym's nose break. Addym roared, and Bregan punched him again. For hurting Pa, for hurting Firin, for hurting however many innocent people had fallen to the bomb.

"Bregan, careful," Jaq said. "You need him conscious."

"You're under arrest," Bregan declared, "for attacking the president of Luisonn."

"You're delusional," Addym said, the words mangled by his bleeding nose. When Bregan flipped him onto his stomach to twist his arms behind his back, he seemed too consumed with ire to struggle. "Fuck, Bregan, you can't tell your arse from your elbow."

"Jaq, go get backup," Bregan ordered. Jaq took off.

Addym released a feral growl. "Whatever happened, it *wasn't* me."

Bregan stiffened. For the first time, he actually *looked* at Addym. The man's chest heaved, pumping blood from his nose onto the street. In a loose tunic and trousers, with the tousled-hair appearance of sleep, he looked nothing like he had moments ago at the stage. He wasn't even wearing a constable's uniform.

Every muscle in Bregan's body liquefied.

Addym hadn't been at the bombing.

Someone else had worn his face.

Firin

Now

Flower petals scattered the stage, paled by dust from the explosion. Dread poured into me like tar as Bregan ran away from his father, disappearing into the chaos . . .

Then I spotted the child.

Blood splattered her thin braids, poured down her temple in an angry river. She stared in the direction of her father, who'd become a lump of clothing in a pile of wood, but her eyes were empty.

Unseeing.

A dozen other bodies lay strewn in the wreckage around her, unmoving. Bile seared up my throat. Slapping a hand to my mouth, I tried to stand and tripped on the toppled podium. My knees slammed back down. Beside me, the president stood swathed in smoke. He brushed dust off his jacket, and for the briefest moment, his lips twitched up.

My rage flared white hot.

"What did you do?" I snarled. But I already knew.

The president had bombed his own people.

Hulei yanked me up by my arm. Pulling me close in a way that would look to everyone around like concern, he said, "I didn't do anything." The words warped in my damaged ears, as if we were underwater. "Draifey did everything, and that's what you will testify."

I should have known he would never be satisfied with a successful play and an election. I should have known he'd never stop until Draifey's fate sat firmly in his iron grip.

He had murdered his own people. Children. His followers.

I had *helped* him.

"Let go of me," I said. "I swear I will—"

Grip bruising, he leaned back just enough to pierce me with sunless eyes. "Don't flatter me with a facade of morals now, Firin."

I stopped breathing.

The corner of his mouth curled. "Oh yes, I know who you are. I know *what* you are, and right now you will come with me to the hospital and testify against Thom Draifey. Then you will win the city for me with a perfect performance of Insei, or I will destroy everything you love. Starting with the Players and ending with your life."

He knew my name. He knew I was a Nodtacht.

And he was using me, just like they had.

"You and I have both just gotten everything we want," he added, spinning me toward the growing group of medics. "Let's not ruin it now."

"Mr. President!" a medic shouted. "Are you all right?"

"Fine, I'm fine." He shoved me toward the man.

Someone wrapped me in a blanket. Someone else took my arm. A terrible pain spasmed inside my skull.

"Vota," someone said, "would you like to make a statement?" A set of watery eyes swam in front of me. I stared at the pen in the man's hand.

Somehow the precipice of everything I'd ever wanted had become a ridge with deathly drops on either side. I could tell this reporter the truth and expose this nightmare, but if Father had taught me anything, it was how to read a man, and the baron wasn't bluffing.

I'd sailed myself into this storm; now I had to weather it.

"Yes," I said, letting my chin quiver, "I would like to condemn Mr. Draifey's horrible attack on the free people of this city . . ."

FIFTY-FOUR

Bregan

Now

The heavy Enlightened Hospital's door swung open on a lobby packed with panicked families. With Jaq a step behind him, Bregan elbowed his way to the line of constables blocking the inner doors. The chaos of light and voices muted the suspicion pounding like a nail against his skull.

He had let Addym go.

He hadn't even thought about it. Bregan knew when Addym was lying, and this time he hadn't been. Addym hadn't been at the bombing. A Nodtacht had attacked the podium while wearing his face. Bregan was sure of it.

He needed to talk to Pa.

When he reached the constables, they recognized him despite the ruined upper-class suit he was wearing. They waved him and Jaq through to the main floor. The doors clicked shut, smothering the cacophony in the lobby with a sudden, rustling quiet. Beds lay in rows like docks, separated only by wheeled curtains.

"An absolute travesty," he heard Hulei say. "An unprovoked attack on a new country."

Bregan halted, scanning for the president. His voice came from behind a curtain, where he seemed to be giving an interview. *Controlling the narrative,* Hulei had put it days ago. The thought punched into Bregan's abdomen.

Had the baron bombed his *own* rally?

Bregan had avoided the question the whole way here, but putting words to the mere suggestion of it sliced him open the way his mother's betrayal had, bleeding uncertainty. Was it possible? Bombing the platform and blaming it on Draifey would give the president a leg up in his campaign. Was it possible he was that terrible? Surely Bregan would have seen it coming?

Bregan pulled aside a young physician with blood up to her wrists. "My father? Dech Nimsayrth." She led him to a cordoned-off bed at the back of the room. Jaq was positioned just outside the curtain. Bregan ducked behind it.

Pa looked as if he were wrapped in a ship's entire sail. They'd bandaged his torso, his head, and half his face. His broken arm had been set and splinted. But when Bregan's boots scuffed the floor, Pa looked up, alert and lucid.

Bregan fell to his knees, clasping his father's good arm to the elbow. Pa strained forward until their foreheads touched.

"You're all right," Pa choked out.

"Saints, Pa. I can't say the same about you." Bregan leaned back. "Why were you there?"

His father's uncovered eye narrowed. "I was following Addym."

"Why?"

"Commissioner's orders."

Pa was the one the commissioner had hired? Bregan felt sick. "I joined the constabulary so you wouldn't have to, Pa."

"I *wanted* to," Pa said. "I needed something to do, and finding Addym was critical to proving Draifey's schemes. I was working on whispers and hearsay until this morning, when Addym came right by my morning tavern. I followed him to the rally, but he slipped through my fingers."

Bregan rubbed his hands down his face. They came away covered in soot. Had whoever'd worn Addym's face lured Pa to the rally on purpose?

"Why keep it from me?" he asked. "I was trying to stop Draifey too."

"I was told to."

Bregan rocked back on his heels, still gripping his father's forearm. He didn't like how the facts lined up. First off, there was no good reason for the commissioner to withhold Pa's work from Bregan's investigation. It didn't make sense. Second, Bregan had checked the entire speech platform for sabotage this morning. Only someone the constables trusted could have planted a bomb *after* the rally started, a bomb that had gone off on the side of the stage opposite where Hulei, Firin, and Bregan had stood—far enough to ensure they'd be sheltered from the worst of the blast but close enough that they appeared to be the target. Finally, everyone knew Addym worked for Draifey; he wouldn't send a Nodtacht to do this job *wearing* Addym's face.

The gears of Bregan's brain turned, trying to see how it could be Draifey's fault, but he kept snagging on a simple truth: Draifey had little to gain from killing Hulei; it would turn the city against him. Bregan thought of the guns and explosives, and his stomach churned. Was it possible Hulei had planted those too?

"Pa," he said slowly. He needed to get this out before Hulei discovered he was here. "The president's been . . . hiding things."

Pa sank back into the bed. "It's his right to, Bregan."

"Not just security secrets."

"I'm sure he has his reasons."

"There are no *good* reasons. Not for this." Not if Bregan was right.

"That's not for you to decide."

"Pa, I'm trying to tell you—"

With a raised hand, his father silenced him. "Listen to me, son. Even after losing his wife and his son, Baron Hulei put everything he had on the line for this country. He supported us when no one else would, when he had no personal reason to. He is the reason the Stav are gone. He may not be a perfect man," Pa continued, "but he is the best future this country can hope for right now, and what he needs from us is faith, not a demand for virtue perfection."

It was the same argument Bregan had fumed over just this morning, after arguing with Jaq and Tez in the kitchen.

What if he used us? Bregan wanted to counter, but Pa's grip shook with a familiar fervor, the kind that had accompanied his arguments with Ma years ago. The sign that he was digging his heels into something and wouldn't be moved.

"I'm surprised you even care, given you abandoned your prospects." Pa released him. "Working for that woman who corrupted your ma."

Bregan stared at him. "*Corrupted* her?"

"It's her whole purpose, isn't it? Teaching people to be two-faced."

"Mezua housed, clothed, and fed me while you sat in a prison cell."

"Right, because that was my choice."

"It *was* your choice."

Pa had *chosen* to risk his life for the movement, and that was fine, but Bregan wouldn't sit here and let him frame Mezua to make himself feel better about abandoning his family.

"No." Pa threw out a gnarled finger. "It was never a choice. The Reform movement was the *only* way I could protect you and your ma; it was the only way to secure *you* a future. One that you're squandering with the same lack of gratitude that your mother showed. Your *ma* is the one who only ever cared about herself."

Bregan reared back. "Then why did she stay here with you?"

Pa didn't hear—or chose not to hear—the question. "I had to lie about joining the Reform movement because she would have stopped me," he rasped. "She always saw it as a threat to the Players, even when I connected the movement with the troupe, even when gaining her the right to perform was half of *why* I was doing it, so she might finally be *happy* here."

Bregan winced. For years, he, too, had blamed Ma's betrayal on selfish cowardice because it gave him a reason to hate her, and the sharp edges of hate kept the torment of missing her at bay. But today, everything he thought he knew had been thrown into a hurricane.

"Why did Ma hate Baron Hulei so much?" he asked.

Pa huffed. "Because he critiqued her performances."

"I don't believe that." Bregan had clear memories of Ma arguing that she didn't trust the baron, and Pa dismissing her fears. What if Ma had known more about Hulei than she let on?

"Fine, Bregan," Pa sighed, sagging into the cot's mattress. "I'm a terrible father, your ma was the perfect parent. I drove her away. I ruined your childhood. I shouldn't have risked my life to fight for freedom, for *your* future. That's what you want to hear, right?"

Bregan's heart suddenly hurt so much he wanted to tear it out of his chest. Why had he come here? What had he hoped for?

Pa thrived on loyalty. When he committed to something, he became singularly focused, all-consumed. Once, that had been Bregan and his mother, but with the Reform movement and Ma's initial lies about joining the theater, his loyalties had shifted. But maybe such fervent commitment led to delusion.

His father only ever saw what he wanted to. When Ma hid her involvement with the theater, he wrote her off as a fame-obsessed liar because that was easier than admitting he failed to make her happy on his own. When he learned Mezua had taken Bregan in, he decided she was taking advantage of him because it was easier than facing the fact that his *own* decisions had made Bregan homeless. When Bregan returned to the stage, Pa decided he was a coward because it was easier than accepting that Bregan didn't want to follow in his footsteps.

Now that nefarious signs pointed toward Baron Hulei, Pa refused to see them. To do so would mean he'd lost his wife, abandoned his son, and gone to prison for the wrong man—that four generations of sacrifice had amounted to nothing.

Bregan braced his elbows on the bed and closed his eyes. He had done the same thing. He had been so eager to put the revolution behind him, and to finally live without always looking over his shoulder, that he had dedicated himself to proving Hulei was the right leader. He had allowed his selfish desire to ignore and explain away all the warning signs.

No wonder Addym and Jaq hadn't trusted him. He never would have listened to them. Just as his father wasn't going to hear him now.

"Nimsayrth, you're alive." The president's voice sounded on the other side of the curtain. Bregan sprang to his feet as the man stepped inside.

"Mr. President," he and his father said at the same time.

The baron shook Pa's hand. Both men beamed as if they'd just won a battle, not survived a bombing. In his slick, ash-smeared suit, Hulei looked every inch the caring politician. How much of this man was an act?

"I'm glad you're all right, son." The president pinned Bregan with a sharp blue gaze. "Any luck tracking down the Taidd kid?"

Jaq appeared through the gap in the curtain, just within earshot, and Bregan felt as if he were standing on the western beaches, facing down the first wave of a storm. If he was wrong about the bombing, he risked losing the president's trust, perhaps even jail time. But if he was *right* and did nothing?

"I lost Taidd, sir," he lied. "In the chaos."

Jaq disappeared again.

The president sighed. "Well, we'll get him soon enough. Now, rest up. You look like death. This country needs something *good* to lift its spirits, so let's give them a stellar opening night."

Bregan left the president with his father. Jaq followed him out of the hospital, into the street, and halfway back to the theater in complete silence. Neither of them spoke until Bregan ducked down an alleyway shortcut.

"I'm sorry I didn't tell you," Jaq blurted. "But I had concerns about Hulei, and you were completely loyal to him. I joined Draifey's campaign to protect Phinnin."

The words landed like blows.

"You lied to him," Jaq added, "about letting Addym go. Why?"

"Because I don't know what to believe."

"Hulei did it, didn't he? The bombing?"

"I don't know. I can't . . ." Bregan's skin stretched so tight over his bones he feared one wrong breath could wrench him open at the seams. "Can you get me a meeting with him? With Draifey?"

"He's deep underground, Breg."

"Can you at least get a message to him that I want to meet?"

"I can try, but he might not want to."

Bregan couldn't blame Draifey for that. "Just try."

He stalked out of the alley alone.

When he reached the temple, he realized how desperately he didn't want to be in the troupe's company. He couldn't bear their worry and questions. So he climbed up to the bell-tower roof.

She was already there.

When Firin got to her feet, the late-afternoon sun silhouetted her like a painting of a Gwyn saint. When she ran into his chest, all the fraught fragments of him melted. He gripped her with all he had.

"I'm sorry," she choked out.

"You have nothing to be sorry for." He had been looking at everything all wrong.

He hovered his thumb over a bruise that purpled one of her temples, pulling out the warmth of her irises and accentuating the single freckle beneath her eyes. Ruined makeup smeared her face. Saints, she was beautiful. Beautiful and hurting. In his grief and desire, he hadn't seen her obvious pain. He hadn't allowed himself to acknowledge it. For years, his father had dismissed Ma's melancholy, pushing it away until *later*, until Reform was over, until the world was safe, writing it off as spite and selfishness so he didn't have to feel guilty for his own role in perpetuating it.

Bregan had done the same thing by painting his own truths about Firin. It had been easier to villainize her than to acknowledge her hurt and the guilt he felt for failing her four years ago. Whatever had happened to her, she wasn't holding it from him out of distrust or manipulation. She was suppressing it because it had edges sharp enough to bleed her dry.

He'd been so dense, so saints-damned selfish.

But his eyes were open now, and he was going to use them.

FIFTY-FIVE

Firin

Now

A few days after the bombing, my acting was the worst it had ever been. A quarter through our show run, Mezua paused to discuss tweaks in lighting. We'd been at it since before daybreak, and the sun had long since set beyond the windows. The air in the room was thinner than a lace veil.

I busied myself placing prop pieces back in their spots and tried to ignore the glares boring into me on every side. The play was almost ready, every part of it near perfect. Except for me.

When my back was turned, the troupe whispered that the bombing had rattled me, that I was terrified Draifey might attack us to weaken Hulei and it was ruining my talent. They were wrong.

We had nothing to fear from Draifey, and everything to fear from Hulei. But I hadn't told anyone, not even Bregan or Mezua. We had no choice but to play the president's games.

"Hey, you okay?" Bregan placed a palm on the lower curve of my back. He knew I wasn't, but for once he hadn't pried. I nodded.

"All right," Mezua finally called, turning back to the stage. "Let's try Insei's beach wake-up scene. I know it's late, but give it your all. Pretend it's opening night."

I strode to the middle of the stage, where the spotlight was trained, and lowered into a pool of red-and-white-striped skirts. I could do this. I just had to focus on Insei, on what *she* was feeling. Waking up on a beach and realizing she'd made a terrible mistake. The light dimmed. I closed my eyes.

And saw the dead girl's bloodied braids.

I slapped a hand to my mouth just as the lights flared. For a few hanging seconds, the theater held its breath; then offstage, Nyfe whispered, "Vota?" Boots scuffed the floor. She knelt beside me. "Come on, just breathe."

When she touched my shoulder, a crack spiderwebbed over the fragile wall between me and my emotions. I pulled away before it could break.

Nyfe turned to the front of the stage. "I think we should pause."

Throughout the temple, actors, musicians, and crew watched with lined frowns and bloodshot eyes. Their compassion had died out long ago.

"I'm fine," I insisted, wiping my mouth. "I can do it. I just need a second."

Mezua sighed. "Everyone take ten minutes."

Before Bregan could reach me, I vanished through the freshly hung velvet curtains and into the dark maze of backstage madness. I ducked out into the hallway and through the first door I could find.

In the empty costume room, I leaned against the door and forced myself to inhale the way Father had taught me to regain control, to stop the hollowness from gouging me inside out.

A soft knock sounded.

"Vota?" a small voice whispered.

When I eased open the door, Phinnin grinned up at me from inside a poof of layered skirts and curls. Crooking her finger, she motioned me down.

I knelt. "What is it?"

"Nyfe said you need a hug." Her tiny arms snatched around me, and the embrace was so tight it reached through the cavern of my chest and enveloped my heart.

I held her to me, biting back a pounding headache. If this play flopped, if I humiliated Hulei, there was nothing stopping him from punishing the troupe to punish me, the troupe that had become Phinnin's family after Taira's death.

"Go back out there, Phi." I tweaked her nose. "Tell them I'll be there soon."

"Will you?" Suri asked, appearing in the hallway behind her.

"Go, Phi," I ordered softly. Once the girl scampered off, I got to my feet. "What do you want?"

Suri crossed her arms over her lacy costume dress. "We're not dense, you know. Clearly something is wrong." She sounded concerned for me. I knew better.

"I'm fine."

"Obviously, you're not. Listen, Vota, if you want to—"

"It's too late to swap." I'd already thought about letting Suri play Insei. But there wasn't time, and the public wanted Bregan and me.

Suri raised an eyebrow. "I was *going* to say, if you need to talk about it—whatever it is—I'm happy to listen." I stared at her. "It's suffocating you. If you don't get it out, you'll keep freezing onstage, and we need you to do well." I could see why the others loved her. Her whole wide-eyed-orphan routine was endearing.

"No, thanks," I said.

But as I headed back to the stage, I knew she was right. Everyone had urged me to open up for weeks—to *go there*, as Bregan had put it. I was afraid merely trying might shatter my self-control, but at this point, maybe shattering was the least of my concerns.

I couldn't trust Suri, but perhaps it was time to trust someone else. Someone who had long ago proved he deserved it.

I stalked straight for Mezua, talking center stage with half the actors. "Give us the night," I said, glancing at Bregan. "Let me train with him." He blinked several times.

Mezua tucked her lips between her teeth, then nodded.

I dragged Bregan to the roof.

We emerged under the stars. On the flat top of the bell tower, Bregan flung out his mother's quilt, as if it were the old days. I hugged myself and stood at the very edge of the roof, shivering despite the humidity that hung warm with the promise of summer.

The smell of him engulfed me right before his jacket did. Slowly, as if he wanted to allow me time to pull away, he draped his arms around the olive-colored fabric, nestling me under his chin. We stared out over the city. A few stars winked through the smog above us.

Questions about technique spun through my mind, but each one was an eager waste of time. He'd already given me everything I needed. I just had to be willing to use it.

"I want to try it," I said. "Using my past."

He pressed his nose above my ear. "Start wherever; I'll follow."

I stepped to the edge of the quilt and turned toward the sea. With a deep breath, I pictured Insei on the palace grounds, staring out at a horizon she couldn't reach.

Alone and unseen.

The moment I thought the feelings, I was back in the rafters at the Grande the night I met Bregan, after Father cut me out of the Hulei con. The world expanded around me, pressing in on all sides until I was nothing more than a shadow. Until I barely existed at all.

"There must be more to this life than duty," I said, with more heaviness to it than I'd ever managed before. "Why am I enlightened with dreams and longings if I'm not meant to seek them?"

"What's a duchess got to wish for?" he recited.

I spun. "Excuse me? Who are you?"

We slipped into the scene.

We'd always been good at this scene, but with a new depth of emotion, it clicked into place. When we finished, Bregan let out a laugh that was brighter than the moon above us.

"That was *brilliant*." He kissed me fiercely. "What's next?"

For hours, we cycled through the show, tackling the happy and effortless scenes first, then easing into the harder ones. The ones with pain. As Insei navigated redefining herself after traveling back in time, I drew on my memories of wandering Luisonn as a thousand different strangers. I channeled from my years working for the Stav, collecting secrets for Eznur, never seeing Father, not knowing if Bregan was alive, forgetting who I really was.

I went deeper and deeper into myself, pulling from the hours Father left me in the shadows, calling on all the moments I wore different faces to try to get him to love me. I even tugged joy from the first time I'd met Bregan. At first, it felt like drinking poison, but then, as the words began to flow, it became more like draining an infection. Like relief.

The moon was high in the sky when we fell silent. Only my hardest scenes remained, floating in the air between us.

"Which one next?" Bregan asked quietly.

I shifted, feeling the quilt between my bare toes. "The one when Insei joins the pirates." The one where she abandons her search for Qoyn, succumbing to a life in a different time, as a different person, without him.

I closed my eyes and conjured up an image of the stage tonight, of Nyfe and the other troupe members dressed as pirates. A shiver shot through me.

"What's she feeling?" Bregan's voice was closer, softer.

"Shame." The word reverberated through my bones. "She feels like it's her fault. She dragged the pirates into her mess, and she has to give up on finding Qoyn in order to protect them."

"Breathe," Bregan said, right next to me. He brushed a thumb over one of my fists. "Find a memory." My stomach sloshed.

I was living it right now.

The Veiled Players were in danger because of me, and my guilt was a rot beneath my skin. But it hadn't started there. I'd lived my entire life in shame: over abandoning Bregan, serving the Nodtacht, helping my father.

"I don't know if I can do this," I breathed.

"You can." He kissed my forehead. "The resistance means you're close. What do you feel?"

In a flash, I was back on Regents' Hill, hauling myself up the steps of the Nodtacht headquarters on leaden feet. The first time I met Eznur in his office, I'd felt just as I had the last few days. "Cold. Numb, even, like I'm outside myself."

"What's beneath the numbness?"

"A burning." The same sensation I had hugging Phinnin. "Like a . . . hollow burning."

"Stay there. Start the scene."

I did.

I moved through the lines in a daze, making and declaring Insei's decision to abort her mission to find Qoyn, asking if she could join the pirates instead. My skin writhed horribly, as if the desires to feel *and* be numb were at war, threatening to tear me in two.

When I stopped, I was trembling. I looked up, and Bregan's whole face was pinched. My heart stopped. "Was it bad?"

"What? No." He took something out of his pocket.

I stared at his handkerchief. "What?"

"Firin . . . you're crying."

When I dabbed the cloth to my face, it came away wet, stained with makeup. I blinked. Then I cracked.

I felt it at the base of my neck, like a hammer to the pressure point of a block of ice. Then heat shot down my limbs, breaking me into pieces like a river in reverence to spring. A tear dropped off my chin, and I caught it with his kerchief; then my limbs went boneless.

"Hey, whoa." Bregan pulled me to his chest. My sobs caught, then tangled, until I sounded and felt like I was choking. Bregan ran a hand up and down my back, and each stroke melted me a little more, until I felt like I would crumble without his arms holding me up. "Do you want to stop? We don't have to keep doing this."

"No," I said, surprising myself with a long, rattling breath. It felt good to *feel* something. "I want to do the end. When Insei goes back to see her mother."

It was the moment I hated the most. The scene where Insei risked both her life and Qoyn's to expose her mother's treachery, but when she came face-to-face with her mother's sick form, she instead forgave her.

When I stepped out of his hold, I felt somehow stronger on my feet. I wiped my palms on the skirts of Insei's striped peasant dress.

Bregan crossed his arms. "What's she feeling when she walks into the sickroom?"

I lifted my chin to the stars. "Empathy."

With a heavy exhale, I tore out the last bolt of the emotional shield from my rib cage and stepped into the truth.

FIFTY-SIX

Firin

Then

I stepped into a very different night, on this same roof.

The night of the insurrection.

"Shit," Bregan said. "There they are."

Straddling the rooftop, wearing Suri's face, I followed his line of sight to the horizon, where ships from the continent spilled soldiers onto Luisonn's shores. In the square below, Stav soldiers poured toward the Reformists meeting in the temple.

This time, I had overheard Hulei say to Heynri Diosi just days before, *our neighbors are with us.* I thought it referred to a business deal, not a war.

Bregan hoisted his gun.

The spell of my longing burst. He was going to fight the Stav. To kill them. There could never be a future for us. Not when he would hate me for what I was. Not when I deserved it.

The temple doors flew open.

The Reformists fired first.

"Get out of here!" Bregan bellowed as gunfire rained down in droves. He jumped into the bell tower, leaving me alone, hypnotized by the scene washed in the temple's orange light.

By *Father*.

He marched in the Stav's ranks toward the gunfire, wearing Restuv's stupid face. I hadn't spoken to him in two years. Half of me wanted to run, to get to my ship, but another useless part of me tilted, tumbling off a cliff.

"Stop!" I screamed. Maybe to him or Bregan or myself.

I skidded recklessly down the roof tiles, thudding painfully to my knees in the square. Father turned, pulled by the sound of my voice, and even though I wasn't wearing a face he knew, his eyes blew open with recognition.

Somewhere behind him, Eznur roared at the Stav to move. They surged around Father, and my insides crumbled as he broke rank to run for me.

"This is it!" he shouted, pushing me toward an alley. "Whoever wins, this is your chance. Go. Hide. Become someone else, anyone. Then you *live*, you hear—"

The first bullet tore through his shoulder, spraying me with blood. The second lodged in his back, shoving him to his knees.

I gaped at him, tasting copper. I didn't want to die. Not in this square, not before I'd had a chance to live. But I was pinned by his molten eyes, by the way his chest caved and his eyes watered. The way blood laced his lips.

"Go, Firi," he rasped.

I ran.

I bolted into an alley and threw myself up a fire escape. As the orchestra of gunshots crescendoed, I yanked my illusion cord and became someone else. I climbed and stumbled over roofs toward the Landings, but the ship I had tickets for was gone, and somehow, miraculously, the Reformists had won.

Then I heard the children. *They're draggin' 'em to the Corners.*

Father didn't deserve the ache in my chest. He didn't deserve my sympathy. Nothing he had ever done warranted me risking my life just to watch him die. But my body carried me to the site of the executions anyway.

I hid on the clock-tower roof as Baron Hulei took the stage, and I realized that somehow, in all my time spying on him for Eznur, I had missed his re-involvement in the Reformists' insurrection. I watched as the rebels led the Stav prisoners onto the bridge in groups of three, as black bags were yanked over their heads and nooses snaked around their throats, as they were shoved over the side. Understanding skimmed the surface of my horror, refusing to sink in.

Then they marched Father out.

One of the Reformists had to hold him up. It was clear he was already dying; he wouldn't make it through the night, and yet Hulei was making a spectacle of him anyway.

When he glanced up at the crowd, he was wearing Mr. Finweint's face.

I fell through the frozen lake of my shock. The questions I'd spent years harboring burst into flight—*Why didn't you tell me? Why didn't we run?* But they were birds that would never reach land, because a Labor was slipping a black canvas bag over Father's head, snuffing out the last chance I'd ever have to know his true face or story.

I was too far away to hear the order that sent him over the edge.

Too far to hear his neck snap.

But I felt it in how his body jerked and the crowd cringed. In the phantom shudder of the world beneath me.

The roar of the people's approval could have been heard across the sea. I braced my limbs on the roof. Everything in me spun. Hulei was speaking, declaring his vendetta against Vorstav to the world, but the ringing in my ears dulled his oratory to a hum.

I withdrew inside myself and found a fire that could burn the world. I was so angry: at Father; at the Stav who'd manipulated us; at myself for my traitorous, gnawing grief. Father was dead. He was *dead* because of his own actions, and if I didn't move, I would be too. The Reformists would notice our brands soon, if they hadn't already, and they would patrol every dock, checking every person who tried to leave. There would be no escaping the island anymore.

Become someone else.

Spite lanced through my veins. I would, I decided, but not in the way Father meant. I wouldn't live like him, slithering from story to story, face to face, never committing to anything or anyone. I wouldn't hide from what I wanted.

With the death of the Stav Regime came opportunity, and I would use it. I would leave everything I had been—my crimes, my mistakes, my father and his betrayals—on this rooftop. I would find Bregan, join the Veiled Players, and finally become the person I had always wanted to be.

FIFTY-SEVEN

Firin

Now

The memories were drowning me, but I swam through the waves with all I had.

"Hear me now, Mother," I recited with a poisoned conviction. "I did not come back here out of spite. I came to free us both. You have hurt me. You have hurt me in so many ways . . ." The line stretched, then broke.

My knees shook as I finally understood why it was so *hard* for me to accept Insei's forgiveness of her mother. I'd spent years refusing to forgive my father. The night of the insurrection, I had thought the answers to the questions that haunted me had been severed at the end of his execution rope, but only because I refused to admit that I already had them. I just hadn't wanted to face them. Despite my father's years of hiding, despite not ever seeing his real face, I'd *known* him.

Father loved me.

In his own poisonous, messed-up way, he had loved me enough to risk his life hiding me from the Stav, training me to survive in a world built to imprison me. Even if I couldn't condone what he'd done, I could understand it—and if I could forgive him, maybe I could forgive myself.

With my heart bleeding through my chest, I fixed my gaze on a spot just beyond Bregan. "But I see the wounds you carry," I recited. "I see the pain they cause you, and the harm they have driven you to cause. And for that, I forgive you, but I will be wounded in your retribution no more."

"Curtain," Bregan whispered.

My knees gave out.

I landed on all fours. He was there in an instant, rubbing my back, and a thick knot of a sob shoved out of me. When he wound around me, I pressed my face into his chest, and my love for him grew talons.

"I made a mistake," I choked out. I'd endangered everyone I'd grown to love to protect myself. To hide from my shame. "I should never have trusted Hulei. He framed Draifey, Bregan. *He* bombed the rally."

The night fell silent. I forced myself to look up, but he didn't look horrified or even shocked. He dropped his chin. "I know."

"W-what?" I turned to face him, sitting between his legs on the quilt.

"Whoever set the bomb was wearing Addym Taidd's face, but it wasn't him. I know it sounds crazy. I wouldn't have believed it possible myself if I hadn't seen—"

"I believe you," I said, swiping at my cheeks. "You don't have to explain."

His throat bobbed. "Well, I'm trying to get in contact with Draifey, to see if there's something we can do. I should have seen the warning signs." He glanced at the horizon, as if blaming himself, which was ridiculous. If anyone was to blame, it was me.

"I lied to the *Daily*," I said.

"I told the papers it was Draifey too."

"But you didn't know. I did." I gripped his knee. "I suspected from the beginning that something was off. In exchange for the patronage funds, Hulei asked me to deliver that envelope, the one you found at the Fingers. I didn't know what was in it, but after the article about the weapons, I realized I had planted evidence against Draifey. He killed them . . ." My voice strained. "Hulei killed his *own* supporters. What would he do to us?"

Bregan massaged my shoulder. "It's all right."

"It's not." None of it was. I needed him to understand.

Father's biggest mistake in all of it had been hiding the truth because he feared it would steal me from him. But if he'd told me, we could have faced it together.

I heaved a big inhale, then dived in. "My father was a thief and a swindler; he lied to everyone about everything, including me. Before, I didn't know how to explain any of it to you. I've done terrible things, Bregan."

"You were a kid," he said softly. "Whatever he made you do—"

I laughed. "I'm not a kid anymore, but I've been acting just like him. I lied to everyone about my name and my past. I framed Suri. I collapsed the set on myself to get her kicked out because I didn't know what would happen to me if I couldn't get her role." The confessions poured out of me, as clarifying as the scenes we just acted.

"Do you think I don't know what it's like to have to survive?" he said. "I was underground for four years, Firin, leading a rebel movement. I've killed people. I've watched good people die because of my decisions. I've done so many things I'm not proud of."

"It's not the same," I said. Bregan had been fighting for something larger than himself.

He shook his head. "You did what you needed to do to stay alive."

I tensed. "You don't know that."

"But I know you."

My ribs caved. *You don't,* I wanted to counter. The other, heavier confessions I needed to make sat like coins on my tongue. But a buried part of me was unwinding, the part of me that believed him. In all my life, he was the only person who'd ever truly seen me.

The wind chilled my wet cheeks. "I love you," I said. "I always have. I should have said it at the Grande, but I felt like I needed to prove I was worthy of it. I thought once *Qoyn & Insei* succeeded, maybe I could be."

"That's ridiculous," he said.

"I hurt you." My voice broke.

"I hurt you too." He ran a thumb down the side of my jaw. "You weren't the only one holding back, Firin. I got so focused on exposing Draifey and securing the new government because I didn't want to lose it all—Pa, freedom, you. But my single-mindedness pushed you and Pa away, it blinded me to what Hulei was doing. I don't . . ." His finger trailed farther, catching on my lip. "I don't want to delay living anymore."

The air between us held its breath. Then his eyes dropped to his finger, and heat shot through my grief like a comet through a dark sky.

Still staring at my mouth, he asked, "Do you want to do the last scene? The one where Insei wakes up on the beach?"

"No." I knew which memory to use now, and no part of me wanted to leave the warmth of his hold. The intimacy of this moment.

When I pressed my lips to his, he tasted like home.

We were still tangled in a knot on the quilt. Without breaking the kiss, I straddled his lap and pulled off his costume tunic. He traced the curves of my torso, pressing kisses to my lips, my eyes, my cheeks. Then his whole palm brushed up my neck, and I moaned.

With excruciating slowness, he tugged the ribbon in my braid, pouring my hair down my back, sending bumps cascading down my arms. Then he undid the back buttons of my dress, and it parted. He traced the shape of my breasts with a featherlight touch that tightened every part of me.

"I didn't savor it before," he said, against my temple. "I didn't savor you."

When his arm slid around my back to lay me down, my muscles pulsed with the desire to succumb, to let him consume me in whichever ways he wanted, but instead I placed my palm on his chest. His exhilaration raced beneath my touch.

"Wait," I whispered.

His whole body went rigid. His eyes snapped to mine.

I held his gaze as I pushed him down on his back, as I slid off his pants and bent over to kiss him, my hair falling around us like curtains.

Groaning, he freed the last of my dress's buttons. When I sat up, red-and-white fabric poured over my shoulders, and when I leaned back, Bregan went as still as the night. His eyes flicked over me.

All of me.

No illusion. No facade.

My pulse rushed as I let the moment stretch. The scar on my bicep, hidden behind the veil of my hair, seemed so small, so insignificant, to the way my whole soul threatened to crack open at the look on his face.

"Firin," he said, a breath and a plea.

I took him inside me. He cursed as my body clenched around him. A *rightness* sang through my bones. I ground deeper, and he let out a husky laugh. I caught it with my mouth, wanting to consume it all—this sense of being seen and known, loved. I was desperate for it, with the sinking fear that it might disappear before my eyes, dissolve beneath my touch.

I tried to move slowly, deliberately, but my breaths quickened with each stroke. Time stretched. Seconds warped into breaths and movement. My mind went blissfully blank, submerged in sensation. For the first time since Bloody Fifthday, it was like I belonged in my own skin.

Bregan's fingers raked down my spine, guiding my hips, slowing me down. Just when I thought I'd go mad from his restraint, his arm slid around my back, pulling me closer. His curls brushed my forehead as he drove deeper, reaching places in my soul I hadn't known existed.

My chin lifted, yearning with the rest of me, ready to break. "Bregan," I gasped, right at the edge. "Please . . ."

"Look at me," he said.

I did, and in the open, depthless pools of his eyes, a tidal wave broke, soaking me to the bone. I let go of everything, every fear, dream, and face I'd ever worn.

There was only now, only him.

We collapsed at the same time. Bregan ran his hand down my back as I panted on top of him, his body slick and warm against the night. Eyes closed, I rode the aftershock, breathing in the honeyed-smoke scent of what had always been, and would always be, where I belonged.

As our racing pulses calmed, each breath pulled a heaviness over the bell tower. Bregan flipped the edge of the quilt over us, and I slid into the crook of his arm, curling my toes around his, wanting to feel every bit of him that I could. My body purred as he stroked my hair, and I marveled at how calm and perfect the center of a storm could feel.

"I don't think I could survive it," he murmured a while later. "Losing you again."

I pulled him closer, digging my nails into his skin, as if that could keep what awaited us at bay. Because down below, in the planes of reality, Hulei was still scheming . . . and in the folds of the quilt lay one secret I had left to share.

FIFTY-EIGHT

Firin

Now

Luisonn woke me with a palm of sunlight across my face. With my eyes still closed, I took a deep breath, soaking in the weight of Bregan's jacket and the press of his hip against my back. I could already tell the day would be the warmest all year, like the spring when we'd first met. I sank into a memory of the first time I'd visited his apartment—the first time I'd tried acting, the first time he'd kissed me—and my heart swelled. If I didn't move, I could almost imagine we'd gone back in time, to our days of pretending the world beneath us didn't exist. But avoiding the world wasn't an option anymore. Not even up here.

When I blinked into the rising sun, Bregan sat at my side, arms slung around his knees. He stared at the horizon like a sailor assessing a coming storm. The sunrise danced over the freckled landscape of his bare chest.

As I sat up, I slid into his coat, hugging the moleskin close over my costume dress, smothering my last secret beneath it. "Morning," I whispered.

He ran a hand down my messy braid, and I leaned into his kiss, savoring its softness, the reverence in his touch. Our foreheads pressed together, and our breaths mingled in the quiet, as if neither of us wanted to step outside our perfect night.

I encircled his wrist with my fingers, my pulse surging. During the night, I had promised the moon I would tell the truth and let him know all of me, whatever the cost. He deserved it. I just needed to find the words.

"We need to talk about it," he said. The world narrowed to the burning pools of his eyes. "Last night you said you knew Hulei was behind the bombing. How?"

I blinked. *Hulei.* Right. "He confessed. I confronted him after the podium stage exploded, and he threatened the troupe if I said anything."

Bregan squinted at the ocean as if in challenge. "How are we supposed to expose the most powerful person in Luisonn?"

"He's the *single* most powerful person." We just had to combine enough opposition to offset that power. The Reformists toppling the Stav was proof of that.

Bregan scrubbed at his face. "Draifey's still avoiding me, so I don't have his side of the story. But we could tell the *Daily* what we do know."

"No. If we tell the papers, Hulei will catch wind of it before it publishes. He'll smother the story. People need to hear it from us directly." I gripped his knee, the answer striking me. "We can use opening night."

"The play?"

"Everyone will be there. He's invited the entire council and all the biggest donors in Luisonn, plus hundreds of Labors who can spread the word. The whole damn city will be there tomorrow. After the show we can expose him, demand his arrest and disqualification from the election, and clear Draifey's name."

"But why would they believe us?"

"Why *wouldn't* they? We have everything to lose and nothing to gain by exposing him. Anyone with half a brain will see that."

Bregan rubbed his hands up and down his shins, glaring back over the city. I stroked the ridge of his spine and added, "You can testify that you checked the rally stage for weapons before my speech. I can testify about his confession and the letter he had me plant on the shipment."

Bregan's face lit up. "I bet the receiving officer at the Landings knows something . . . If we bring someone in to testify that the weapons were planted, we'll build more clout. Did you meet him when you delivered the envelope?"

"Not exactly." I had, but wearing a different face.

Bregan launched to his feet. "I'm sure Hulei used some of the confiscated explosives. If I can get into the constabulary and prove the inventory I picked up is missing some, we can present that evidence too."

I played with the cuffs of his jacket, which had been reinforced by strips of stained cotton. It was the start of a plan, but it wasn't foolproof. Hulei was smart enough to weasel his way out of hearsay from a couple of actors and a dockworker. We needed something else. Something big.

"What about his inner circle?" I asked, watching Bregan pace. In the morning light, freckles winked tauntingly up and down the ridges of his torso. "Do you think anyone high up would be willing to testify?"

He shook his head. "I doubt it. If my pa is any indication, they're all drinking the same story. I'm positive the commissioner is in on it, and the constabulary board is . . ."

The commissioner.

Bregan kept talking, but I stopped hearing him. The commissioner was a continent man with no loyalties to the Stav *or* a single party in the new government, someone who would believably know *all* Hulei's schemes, and have everything to lose by coming clean.

He would never do it . . . but I could do it on his behalf.

Bregan told me weeks ago that the commissioner, like Hulei, knew about illusion. If Bregan was right about someone using it to bomb the rally, then they had a Nodtacht in their pocket. If I took the commissioner's face to confess onstage, he would know exactly what had happened but be unlikely to deny it in order to protect his Nodtacht asset. If it all worked out and Hulei was arrested, the commissioner would stay silent just to avoid going down with the ship.

It could work . . . but Bregan would never agree to it.

"Firin?"

I startled out of my thoughts. "Sorry, what?"

"What about Mezua?"

"What about her?"

"Shouldn't we at least warn her?"

"No." Mezua would never let us expose Hulei on her stage. The Veiled Players had money and stability for the first time. She wouldn't risk it.

"If we fail," Bregan argued, "and Hulei comes out on top, he could punish the entire troupe."

My ribs constricted. He was right, of course. But the baron could take everything away from us at any time, for any reason. He had already threatened to if I didn't perform well. I'd thought that seeking his patronage would secure our future and free us from worry, but instead I'd only made us vulnerable to his whims and manipulations. He had murdered his own supporters to frame his opponent. As long as he was in power, the Players weren't safe. If there was a way to take him down quickly and smoothly, we had to take it—and this was as good a shot as we were going to get.

"That's exactly why we can't tell her." I stood and took Bregan in my arms. The ropes of his back muscles were taut. "The less Mezua knows, the better. If it all goes sideways, she can claim ignorance and blame us instead."

Bregan stared at me, forehead pinched, as if searching for some kind of permission.

"We *will* tell her everything," I promised. "Once it's done. But if we're going to succeed *and* keep them safe, we can't let her in. Not yet." This plan needed to be waterproof. If we had one leak, one weakness, we'd go under.

Which meant I couldn't tell Bregan the truth any more than we could tell Mezua.

He would never agree to using illusion to expose Hulei, but we had to sink the baron without a doubt. We *needed* the commissioner to testify, and that would only happen if I impersonated him myself.

"What is it?" Bregan asked. I'd gone silent for too long.

"Bregan? Firin?" Nyfe's voice reverberated off the bell beneath our feet. "Everyone's looking for you."

"Coming!" I shouted, smoothing the creases in my dress. Nyfe was going to kill me for wrinkling it. "I might have someone," I lied to Bregan. "Someone in Hulei's inner circle."

Bregan froze with his shirt halfway on. "Who?"

I dropped through the roof hatch.

One last con.

The promise slid through my mind, over and over all day. The rhythm of it carried me through cleaning the nave, prepping the show, and bringing the emotions I'd unearthed last night to the stage. Every time Bregan smiled at me from backstage, or Mezua beamed from the pews, I silently repeated it, holding on to it like a Gwyn prayer.

One last illusion to get rid of Hulei; then I'd come clean. Completely.

Our dress rehearsal ended with a fierce kiss and the swishing of thick velvet curtains. As we dropped into darkness, Bregan held me for several seconds longer than necessary, his lips sliding from my mouth to my ear.

"You did it," he breathed.

A thrill sang through me, but it had less to do with my performance than what I'd seen in the pews right before the curtains closed: Hulei, grinning from ear to ear, and the commissioner arranging security at the back of the room.

The pieces I needed were here.

Behind the closed curtain, fabric swished and shoes shuffled as the cast arranged in the dark for a final bow. A question lingered in the way Bregan ran a thumb down the back of my hand. I'd managed to avoid being alone with him all day so I wouldn't have to tell him who my "contact" was. I would tell him *after* I'd gotten the commissioner out of town.

With a surge in the music, the curtains flew back open. Lanterns accosted us in a wave of firelight. Bregan took my hand as the troupe swept into an ensemble bow. When we straightened, he squeezed my fingers. *This is when,* the gesture said. Right after our last bow tomorrow night, he would step forward for our "special announcement," and I would slip backstage to "collect" our witnesses, reemerging as the commissioner.

When my vision adjusted to the light in the audience, I saw Mezua first. Her eyes were brighter than her smile, and the pride in them burned my skin.

I wished I could feel her triumph.

I wished Hulei had been what he'd promised.

But at least we'd already used the baron's money to restore the temple. Once he was behind bars, our role in exposing him and our success with the first show would attract new patrons. It would all be worth it in the end. It had to be.

"Incredible." Hulei's applause stretched into a solo as he strode down the center aisle. "*Qoyn & Insei* as it's never been seen before."

"Wonderful, everyone—absolutely wonderful," Mezua said. "I have some last-minute notes for Luka. Everyone else, go rest up for tomorrow." The troupe surged offstage, spilling into the pews and hallways.

"We need to talk," Bregan said, gripping my hand.

I shook my head, one eye on the baron. "You should go. Use every minute you have." He needed to check on the confiscated explosives before the commissioner returned to the constabulary headquarters. Before he could argue, I jumped offstage.

"Vota!" Jaari crashed into me with a wild cackle. "That was *incredible*."

I went rigid, so startled by her iron-tight hug that I didn't notice the other troupe members until they'd pummeled into me too. Nyfe hugged around my other side, her cheeks streaked with tears. Phinnin clung to my leg, shrieking in a child's manic glee. Tez's guffawing laugh filled the whole nave while Jaq and Suri gave me half smiles. Even Luka, standing onstage with Mezua, nodded toward me. Mezua's lips twitched.

I'd done it.

I swayed a little, leaning on Jaari. Digging into my past and pulling from my own emotions had brought Insei, and this entire production, to life. We'd created something incredible, something beautiful. *I* had.

Finally, I had a place where I was welcome, supported, and celebrated—and yet, as the troupe squeezed and heckled me, I felt like that seven-year-old, staring into a bakery at a mother and her daughter, wishing that Father's and my con was real.

I swallowed the lump in my throat.

One last con.

"Vota," the baron said in his clear, announcer-style voice. The troupe sprang apart, clearing space between us.

"Mr. President," I said. We hadn't spoken since he threatened me on the rally stage, but the troupe watched us in rapt curiosity, so I added, "Thank you for this opportunity."

"No, thank *you*." Hulei clasped my arm, right over my scar. "You're putting on an *excellent* show."

"It's only possible because of you," I crooned, leading him back up the center aisle. At the end of it, the commissioner—a massive man with little hair and a lot of flesh—chatted with some constables near the doors to the lobby. This was my chance. "Can I have a private word?"

Hulei's smile didn't falter. "I unfortunately have to get to a meeting at Regents'."

I lowered my voice. "I've had word from some of my old . . . associates. I thought you would want to hear it." When his eyes snapped to mine, I held them.

With a subtle wave, he directed the commissioner to meet us in the empty lobby. The commissioner closed the large doors, then eyed me curiously. "What's this?" he asked. I mentally cataloged the scrape of his voice.

"Vota has information for us," Hulei said, dragging out the syllables of my fake name.

I assumed the commissioner knew everything Hulei did, so I said, "I got a message from one of my old Stav associates, one who's in hiding with the Labor Party. They claim Draifey has proof about who planted the bomb."

"What? What proof?" Hulei said.

I shrugged. "The message was a plea for me to meet with them. They figured I might have inside information on you."

"Join them where?" the commissioner grunted.

"Nusias." The small, impoverished fishing island was an ideal place for rebels to hide.

Something unspoken passed between them. Then the commissioner nodded, and I knew I'd won. Hulei wouldn't send anyone else to Nusias to check on the rumor. The commissioner would go himself. Tomorrow night, during the play's opening, he wouldn't be here to counter my story.

FIFTY-NINE

Bregan

Now

The sky was dark when Bregan burst from the constabulary headquarters and hurried down the steps. The commissioner had returned right as Bregan left the evidence closet. Somehow, Bregan had managed to leave without crossing his path.

"What'd you find?" Jaq asked, joining him in an alley, coat collar flipped against the wind.

"Three packages of explosives are missing," Bregan said, "but the paperwork says otherwise."

"So that's proof. He used the weapons he claimed were Draifey's to frame Draifey for the bombing?"

"That's what it looks like."

Jaq removed his glasses and rubbed his eyes. "Shit."

Before they emerged in the Commerce Block, Bregan stopped and faced his friend. Jaq looked as exhausted as he felt, and Bregan wondered what else he'd been doing besides *Qoyn & Insei*. Had he, like Addym, been working for Draifey directly? For once, Jaq was unknown to him, and Bregan had only himself to blame. But there was no time for questions now.

"Did you talk to Addym?" he asked. To reach Draifey, he needed to go through Addym.

"He said he'll be there." Jaq shifted his weight. "Breg, what are you planning?"

Wind whipped at their coattails. Bregan didn't want to lie to Jaq, but Firin was right. The troupe was safer not knowing their plans. He didn't want to tell Jaq anything that could get him or Phinnin in trouble. "Are you sure you want to know?"

Jaq scratched at his jaw. "You sure it'll work?"

"It'll have to." It was the most honest answer he could give.

With a nod, Jaq stuffed his hands in his pockets. "Find me if you need me."

Under the clearest night in days, Bregan descended the steep roads and stairways to the Fingers. Bright moonlight shone down on the eerie docks, which spread out like hands beckoning him to sea. Once on the shore, he wove through sparse crowds of fishermen and dockworkers, feet dragging. He had barely slept last night and hadn't sat down all day. But now that he had confirmed the explosives were missing, he had no doubt the president had bombed the rally. Without proof, however, it was his and Firin's word against Hulei's. They needed witnesses.

Hopefully, Firin could get someone close to Hulei to talk. Bregan had thought of himself as inside Hulei's inner circle, and he couldn't imagine who might betray him, but if Firin had been doing deals with the president, maybe she had connections he didn't.

"What the fuck could you possibly want?" Addym hopped off the front porch of a tavern that was spilling patrons onto the boardwalk. "I'd shoot you right now if Jaq hadn't insisted I hear you out." One of his black-and-blue eyes was swollen shut. Bregan winced at the sight of it, and his knuckles throbbed, but he bit back his apology. It wouldn't be well received—not yet.

"I have a lead," Bregan said, continuing down the walk toward the receiving officer's shack. A light was on inside. "Someone who might have evidence that Draifey wasn't behind the bombing. Thought you'd want to join me to question him."

At the receiving office, Bregan rapped his knuckles on the window. It slid open.

"What is—" The old Merchant-class man blinked.

"I have questions about that shipment I confiscated the other night," Bregan said.

"Told you everything already." The man started to close the window, but it hit the palm of Addym's hand.

"I'd like to hear it too," Addym said, glaring through his one open eye. "Let us in."

The tiny shack barely fit the three of them, forcing the receiving officer to sit on his stool in the shadow of their combined bulk. His beady eyes flicked between their faces.

"You knew those weapons weren't Thom Draifey's," Bregan guessed. The signs were there in how the man had acted that night; Bregan just hadn't paid attention. He'd mistaken the man's confusion for fear.

"Don't know that I'd say I *know* anything like that," the officer said. He glanced at their wrists, where their Labor-class bands once sat. Addym shifted, jacket falling open just far enough to show the pistol hanging at his belt.

"What *do* you know?" Bregan said quickly.

The former Merchant's jaw tightened; then he spit on the floor. "Look. It was weird from the beginning. The moment the guy dropped off the freight slip, I suspected it. Who needs a decade's worth of salt? Figured it was some Lower scheme to get—"

Addym laughed darkly. "Because only Labors trade on the black market?"

"Tha's not what I said," the man grunted, even though it was exactly what he'd said. The Merchants who owned and ran the Landings' quarters often reported illegal trades run by Labors, but not those run by the upper classes.

Bregan glared at Addym. They needed the officer to talk more than they needed to put him in his place.

The Merchant-class man sniffed. "Was hoping to get some cash from the Trade Office for reporting it, but when I followed the bastard, he went straight to Regents' and got into some gods-damned fancy carriage. Realized it wasn't no run-of-the-mill Labor deal. Somethin' bigger was going on. Dangerous, probably. Got weirder when that envelope showed up, and then when you told the papers them guns were Draifey's. The guy didn't look like no Labor Party member. But I didn't look into it. Didn't want to get mixed up in whatever it was."

Bregan put a piece of paper with the temple's address on top of the man's desk. "You're going to testify to everything you just said here tomorrow night."

The man straightened. "Now, wait a minute, I'm not gonna—"

"Here's the thing," Bregan said. "The man who *did* order those crates will soon find out you know more than you should, and given that he just murdered his own supporters at his own rally, I doubt he will hesitate to silence you."

"Wait . . ." The officer's face went slack. "You're saying the *president* did that bombing?"

"It's in your best interest to help us," Bregan said.

"Why? What are you gonna do?"

"Don't worry about that."

The officer's jaw worked. He looked at Addym's gun. "Fine."

Outside the shack, Addym stuck to Bregan's heels, boots thumping on the boardwalk planks. "What the fuck was that?"

"I'm going to tell the audience what Hulei did, tomorrow night after the opening of *Qoyn & Insei*."

"Whoa, whoa, *what?*"

Bregan pointed to the abandoned shop front he had squatted beneath nights before. They didn't need the entire Landings listening in on them. When they were swathed in the privacy of the building's eaves, he said, "Vorkot told me Draifey was working with a Nodtacht."

Addym stiffened. "That's why I haven't trusted him. Vorkot said he overheard Draifey talking with the Nodtacht about recruiting more to his cause."

With a sigh like a curse, Addym shoved his hands in his pockets and leaned against the wall of the building, sagging in on his own bulk. "One of the prison guards was a Nodtacht," he admitted, "but he was a turncoat. He helped us get the names and locations of as many Nodtacht as possible so we could arrest them the night of the insurrection, before they had a chance to slip through the cracks. How do you think we managed to catch so many of them so fast?"

It was almost painful, how simple the truth was.

"Why didn't he tell the rest of us?" Bregan asked. "Or the council?"

"Because he didn't trust them and, it turns out, with good reason. After our attack on Central, I discovered that half the Nodtacht we had names and locations for were already in custody, indicating that Hulei had someone on the inside too." Likely whoever had taken Addym's face the other day.

Bregan joined him in leaning against the dilapidated building. The sea accosted them with harsh, edged gusts.

"Draifey volunteered for the prison break to protect the guards, you were right about that," Addym said. "But they took a real risk keeping the Five alive and helping us get the locations of Nodtacht agents. Draifey was worried Hulei would have killed them anyway." It was exactly the explanation Draifey had given when Bregan questioned him; he'd just been too desperate to believe in Hulei to listen.

Even in the dark, even beneath his wounds, Addym's cheeks were ruddy pink in the cold. His hair was longer than Bregan had ever seen it, just brushing his ears. The beard on his face was patchy, untrimmed. Bregan felt a pang for him and his son, still living in hiding because Addym was doing what was right.

"I'm sorry about that," Bregan said, gesturing to Addym's face. "You were right not to trust me before, but I'm trying to fix it. I could use your help. Yours and Draifey's."

"It's not that simple, Breg."

"Why?"

Addym sighed. "You *smeared* Draifey all over the papers with out-right lies. Do you think we can just take you in now? Tell you all our plans? Just because you've stopped long enough to think it through?"

Bregan laughed humorlessly. "As if you've never acted on instinct."

"Don't." Addym's boots crunched rock and shell as he pushed off the wall. "I didn't come here to be—"

Bregan raised his hands. "I swear, Addym. I'm trying to work *with* you. I've got three separate witnesses, myself included. Possibly one more. We're going to expose Hulei tomorrow before the whole council and half the city's wealthiest, most powerful citizens. He won't be able to do a thing without damning himself. Go up there with me. Testify on Draifey's behalf."

Addym shook his head. "For saints' sake, you really think this will work."

"Of course it will." It had to.

"This, right here"—Addym tossed a hand in the air between them—"has always been the difference between us."

Bregan tensed. "What?"

"While you were traipsing around in costumes and fucking song, I was breaking my back on factory floors. I don't have the luxury of ideal-ism. None of us in Draifey's camp do. Labors don't get to believe the *best* of people, to *hope* you or that council of Uppers will do the right thing."

Bregan flinched at the implication that he didn't belong in the Labor class, but Addym wasn't wrong. Bregan had spent a mere couple of months in a factory when he was twelve. He'd left that work for the theater with a profound sense of relief, but Addym and the other boys hadn't had that choice.

"Addym, come on," he said.

"I'm not walking into a trap, Bregan."

Bregan wanted to argue, but Addym's distrust was his fault. "All right, I get it. But we're going up onstage regardless. Can you have

Draifey prepare something? A statement for the *Daily* with *his* side of the story? You can publish it after the dust settles." Once they knew if the truth prevailed.

"Fine." Addym turned to leave.

"One last thing?" Bregan said. Addym paused. "Could you have someone ensure that asshole makes his way to the theater tomorrow night?" Bregan jerked his chin toward the receiving officer's shack.

"Gladly," Addym said.

For a moment, the years swirled between them in the sea air, a relationship of tension and reliance that they'd inherited from their fathers and their grandfathers before them. Unlikely allies in an exhausting, endless battle. Bregan wished, with a wave of regret, that they'd realized earlier that they weren't their fathers. But at least, in the end, they were truly on the same side.

A few hours later, when Bregan dragged himself back into the sleeping temple, he found his cot bare. A note lay on his pillow.

Following my lead.

Who was Firin after?

SIXTY

Firin

Now

The costume room throbbed with life. Racks of clothes had been shoved aside to make space for a long table of mirrors and benches. Half-naked troupe members crowded its benches like birds on a clothesline, primping and preening. Perfumes and powders tickled my nose as, off to the side of the room, Nyfe spun me around.

"You're lucky I was able to get the wrinkles out," she joked, surveying the red-and-white-striped skirts of Insei's peasant dress—the one Insei wore when she sneaked off royal grounds.

I blushed. "You don't think the sweater is too big?" The threadbare sweater I'd donned over the dress wasn't the one I had planned to wear, but Phinnin had poured paint on that one this morning. Nyfe had given me this one from her trunk.

"No, it's perfect." She licked her thumb and wiped something off my cheek. I tried not to fidget. I needed to double-check the commissioner costume I had hidden backstage before the show started.

"I need to check my props," I reminded her.

"Right, of course," she said, but when I turned to leave, she didn't let go of my arm. A sheen fell over her eyes. "Thank you, Vota."

My insides recoiled. "I didn't do anything."

"You did everything. We're here because of you. I just want you to know that you don't have to prove anything to us. You never did."

I kissed her cheek so she wouldn't see my failed return smile.

"Costumes should be done!" Mezua shouted.

"Go." Nyfe winked.

As I navigated the racks, benches, and bodies, my ribs bowed beneath the pressure of my secrets. Rubbing the heel of my palm into my sternum, I headed into the hall.

I bumped right into Bregan. He was in a full old-Iaqunsiad costume: a yellow tunic unlaced at the top, biceps peeking through the short-cut sleeves, dark trousers clinging to the curves of his legs. Kohl lined his eyes, accentuating their intensity.

"I was just looking for you," I lied.

"The receiving officer—"

"Not here." I led him through the curtained door that led backstage.

"The receiving officer agreed to testify after the show," he reported in a rush. "Where were you last night?"

"I had to put some pieces in place." I had trailed the commissioner from the theater to the constabulary to study his mannerisms and voice. Once I had found and hidden a costume suit that would work, I slept in the nave. If I had gone to the basement, Bregan would have needled me with questions. At least now, with two hours until showtime, it was too late for him to do anything with the truth. "The commissioner is going to testify against Hulei," I said.

"The *commissioner*?" His pupils bounced between mine. "How?"

I had prepared an entire speech about how the commissioner regretted his decision to support the president, how he had thought no innocents would be injured in the bombing and wanted to atone, but the lie wound in a knot, refusing to budge.

"I'll explain later," I said. "He'll be backstage after the curtain call, with the receiving officer."

The moment Bregan relaxed, I felt sick. "I think this might work," he breathed.

"It *will* work. Now, go find Tez. He was looking for you earlier."

Once he was safely out of the way, I found my commissioner clothing right where I'd left it: shoved between the wall and the witch's hut, where no one would stumble upon it and I could quickly change after our last bow. I clutched the fabric in a fist until my hands stopped shaking. Everything was ready to go.

Time passed in a haze.

Then Mezua called all of us to our places.

Deep in the dark of backstage, I paused to collect myself, kneading my knuckles into my palms. The temple trembled in a sea of vibrations so loud I could barely hear my own breath. According to Jaq, every seat was full, and then some.

"You ready?" Bregan said into my ear. I jumped, then relaxed as he tucked me under his chin, smelling of fresh soap and makeup oil. In his arms, my knees felt strong. Grounded. I *was* ready, for all of it.

"Let's go break their hearts," he said. With a final kiss, he disappeared in shadow.

I crept through the back curtain and climbed up onto the set cliff. As I arranged my striped skirts, the auditorium lights dimmed beyond the front curtains. The theater fell into a rustling quiet. Hulei's boots clicked on the edge of the stage. A spotlight flared, and I could see just the heels of his polished shoes; then he was waxing poetic about the play, his campaign, and Thom Draifey. The audience clapped and cheered as he spun lies into threads of gold.

But no one would cheer for him later.

After his speech, his boots clicked again, and the temple darkened. My pulse pounded in my ears. Then the front curtains swished open in oiled silence, the row of lamps along the front of the stage flashed to life, and a sea of faces opened before me, filling every corner of the building. Thousands of eyes, pinned on me. I focused on a distant, empty point and tugged Nyfe's too-big sweater tight against a phantom wind.

Then I let Insei sweep me away.

Bregan

Now

Peeking between curtains was forbidden. If Mezua spotted him, she would wring him out like a rag, but Bregan couldn't help himself. Firin was incredible.

Through the smallest split, he watched her wake up center stage after taking the wrong potion. The orchestra played a piece that sounded like the crashing of waves as she rose on the fake beach, looking for Qoyn.

Her chin swiveled, her eyes widened, and then a tremor racked her whole body as she tripped to her feet. Nyfe strode out as the pirate captain and informed her that she was not in her home country anymore. In fact, her home country didn't exist yet. She'd gone back two hundred years in time.

Her dawning horror was utter perfection. The way a weight slipped onto her shoulders and her voice broke. As she started to shake, Bregan could *feel* it: that need to escape his skin, to abandon the imploding world and the reality that it was his fault. It was exactly how he'd felt at the hospital after the bombing.

During their night on the roof, Firin had fractured her armor, but now it seemed like she was stepping out of the wreckage, baring herself to the world.

"Whatever you did, it worked." Suri appeared at his side.

As Firin fell to her knees with a wrenching sob, Bregan realized this was the only scene they hadn't practiced together. He wondered what she was pulling her guilt from. Maybe he'd ask her tonight, after everything was over. For once, he believed she might answer.

In the glare of the light, Bregan couldn't see Baron Hulei on the balcony. But he imagined him, beaming from ear to ear, convinced he had finally conquered the world. Constables guarded every doorway. Bregan didn't see the commissioner among them.

The commissioner was the last person Bregan would have expected to testify against Hulei. He had *helped* with the bombing, had covered up the weapons shipment and stolen the explosives. He was as deep in the scheme as Hulei was, and exposing the baron would mean exposing himself. Perhaps he truly felt remorse, or maybe he just sensed the way the cards would fall and hoped to preserve himself.

I don't have the luxury of idealism, he heard Addym say.

Either way, Bregan could do nothing except pray Firin was sure. Soon enough, they'd find out.

Firin

Now

I cracked my soul wide open.

The show carried me like a current. I danced with first love, adventured with pirates, and fell headlong into despair. Memories poured out of me through Insei's character—less like an open wound and more like a hidden flame suddenly exposed to air. The lines blurred where I stopped and she began.

I forgot about the audience.

I forgot about Hulei.

Moments became minutes, which became hours, until suddenly I stood at the edge of the set cliff again for the show's final moments, the oil lamps lighting up my red-and-white-striped skirts from below.

The audience held its breath.

"What do you want?" I asked Qoyn.

Bregan stepped up the cliff. "You," he said, his love as open and eager as when he'd confessed it after we fled the Grande. "Only you. Forever with me."

We met halfway, and the kiss was the sweetest thing I'd ever tasted, as real as it was performance. His thumb brushed my ear, out of sight of the audience, and I clung to him as if we could live in that moment forever.

The temple lost its mind.

The standing-only Labor section thundered. The balconies cheered. Exhilarated joy filled the building, bright enough to swallow a storm. No one stopped clapping, not when the lights went out, not as the curtains fell or we plunged into darkness. I couldn't even hear myself laugh.

Bregan kissed me again, his whole body folding into mine, and even in the face of what came next, I had no fear at all. Everything felt possible. Even Hulei's demise.

Bregan led me off the set cliff by feel. The headiness of it all made me unsteady, and when we hit the stage floor, I ran into the pirate ship. Something sharp snagged in Nyfe's sweater and pierced my flesh. I pulled myself free.

We took center stage, and the troupe flowed out around us like a dark wave. When the curtains swung open, we swept into a bow as one. Anyone not already standing leaped to their feet. Up on the balcony, Hulei headed for the stairs, coming down to give his final speech.

This was it. I had to get offstage. I had to change.

I reached for Bregan's hand, for our last bow together—

My fingers closed on air.

His face had gone bloodless, paler than a full moon. The applause warped into a deep, droning warning. He was staring at my arm.

At the sleeve I'd just torn.

At the Nodtacht scar shimmering in the oil light.

ACT V

SIXTY-ONE

Bregan

Now

The world tilted as if the stage were a ship and the night were a storm.

Firin snatched at the tear in her sweater, and Bregan's mind severed from his body, clutching for something, anything, to stop this moment from swallowing him whole. A heartbeat later, he realized he was waiting. For the commissioner.

But the commissioner wasn't coming.

In the split of the back curtains, the receiving officer stared out, awaiting instruction, alone—and suddenly Bregan knew, in his bones, that it had all been a ruse. Firin had planned to frame Hulei with false testimony by wearing the commissioner's face.

She stepped forward, and Bregan bumped back into Tez. The entire cast stared at them. Him and Firin. Their plastered-on grins flickered.

The front curtains flew shut, blocking the light but not the sound. Bregan stumbled backstage as applause distorted in his ears, throwing him off-balance. He launched for an exit, any exit, but there was no escaping what he'd just seen.

Firin was a Nodtacht.

I've done terrible things.

He tripped into the edge of a set table, pain stabbing his ribs. He slapped a wrist to his mouth, fighting the gravity that wanted to pull him to his knees. He'd told her that he knew her, that he loved her. He thought he had.

The door to the back hall beckoned in a dim rectangle of light. Bregan headed for it, but then she was there. Silhouetted by the frame.

She said his name.

When she reached for him, her hand became his mother's, begging on her knees. But Firin wasn't his mother. She was worse.

His mother had spied for the Nodtacht.

Firin *was* a Nodtacht.

"Don't touch me," he snarled, backing into the table again. Her hands shot to the base of her neck, her knuckles bled white. Tears smeared her makeup. Her mask.

Was this even her real face?

"I was going to tell you," she choked. "I swear, I just—"

"Was *any* of it real?" He gasped for air, but she'd stolen all of it.

She had never let him meet her family. She hid her name and past. She flinched from his touch, disappeared for weeks on end, only undressed in the dark. The signs had been *everywhere*.

"I can explain. Please—"

"You had every chance." He tried to step around her.

"I didn't mean to," she sobbed. "I swear. I didn't mean for any of it to happen. Father tricked me. Then *they* tricked me, and I never would have told them about your pa, but—"

Bregan reeled back. "My *pa*?"

Firin looked at him with a violent storm of shame in her eyes, and it reverberated through him. It was the exact same expression she had worn onstage when Insei realized her mistake. This was the guilt she'd pulled from.

"It was you," he breathed. "On Bloody Fifthday, *you* turned Pa in."

Her lip trembled, and the ground disappeared beneath his feet.

SIXTY-TWO

Firin

Bloody Fifthday

In the Nodtacht's interrogation room, a halo of lamplight illuminated Eznur as he gazed down his pocked nose at me. Somewhere nearby, Father squatted behind bars, his secrets freshly unveiled.

"What do you want?" I demanded.

"You," Eznur said.

He wanted me to *join* them.

"I'm not a Nodtacht," I said. Lying to Bregan about Father's cons was one thing, but serving the Stav? I wouldn't do it.

Eznur's chair creaked as he leaned over the table. "That's debatable. You have the brand; you have illusion; you even helped us with missions, if unknowingly. Reckless, on your father's part, but you're cleverer than he is, aren't you?"

I didn't need this man's approval. I didn't need anything except for him to let me go and maybe reveal Bregan's location. "What happened to the Reformists?"

"We caught many, executed some. But I was under the impression you didn't care much for the Reformists, given that you helped us infiltrate their ranks. You revealed Quan Kenkitu's location, gathered important intel on Baron Hulei, and even showed us Esmai—"

"I didn't con Esmai."

Eznur raised a brow. "No?"

Shit. Esmai couldn't get blamed because of me. "She's not a Reformist. She's just an actress."

"The theater harbored the Reformists."

"No. She didn't like it. She didn't want to be in the movement. She always said it was too dangerous. But Dech—"

"Dech Nimsayrth?"

My heart tumbled. "No. Dech isn't—"

Eznur's chair screeched.

"No, please."

"You've managed to evade us simply because we didn't know of your existence. But now we do." Eznur straightened his suit vest. "If you try to run or hide, you won't like the consequences. We will always find you. You are one of us now."

"W-wait."

He knocked on the door. The Stav soldier returned.

"No," I gasped as she hoisted me to my feet. "Dech isn't a Reformist."

"Give her to her father," Eznur said. "Keep eyes on both of them."

"Please." I fought the soldier as she hauled me into the prison's lobby.

"Dispatch to the Shipyard," Eznur told a loitering unit.

Bregan's apartment.

I caught my scream on the edge of my tongue. I wanted to rail against the soldier's sharp nails, but I forced myself to go limp, tears streaming down my face.

"No," I moaned. "Please . . ."

She shoved me into the pitch-black night, and I kept myself meek and malleable as she brought me to Father, who waited on the steps as Restuv. Then, in the split second when she handed me to him, I twisted free and bolted into the city. Shouts shot through the dark, but I pounded the cobblestones as fast as I could.

Who are you, girl?

Who's your pa?

Dech's frantic distrust bounced in my skull. I had to warn him. All of them. If the Stav got to him before I could, then he'd have been right about me all along. They might even punish Bregan too. The Stav had killed his cousin because of his uncle's involvement with the Reformists.

I vaulted to a low-hanging roof, then leaped across the Merchant District, toward the Labor streets and the apartment that had become my home.

The shouts reached me first.

I skidded to a halt at the edge of a roof, and the moon cut through the clouds, spotlighting the scene in the square outside Bregan's apartment building.

I was too late.

A dozen Stav soldiers wrestled Dech to the ground. He didn't fight. His legs buckled as they shoved him. His back rounded as they shackled him. Eznur watched from beside a black prison carriage, hands clasped behind his back. The Nodtacht looked up, spotting me with a knowing sneer.

He had known I would come here. He wanted me to see.

"Pa!" Bregan screamed, hurtling from the building like a sparking ember. A Stav soldier caught him around the waist, slammed a fist into his gut. I twitched, as if to run to him, but I couldn't do anything. A heaviness poured over me like a wave, and I fell to my knees on the roof.

What had I done?

"Stop." Esmai raced out after her son, her hair a tangled, wild flame. She was still wearing her costume. The soldiers stuffed Dech into the carriage. Esmai raced for Eznur, but a Stav soldier shoved her to the cobblestones. She clawed at him like a caged fox. "Let him go!"

"You broke the terms of our deal," Eznur said, flicking his cigarette to the ground.

I wanted her to deny it, to tell him to go to saints-damned hell, but she only scowled up at him with a hateful recognition. "You promised," she said.

"Yes, well, you didn't tell us your *husband* was a leader of the movement."

The carriage driver snapped the reins.

"No!" Bregan clocked his Stav captor in the chin. He broke free and battered his fist on the carriage door, but it kicked into motion, and he tripped, falling hard.

A moan slipped out of me. I wanted to call out but couldn't find my voice. The lines of his face were twisting in a way I'd never seen, a way that tore through me like a hurricane. With groggy slowness, he turned his blotchy face toward his mother. She reached for him. He flinched.

Esmai made a sound that was half cough, half choke. I slapped my palm over my mouth as Bregan spit something and disappeared back inside.

A hand fell on my shoulder. "There's Nodtacht watching us," Father said in Sniq's gruff drawl. "We need to go."

I shrugged him off. "No."

"There's nothing left for you here, Firin."

The truth of it shattered me.

SIXTY-THREE

Bregan

Now

There was a hook in Bregan's rib cage, pulling him down with every step into a darkness ready to smother him, a depth he couldn't climb back from.

Firin had betrayed his father.

She was the reason Pa had spent four years in prison.

"Wait, where are you going?" she begged. "What are you going to . . ."

He needed air. He needed space. In the back hallway, concerned hands reached for him, voices bled together, but he shrugged all of them off and wound through stacks, crates, and piles of all the *shit* the baron had bought them to pull off this play. This perfect facade.

His elbow sent a box of props flying. It popped open, items shattering. The sound shook him, evoking an urge to break everything, to make the world look like his heart. Usually, he would escape to the roof, but that was the first place she would search, so he headed to the kitchen instead.

Tez was inside, blocking the door to the street. "Bregan, you need to calm down. Let's talk about this."

"Did you know?" Bregan demanded. Tez had been right behind him onstage. He'd had the exact same view of the scar hidden in the cut of Firin's sweater. But Tez revealed no surprise. No pain. He bore no sign of betrayal.

Tez turned his beefy palms skyward. "I suspected, when she showed up the night of the insurrection. But it's Vota's—"

"That's not her name."

"All right, okay. But what was she supposed to do?"

"She's not a child."

"Take a deep breath. *Think* before you turn her in like you did Suri."

Bregan flinched.

The girl the night of the insurrection.

The girl at the tavern.

She looked just like me.

He laughed. "She framed her. She *framed* Suri."

"Slow down, Breg. I'm sure Vota—"

"That's not her *fucking* name."

This time, Tez didn't stop him. Bregan escaped to the street, footsteps racing ahead of his heart. He turned down an alley and collapsed against a wall, gasping for air.

He'd done it again: seen only what he wanted to. He'd told Firin that whatever she was ashamed of, whatever she had done, had only been to survive. He told himself that she was redeemable because he wanted to believe it, because vague generalizations of her sins were easy to dismiss when you didn't have the details, the awful truth. But just because you wanted something didn't make it possible; just because you believed something didn't make it true.

Everything was a facade.

Hulei. His mother. Firin. Tez.

He didn't know what or who to believe anymore.

"Bregan?" Suri stood at the end of the alley. Starlight danced over the pinch of her brow. Bregan's chest caved. How could he have thought *she* was a Nodtacht, after everything she'd done and lost for the movement? "Are you okay?" she asked.

"No."

As he pushed off the wall, Suri caught his arm. "What's going on?"

He had loved Firin with every part of his soul. But had it been love? Could you love someone you didn't know at all? He swiped at his eyes, head throbbing. However much he feared it, he felt he knew the answer.

Deep down, he knew what he had to do.

SIXTY-FOUR

Firin

Now

When I rushed after Bregan into the backstage corridor, bodies, costumes, and whoops of exhilaration sent me staggering into the wall. I held the threads of my torn sweater sleeve closed. When I got my bearings, he was gone.

"Vota?" Jaari asked, steadying me. "What's wrong?"

Behind her, half the troupe gaped at me. With a sob, I wrenched free and rushed in the opposite direction, my vision blurring with tears. Halfway to the corner, someone grabbed my wrist.

"Vota, I need you to talk to the patrons." Mezua spun me to face her, shining brighter than the sun. She was happy. Of course she was happy. Everything I'd ever wanted, everything she'd ever dreamed of, was crumbling, but Mezua had no idea.

"What is it?" Her tone sharpened. "What happened?"

"Bregan," I choked out, still gripping my sleeve. "He knows."

With a breathless curse, she released me.

I raced to the basement, the one place in the building that wasn't full of people. I stumbled into Bregan's room, and sobs rolled out of me like stones. Dim moonlight pooled half shadows over his dresser and his cot. His old jacket. Above me the building shook with voices and footsteps.

Was any of it real?

He would never forgive me. I had wanted to tell him. I really had. But wanting wasn't the same as doing. I'd ripped his family into shreds, served his enemy, lied to him about it again and again. If I didn't get out of here, I wouldn't survive to see tomorrow.

I sucked in air as if it could buoy my sinking heart and took in the whole of his room, the space that had also become mine.

Except there was no sign I'd lived here at all.

I had come to the temple with nothing more than the dress on my back, a dress Nyfe had burned. All my clothes were Nyfe's and Jaari's. Everything else in this space was Bregan's. I had nothing, except for Father's pocket mirror and my hidden knife, both already concealed in the folds of my costume. I had less to my name than Suri, with her wooden ball and stupid pressed flower. But that wasn't new, was it?

This was how I'd lived my entire life. Like a shadow.

I swiped at my face, scrubbing away some of the conspicuous grief. Then I stole Nyfe's brown coat and slipped it on over my striped costume. I nicked one of Luka's hats and a pair of Jaari's boots. I bounded past the eight blank, judging faces of the Kirru gods and up the basement steps, considering my illusion options.

A dozen guns clicked.

Constables lined the hall, weapons pointed at me. I leaped back, almost toppling down the stairwell, as Baron Hulei strode forward with a razor-thin smile.

He knew.

Somehow, he knew that Bregan and I had planned to expose him. In the wake of the last few minutes, our scheme felt so distant, like another lifetime, but now it was coming back for revenge.

Down the corridor, Mezua stood with Nyfe and Phinnin. They gaped at me. Nyfe peered at my coat. Her coat. Phinnin tried to step toward me, but Mezua yanked her back. I'd known the director wouldn't help me, *couldn't* without condemning the troupe, and still it burned.

"Vota," Hulei said, "you are under arrest for suspicion of being a Nodtacht."

Then the constables were on me. A dozen hands grabbed me in a dozen places, contorting me into submission, shoving me toward the theater's lobby. As soon as we rounded the corner, still-mingling audience members erupted in horrified chatter. The sound warped in my ears. I felt sluggish, underwater, as they led me across the lobby and into the western corridor.

He was going to execute me.

"In there," Hulei ordered.

They pushed me into the costume room. In a flash of memory, I was a child again, being shoved into racks of clothing by Father. My mouth filled with the sour taste of fear.

"Leave us," the baron said. The door closed.

"Listen," I said, "whatever Bregan told—"

A slap killed my words.

"You *imbecile*. I don't know what trick you were planning to pull tonight, but telling *him* what you are was unacceptable."

I pressed fingers to my burning cheek.

Hulei didn't know about our plan.

Bregan had told him that I was a Nodtacht, but he hadn't outed what we'd planned to do. He'd sacrificed me to protect himself. A weight landed on my chest, weakening my knees.

The baron shook out his hands, as if settling. "Now," he said, smoothing his hair, "our *Qoyn & Insei* plan isn't going to work anymore, but there are other avenues that might salvage the end goal. Vota will be executed tomorrow, but *you* may not need to be."

He wasn't going to kill me.

He was going to use me.

Of course he was.

"My associate here insists you have many skills." He waved at the corner of the room. Someone I hadn't noticed lumbered forward.

"It's good to see you again," the commissioner said, his voice like gravel.

I stared at the fleshy, beardless face I'd planned to wear tonight. What did he mean? We didn't know each other.

"I'm disappointed," he added, and the shape of his sneer curdled my blood.

With a deliberate, torturous slowness, his face started to shift. His cheekbones widened, pockmarks dug into his flesh, a dark beard flicked into place, followed by a hook-shaped scar.

I backed into the nearest costume rack.

"Hello, Firin," Eznur purred.

SIXTY-FIVE

Firin

Now

"No," I choked out.

This had to be a nightmare.

"You've done well," Eznur said, as if I'd just completed a Nodtacht mission, as if he still owned me. He stepped forward until his shadow swallowed me.

"H-how . . ." I'd watched him hang.

How was he alive?

How was he with *Hulei*?

"Eznur has worked for me for years," the baron said. "He was instrumental in the Reformists' success."

"But . . . the Five," I said. Eznur had ordered Dech's arrest on Bloody Fifthday.

"I had no choice," Eznur grunted. "Hulei was supposed to secure leadership of the movement that night, but *you* set us back four years. Esmai was spying for the Stav, but she was also strategically hiding things from them. When *you* told your father she was an actress, he put two and two together. He told Stav leadership that the Reformists were hiding with an illegal theater troupe, and by the time I found out about the raid, it was too late to stop it."

I shook my head. It couldn't be true.

"Bloody Fifthday was your fault, Firin."

You are a Nodtacht.

How many sins could a person commit without knowing?

"Why didn't you tell me?" I asked, shaking. "Why didn't you use that to bully me into working for you too?"

Eznur smiled. "Your guilt over Dech Nimsayrth's arrest proved more than enough. You pledged to us the very next day, remember?"

"But you made me spy on *him* for years." I glared at Hulei.

"Oh no," the baron said. "We fed you information."

That wasn't possible. All the times I'd tracked Hulei, all the dinners with patrons and meetings with Diosi, the plays and the—

I nearly fell over.

Eznur was wearing Heynri Diosi's face.

The handsome illusion's lips curled into that signature grin, and I backed into the table, rattling mirrors. "Diosi was never real, Firin," he said.

"We made sure that you heard what we wanted you to hear," Hulei explained. "See, I knew the Labors in Luisonn would eventually attack the Stav. In Qunsii I saw what happens when the poor take over. The factory workers there toppled the royals, then murdered everyone with royal blood and anyone with family money. Luisonn's Labors are no different. They don't want *equality*. They want revenge. I knew I needed to take charge of the Reform movement to prevent another mess. Unfortunately, after Bloody Fifthday, it was difficult to reorganize when the Stav had eyes on me."

"So we used you," Eznur said. "I knew from the moment I caught you that you'd never truly be loyal to the Stav. I tested you by planting information on the Reformists within your reach, and every time you came across it, you lied to Skavka to protect them. So I eventually set you to tail Iulei."

Memories rose like a tide until I was drowning in flashes. The nights of isolation. The glint of knives. Rope burning my wrists as I writhed against restraints. Eznur had let Skavka *torture* me for information on the Reformists—not because he'd wanted the information, but because he wanted to see if I would break.

"Your false reports about what he was up to kept the other Nodtacht off our scent," Eznur continued.

This was why I hadn't seen the insurrection coming, why I hadn't known Hulei was back with the Reformists until he emerged as president during the revolution. They had played me like a pawn in some messed-up game.

"After we overthrew the Stav, we assumed you were long gone." Hulei folded his hands together as if this were a business meeting. "It wasn't until the Salted Crown that we realized you were right under our noses. It was clever, taking Diosi's face, but I knew right away you weren't Eznur, and when you went on about *Qoyn & Insei*, I knew where I'd find you."

My windpipe was constricting, bowing under an unbearable pressure.

"Vota will die tonight," Hulei continued matter-of-factly. "Now that Bregan knows your identity, we can't trust it will stay secret. But *you* don't have to die. Tomorrow morning the *Daily* will announce that I caught a Nodtacht in my own theater, that you were with Thom Draifey's campaign and that he's working with the Stav to undermine me. After that, if you'd like, you can adopt a new identity and help me secure Luisonn's freedom."

I almost laughed. Hulei didn't want freedom. He wanted control.

"What's in it for me?" I hedged. "Other than my life."

"Everything." Hulei smiled broadly. "You betrayed the Reformists on Bloody Fifthday. You were complicit in who knows how many Reformists' executions and arrests, including Bregan's *father*. There's no going back from tonight for you. You cannot salvage Vota. But"—he flung out a finger—"work with me, take on a new identity, and you can act for the Players or the Grande, wherever you want. You can become the city's new darling again, maybe even court Bregan as your new self. That's what you've wanted, is it not? The chance to erase your past?"

My chest was so tight it was a miracle my ribs didn't splinter. Since the insurrection, I had bent myself in knots trying to erase my past, hoping that if I did, I could finally belong in Bregan's world—be worthy of it. I'd yearned for some kind of validation that I deserved my own dreams. But seeking absolution had only led me to the end of yet another leash.

When I was a child, Father had warned me: There was no world in which I was safe. People would always try to kill me. Betray me. Use me.

I was so tired of being used.

I was even more tired of being blamed for it.

The world might never understand or forgive me, and maybe I would never truly be safe, but it was time to stop carrying shame for a brand I'd never asked for. Perhaps, instead of trying to erase my past, it was time to embrace it.

Maybe it was time to become who Father had raised me to be.

"You're right." I lifted my chin. "Vota has to go. But if we're to successfully stage her death, you'll need another body. Hang it from the bridge in one of the same black bags you used after the insurrection. Make it symbolic. Do it fast. You can dress the body with . . . this." I gestured to my red-and-white-striped Insei costume.

Hulei stirred first. "Yes. We'll make the arrangements."

Only one of Eznur's pockets bulged, in the shape of a gun. He didn't appear to have handcuffs, so I held an arm out to him. "We should leave," I said. "The whole temple will be gossiping about what's going on in here by now."

With a nod from Hulei, Diosi's features contorted, shifting back into the commissioner as he took my forearm. Hulei opened the door on a line of constables, and Eznur led me to a man with more pins than the rest.

"Handcuffs," he said.

The man reached into his pocket. I withdrew, as if afraid, and Eznur shoved me forward. Right where I wanted him to.

I stabbed my hidden knife into his wrist.

The cuffs clicked shut on air, and I dived through a curtained door into the pitch-black maze backstage. Eznur roared at the constables to find me, and shouts overlapped as they tripped on boxes and set pieces, unable to see the winding path I knew by heart.

I emerged onstage. A few show attendees still lingered in the back of the near-empty auditorium. The gas lamps that lined the front stage were on full blast, flames licking their glass covers. Footsteps thudded behind me. I'd never outrun them, but I didn't need to.

"Find her!" Eznur ordered.

The temple stretched around me: the pews where Reformists had died, the kitchen where the troupe had welcomed me, the office where Mezua had embraced me, the basement where Bregan had held me, the roof where I'd finally set myself free—all of it sanded, painted, and polished to perfection.

The constables charged onstage.

I drove my foot into an oil lamp, sending it straight into one of the velvet curtains. It erupted in flame. The constables reared back. Heat billowed like a blacksmith's forge.

Then Eznur emerged.

A monster stirred deep in my soul as I kicked another lamp, right at his chest. Oil sprayed his tunic. Fire licked his gray uniform. His shriek was otherworldly. He fell sideways, landing in a pool of lamp oil. The other constables slapped at the flames, but the acrid smell of burning flesh danced with his screams.

I watched him burn.

His visage shuddered. A thin, dark-haired man flickered through. He gaped at me, clinging to his facade as long as he could—but the knowledge of his *true* self, of his *true* face, filled me with an acrid glee.

What had Father looked like, in the end, beneath that black bag? Before Eznur and Hulei had killed him?

His illusion died when he did.

I struck a third oil lamp. Then a fourth. Until a wall of fire consumed the stage. Until the temple was crumbling beneath a blaze feral enough to finally turn my shame to ash.

SIXTY-SIX

Bregan

Now

The fire demanded retribution.

It burned the way the priests and poets described the Great Cataclysm, billowing off walls and ceilings that had been oiled until they shone, searing the hair from Bregan's arms, scorching his eyes, blistering his lungs. He thrashed as constables pulled him from the collapsing temple, but they held firm as they dragged him down the front steps and out into the crowd that edged the square, gaping at the monstrosity of flame. Bregan clawed at the hands binding him.

Firin was in there.

He had to get to her.

When Hulei had led her and an army of constables to the costume room, Bregan instantly understood his horrible mistake. Hulei would kill her, right after he used her in his political games. Bregan had tried to follow them, to stop him, to fix it, but a dozen constables had appeared from nowhere. They'd bent his arms behind his back and forced him back into the lobby. They were *his* constables, the boys *he* had trained, but their grips were iron.

When he demanded they release him, they'd refused.

President's orders, they'd said.

When the fire erupted, they still hadn't let him go.

But Bregan needed to get to Firin. He wasn't *finished* with her yet. He needed to scream at her until the edges of his anger dulled, until she understood. He needed to kiss her until they suffocated, until she broke, until he got answers to the questions that were gouging him from the inside out. Answers the fire was consuming.

Distantly, Bregan knew he was in danger. If Hulei had ordered the constables to restrain him, then he likely knew Bregan had planned to expose him tonight. But every wounded piece of Bregan's heart was within the walls of the temple, and danger was the last thing on his mind.

The deafening crack of the temple's roof sent everyone in the square to their knees. Flames shot to the sky. Sparks poured down like rain. The constables released Bregan to protect their own faces—and Bregan broke free.

When he reached the temple's front steps, the doors groaned open. A plume of black, acrid smoke poured out, enveloping Hulei and another handful of constables as they staggered out, coughing and gagging. Firin wasn't with them. Bregan raced past, up the steps.

Tez caught his shoulders.

The actor was covered from head to toe in soot. The stark whites of his eyes flashed as Bregan tried to push around him. "You can't. It's coming down," Tez bellowed, his voice breaking. "I'm so sorry, Bregan."

That's when he saw the fabric.

The stripes.

The burned piece of Firin's costume in Tez's hand.

Bregan plummeted into a winter sea. Icy water engulfed him, blocking out the screams and cries, the splintering wood. He couldn't breathe, couldn't feel, couldn't think.

All he could do was float.

Tez got him off the steps. The constables imprisoned his wrists. Someone pressed a warm, wet cloth to his forehead. He found himself seated on a crate outside a shop, armed men and women in a circle around him.

Rain began to fall—light at first, then as heavy as grief.

A blessing, people around him called it.

Ash seeped in rivulets out of the smoking temple like blood from the severed veins of a beast. Bregan watched as it pooled, split, and curled around his boots. Rainwater streamed off his chin. When a wind whipped the soaked fabric of his shirt, he didn't have the energy to shiver.

By the time Hulei approached, the clouds had shifted from black to gray. Though ash stained his hair, the president was in a new suit, dry beneath his umbrella. Harried, but in control. He looked like a martyr people could rely on. *You should get cleaned up,* he had told Bregan after the insurrection. *We want to show the public strength and stability.*

All of it a game. A show. A facade.

Bregan watched the baron, waiting for an order, for handcuffs. But with a wave of his hand, Hulei sent the constables away.

"I'm sorry I had to restrain you," he said, projecting over the patter of the rain. "But people do stupid things in love." He squeezed Bregan's shoulder, and Bregan didn't even have it in him to flinch. "Get some rest, son. Grieve. We're going to need you soon."

Bregan stared at the president's receding back.

Hulei headed for the temple's ash-covered steps. As reporters, supporters, and well-wishers closed in around the president, Bregan spotted the Veiled Players huddled together beneath an awning on the other side of the square. Jaq had Phinnin in a death grip. Nyfe was covered in bandages. Mezua met his eyes. Her mouth thinned.

A spark flared in Bregan, a flint against a snowstorm.

If Tez had known about Firin, Mezua probably had too.

"Thank you for coming," Hulei said to the reporters. "It is now confirmed that the star of *Qoyn & Insei,* known as Vota, was a Nodtacht agent of the former Stav Regime." The spark in Bregan's chest grew, as if in defiance. "Before she turned on those arresting her and set fire to the temple, we confirmed that she was working with my opponent, Thom Draifey, in an attempt to reinstate the Stav through his election campaign."

Bregan stood. Whatever Firin had done, she hadn't worked for Draifey. Hulei was using her to his advantage, even now.

He couldn't listen to this.

Debris crunched beneath his steps as he headed for the back of the building. The soles of his boots started smoking as he climbed through the jagged remains of what had been the kitchen door. The temple gaped open to the sky, scorched and gouged, a husk of itself. Audience seats smoldered. Ash coated his mouth.

Half of the nave had collapsed into the basement. Despite the danger and the hot wood burning his palms, Bregan dropped down, landing in a lake of wet ash. He waded his way to his bedroom.

His cot still stood.

The sight of it, sitting in a pool of water and twilight, made him feel raw and chafing, like intimacy exposed. The edges of his mother's quilt were scorched; wet ash stained his olive jacket. He stared at the place where he'd touched and kissed Firin, where she'd slept when he refused her, where he'd watched her, night after night, imagining her secrets and never coming close to the truth.

The first time he'd seen her lying there, he'd been sure she would disappear.

Now she had.

Agony lurched inside him, a surge of sea through a hole in a ship. He sank beside the bed, folded over it, and bit his knuckles, as if he could cork the grief, but a sob broke through anyway, then another, wrapped in thick knots of shame.

By the time he stopped crying, the rain had passed. Bregan wiped sodden hair off his face and blinked against an onslaught of morning sunlight he couldn't feel. He pulled his jacket on without bothering to brush off the ash and stuck his hands in his pocket.

His fingers brushed rope.

Bregan stopped breathing. He pulled out a three-strand bracelet that hadn't been there before, an honoring to Saint Chyira he would have known anywhere. He'd braided it as a child, but he hadn't seen it in four years.

It was Ma's.

SIXTY-SEVEN

Firin

Now

Hulei won the election.

Seated on the same clock-tower roof where I had watched Father die, I observed as the city poured into the Corners for Hulei's inauguration speech. People from all districts stuffed into the square, until they were shoulder to shoulder in a crowd nearly as large as the one the night of the insurrection. As I glared out over their brimming ecstasy, the heat rushing beneath my skin surged closer to boiling.

None of them knew the monster they'd elected.

A podium perched at the edge of the canal, right where the statue of Emperor Dreznor'proska'ed'nov had once stood. Light from the setting sun pooled over it like a spotlight as Hulei strode out to greet his adoring citizens with a suave winner's grin. A team of private security guards surrounded him, a barrier even from the constables lining the canal. Just last week, he had announced in the papers that the Nodtacht were branded with X marks, that a few were still on the loose in Luisonn, and that he intended to smoke out every last one.

I wondered if he was afraid of them, or if he was afraid of me.

Because he should be.

Although he'd announced my death more than a month ago, I doubted he believed it. Either way, he'd gotten what he wanted. After spinning stories connecting my death to Draifey's alleged treason, he won the election in a landslide. He was now the official president of Luisonn.

But I didn't intend to let him stay so for long.

"People of Luisonn," he called out, "today marks a brighter future. Together, we have cleared corruption from our . . ."

I stopped listening.

Instead, I searched the edge of the crowd and laid eyes on Bregan for the first time since the theater fire. He stood at attention with the other constables, straight-backed and certain, as if he believed the baron's bullshit, as if nothing we had uncovered meant a thing. Maybe he was loyal to Hulei again, or maybe he had merely given up, but in the end it didn't matter.

An ache pulsed through the mess he'd made of my heart. He'd told me he knew me, that he loved me, and the worst part was that it had been true. I'd been more myself with him than anyone else in my entire life. The person he loved had been *me*.

It still hadn't been enough.

At the podium, Hulei spun his own brand of illusion, and a thread inside me started to unravel. I dropped into the square and wound through the enraptured crowd, heading for Bregan. Warnings scraped the numb edges of my mind—this could ruin every plan I'd slowly started to put into motion—but my feet kept moving, one step in front of another, like a lapping tide pulled by the moon.

Bregan had cut his hair close to his scalp, shorter than I'd ever seen. He sagged beneath the weight he always insisted on carrying and observed the crowd with that *look*, always seeing more than he should.

When I drew close enough to make out his freckles, a steel ball ruptured inside me, its scalding insides seeping out, burning through my illusion cord until it went slack.

Then he saw me.

His eyes widened, dark as the void between stars, and I suddenly realized why I had risked coming here today—I wanted *him* to be the last person in this world to see my real face.

Two heartbeats later, I spun away from him and pushed through bodies. I made it through three rows of people before his fingers closed on my arm. The heat of him enveloped me. His freckles filled my vision. I shrieked.

"Wait. Stop." He choked on his next word, taking in my illusion: something like my own face, but all wrong around the edges.

"Let go of me," I snarled in a Kirru accent.

It took everything in me to pull away, to allow his fingers to slacken, and cold to rush between us. I tightened my shawl, caving beneath the pressure of a sudden, horrible emptiness, as if, in the space of a breath, all the hatred keeping me upright had bled out.

It dawned on me then how easy it would be for him to yank off my sleeve and see my brand. Arrest me. Kill me, even. But Bregan didn't move, even as the people around us murmured in apprehension. He didn't seem capable of speech. He looked at my carefully illusioned face as if I were a ghost.

Good, I thought. I hoped I would haunt him forever.

When I slipped into the crowd, he didn't follow.

"Thank you," Hulei said onstage. "May the gods and saints measure you justly."

The distant sun slowly dropped over the horizon, sliding a line of shadow over the audience, like a curtain closing on a years-long performance.

But the finale of Hulei's masterpiece was just the prologue to my own—and in this story, I wouldn't be the victim.

ACKNOWLEDGMENTS

I was daydreaming about another story on a hike when Firin elbowed her way in and demanded I tell her tale. At first, all I had was a con woman and the man who loved her despite not knowing her whole story. I had no idea where they would take me. During the journey, however, I was never alone. There were those who supported me, those who pushed me along, and those who dragged me forward, even when all I wanted to do was turn around. I'm so thankful for every single one of you.

I am forever grateful to my agent, Laura Dail, for taking one look at Firin's story and truly seeing her behind all her masks. Together, we leaned into her darkness, and in doing so, let her humanity shine through. I'm equally thankful for my editor, Adrienne Procaccini, for her instant appreciation of this story's politics and historical echoes, to Lindsey Faber for helping me shape Firin and Bregan's romance into the dream it now is, and to Marilyn Brigham for welcoming me with open arms. My whole team at 47North is amazing.

My writing community is an absolute dream. Without Rachel May, this book wouldn't exist. We've come so far together the last couple of years, as writers, coaches, and a team—I wouldn't know what to do without you. Mary and Corrie, thank you for cheering me on from the first day I decided to write, even when you were the only people on the planet who knew. A big thanks to Chris for the late-night nerd sessions—I'm a better world builder because of you—as well as to McKell and Carly for loving my characters even more than I do and holding me up during the query days. To Tenacious Writing: you've all shown me what an unconditionally loving writing community looks like; thank you for being in my corner. And to Annie, for being the first person to read and support Firin's story, I'd give anything for you to read the final version. I think you'd love it.

A deeply heartfelt, and utterly inadequate, thank-you to Jess. What a *journey* this has been. Without your daily (read: hourly) polos, long-walk chats, and endless support, Firin and Bregan would still just be dancing on rooftops in the back of my mind. They're out here, on paper people can read, because of you. Thank you for being half of my brain. I used up a lifetime's worth of luck the day I slipped into your Twitter DMs.

Last, thanks to Mom and Dad for showing me that I could do absolutely anything I set my mind to. To my husband, David, for the endless patience and support you've shown me through this process; I'm so lucky to adventure through life with you. And to my daughter, Bailey, for reminding me what's truly important and why I do what I do. I love you.

ABOUT THE AUTHOR

E.B. Golden has always been a wanderer, both inside and outside her imagination. Though born and raised on the coast of Maine, she spends most of her free time exploring the mountains of southwest Colorado with her husband and daughter, and sometimes their cats. Since she could hold a pen, she's used speculative fiction to make sense of a non-sensical world, and when she's not writing, she's usually traveling or coaching other writers, because the world always needs more stories.